I0673154

THE ANMORIAN LEGENDS

LEGACY OF THE SENTINELS

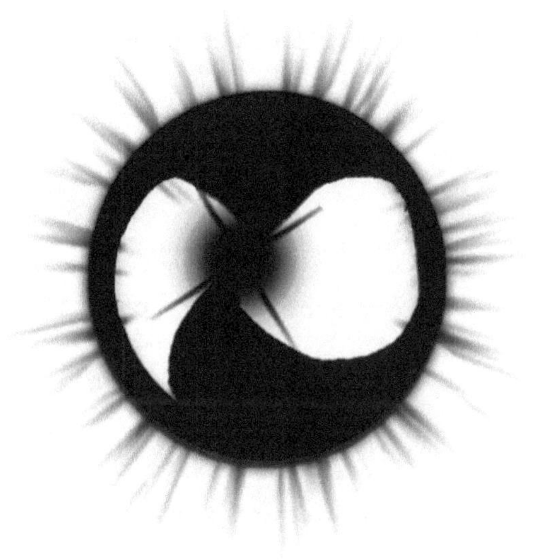

D. N. Pillay

The Invictus Group

First published in South Africa 2018

ISBN: 978-0-620-79562-3

The Invictus Group

Cover design by Larry Wilson

Edited by Createspace

Typeset by The Invictus Group, Durban, South Africa

Printed by Createspace

First edition

http://dhesanpillay.wix.com/dhesan-pillay
www.facebook.com/anmorianarchives
Follow us on Twitter: @anmorianarchive

To my parents, Kevin and Sandra, for teaching me the magic of imagination, my brother, Kavesan, for the best companion through any journey and my fiancé Melisha, for her unwavering love and support in this journey. Your love has been the greatest magic I have known.

CHAPTER ONE

REDEMPTION

A drumroll of thunder sounded from the depths of the dark clouds, morosely skulking after the lightning that flashed across the blackened sky.

A single bolt sharply broke the dense shroud of the storm and struck a lone tree, setting its boughs alight. Fires crackled in the silence of this gloomy realm, briefly lighting the ghastly bastion of black steel that was the source of the ubiquitous evil in this once-sacred world. What had stood proudly as the Antarika Citadel, the outpost of the Light, was now in the clutches of a foul-hearted monster.

The lament of the clouds, a sorrow-filled melody of slow thunder and bitter sobs of rain against the somber crackling of fire, was the only sound amid the grave stillness of this lonely world. The ethereal chorus of the free souls who had found peace in the Nuhremorn no longer sang aloud, adopting instead a more taciturn manner and retreating to the far corners of this realm. Whatever natural beauty had once existed here had withered into lost memories.

Ash from the burning tree rose slowly on a choked gust of wind, rising ever higher as it climbed the walls of the corrupted Sanctum. Rain fell with greater intensity as the ash drifted upward past the fallen hero in an upper turret who had led the realm to this dire state. The heavens' cold tears ran along his soaked brown hair, passing along his face and his exposed torso.

He slowly turned his head aside as the water dripped off the tip of his nose. The rumbling thunder sounded again, this time with greater gusto as the storm attempted to rouse the fallen hero. He alone could correct the disorder that plagued this mystic realm.

Rezaaran Valhara opened his eyes to a familiar walkway. The wind felt cold against his bare chest. This and the gentle caress of water running down his arms and face began to rouse his mind. There was a reason he was here, but he could not quite grasp it. He attempted to draw his hands over his face but felt a strong resistance as he tried to move them. Looking upward, he saw glowing red energy bands binding his wrists to the walls. The young War Mage closed his eyes and clenched his fists.

His last memories were of meeting Lord Salvidawn, who had granted him another opportunity to return to save Kashari. The Guardian King had been emphatic that Rezaaran rescue her. Unfortunately, his return to the Maelinthian had been brief—he had passed into unconsciousness upon the outskirts of Prashorida and mysteriously awoke in the Antarika Citadel.

He drew a deep breath and tried again to pull free of his bonds. Once more, he could not muster the strength. Rezaaran let out a weary sigh, and his shoulders slumped in defeat.

How had it come to this?

The power lust he had sworn never to succumb to had been his undoing. It had been the cause of his drifenira's demise. At his core, he felt too fractured, too shattered, to summon any real resolve to contest the dark magic that was holding him prisoner.

The cool water on his skin cleared his mind. His thoughts soon transcended the regrets of the past and entered a more lucid state. Despite the shadows around him, he sensed two echoes from across the bastion. The stronger was the unmistakable presence of Yudhara, the false mentor who had led him astray. The other was the waning echo of the Elder Mage, whose goodwill, trust, and friendship he had betrayed in a quest for power. Whatever his intentions may have been, the truth remained that they had been at the expense of Kashari. For all her sacrifices, she deserved a better-quality student than what he had become.

He was the cause of her suffering, and he alone could be her salvation.

He had betrayed her once.

It would not happen again.

Rezaaran concentrated his strength and started pulling his shackles from the wall. The muscles across his arms and torso tensed, pushing the veins to the surface. With nothing but his indomitable will, he forced himself to power through the burning in every sinew. He would not submit to the pain—not when his friend needed him most.

That last thought was what he needed to rip the energy shackles completely from the wall. He fell to ground in a crouch and gathered his breath. The War Mage rose, feeling rejuvenated and ready to do what was necessary. Feeling the rain upon his face, he looked up, taking in the stormy skies.

Antarika was no longer the beautiful citadel in which he had met Kashari at the time of his ascension. The very walls of the fortress had warped into a malevolent monument of steel and ire. The symphony of the free souls in song was now but a memory. There was only despair across this land. Beyond the walls of the fortress, against the backdrop of a dead forest, a solitary burning tree poignantly symbolized the affliction wrought upon the realm by Yudhara's pernicious presence.

Beyond this place of wickedness, wrath, and horror, Rezaaran sensed a flicker of hope that the Light would return. It resided in the presence of Kashari. She was the custodian of this realm, the mentor and dear friend who had saved him numerous times through her surreptitious interventions, never once asking for gratitude or recognition but selflessly fulfilling her role. It was now his turn to reciprocate the kindness the Elder Mage had shown him.

Rezaaran set off at a run down the ramparts, his bare feet noisily splashing through puddles as he sprinted to the courtyard—where he sensed Yudhara.

The soft sobbing of an Elder Mage who had once called this fortress her home provided a somber undertone to the Nuhremorn's lament. Once the respected and powerful leader of the Vokarii Order, now she stood alone, in the very courtyard wherein she had met Rezaaran not long ago, awaiting her end due to his actions.

Fate, it seemed, was not without a sense of cruel irony.

In her two centuries of training Vokarii apprentices, the young War Mage had been her most esteemed student. Alas, her pride in watching him flourish had blinded her to the growing darkness within his heart. Perhaps she ought to have been more vigilant. But what did that matter now? The events since Voltfes had frayed their bond to its final thread. She could not reach out to Rezaaran. But right now, his help was what she needed most.

The Emissary towered over her, his looming wings casting an ominous shadow over his ragged victim. The Elder Mage lay weakened, but she had to hold on. She had to believe that Rezaaran was still alive. She had to fight down the urge to submit. For her student.

For her friend.

"You're growing weak, my dear." The words seeped from between the Emissary's pointed teeth against the backdrop of the rolling thunder. "How much longer do you think you can withstand my power?"

Kashari caught her breath and emerged from her reverie with renewed resolve.

"I am a departed soul. I fear no death."

"Perhaps," replied the Emissary, admiring his black claws. "But I intend to break your spirit. And when I am done, you will be begging me for a reprieve from this pitiful existence."

He unleashed yet another agonizing blast of red electricity upon the Elder Mage.

Kashari cried out in anguish at first, caught by the surprise of the assault, before she fought down the rising panic. She had to endure this torture with the mental serenity she had taught Rezaaran. She would not afford this Obsidious creature the satisfaction of knowing his torture was eroding her soul.

Suddenly the Emissary ceased his assault and appraised her slow-breathing body. "This battle of wills grows tedious, Mage. I have made my demands; you would be wise to comply."

"Perhaps if you had more brains beneath that bone-laden helmet of yours," Kashari wheezed, "you may be able to endure such a battle."

The Emissary scoffed at this. "How cute. Cute…yet undeniably pathetic that the great mage Kashari Alda-Fyre has to resort to meek insults. Do you finally realize that your feeble Zenorian experimental charms have no power to resist the might of the Obsidious?"

"There is still some fight to be found with the Zenorians," Kashari whispered, attempting painfully to stand.

"Why do you cling so dearly to this apprentice of yours? Such loyalty would be admirable were it not so foolishly misplaced."

"At least I know where my loyalties have always been. Can you say the same for yourself?"

The Emissary contemplated this as he pressed his heavy foot against Kashari's back to keep her down. "I believe I can. My loyalty has only ever been to my true master. It is by his will that I am here now, serving the orders of Thaedis himself."

"What master?" Kashari asked as she unsuccessfully attempted to shrug off the Emissary's foot.

"Ah, yes…I forget you are merely a Zenorian mage misled by Tyrel Salvidawn's skewed perception of the truth. That aside, he is not the one you have bound yourself to. No—he was your lord in an era long past. Now you serve the Valhara boy. He is the reason for this obstinacy, is he not? Do you somehow believe your lost apprentice will arrive and save you from the big, bad monster of the Obsidious?" The Emissary released Kashari, guffawing at the notion.

"Rezaaran has not been lost. His soul remains true to the Light."

"If this is true, then where is the boy now?" asked the Emissary, theatrically spreading his arms to indicate the empty courtyard. "If he was bound to the Light, how has he allowed you to stand defenseless before me?"

Perhaps there was some shadow of truth to the Emissary's words. But Kashari could not let herself believe it. His words were a dark poison. They had corrupted Rezaaran before, and if she allowed him a foothold in her mind, it would be disastrous for her friend.

No.

She had to believe in the purity of her friend's virtue. The only weapon that could defeat this monster was the strength of their bond. She would not forsake that now. No matter the cost to herself.

The Emissary seized Kashari by the neck and drew her close to his red face. She looked into his soulless slate-gray eyes and felt her skin crawl as his venom-laden words flowed onto her cold skin.

"My patience grows thin. I do not care for this tiresome war between the mortals, your weak apprentice, or the empty words of a powerless and broken woman. All I want is what Thaedis has sent me for so I can leave this insipid realm and return to the comfort of the Obsidious."

"Oh, you will find your way home, Emissary—and by Rezaaran's hand, I am sure. But you will not get what you seek from me."

The Emissary threw Kashari to the ground and snarled menacingly. He unleashed another blast of red electricity upon the mage, letting her taste his growing displeasure. "You may not be able to die in this realm, for your soul is already departed. But I can tear you apart piece by piece until your soul has disintegrated into oblivion."

This caught Kashari's attention. She looked down at the stump of her arm, a grizzly reminder of her first encounter with the monster.

"Yes, I think that will be a fitting levy for your obstinacy. Now tell me where the Sentinel's conduit is, or I will hack what remains of your pathetic presence—"

The Emissary abruptly ceased his tirade and sniffed the air.

He had sensed a ripple in the Vaux earlier that he had chosen to ignore. Yet there was no ignoring the unmistakable mortal scent of the last Vokarii War Mage.

Rezaaran looked out the archway, baffled by what he saw. He was certain this staircase led to the courtyard where he usually met Kashari, but now he was looking through the darkness upon a field shrouded by a veil of mist.

Stepping carefully through the steel archway, he felt his bare feet touch damp grass. No remnant lingered of what ought to have stood in place of this field, save the memories in the War Mage's mind. But the fell deception at work here did little to beguile the young mage.

Occasionally the mist flickered as it drifted around him. Steam hissed from the ground, and the grass beneath his feet intermittently revealed the cold touch of stone. The Vaux was writhing from the gross distortion it was undergoing. Rezaaran could feel the fractures beneath the probing touch of his mind. Something was amiss.

He faintly heard the whispers of Kashari, but someone was making a great effort to mask the Antarika Citadel in shadows that stifled the Elder Mage's voice. Although he could not hear her, he still remembered her teachings. Deception was a shroud strengthened by fear and destroyed by the eye of a calm mind.

Rezaaran drew his breath slowly, stilling his mind. The mist around the War Mage crept aside, and his calming psyche repaired the integrity of the Vaux around him to restore normality. The purified zone continued expanding, at last revealing a familiar stone courtyard. But the intruder to Antarika was tenacious. The mist hung ominously upon the peripheries, oscillating as the conjurer and the savior contested wills.

Now that he had drawn the weaver of this deception into the open, Rezaaran sensed the distinct echoes of two powerful entities. One was definitely Kashari, who was attempting to dispel this mist with what power she could spare. Rezaaran sensed that she was enduring great agony, yet her will to help him gave her strength to resist her torturer.

The other was a presence he had grown all too familiar with lately. It was clear that Yudhara was the conjurer of this mist—an attempt to dissuade Rezaaran from his course of action so that he would have ample time to break the Elder Mage. But Rezaaran would not allow it.

If Kashari's will could resist Yudhara's torment a little longer, then together they could escape this entanglement.

Rezaaran searched deep within himself for the strength he had once shared with Kashari. He closed his mind to the coldness of the mist and rain that relentlessly raked his bare chest. He shut out the booming thunder that echoed from the darkened heavens, for there was only one task his mind needed to fulfill now. However, more than a cruel storm contended with him in this misty field.

The War Mage opened his eyes sharply. Something had moved near him.

Pools of bubbling black sludge formed around him. The sludge congealed and rose, forming viscous, mangled corpses armed with various ancient weapons. Their slow, rasping breaths pressed in on Rezaaran, and they dragged their defiled vessels onward. The lashings of Yudhara's dark magic spurred each slumping step they took.

The War Mage closed his eyes again and ignored their advances. These resurrected souls were an extension of Yudhara's morphed reality. If he shattered the warlock's tapestry of illusion, these shades would no longer exist.

He returned his attention to reforming his bond with Kashari, for in this bond lay the only cure to the plague of darkness that afflicted the Nuhremorn. Rezaaran felt her spirit reach out to him, and as he accepted her presence within his core, her muffled whispers found a clarity he had not heard since Voltfes.

Kashari, can you hear me?

He felt a surge in the connection. The Elder Mage's will immediately strengthened at the sound of his voice, and the purified zone around the young War Mage expanded.

Rezaaran? I knew you were not lost to the shadows! It is good to hear you again, but I do not know how much longer I can resist.

Do not worry, my friend; I am here now. Where are you? And how do I get back to the citadel from this field?

You are in the citadel, but an illusion is keeping you from seeing what is truly around you. The Emissary holds Antarika in his tainted grasp and can alter the truth within the citadel—unless you contest his will with your own. I fear it will not be much longer until he breaks this link. Hurry! I need your help!

Kashari's agonized scream filled the War Mage's mind, and he felt the anguish of her torture as his own. His actions had released this evil upon the Nuhremorn, and now he would see it destroyed, regardless of the cost.

And as this thought left his mind, just as had been the case on Imperitus a year ago, a familiar force began to manifest. When the situation around Rezaaran was most dire and friendship had been all that mattered to him, the bond between War Mage and Elder Mage was forged at maximal strength.

Within his core, Rezaaran felt a warmth explode from his rain-covered body.

He opened his eyes and watched a wave of white light obliterate the mist. A shadowy corpse standing before him with its broadsword poised to deliver a killing strike was instantly reduced to smoky remains that rolled away with the purged mist.

Rezaaran rose and looked around warily, relieved to find himself surrounded by the familiarity of Antarika. The hatred and ire that cloaked this building did well to hide its beauty, but it could not expunge Rezaaran's memories of his conversations with the Elder Mage when they walked here between training sessions. Regardless of the evil he was soon to face, he knew he would destroy it. Not in wrath, nor for glory, but for the sake of saving Kashari.

He turned his attention to the two Zenorians of an era long past. Yudhara held a limp Kashari by the collar and seemed mildly surprised at Rezaaran's appearance.

"Weren't expecting me, were you, Yudhara?"

The warlock considered this as he dropped Kashari to the ground and stepped toward the War Mage. "Well, I would not consider this a complete surprise. You Zenorians are particularly irksome to eradicate. But I am amazed that you arrived at this courtyard before I intended you to be here."

"The ties of a true friendship cannot be undone by deception," Rezaaran replied as he cast his eye over Kashari. She was still breathing, albeit slightly.

Yudhara laughed loudly at this as he too glanced at Kashari. "You continue to astound me, Rezaaran. There is such potential within you, yet you place loyalty in the hearts of weaker companions. Orin, Kashari, Ashana—you would do anything to protect these people. But you fail to realize that your attachment to them stifles you. Yet perhaps your greatest undoing is your attachment to Zaran."

This piqued Rezaaran's interest. "What do you know about my father?"

Yudhara smiled smugly. He knew he had the War Mage's attention now, and he was all too familiar with this vantage point.

With only a slim foothold, he would be able to easily sway Rezaaran's allegiance to the master's plan. "I know you witnessed his death at the hands of Thaedis. That you have been reliving that memory every night. You would do anything to reap vengeance for his murder."

"What are you talking about?" Rezaaran asked hesitantly.

Yudhara's jeering laughter was calculated to goad Rezaaran into acting rashly, but the young mage remained calm. Anger would slow his mind. At some point, the warlock would lower his guard for only the slightest moment, and Rezaaran would need to be ready to seize the opportunity.

"What is this plan your master has?" Rezaaran asked calmly.

"You are different from my memories of you," replied Yudhara shrewdly, ceasing his mockery and appraising the War Mage. "You are no longer directed by emotion. Purpose now drives you. Perhaps there is some use for you after all."

Rezaaran awaited the answer to his question.

"Well, if you are to join us, the substandard education you received from that whimpering whore will not do. You are most probably thinking I refer to Thaedis, but he is not the master of whom I speak. Thaedis Silvermire is perhaps the most powerful mortal, but he too must answer to a superior. My true master is Nethriziin, the Great Scion of Darkness. Born from within the Vaux, he has been the ever-present shadow since the dawn of Anmor's creation. He is the father of my people."

As he spoke of the Scion, Yudhara held a reverence about him, respectful even though he was beyond his master's gaze.

"For the longest of ages, Nethriziin has had one purpose: to see Anmor burn in Obsidian fire. To this end, he embarked with an army of Edarians on the grandest of wars to fulfill his destiny. Alas, we met countless failures at the gates of the Aetherealm—until Thaedis Silvermire joined our conquest. Thaedis showed Nethriziin the flaws in the Anmorian Guardians, and this allowed my Edarian kin to overwhelm the pious Guardians, corrupt their reason, and enslave them to the Obsidious. Thus ended the rule of the Guardians, and the time of the Archlords began."

"The Archlords...are actually the Anmorian Guardians?" Rezaaran asked blankly. He had been slaying the beings charged to protect Anmor against horrors such as Thaedis and Yudhara.

"Well, they are nothing more than vessels now for the Edarians who control them. With these incredible war machines at our disposal, we were ready to fix our gaze upon the last realm: the Maelinthian. However, the instability of the Vaux posed a problem for our kin. Those who held the Archlord vessels could enter the Maelinthian but could spread our rule only one world at a time. Nethriziin was not impressed, but he was patient, and between the Archlords and Thaedis, we have slowly edged our cause onward...until the day you took the sword on Imperitus. That was the day it all changed."

"Why?"

"When you grasped that sword, it sent a roar through the Vaux that alerted Nethriziin to the presence of another mortal who could advance our cause. He instructed Thaedis to recruit you. Yet to do this, we needed a means to sway you."

"My father's death was that means to your end," Rezaaran remarked grimly. The scheme was materializing before his eyes, and he not could believe how blindly he had played into it.

"I must commend Thaedis on whatever he did to you before you arrived here. You are far quicker on the uptake than I remember. I traveled to the Nuhremorn, where I gravitated to the stream of your memories surging through this dreary world. For the most part, your recollections were equally droll. Yet I soon came to learn of your idolization of your father. You had all but forgotten that Thaedis had killed him when he was regenerating. You were too young to have taken in everything amid all that chaos. I very carefully fished that detail forward so that you could reexperience it, to get some hatred bubbling within you."

"Why would you want me to see that?"

"Revenge is a powerful motivator."

"I did not start this seeking revenge."

"What were you pursuing, then? Justice? The chance you could prevent a similar fate occurring elsewhere? Call it whatever you want,

Rezaaran, but were it not for that memory, you would never have hunted Thaedis with such vigor. I needed to ignite that fire in you. I had to turn you into a weapon worthy of Nethriziin's great plan."

"What? Now you want a thank-you?" retorted Rezaaran.

"No need to be bitter. I would say that you turned out for the better. Admittedly this transformation seemed impossible at first. But after I saw the results of my little intervention, I realized that you throw rationality aside when your father is concerned." He paused a moment, allowing his last point to sink in. "However, breaching the citadel proved more difficult than expected. Powerful, ancient magic permeated these walls—the joint effort of Salvidawn and the Elder Mage to protect a conduit of power that none knew existed. I reported to my master my suspicions of what this fortress had been built to house. Nethriziin ordered me to secure the conduit along with you. However, I needed entry through the barriers. I attempted to sway you on Zeema-Tamius when I fabricated your father's spirit. I knew that slaying the Archlords would augment my power, and with the memory of Zaran, I urged you to do so. I expected you to heed your father's advice without question. However, your empathy for that brat was something I had not anticipated."

"Perhaps you weren't as powerful as you thought," Rezaaran said with a smirk.

"Normally I would flay the skin off your face for such insolence, but in this instance you are right. There was a self-righteousness lying dormant within you that I had not foreseen. It fortified the Elder Mage's barriers of this citadel and made it impenetrable to my influence. I knew I needed patience and more power."

"The darkness in the shards," Rezaaran whispered to himself, remembering the uneasy feeling he'd experienced after defeating Arlen and Sephiron.

"Indeed. With every Archlord's power you gained, you also took a darkness into your being that strengthened me. After Sarganium fell, I had enough might to breech Antarika's defenses, and I lay in wait for your arrival to offer you my aid."

Rezaaran said nothing. Words did not matter now.

Despite intending to be a symbol of light in these times, he had unwittingly opened the floodgates for shadow to creep in. He had played right into the cold hands of the Obsidious. Each victory had been a farce. Every action he had carried out under Yudhara's instruction had merely been part of an elaborate ploy to entrap Anmor within the Scion of Darkness's plan.

"Ah, well…my time here is nearing its end. I have a fair idea that the conduit is within this fortress. Nethriziin will be able to dismantle the protective charms and do as he wishes with it. I need a reprieve from my year in this banal realm. What will it be, young Zenorian? Will you bow before my master and accept your place in his army? Will you stand beside Thaedis as he purifies the Maelinthian? Will you join us in our last battle as we conquer all of Anmor?"

"You want me to stand beside the monster that tried to kill me? After all that you've done to me, I should just forgive the Obsidious and accept this offer?"

"Well…yes." Yudhara seemed surprised that Rezaaran had to ask this. "Look, the business with Thaedis on whatever that backwater world was called—most regrettable, I must admit. However, a bigger plan is in motion here. Thaedis acted rashly in trying to kill you, but if my master decrees you his ally, Thaedis will have to obey. Once the Maelinthian falls into darkness, Nethriziin will not care which of you lives. You will be free to destroy him then. I am offering you a way out of here, boy. I suggest you take it."

Rezaaran considered this carefully. This was a familiar position. Yudhara's dark whispers had veered him off course once before. But he had been waiting for this opportunity. He had to do what was necessary for survival.

"So your master will just accept me with open arms, and we will all just be friends?"

"Well, now that you mention it, there is a matter of a tribute to pay."

"Name your price."

Yudhara looked behind Rezaaran at the Elder Mage.

Kashari was slowly raising herself with her one arm. Although she was alive, the tussle with Yudhara had severely crippled her.

The warlock returned his cold eyes to the War Mage. Rezaaran had cast her aside once before, but if he was to join the ranks of the Obsidious, he needed to sever all ties to the Light.

"Bring me her head," he said with a cruel smile. "Oh, better yet—I believe this would be more fitting."

Yudhara held his hand aside and, with an explosion of black fire, summoned Harkenathor to his grasp.

Rezaaran looked at the blade he had wielded as his own, surprised to see the sacred weapon once more. The warlock telekinetically passed the blade to him. He looked down and took the sword; it felt foreign in his hand, yet in his heart, he felt the stirring of the power he had once known.

"As you wish."

Rezaaran walked toward Kashari, clearing his mind. He knew there was only one course of action to take. The distance was a matter of only a few paces, yet the walk seemed to take an eternity.

He came to a halt before the weakened Elder Mage whom he had once called his mentor—the spirit that had sworn the most solemn vow to him and that he had known as his friend.

She raised her glassy eyes toward the young War Mage. She was too weak to find the words to plead her case, and the look in her eyes told of a will too shattered to fight the pain of another betrayal.

Rezaaran placed the sword at his side as he considered what he was about to do. The weapon seemed much heavier than it ought to have been, compounded by the gravity in his heart of the actions to come.

"Forgive me, my friend," Rezaaran whispered as he came to a decision.

"Do not tell me you have cold feet now," Yudhara remarked as he crossed his arms. "Do you not see that she holds you back from the power you deserve? Just get this business over with, and we will leave. She is not important to us."

Rezaaran raised Harkenathor over his shoulder, preparing to deliver the final strike to the mighty Kashari Alda-Fyre.

Yudhara looked on with a self-satisfied smile. He may have failed to find the exact location of the conduit, but when Nethriziin learned that Rezaaran had joined them, that failure would be forgotten. His pride blinded him to the deception at the fore of the War Mage's mind.

Kashari dejectedly looked at her student, who offered her a surreptitious wink. He slammed Harkenathor down in front of her, releasing the hilt as the sword sparked off the steel floor. He stretched his arms aside, taking aim at the older Zenorians.

"There is nobody who is *not* important to me," Rezaaran whispered as he reached deep into the Vaux to snare Yudhara's soul.

The warlock had grown complacent awaiting Rezaaran to strike down his mentor and, his guard lowered, was unable to fend off the spell.

Rezaaran siphoned the life essence of Yudhara into Kashari, using his soul to filter the darkness of the warlock's life force. The evil Zenorian's attempts to resist were futile.

But this powerful spell was not without cost to the caster. Every vein on Rezaaran's face surfaced as blood dripped from his nose beneath the strain of the power he was handling. A dusky dye seeped through the engorged vessels as black pearls of Yudhara's energy coursed through the War Mage's body.

For a flicker of an instant, he felt the roaring battle hunger reignite, demanding violence to quench its appetite. Yet he remained steadfast. He had seen what that temptation had led him to before, and he would not walk that path again.

Using the might of his will, he contained the darkness within him. A white ribbon of pure light flowed to Kashari, bearing no taint of the warlock's spirit. This sanctified power was healing her battle wounds, even allowing her arm to regenerate.

However, the foul essence of Yudhara was not making the young War Mage's sequestration easy. Rezaaran bound the evil within his soul and took the tormenting forces deep within himself. He could feel that darkness attempting with all its fell might to break the confines of the prison he had crafted for it.

Rezaaran ignored the pounding within his skull and blocked out the mad rattling of his heart against his ribs. Reaching deeper still, he ripped apart the last shreds of Yudhara's existence.

The warlock dispersed with a loud explosion amid a cloud of smoke and cinder.

Rezaaran took the moment to gather his breath. He looked at Kashari. She had collapsed from the rapid infusion of power she had received, and it would take her some time to regain consciousness. Yet something in the pit of his stomach told him that he might not have time to wait. A sinister force had roused, drawing closer to the War Mage. And Rezaaran was uncertain that he would be able to contest this foe on his own.

From the shadows of the courtyard stepped a phantasm born of the deepest enmity. Nethriziin himself had crafted these creatures in the black fires of the Obsidious to exude despair as they swarmed across battlefields in his name.

A powerful flap of its red wings instantly cleared the smoke and brought it to stand before Rezaaran. It lowered its slate-gray eyes to look at the War Mage, revealing its needle teeth in a malevolent smirk.

"So…you chose to reject my offer." His drawling voice echoed the smugness of Yudhara, but this creature was far from being a Zenorian. "Well, a simple no would have sufficed; the theatrics were a bit much."

"What the hell are you?" Rezaaran asked, tightening his grasp on Harkenathor.

"Well, since you so rudely destroyed my vessel, I have had to resort to my true form. Have you any idea how long I'd kept that vessel intact, you obnoxious bastard?" The creature's snarl was an attempt to intimidate Rezaaran, but it knew such an act would meet little success against the brazen soldier. "I am an Edarian, the original inhabitants of the Obsidious created in the image of Nethriziin's perfect army. Now, this is my final offer to join our cause. I am being benevolent, boy, but you are testing me."

"Drop the act, for it will not absolve you for your crimes against Kashari. Now…who *are* you?"

"I am curious to see whether your heart will bleed like this when I tear it from your chest. My true name is Tolbetrius. Some call me the

Emissary of Darkness, for I go where I must to carry forth the will of Nethriziin, the Great Scion of Darkness. Well, if you will be calling me by my true name, then it would be fitting that I return the favor…Loradún."

"What did you call me?" Rezaaran asked, staring blankly at the Obsidian messenger.

"Your soul bears a unique name, for it is one of few bound to the conduit of this realm, and through that tether is its secret to wielding such great power. This is why we need you, Loradún. A soldier of your might would be a fine addition to our ranks."

"I will use every ounce of strength I have to fight the Obsidious across every realm of Anmor. I will lead IRIS in however many battles it takes to contest Nethriziin at every juncture. But I will never join you."

"Tell me, how will you be leading them when you are too busy fighting them as my vessel?"

Tolbetrius hurled a screeching shadow of himself at the young War Mage, but Rezaaran was unperturbed. He leveled Harkenathor, preparing for battle.

"I am impressed. You can resist my terror shackle, which was more than your Elder Mage could do. I will relish the challenge of enslaving you!"

The Edarian thrust himself skyward and unleashed a surge of red electricity upon the youngster. Rezaaran raised Harkenathor, absorbing the spell into the dark-gray blade. The runes burned a bright blue as magical energy overcharged the weapon.

Tolbetrius plummeted to the ground, driving his fist through the empty space where Rezaaran's head had been seconds earlier. But the War Mage was more agile than the lumbering monster. Rezaaran rolled aside.

Harkenathor flashed through the air as lightning crackled overhead. Tolbetrius evaded the slash and swung a heavy tail into the Zenorian's chest. Rezaaran steadied himself and unleashed a flurry of slashes, which the Emissary parried with his heavy talons.

Tolbetrius caught Harkenathor's edge in his armored hand and ripped it from the War Mage's grasp, punishing the stunned warrior with a series of punches to the midriff. Swinging his tail, he thrashed the battered fighter aside.

The Emissary looked at the sword in his grasp with disdain and threw it to the War Mage. "It has been a while since I have been entertained in this place. I may as well make the most of it."

Obsidian fires ignited along his outstretched arms, and two large pools of the black, viscous liquid formed beside him. The Emissary raised his hands, summoning the sludge higher to congeal into two heavily armored knights brandishing axes.

Rezaaran shifted his gaze tentatively between the two adversaries lumbering toward him. "I hate these things," he mumbled, holding Harkenathor firmly before him.

The young mage charged forward, meeting his foes with the valor for which Zenorians were renowned. He dodged the first swing, sinking Harkenathor into the belly of the aggressor and drawing the blade to deflect the strike of the second minion. However, his slash afflicted no damage, and the first viscous knight pulled Rezaaran's feet from under him with the handle of his pole arm. Rezaaran crashed to the ground, the wind knocked out of him.

The Obsidian knight lifted his ax and brought it to bear upon the Zenorian, who narrowly evaded it by rolling deftly aside. He leaped to his feet, and Tolbetrius struck him in the face with his bone-plated gauntlet. In a quick follow-up, the Emissary flung Rezaaran skyward, where a wyvern made of the same viscous black liquid caught him in its claws and carried him higher. Rezaaran swung Harkenathor, slicing the winged beast's feet to free himself. But another wyvern bearing an Obsidian knight caught him on its back midfall.

The War Mage fiercely dueled with the conjuration, attempting to knock his adversary to the ground below with a spectral blast—but to no avail. He still could not use any of his abilities. He dodged another swing of the battle-ax, losing his footing on the wyvern's back and falling toward the citadel.

Ready and waiting, Tolbetrius caught him with two hands around his throat and sped them toward the cold metal floor of the courtyard. Using his great wingspan to break their descent, he landed, his heavy feet powering into Rezaaran's chest before rolling aside.

The War Mage spluttered blood and gingerly clutched at his chest. Rain beat relentlessly upon him as he realized the fight was too much to handle. Without his powers, he was nothing more than a pile of flesh for three hungry predators.

"Ah, well...this has been fun. But in the end, you were born to be broken by my superior might. Good riddance, you useless bastard!"

The wyverns screeched as the Zenorian raised himself, using Harkenathor as a crutch. Rezaaran looked toward the wyverns, which were almost indiscernible against the inky backdrop of the stormy sky.

If this was to be his penance for the darkness he had brought to this realm, then he would face it with the courage of a Zenorian warrior, regardless how unfairly weighted the skirmish had been.

The wyverns flew toward Rezaaran, preparing to claim their prize. But the young War Mage did not stand alone. An enormous broadsword made of pure light flashed through the air, cleaving one wyvern in two. Another similar sword flew through the air to skewer the other conjuration into the steel floor. Seven more swords of light energy appeared out of the stormy sky and embedded themselves around Rezaaran and Tolbetrius, forming a warding dome that bound the Edarian in place.

The Emissary growled as he appraised the situation. The pure light that formed these swords would incinerate him on contact. He was trapped. But this was impossible! The boy had no power in this realm. Unless...no, it could not be!

Kashari stood boldly beyond the dome of light swords, fully healed and at her student's side. "Your corrupting touch will be lifted from this realm. The Obsidious will never prevail!"

Four concentric rings of light formed over the dome. Sirantanian runes appeared between the rings, and at the center of the middle ring, a powerful white light glowed with gathering fury.

Rezaaran, this spell will obliterate all who are composed of Torementhicite. It will destroy Tolbetrius, but I cannot guarantee that it will leave you uninjured.

Kashari, if you have the shot, take it. We cannot allow him to survive after the havoc he has wreaked already.

When the swords part for the cataclysm to release, he will have a fleeting moment to escape. You need to keep him contained so that the spell can make a direct hit.

Rezaaran watched the Edarian turning frantically, seeking a weakness in the prison that held him. The War Mage charged forward, slashing at the monster with Harkenathor, but the blade only embedded itself in his bone-plated armor. With some annoyance, Tolbetrius turned around and slapped Rezaaran away. But the young Zenorian was unrelenting. Using Harkenathor as a brace to bind him, he locked his arms around Tolbetrius's waist, using all his strength to keep the beast in place as the Emissary struggled to free himself.

"You fool," Tolbetrius grunted as he tried to break free. "What are you doing? If that spell is unleashed, it will disintegrate all Obsidian Valinthicite. Mortals are composed of as much Obsidian as Aethereal Valinthicite. You will die in this act!"

"If that is the price of taking you down so you may never hurt anyone else again, then it is a price I am willing to pay."

"You're insane! *You* may have a death wish, but *I* do not!"

At that moment, the light swords parted, and Tolbetrius glimpsed his fleeting opportunity to escape. The Emissary opened his wings wide, breaking free of Rezaaran's bindings.

Rezaaran lunged forward, thrusting Harkenathor into a chink in Tolbetrius's bone-plated armor.

The Emissary roared with rage as the blade pierced his tissues. He spun around, slashed Rezaaran across the face with heated talons, and ripped the blade from his flesh. Too late, he looked woefully skyward as the giant cataclysm of power was unleashed upon them with a burst of light as bright as if every star had exploded.

Kashari lowered her hands as the scouring light of her attack faded. The sheer force of the blast had disintegrated the steel floor, awakening the flagstones from their dormancy. She no longer sensed the echo of the Edarian, but she also had trouble locating her apprentice.

She had warned him of the risk, and he was right when he'd pointed out that they could not allow Tolbetrius to escape. The Emissary knew of the conduit, and if left alive, he would pass the information on to Nethriziin, leaving little hope for Anmor's fate. Despite the necessity, she felt her heart grow hollow as realization dawned that she had lost her greatest friend.

But as the glow faded, there—where the cataclysm had landed—stood her apprentice, looking skyward.

Rezaaran turned to face his mentor. He chuckled lightly and ran over, dropping Harkenathor to embrace Kashari.

Tears sprang to her eyes, and the Elder Mage held her student tightly, glad that he was safe once again.

The young Zenorian looked Kashari in the eye and smiled warmly. A cauterized wound ran across his face, beneath his eyes and over his nose. But despite the grievous wound, he glowed with the warmth he'd had the first time they had met.

"I am so sorry for everything I have said and done to you, my friend," he said, meaning every word that passed his lips. "Despite it all, you never gave up on me."

"And I never will. What matters is that you are safe once more."

They looked back at the site where the light array had landed and blasted away the black steel, revealing the original beauty of Antarika. The steel casing around the citadel began to crack and fall away as the last outpost returned to the Light.

"You did it, Rezaaran! You won back the Nuhremorn from the Obsidious."

"*We* did it, Kashari," he corrected her with a smile as they watched the rain falling over the forest beyond the citadel. "I feel clearer than I have in years."

"Your echo is also far purer. The Light magic from the cataclysm seems to have eradicated all traces of Obsidian Valinthicite from you and healed your wounds. I am afraid, though, that the mark Tolbetrius scarred you with cannot be lifted. It is beyond my healing powers to remedy such evil."

"Ah, well...I am sure I will be able to live with this," Rezaaran remarked as he ran his fingers across the wound. Secretly, though, he felt that perhaps he deserved the mark to remind him of the price of his ambition.

"There is only one thing I am uncertain about," Kashari said.

Rezaaran passed his mentor an inquiring look.

"How did you arrive here? Ordinarily you cast your soul to the Nuhremorn through meditation and using our bond. But this time you did not consciously will yourself here."

The War Mage looked back over the Nuhremorn with alarm.

"Will I be able to return to my body?"

"I do not know the answer to that, Rezaaran."

CHAPTER TWO

A DARK DEAL

Thaedis stood alone at the helm of the *Sedah Destroyer*, idly looking at the blade in his hand. His cold fingers traced the dull runes etched along the blade. Such a beautifully crafted weapon—perfectly weighted, a relic of an era long past. And the power it contained was a calamity to behold. It befitted him in every manner. The weapon he had coveted for almost a year was finally his, yet every time he grasped the hilt, he felt haunted by the battle in which he had claimed it.

When he had faced Rezaaran on Zynoo, he'd expected victory. He knew that the young boy would pose little threat to his reign. However, the War Mage's barbed comment about his father's likely disappointment in him had wounded Thaedis deeper than he'd cared to admit.

Fueled by insatiable rage, he'd scorched Prashorida into oblivion. Yet the destruction had done little to quell his fury. He had flown to Meston and flattened the city with his newly acquired weapon, amazed by the power contained in such an innocuous artifact. With a swing of the sword, he disintegrated all before him and directed blasts of Obsidian fire greater than ever before.

IRIS had grown in influence across the Maelinthian and inspired several other rebellious organizations to emerge on worlds previously claimed by the Dominion. He had personally ensured that they would serve as an example for any who dared to oppose him.

Thaedis had led the battles against the various rebel factions across the Dominion's worlds. The display on Zynoo of what this sword could achieve had incited him to be more adventurous with his destruction, and the weapon responded accordingly by augmenting his dark magic.

Intrigued by the weapon's capacity for destruction and unable to shake the feeling of great familiarity about the relic, he'd withdrawn to the *Sedah Destroyer* to investigate further. Yet what he had learned further stoked his anger.

Poring over the journals he had claimed from the captive Thyrillian scientist, he'd learned that Itara Zelzo had some knowledge of the weapon. Despite possessing him for almost two centuries, the Edarian within could not suppress the Arkanian war chief's memories.

The notes detailed that when Tyrel Salvidawn had stripped Thaedis of his Guardian power and exiled him, he had kept the Valinthian shard, unsure how to dispose of it. During a session of meditation, he had glimpsed a vision but had provided little information to his fellow Guardians. He'd left their realm with the shard in his possession, and that was the last Zelzo saw of him before he lost control of his being to an Edarian.

With this information and the familiarity enshrouding the blade, Thaedis was certain Tyrel had used the Valinthian shard containing his Guardian power to imbue the weapon with its magic. The thought of this sickened him to his core.

It was not enough that Tyrel had betrayed Argur Silvermire's trust when he handed Thaedis's father to the Triad of Phantoms. No, the devious Guardian King had compounded his deception and stripped Thaedis of his magic to empower his anointed mortal pawn. While Thaedis existed in exile, cast from the Aetherealm to scrounge a living off rocks in a wasteland, Tyrel had bestowed his immense power upon an arrogant child who had no inkling how to wield such might. More than mere magic lay within this sword. That Valinthian shard had imprisoned fragments of his *soul.* It was rightfully his. The thought that Rezaaran had so ostentatiously flashed this weapon as a token of his induction into the ailing Vokarii Order was repulsive.

Enraged by his findings, Thaedis had led the Dominion on a rampage. He was not interested in subjugation or eternally enslaved souls. He had ensured that Anmor suffered for Tyrel Salvidawn's deception and Rezaaran's arrogance. Over the past month, he had led his Harbingers on a bloody crusade. They had leveled civilizations and culled billions to reclaim once-freed quadrants.

Yet after every battle, although he had stood victorious and watched the smoke rise from the battlefield, Rezaaran's last words haunted him. In time, each plume of smoke carried a fleeting but uncanny resemblance to the face of his departed father—and in every instance, the nebulous apparition looked at him with disdain before dispersing.

He had slain the War Mage by his own hand, but this had not brought him the peace he had imagined it would. None remained to contest his spreading rule. He would bring Anmor to order, and there would be peace.

Despite this, after his most recent conquest a few hours earlier, the look in the eyes of his father's smoky apparition lingered in his memory.

Thaedis sighed heavily and looked out into the darkness of space. "What would you have me do, Father?" he thought aloud. "I am on this quest to rid all corruption and evil from Anmor. Perhaps that idiot War Mage was correct. Perhaps my methods have gone amiss of all you taught me. But I have come too far now to turn back. I have sacrificed too much."

The air beside Thaedis rippled, and a familiar cloudy apparition with glowing yellow eyes formed beside him. The sorcerer stood tall. He had not expected Nethriziin and wore only his black ceremonial suit.

"Master," he murmured, bowing. "How may I serve?"

The apparition issued a deep rumbling, like a growing storm cloud.

"I do not understand—"

Suddenly a humanoid mass burst forth from the smoke. Its body, forged of black igneous rock and orange magma, pulsed between fissures across its exterior. The volcanic spawn rose to face Thaedis, whose pale face showed no sign of apprehension as he stood before Nethriziin's physical manifestation.

"Then I am forced to take this form and speak in your guttural language to remind you of our mission. Of the deal that we made."

"I have not forgotten our arrangement, Master."

"Your actions of late make me think otherwise, and so here I am to remind you. When Salvidawn exiled you to the Maelinthian, stripped of your Guardian powers and afflicted by mortality, I came to your aid. I offered you the greatest power to return as an immortal in a mortal realm. I gave you the vengeance you sought—in exchange for your joining in my conquest of Anmor."

Thaedis silently stared at the magical entity he unwillingly had come to call his master.

The Scion continued. "I made you the greatest weapon to bring me the final realms of Anmor. You have done more than the countless legions of Edarians who came before, for now I am able to manifest in the Maelinthian. But do not mistake my praise for acceptance of your current weakness."

Nethriziin seized Thaedis's wrist. The pale white skin of the sorcerer withered to a black skeletal form. He observed the transfiguration with horror but concealed this from the Scion.

"I preserved your soul when it was on the brink of death, embalmed it in darkness, and bound it to carry forth my will in the Maelinthian. Do not forget this. I hold the power over your soul and can easily revoke my benevolence, abandoning you to the ravages of time. With all you have done, you know your soul's destiny. How long do you think you will last among your victims?"

The Scion released Thaedis from his grasp and sneered. "Were it not for that confounded box, you and your ilk would never have had a hope of conquering the Obsidious. I cannot believe that the likes of you could incarcerate me. Now, at last, the natural order is restored."

With that, Nethriziin stepped into the gray cloud from which he had emerged and returned to his throne in the Obsidious.

Thaedis flexed his fingers. His pale flesh had returned to its original consistency. How he rued the day he had handed control of his soul to that arrogant specter.

Suddenly the stolen sword flew from his grasp and escaped the chamber. Careering along the length of the *Sedah Destroyer*, it breached the hull and disappeared from sight.

Obsidian fire ignited the air beside Thaedis, and Tolbetrius stumbled onto the deck. The Emissary's wings were incinerated, his bone armor shattered, and his body marred by countless cuts.

"What in the four realms happened to you?" Thaedis asked with surprise as he watched the battered Edarian struggle to stand.

"He lives," Tolbetrius wheezed.

"What?"

"That little bastard and his bitch of an Elder Mage."

"Tell me what happened—*now*!"

Yudhara took a deep breath. "I was in the Nuhremorn, as the master ordered…when the boy emerged. Somehow he survived Zynoo."

"That is impossible."

"Is it really? A surreptitious force works to guide him on his quest, and it reeks of your old friend."

"Tyrel," Thaedis seethed, narrowing his gaze.

Tolbetrius held his chest between guarded breaths. "His appearance was an inconvenience, but I did what I was created to do. I attempted to find opportunity in a difficult situation. I tried to convert the boy to our cause."

"Oh, really? And will he be enlisting anytime soon?"

Tolbetrius ignored the sardonic jab. "I gave him the sword with the order to execute his Elder Mage. If he were to join us, he would need to sever all ties to the Light."

Thaedis looked out the view panel with growing rage. Mere seconds earlier, Nethriziin had threatened him, and now, to add insult, his closest ally had betrayed his trust. He felt his pulse quicken, and the dull throbbing in his head grew sharper. Heat rose from his normally cold form and misted the glass beneath his clenched fist.

When Nethriziin had incarcerated him as a mortal, he had been gifted a few of the powers he wielded as a Guardian. The ability that proved most useful in the Maelinthian was his power to ignite with a touch the Torementhicite within mortals. This allowed him to intimidate his subordinates and punish those who wronged him. Except in one key instance…

"He did not burn," he murmured to himself.

"What? No, he did not burn. Somehow he was immune to the Elder Mage's spell."

A spectral blast knocked Tolbetrius across the deck.

"That is but a consequence of your blunder. The plan was brilliant. When the War Mage defeated the Archlords, I knew he would absorb their essence. Every Archlord bears the darkness of an Edarian that he would have taken into his being. He should have been burned to a crisp. But that darkness never found a way into his soul at all, did it?"

The Emissary rose and struggled to steady himself. "You are right. That power never did find a way to the Zenorian boy. He would have squandered such a commodity. I took it as my own. I needed it to break down the defenses and reach the conduit, as the master instructed me to."

"Did you achieve this?"

Tolbetrius hesitated for a moment. "No. And I fear the cost of not finding it is greater than anticipated."

"You returned the sword to him. Do you have any idea how powerful that weapon is?"

"It is worse than that. He knows."

"He knows what, exactly?"

"He knows about the conduit...and the Sentinels."

Thaedis felt his pulse throbbing in his temples. "I made my orders to you very clear, Tolbetrius. Your recalcitrance has cost me dearly."

The Emissary snorted incredulously. "I have always been an obedient servant...but never to you. My will has always been to serve the interests of Nethriziin. I doubt you could say the same."

The control bridge darkened rapidly. Thaedis's growing fury drew the cloak of the Obsidious in his wake.

"You could not really have expected me to swear fealty to you over my own creator?" Tolbetrius continued. "Even less so when *I* created *you.*"

Thaedis cast the Edarian a frigid glare, and his white-knuckled fist drew in tighter.

"Yes, you heard me correctly. Nethriziin had conceived of an ideal mortal soldier to further his crusade. I saw the potential in you when you were a mere wisp in time. Your heart held the promise for great darkness. All it needed was a catalyst—which I handed you by being the mystic who schooled the Triad of Phantoms in dark magic."

Tolbetrius allowed himself a small smile as he saw a snarl flicker across Thaedis's face. "The great destiny you have relished was crafted for you by the Obsidious. You are but a mortal that gained the favor of my master for your vengeful desire. It would be wise to remember that, for when you are at your weakest, he will discard you for another. I am one of his own children; I am the one who handed him his perfect weapon. The Great Scion would never take a pitiful mortal over one of his own creations."

Thaedis crossed the distance to the Emissary in an instant, reappearing in a burst of smoke and laying his hands on the face of the Edarian. His stare pierced the slate-gray eyes of the Obsidian creature.

"Then I shall hurt him as I have so many before—through his child."

The sorcerer's eyes flared orange, and his touch incinerated the Torementhicite within Tolbetrius. The Emissary's red flesh turned to cinder, and his face contorted in fleeting agony and horror before his eyes grayed.

Thaedis bowed his head before the ashen cast of his former ally. "Know that I took no pleasure in this. But it was necessary."

He raised his hand to the face of the cast and, with a spectral blast, obliterated the ashen remains of Tolbetrius. However, the Emissary's death did little to fill the gaping hollow within him.

How had he allowed supposed allies he had known for so long to betray him? Nethriziin had manipulated and controlled his fate at every juncture of his life. His father's death at the hands of the Triad of Phantoms had been a result of Tolbetrius's interference. Nethriziin's venomous whispering when he was Guardian, urging him to seek out the soul of his father's killer, was no act of friendship on the Scion's part. The specter knew he would swoop to vengeance, and when he did, Nethriziin would find his weapon.

This was no benevolent Scion. His salvation from damnation had never been a charitable act, and he had been foolish to think otherwise. Now he was doomed to serve the fiend who had masterminded the execution of his father and had slain so many of his people. He should never have freed him from that durance.

This thought brought forth a recent memory. Nethriziin begrudged the Guardians for usurping him from his throne in the Obsidious. The specter had made one mistake by callously mentioning an artifact Thaedis had long since forgotten. It was through the Ark of Torementhias that the Guardians had learned how to imprison the Scion. However, the location of the Ark had been lost in time. When the Edarians stormed the Aetherealm to defeat Tyrel Salvidawn in his defiant last stand, they searched for it, but to no avail.

Tolbetrius had believed the Ark destroyed and never investigated further. Yet now that Thaedis thought more on the matter, he recalled that as Guardians, they had learned the Ark was indestructible. Perhaps his old friend, gifted with future sight, had witnessed Nethriziin's plan for Anmor and hid the Ark from the Scion's gaze. If he were to locate the Ark, he would gain freedom from Nethriziin and become the master of his destiny once more. He would be free to bring Anmor to order, as he had been born to do. But to find the Ark in the vast expanse of the Maelinthian would not be easy.

Although the Scion could manifest in the Maelinthian, he currently lacked the strength to maintain his presence. The ongoing war would change that. Furthermore, Rezaaran was now aware of the conduit and the role of the Sentinels. If he marshaled them, united under a common banner, they would overthrow the Dominion and all that he had worked to achieve. Only a handful of Archlords remained. The new legions he commissioned could contain IRIS but would taste defeat against the Sentinels. He had heard whispers of their collective might through the Vaux and dreaded having to contest them along with a fully powered Nethriziin.

The situation was slipping from his control, and although the Ark would change his fortunes, he needed time to find it. In the interim, he would hand control of the legions to the Harbingers. With the Ark in his possession, he could swiftly recoup any losses they incurred.

However, he would need someone with a specialized skill set to handle Rezaaran and the Sentinels.

"Eknarl!" he roared, calling the Dusanian spirit. "Send in my hunter."

CHAPTER THREE

THE ATMARI ALTAR

"Where are we going?" Rezaaran asked his ethereal mentor, walking beside her as they descended a spiral staircase.

Kashari had a distance about her before she answered, emerging from a reverie of memories she had thought forgotten. "When I was first cast into the Nuhremorn," she explained slowly, "this realm was a vast arboreal expanse. However, an incomprehensible magical power was also present. It existed as a great pillar of light that burned from the sky through the ground of this world. Alas, I have been in hibernation for almost three thousand years, and such a time has led me to forget a great many things. Recent events have helped remind me of the truth."

Rezaaran looked at the walls curiously as he followed Kashari deep into the caverns below the citadel. A glowing orb of light hovered above her hand, illuminating their way. Just ahead, an enormous stone carving depicting an explosion and the formation of four planes joined by a central streaked pillar adorned the wall.

"What is this, Kashari? I never saw this place before when we trained in the citadel."

"That is because I had forgotten it existed," Kashari admitted with mild embarrassment. "This citadel was constructed by three of the Anmorian Guardians: Lord Tyrel Salvidawn, Itara Zelzo, and Lady Luminara. The mural you see on the walls was left by Zelzo as a reminder of the history that transpired and what had necessitated the construction of this citadel."

Rezaaran followed the story captured in the ancient rock foundation. An army of creatures identical to Tolbetrius moved along the streaked pillar, their sights set upon a solitary figure who stood fast with a glaive aloft.

"Is this Lord Salvidawn?" Rezaaran asked, in awe of the warrior who stood valiantly against such a vast army of Obsidian creatures. One of them alone had been impossible to defeat; Rezaaran could not fathom the power this defender must have possessed to stand against a legion of them.

Kashari turned her attention to the mural, and the orb wandered from her hand across the sculpture. "No, my dear friend. The being you see before you is Alaris, the great Scion of Light. At the dawn of creation, there existed two stones: the Valinthian stone in the Aetherealm and the Torementhian stone in the Obsidious. Each of these stones generated its own magical power, which in turn gave rise to the primordial entities who came to be known as the scions Alaris and Nethriziin."

"Nethriziin..." Rezaaran mused. "That's the name of—"

"Tolbetrius's master," Kashari said. "A fact I too was made aware of recently. The Vokarii had thought him a mere myth, a shadow of legend. Alas, this is not so. It appears that the only truth of our place in Anmor, even of Anmor itself, is found in this mural."

Kashari continued down the last few stairs, which terminated into a long corridor, the mural accompanying their journey through the forgotten passageway.

"So...if Alaris could hold her ground against an army of creatures like Tolbetrius—"

"Edarians," Kashari corrected him.

"An army of Edarians, then why doesn't she contest Nethriziin? Or even Thaedis?"

The orb of light flowed to a depiction of Alaris with arms wide open and wings aloft. Rays of light reached from her chest to twelve individuals who looked toward her.

"Alaris grew weary of the conflict against the Obsidious. She was growing weaker with each passing century. Nethriziin knew he needed to augment his strength to defeat Alaris; however, he had gained all he could from the Obsidious and so turned his sights to the Maelinthian. His pernicious influence spread through the mortal realm, no doubt by way of Tolbetrius. The Obsidian touch fell upon emerging civilizations as whisperings of treachery, sparking violence. The growing bloodlust and hatred strengthened Nethriziin and his armies further in their efforts against Alaris. She could not defend a people she did not understand. Therefore, she anointed the Anmorian Guardians in her stead. To each she gifted command of elements within her control and scattered her essence between them and the Vaux.

"In a surprise assault, the Guardians marched on Nethriziin's fortress at Torementhias and sealed him within a prison in the Obsidious. The Edarians relinquished to the will of the Guardians. Salvidawn and Thaedis decided together to spare their lives."

"Thaedis is a Guardian?" Rezaaran asked incredulously.

"He was the most powerful of the Guardians. Lord Salvidawn felt that Thaedis far surpassed him in every measure. Thaedis Silvermire was once a valiant and honor-bound warrior, a champion of truth and justice. He averted numerous cataclysmic wars and with Lord Salvidawn oversaw the longest era of peace Anmor ever knew."

Rezaaran's eyes swept over a hooded figure surrounded by Edarians, his sword drawn and his gaze looking upward toward the Aetherealm. "What happened to him?"

Kashari looked at Rezaaran hesitantly. He had come so very close to following Thaedis's path and now stood at a precarious point in his journey. "He was seduced by the Obsidious, swayed by his thirst for vengeance. Thaedis believed that the Anmorian Guardians had conspired against him and led an attack upon them with an army of Edarians at his command. He was swiftly defeated at the hands of the Guardians. They stripped his powers and banished him to the Maelinthian. During this time, Lord Salvidawn foresaw his return at the forefront of a great evil and knew that the Guardians would not be able to contest his wrath."

Rezaaran gazed at the figure draped in a billowing cloak who had killed his father. The Exiled. "If the Guardians could not defeat him, how does Salvidawn expect a mortal to undertake such a task?"

"Indeed, such a quest would be impossible for one mortal to perform, regardless of his or her individual power."

The War Mage turned his gaze from the depiction of the Antarika Citadel to his mentor. "What do you mean, Kashari?" They had entered a new chamber. It was cold and dim with a wisp of steam in the distance. "What is this place?"

Kashari smiled benignly and walked down the pathway alongside Rezaaran. The young War Mage felt the cool touch of water around their path.

"Lord Salvidawn knew that Thaedis had to be defeated, that the Light had to prevail. Together with Zelzo and Luminara, they constructed a safe haven for five powerful souls. These five warriors, these Sentinel souls, would walk the mortal plane but be gifted abilities far beyond any mortal. Together they would be able to defeat Thaedis and Nethriziin. Together they would return the Light to Anmor."

"There are others like me?"

"In a manner of speaking. The Guardians created the Sentinels to be powerful and to inspire hope in the hearts of mortals. However, each of you was unique."

"So...what is this place?"

"Behold the Atmari Altar."

The orb of light flew from Kashari's hand to the center of the chamber and exploded above a pedestal. Five blue fires burst alive, each at the foot of a giant statue. Each statue occupied a pentagonal base connected to a central pentagon by a walkway, with a pedestal in the center of the altar. The entire monument rested atop a still lake.

Rezaaran approached the altar in awe of its sheer size. From within the black marble figures, he felt the whisper of subdued echoes.

"This place has been under the citadel the whole time?" he asked incredulously, gazing upon each statue in turn.

"Indeed it has, my friend. As I said before, after hibernation in this realm for so long, I have forgotten a great many things. However, Lord Salvidawn reminded me of the purpose for which he bound me to the Nuhremorn. I was to protect the Sentinels."

"I can feel the traces of a great power lingering in this chamber."

"When Tolbetrius gained enough power to take the citadel," Kashari explained, "I knew he could never be allowed to gain access to the altar. I dampened the echo of the altar to hide this chamber. I did what was needed to preserve all of you."

Rezaaran felt a pang of guilt. He remembered how enraged he had been on Zynoo that Kashari had subdued his powers. Yet now he understood that she had done it to protect him. She had saved them all from the monster he himself had allowed to enter this sacred world. He was not worthy of her forgiveness.

"Kashari, I—"

"You defeated Tolbetrius," Kashari replied with a warm smile, resting her hand on Rezaaran's shoulder. "You preserved the last hope for the Light to return to Anmor. You lived up to every hope Lord Salvidawn and I held for you."

Rezaaran lowered his gaze. He could not stand to meet his mentor's eyes, ashamed at how he had treated her after Voltfes.

"With the Guardians fallen to the Obsidious," Kashari continued, "it now remains to these few souls to come together and fight this ancient battle. Now is the time for the legacy of the Sentinels."

Rezaaran approached the pedestal, which proudly bore a steel plaque that read: "Here stand the five who shall guard Anmor in our absence: Loradún the Bold, Mergen the Wise, Morak the Faithful, Diothur the Just, and Dilisin the Kind. May these Sentinels be the Light when darkness surrounds us."

The War Mage placed his hands on the circles beside the plaque. The steel plate revolved to expose a bare surface with the inscription "Their spirits shall bind them in purpose."

"*Our* spirits," Rezaaran whispered, remembering his journey to the palace of Kel-Ardimus with his grandfather.

He drew Harkenathor, quite sure this was where the blade was meant to find its home. Rezaaran set the blade upon the plate. The marble pedestal rumbled briefly, and five domed stones rose in front of the metal plate. The names of the Sentinels glowed below each stone.

Rezaaran held his breath, and his fingers apprehensively touched the stone marked "Loradún." The name Tolbetrius had called him.

The flames at the feet of the statue holding a raised sword flared alive, and the lake shimmered. Rezaaran turned his attention to an image of himself at the altar that was projected across the lake and mirrored his actions and astonishment.

"This is incredible!" he gasped.

Kashari allowed herself a small smile. It was good to see remnants of the wonderstruck young mage she had encountered for the first time last year. There was hope yet for Anmor.

The War Mage's hand passed to the stone marked "Mergen" and activated the flames at the base of a statue with a pensive finger to its downcast forehead. The lake shimmered and displayed a red-haired scientist wearing a large pair of spectacles. He was at work in a laboratory on what appeared to be a suit of armor that bore an unusual familiarity to the armor Rezaaran had worn during his missions with Ashana.

He activated the next avatar, Diothur, who held an appraising hand aloft and a drawn dagger in the other. However, when the fires at the foot of the statue flared alive, the lake did not shimmer and depict the Sentinel as it had previously. Instead, it showed only smoke and cinder.

Rezaaran looked at his mentor anxiously. "Why can I not see this Sentinel?"

"In truth, I do not know, my friend. Whatever the reason may be, they are lost beyond the gaze of the Light, perhaps fallen in battle."

Rezaaran thought on this solemnly. As a slave on Mar-Karatheer, he had always felt alone. He had always yearned to find people with whom he could connect. When he joined IRIS, Ashana had become such a person. So too had Kashari. However, something about this altar and the Sentinels seemed to transcend friendship. Each time he touched these stones and saw the souls, he felt he had known them for a lifetime…and possibly in lifetimes before. Even though he had not known Diothur in this life, the thought that she had died created a void in the depths of his soul.

His hand passed over the next stone, and a blue flame illuminated the statue of Morak, a stoic figure with a fist firmly pressed against his palm held before his hooded face. The lake shimmered again and revealed the mortal identity of the Sentinel.

"Jet!" Rezaaran exclaimed incredulously. "Jet is a Sentinel!"

Kashari had never seen her young apprentice so excited. "Do you know this...creature?"

Rezaaran looked at her sternly. "Kashari, he's a person. He was my closest friend on Mar-Karatheer—the reason I kept my hope for a better tomorrow. Yet now it seems he needs some of that hope for himself."

Jet had his head down on a countertop. Four empty bottles of different liquors lay toppled around him, and an ash pile spilled from its dish onto the counter. Rezaaran felt as his own the despair and sorrow brewing within his friend. How had this become the adult of the exuberant and excitable young rebel he had befriended on Mar-Karatheer? What tragedies had befallen Jet to break him so?

Suddenly Jet grunted and sat up. Bleary-eyed, he looked around and murmured Rezaaran's name.

Rezaaran immediately released his hand from the stone. "Can they see me looking at them?"

"No, they cannot. The Nuhremorn exists outside time and space. Zelzo explained to me once that should a Sentinel touch the bulbs to commune with their counterparts, the soul who was reached would experience a feeling of remembering the one who called out to them."

The War Mage thought about this as he reached for the last stone. He turned his eye toward the remaining statue, vaguely seeing its form in the glow of the others. Dilisin's statue, a hooded figure with a half-drawn bow, flared alive at his touch.

Rezaaran's heart skipped a beat as he saw the scene in the lake. Tears welled in the corners of his eyes when he saw Ashana sitting beside his own unconscious body in an infirmary. She had fallen asleep at his bedside with his hand in hers. Rezaaran felt a flood of emotions at seeing her from this distance: guilt for how he had treated her on Voltfes, shame for how he had manipulated her trust on Zynoo, and self-loathing for how he had taken her love for granted. Yet despite everything he had done, she had neither lost faith in him nor wavered in her affection. He felt the love she felt for him—and her sincere hope that he would return to her.

A tear ran from his eye, and he longed to hold her once more, longed to make everything right again.

"Ash," he whispered. "I miss you."

Ashana roused slowly and looked toward Rezaaran's body. She gently stroked his hair from his face and reassured him that all was well, that she was not going to leave his side.

Rezaaran withdrew his hand reluctantly. He took a moment to compose himself, and then a thought wandered through his mind. "Did you know that Ashana was a Sentinel?"

"I only learned who the Sentinels were when I came to depower the altar and hide its existence from Tolbetrius."

Rezaaran swiftly stepped toward Kashari and held her in a tight embrace. "Thank you. Thank you so much for keeping her safe. I know it was my fault—"

"Don't start doing that," Kashari interrupted, releasing her student from the embrace. "The mistakes we make shape us into the people we become. I have forgiven you for what has happened. And just as the blame is not yours alone to bear, so too is the forgiveness you seek not mine alone to grant."

"Of course. I need to make things right with Ashana as well. I understand that clearly now."

"That is commendable and gallant to be sure. However, what I mean is that you need to forgive yourself."

Rezaaran realized Kashari was right, as in her wisdom she frequently was. However, he knew the only path toward forgiveness lay in his repenting and redeeming himself through his actions henceforth.

"Besides, I would never allow anything to destroy the beautiful bond you and Ashana share," Kashari added. "As I have told you before, my friend, the love you and Ashana share is your anchor through any storm."

Rezaaran looked at her sharply, and his face began to beam.

Kashari smiled tentatively. "You have that look. Like you are about to attempt something impossible."

"I have an idea! Come with me, Kashari!"

Rezaaran and Kashari arrived at the ramparts of the citadel a few moments later. To the delight of both Zenorians, a familiar view greeted them. After it had scoured Tolbetrius's pestilence from the land, the storm had abated and returned the Nuhremorn to its original pristine state. In the distance, the chorus of free souls found its voice once more. The skies remained gray as always, yet they no longer evidenced the foreboding that had accompanied the emergence of Tolbetrius. Instead, they now drew the hopeful gaze of one War Mage.

"What do you plan to do, Rezaaran?"

"Something at the altar stirred an instinct within me. I felt that the Vaux showed me that this is what I have to do. I know that probably sounds crazy."

"Not in the least. The Vaux directs all mages in life, and those who choose to listen to its counsel find what they are meant to."

"I believe that if Ashana is my anchor in my journey, then just as she could feel my presence at the altar, I can reach her from beyond the altar as well."

Rezaaran took a deep breath and calmed his mind. Opening his arms wide, he thought of the image he had seen at the Atmari Altar. He pictured Ashana beside him in the infirmary at the IRIS base. He remembered the feeling of her fingers between his own. Memories flashed through his mind of every moment they had shared to this point. He remembered the floral scent of her hair, the same fragrance that had permeated the *Larkesian Liberator*. He remembered how her smile would illuminate any room. He remembered holding her close when they watched the stars on Artherikas.

"Ashana, if you can hear me," Rezaaran said toward the gray firmament, "I want you to know that I am alive. More than that—I want you to know how sorry I am. I have taken so much for granted of late, and you were the one who suffered most for my selfishness. I was cold and callous. I pushed you away when what you needed most was compassion. I allowed my ambition to overcome my reason and lost sight of what was important. Despite everything that I learned from my Vokarii training, the most wonderful magic I have ever experienced occurs when I am with you. You are the piece of myself that has always been missing, and you are the reason I want to push myself to become better than the man I have been. I want to become the man you know I can be, the person you have never lost faith in my becoming. Despite the distance that separates us now, I will find a way back to you. I will always find my way back to you, because you are the one my heart will forever be tied to."

Ashana awoke with a start and looked at Rezaaran. She gently brushed his hair aside and took his hand in her own.

"Don't worry, Rez," she whispered as she kissed his hand. "I'm here for you."

She closed her eyes once more, reflecting on the strange dream she'd just had of Rezaaran wandering a dark corridor toward a marble monument. The scene had then fragmented, and she'd seen him standing at the edge of a great stone fortress, looking toward the sky. However, during the unusual dream, she'd had a strange feeling that Rezaaran was there with her in spirit and that she had heard his voice calling out to her.

Maybe she just needed something to drink. A shower would probably not hurt, either. Most likely her anxiety about Rezaaran's state had caused these strange dreams. For what else could they be? They most definitely were not memories. Neither of them had ever visited a place that looked at all like the scenes she had glimpsed.

Ashana stood to leave. However, as her fingers reluctantly released Rezaaran's, she had a premonition, the wind gushing around her. Unlike the portents she'd had previously, this was more of a feeling within herself than a visual foresight. She felt a warmth within her core that reminded her of how she felt about Rezaaran whenever they were together.

She sat beside him once more, looking intently at his closed eyes, and squeezed his hand between hers. She was certain she'd felt a flicker of movement in his hand. Yet adding to her concern was that within an instant, a new scar had formed across his face. What was happening to him?

"Come home to me, Rez," she whispered quietly.

A beam of light broke through the clouds and landed on Rezaaran's chest. In the distance came a rumbling from beyond the clouds, too soft to be thunder and yet too indistinct for him to clearly discern.

Rezaaran kept his mind focused on thoughts of Ashana, homing in on her echo. He felt the Antarika Citadel drift away, and a warmth swept over him. The light around him brightened, and the sound from the distance clarified. Ashana was calling out to him.

Kashari watched in amazement and delight as Rezaaran levitated above the ramparts and the mysterious pillar of light drew him in. She had read once of magic so powerful that it transcended the physical realm. Yet seeing it with her own eyes was an experience she had never anticipated.

"Come home to me, Rez." Ashana's voice pealed through the heavens as the young War Mage floated in midair.

A thunderous crack resounded across the sky with an accompanying brilliant flare. Rezaaran awoke with a start and looked around in bewilderment, but he found his bearings immediately as his gaze fell upon Ashana.

She gasped in astonishment and embraced him tightly. "You came back!"

"I don't intend to leave anytime soon. I have missed you, Ash!"

CHAPTER FOUR

WHAT WAS LOST TO THE DARK

"Is this really necessary? I am fine! Really, I am!"

But Rezaaran's bravado fell upon deaf ears. Four small silver orbs encircled him, navigating their course from his head to his feet. They relayed their scanned information to a series of monitors that Xephyrus scrutinized.

"Most of your physical injuries healed rapidly due to your latent regeneration," Xephyrus said. "However, for some inexplicable reason, you remained in stasis. I attempted to heal you with light magic but to no avail. Honestly, without your regenerative abilities, you would not have survived. We pulled you from under a rockslide."

A silence followed Xephyrus's explanation while he accessed the menu to read the older reports on Rezaaran's state. Rezaaran realized that had Lord Salvidawn not intervened when he did, the War Mage would not have been able to regenerate.

Xephyrus spoke again. "When we realized you were not improving, we transferred you to this secret medical facility on a moon orbiting the planet Inyas. Ashana and her former legion stayed on to guard the facility and you while Albeinius supervised the initial setup of the facility. Based on the initial scans performed on your arrival, you suffered an unusual neurological injury with a resultant dissociation of several distinct regions of your brain."

"I thought you weren't a doctor."

"I am not," Xephyrus murmured, reading the latest report generated by the computer. "These droids perform a thorough systemic scan and then generate an assessment and solution that the medical droids then enact. According to their assessment, your condition is stable. However, they cannot explain how you developed that scar you now sport."

"Well, that's a relief to hear. As for this scar, that's quite a story to tell. Are these scanning droids your brother's new invention?"

"You would think so," Xephyrus replied. He closed the reports and turned to face Rezaaran. "However, this set of intriguing technology was created by a new addition to Albeinius's team."

"Since when does he have a team?" Rezaaran asked with a cocked eyebrow and a bemused expression.

"There's a lot to catch you up on, Rez," Ashana replied with a smile, taking his hand in her own.

"It's only been a few days. How much could have really changed?"

Ashana and Xephrus exchanged a silent, concerned look.

"What?" Rezaaran asked.

"Rez, you were in a coma for a while," Ashana said gently. "You've been here for three months now."

Rezaaran looked at her in disbelief. He shifted his gaze to Xephyrus, who offered a curt confirmatory nod. "Well, I guess there is a lot that we all have to share."

"Like Xephyrus said, we found you buried beneath a pile of rocks," Ashana said. "Was that because of Silvermire?"

"Yes," Rezaaran replied mirthlessly, avoiding the gaze of his friends. "He defeated me and took Harkenathor. I…I remember the screams." Rezaaran closed his eyes, and tears rolled down his cheek. Ashana held him comfortingly around the shoulders. "Their screams were so loud. All of them. Did anyone survive what he did to Prashorida?"

He looked with hope for some indication from either of them that some mercy had been shown, but he knew it was only a fool's hope. Xephyrus grimly shook his head.

"He obliterated the city. There were no survivors."

Rezaaran held his head between his hands. They had not deserved such a fate. They had been freed of Zelzo's curse only to be scorched from existence in Obsidian fire. It was his fault. "What else happened?"

"Rezaaran, there is nothing that can change what has been done."

"Xephyrus," Rezaaran whispered with a choked voice. "I need to know."

The Elder Mage remained silent, reluctant to say anything more. He knew it would only cause Rezaaran more heartache. However, Ashana knew that despite the pain and burden it would place on his shoulders, he needed to know the truth.

"We've lost many of the worlds we once liberated," she said. "Following Zynoo, Silvermire wanted to make a statement that the Dominion would not tolerate any challenge to its rule. He forcefully recaptured Voltfes, Xorax, and Balkavis Seven, along with most of the liberated worlds in quadrants one and three. We lost many soldiers in the battles."

"How can this not be my fault, Xephyrus?"

The Elder Mage remained silent and afforded Rezaaran the opportunity for reflection.

"I was so certain, so arrogant in my belief that I could defeat Silvermire," Rezaaran said. "I kept goading him, kept riling him to greater rage. I lost more than the battle. I lost my way, my purpose, and my discipline. So many have suffered because of my foolish selfishness."

"Yes, many have suffered." Xephrus spoke slowly, carefully weighing his words. "Yet the war is not lost. As long as we keep fighting, hope remains. You inspired so many within our ranks after your success on Imperitus. With every world that you freed, the tales of what people witnessed spread. So too did hope. Yes, you strayed from your purpose, from your teachings. It happens to us all at some point. What matters more is that you realized the error of your actions and committed to change. I know you, Rezaaran. You have a righteous heart and will always see that truth and justice are upheld. You are a hero. We will never stop believing that about you."

Rezaaran dried his eyes. He clasped Xephyrus's hand in his and brought him into an embrace with Ashana. "I am grateful to have people like the two of you in my life. I know there is no blood between us, but were it not for IRIS, I would truly be without a family."

"You'd better get used to us, then," Ashana said with a smile, "because you are stuck with us for a very long time."

"I concur," Xephrus replied with a small smile. Rezaaran truly had a fiery spirit, but he worried that this news may serve to break it.

"I wouldn't wish it any other way. I suppose we should choose to look at the positive side."

Ashana and Xephyrus looked at him curiously.

"Xephyrus, are you sure those scans show a normal brain?" Ashana asked with a trace of cynicism. "What was possibly a good thing in any of what we told you?"

"Silvermire no longer holds Harkenathor," Rezaaran replied with half a mirthless smile.

"You know this how, exactly?" she asked.

Xephyrus, his arms crossed, had a skeptical look upon his face.

"After my injuries on Zynoo, I was visited by Lord Salvidawn."

Xephyrus's eyes widened. "Lord Salvidawn?" he asked. "King of the Aetherealm? The ancient Zenorian prince who was appointed as a Guardian, safeguarding peace and freedom across all time?"

"The very same one!"

"I thought he was a myth."

"No, Ash. He's very much a real person."

"What was it like to be in his presence?" Xephyrus asked.

"It was..." Rezaaran thought for a moment, considering how to adequately explain the surreal nature of meeting such a powerful being. "It was majestic. *He* was majestic. In his presence, it felt like you could glimpse all of eternity."

A distant but blissful look crossed Xephyrus's face at this thought.

"What happened next?" Ashana asked.

"He returned me to life. Briefly, anyway. I returned to Prashorida for a few moments before fading into unconsciousness."

"That's when I found you."

"The next thing I remember was waking up in the Nuhremorn."

"The plane between the Aetherealm and the mortal realm?" Xephyrus asked with a raised eyebrow. Although he knew Rezaaran would not lie about such an experience, this required a tremendous suspension of disbelief on his part. Everything Rezaaran had mentioned thus far was enshrined in the oldest of Vokarii writings but deemed mere mythology by modern scholars.

"The very same, Xephyrus." Rezaaran spoke solemnly. "I met Kashari, the spirit bound to Harkenathor. However, a creature of the Obsidious had corrupted the Nuhremorn. That is the reason I bear this scar. The creature called itself an Edarian."

"The ancient tomes mention these creatures," Xephyrus murmured as he recalled the description. "According to the legends, they were the denizens of the Obsidious. Tales foretold that their presence would exist as the sway upon the hearts of weaker men. Despite this, they could never emerge in the mortal realm due to the fundamental forces of magic."

"That is true...to some extent, anyway. The Edarian I encountered said that the Archlords I have fought are Edarians possessing the former Anmorian Guardians." Rezaaran paused and allowed Xephyrus to process this.

"So...the protectors of Anmor," Xephyrus began slowly, "are all enslaved to creatures of the Obsidious?"

"Well, not *all* the Guardians. One survived the war against the Obsidious because he initiated the conflict—Thaedis Silvermire."

"Silvermire is a former Anmorian Guardian?" Ashana asked, awe and terror glazing her face. "Then how do we defeat him?"

Rezaaran looked at her curiously.

"What?" she asked. "I may not be a Vokarii, but that does not mean I am unaware of the legends. The ancient scripts of every magical order on Zenor chronicled the immense power of the Guardians. They draw their strength from the most fundamental magic, from the very reality of existence itself. If Silvermire really is one of these Guardians incarnate, then how can we hope to stop him?"

After his jaunt through the Nuhremorn, Rezaaran realized he did not require proximity to Harkenathor to call upon the bond with Kashari. In moments like this, her counsel proved invaluable.

Should I tell them about the Sentinels?

Not at present, my friend. There is much we still have to learn. And alas, I am not the one to teach you in this venture. We will know when the time is right to reveal Salvidawn's plan to the others.

"I trust in the strength of IRIS," Rezaaran said simply, "and that our answers will be revealed through the Vaux."

"Fair enough, I suppose," Ashana said slowly, regarding Rezaaran with a shrewd eye. She felt more was at play than what he'd divulged, but she trusted his judgment. "So how do you know that Harkenathor is no longer in the command of Silvermire?"

"I sense its echo nearing. It calls out to me. Actually…" Rezaaran looked out the window. Suddenly he leaped off the table, caught Ashana in his arms, and rushed aside. Harkenathor shattered the tall glass panel and embedded itself into the metal floor of the infirmary.

Several soldiers of Legion Ninety-Nine stormed the room with their weapons readied. However, once satisfied there was no imminent threat, they relaxed and greeted Rezaaran cordially before they exited the medical bay. Many were glad to see he had recovered, and more than one remarked that now Ashana could rest easier.

Rezaaran drew Ashana into a loving embrace and gently ran his fingers through her hair as her head rested against his chest. "I'm glad to be back here with you."

Xephyrus cleared his throat. "Well, I shall let you two catch up." His cheeks were flushed. "We will be leaving tomorrow at first light for a council meeting aboard the *Metrovia*."

Xephyrus made a hurried departure, leaving Rezaaran alone with Ashana for the first time since he had awoken.

"There's so much I need to tell you, Ash," Rezaaran began, "so many things I did not have a chance to say before—"

Ashana pulled him close and kissed him passionately. Rezaaran closed his eyes and took in the moment, feeling everything else fade away, lost in the ecstasy.

Rezaaran awoke a few hours later, drenched in a cold sweat. Flames and gunfire and a great shadow overhead had surrounded him. Yet now he realized it had merely been a dream. He climbed out of bed, taking care not to disturb Ashana, and quietly donned his thermal suit. He watched her sleeping peacefully. He was genuinely happy to be with her again, but he had a foreboding about events to come. He needed guidance.

The doors to the infirmary parted for the War Mage. Nobody had attempted to remove Harkenathor, and the soldiers of Legion Ninety-Nine had posted themselves around the perimeter of the facility after the sword had crashed into the infirmary. A blaster shutter sealed off the broken window and insulated the infirmary from the outside world.

In the silence that surrounded him, his thoughts flashed back to the nightmare from which he had awoken. Had it truly been a nightmare? It had felt so real. He recalled the screams, the explosions, the fire fights. He had been on a battlefield, but the objects around him were blurred shadows too indistinct to identify. Despite the uncertainty, a definite foreboding about the surreal experience now haunted him. Had he glimpsed the future? Had he gained some of Ashana's abilities? They had been together that night, but surely being together physically could not transfer magical abilities. Although the experience had been magical in itself, he doubted he had gained future sight by such a means. He could always ask Kashari, but he was not entirely comfortable having such a conversation with the aged mentor.

His fingers closed around the leather hilt of Harkenathor. The familiar, solid deftness of the weapon was a welcome reprieve amid the uncertainty that enshrouded him. He felt a stirring between himself and the sword, a rekindling of spirits after their lengthy separation.

Rezaaran attempted to draw the weapon from the floor, but it held fast, relentless in resisting his repeated and increasingly forceful attempts to dislodge it. Frustrated, he reluctantly released his grasp. Maybe in the morning he could find some heavy-duty equipment to extract the blade. Then he recalled his grandfather's words to him on Zenor last year.

"Strength alone will not help," Rezaaran murmured. "It is your spirit."

He regarded Harkenathor carefully. After his trial through the Nuhremorn, he expected his bond with Harkenathor to be stronger than ever.

Our bond is as strong as you believe, my friend. However, your spirit remains fractured, and as long as that is so, you will never be able to wield the might you once knew.

"I don't understand why I feel conflicted about my destiny. In the past, I had such certainty about my actions, but now I feel lost."

As I said before, Rezaaran, the first step to redemption is forgiving yourself. Let go of the guilt and the sorrow for the past, and embrace the future. You are the one destined to lead the Sentinels in the forthcoming battles. This is no trivial feat, and you cannot undertake this with a heart in conflict with itself.

"You're right," Rezaaran said, seating himself on the edge of an examination table. "I've made so many mistakes trying to create peace through my quest. My actions and indiscretions are directly responsible for so many deaths of people I ought to have protected. In the wake of what has happened, the Sentinels are the only source of hope. If I am to walk this road to my redemption, then I need to accept that all the actions that led to this point are part of my history. I need to learn from them and safeguard myself against succumbing to the same vices of pride and power lust."

How do you propose to do that?

"By having the humility to accept that I cannot do this alone. It was arrogant and foolish to think otherwise. I am glad to have you guiding me in this, Kashari, and I will endeavor to be the student you held in such high regard. I believe that in uniting the Sentinels and rallying us to defeat Thaedis, I can open myself to depend and trust in others."

Rezaaran, you will always be my greatest student and the highest source of pride for me. You were born to be a hero, just as I was born to guide you. Together we can defeat Thaedis! The Light will prevail!

"With you and Ashana as well as the Sentinels by my side, I know we can achieve peace in our time. Let's do this...together!"

A fire roared alive in Rezaaran's heart once more. With renewed purpose, he grasped the hilt of Harkenathor and effortlessly reclaimed his weapon.

Rezaaran felt his conviction burn stronger than ever within himself, and he welcomed the comfort of the familiarity. With

Harkenathor at his side, he returned to the chamber he shared with Ashana. Tomorrow he would meet the council, and he did not require Ashana's future sight to know that it would be an unwelcoming affair.

The soldiers disembarked from the shuttle into the bustling hangar deck of the *Metrovia*. Rezaaran's gaze shifted across the throng of people before him and admired the vast expanse of this phenomenal structure crafted solely to house the liberated people. Yet he remained painfully aware of the uncomfortable situation that crept steadily closer.

"Are you all right?"

"Yeah, I'm fine," Rezaaran replied quickly as he and Ashana entered a lift to the main deck. "Why do you ask? Is it your future sight?"

"I don't need my future sight," she replied kindly with half a smile. "I know you, Rez. What's wrong?"

"After everything that happened since my defeat on Zynoo, we can guess the likely course this council meeting will take."

"You've battled monstrous Archlords with the power to devastate entire worlds, but you're worried about a group of egomaniacal soldiers?"

"Well, that was different. I had you at my side in each of those battles."

"You still do," she replied with a bright smile, interlocking her fingers with Rezaaran's.

"I thought this was a council meeting."

"It is, but I'd like to see them try to keep me from being present. We are in this together, Rez, through whatever comes our way. I am going to be here with you...always."

Rezaaran beamed and kissed her.

The pair of young soldiers entered the council chamber in solemn silence—the expected decorum. However, what greeted them within the chamber most certainly was not.

"I guess we are just very early."

Ashana's tart remark did little to mask her surprise or irritation at this insult. Despite the summons for a council meeting and their arrival at exactly the time Gerrin had indicated to them, they were alone. They took their seats next to one another at the empty table.

Sometime later, the doors parted for Leta and Moraya. The former offered a curt nod of acknowledgment while the latter greeted only Ashana. Rezaaran cared little about her disregard of him. Ashana was right: after everything they had endured together this past year, the petty actions of the egocentric council members were laughable in comparison.

A portal shimmered into existence, and Gerrin emerged, draped in his hooded silver cloak and with his lance strapped to his back. He drew back the hood and regarded the pair of young soldiers with a derisive snort.

Rezaaran braced himself, knowing that Gerrin was the one most likely to get the better of his temper.

"Glad you could make it. I hope you are ready to start cleaning up the shitstorm you threw upon us while you decided to take a nap!"

"Gerrin, that's a bit uncalled for, don't—"

"I don't remember asking your damn opinion!" Gerrin snapped at Ashana, fury flaming in his eyes. "Nor do I recall you being appointed to this council!"

"I have offered my fair share to IRIS in my time," Ashana replied firmly, rising from her seat. "And I have spent the better part of this past year on the mission with Rezaaran that Orin assigned us."

Gerrin sneered at the War Mage. "Happy to let your little girlfriend here fight your battles for you, boy? Well, I'm not surprised, given your show of incompetence that led us to this state. Years of work, of our hard-won victories, lost in a few months because this glorified imbecile failed!" Gerrin slammed his hands onto the table and glowered at Rezaaran. Then he turned his rage on Ashana once more. "As for you and your bogus mission—while you two are merrily trooping across the galaxy chasing fantastic tales, the rest of us are making hard sacrifices to advance this war. Meanwhile, Orin protects and submits to you because of your lineage. Well, you are not *my* princess. I am not from Sylvoria, and the Kingdoms of

Zenor are no more. In IRIS, I am your ranking officer, and I will not tolerate this insubordination!"

Rezaaran cast a sideways glance at Ashana. He could not believe she was the princess of Sylvoria.

Gerrin detected the disbelief like a ravenous anarchist predator scenting new prey. "Ah...you didn't know," he sneered. "Perhaps that is something the two of you can discuss on your next escapade as you continue this tryst!"

Rezaaran abruptly leaped to his feet, his arms alight with flames. However, Gerrin's sneer was erased by a blue bolt that struck his golden loop earring and spasmed his face.

Everyone turned to face the doorway, where Aloric Melias stood with his pistol still aimed at Gerrin's head. A disappointed Xephyrus, a solemn-faced Stryker, and an irate, growling Muraka flanked him.

"Take your seat, Gerrin." The Gundancer's commanding voice resounded throughout the room. "*Now!*"

Gerrin slowly drew his chair. His eyes remained fixed on the young soldiers while his spasm abated.

"I am highly disappointed in you, Gerrin. Fortunately, Orin was not yet transmitting, or he would have had to witness your disgusting behavior. Rezaaran is a council member by Orin's order. Having fought alongside him, I will adamantly vouch for his position. Regarding his mission, this is no mere tale of fantasy or escapism. I have faced just one of the monsters Orin tasked Rezaaran with defeating. Are you calling the general and me liars?"

"No, sir," Gerrin replied stiffly. His cheeks became duskier with each moment that passed.

"As for your insults to Princess Ashana, count yourself lucky that Commander Muraka is merciful. She has proven her worth to IRIS as a leader and a committed soldier. She gains no preference from anyone because of her lineage. Yet we cannot forget our heritage, and we will not tolerate such disrespect. You are a council member. Act like one."

"Yes, sir," Gerrin murmured with a downcast gaze. "I am sorry, Princess Ashana." It was clear he uttered this forced apology only because he could not bear to meet the fearsome glare of the burly Muraka.

Rezaaran felt his rage abate, and the fires dispersed from his arms. However, he had lost the sleeves of his thermal suit—a point nobody dared mention in the wake of Aloric's harsh words.

"Well, if this juvenile business is behind us," Xephyrus said, taking his position at the table's head, "we can proceed to the reasons we are gathered. Orin is on a liberation mission with several of our detachments. The general has requested this meeting for an update on all our current missions. Furthermore, Rezaaran has some new information to share with us regarding the leadership of the Dominion. Finally, we have received intelligence reports from the Zamtians about Dominion activity on Hysforth. We have a lot to get through, so let us focus and proceed, please."

The soldiers walked in silence along the corridor. The scalding council meeting they'd endured had erased the blissful memories from a few hours prior. Yet despite everything that was said, one topic remained at the forefront of their thoughts.

"Why didn't you tell me, Ash?" Rezaaran asked, breaking the silence.

The archer sighed as they entered an elevator. "I really am sorry. It's something you should have known about me from the outset. I just...I lost that life a long time ago. Ever since being brought to IRIS, I have had to distance myself from all the pain that followed my losing everything and everyone I had ever known. Orin felt it was best that I leave my original identity behind me and adopt a new one, that I would be safer if nobody knew I was the princess of Sylvoria. I was happy to become someone else. I never wanted people to pity me or to give me any special treatment because of my past. I had no ties to my past. Besides, the royal family of Sylvoria raises their children with the ideal that we rule as one of the people, never above them. Orin's way felt like the right path to become one with the survivors of Zenor. I didn't want people to revere, worship, or die for me. I wanted to be part of the fight for our people. I wanted to be a leader like Orin. The people of Zenor shouldn't follow me out of obligation.

I should be someone they follow because I am a leader that inspires followers to a just cause."

As Ashana explained her stance, Rezaaran found himself falling for her so much more. He knew that when the day came for Zenorians to return to their way of life, she would rule as a fair and just queen. Not only did she fiercely stand for her views, she also proved to be the quintessence of compassion, like her Sentinel soul.

"Well...as long as you don't expect me to start calling you any royal titles from now on."

"You start doing that, and I'll have Gunner slobber oil across your face while you sleep." She turned to face him as they exited the elevator. "Are we going to be all right after this?"

"Of course," Rezaaran replied with a smile and brushed a stray stand of hair from her face. "I understand the pain you feel from losing your family, and I understand why you would want to leave that life behind to become someone else. I also know that when the time comes, Zenorians will cherish a leader who took the time to become one of them."

"Thank you, Rez," she said, squeezing his hands before they continued down the corridor. "By the way, it's Binarjiin."

"What's that?"

"My surname. My real one, at least."

"Very well, Ashana Binarjiin. Where are we off to?"

"Albeinius wanted to see us before we leave for Hysforth."

The scientist's eyes narrowed and his brow furrowed as he watched the nanobots constructing his device. His attention flashed to the monitor on his desk. It seemed that the construction was on the right path. For now, at least.

"My fiery-haired wonderfriend," his fellow scientist remarked with a laugh, turning his hovering chair to face him. "I sense a lot of agitation in you. Relax. These droids know what they are doing."

"And how can you be so certain that they will not make a mistake?"

"Well, it's simple," replied the second scientist. "I built them myself."

The red-haired inventor rolled his eyes but chuckled lightly. It was a pleasure to have company once more.

"What are you working on there, anyway, Dr. Zefrityn?" Albeinius asked.

"I have told you before—you can just call me Quirt. I decided to replace the antiquated goggles I had used these past three years and create something more modern and useful. These lenses will be able to fit onto my eyes and relay information across my field of vision that can be fed from one of the interfaces you created."

"Well, only a mind such as yours would be able to handle the constant flood of data you will be receiving with such a device."

"We shall soon find out."

"Shall I discard these for you?" Albeinius asked, picking up the five rotating lens goggles that Quirt had been using.

"No…I would very much like to hold on to that, please," Quirt replied with a sorrowful distance about him. "It reminds me of Griff."

"I understand," Albeinius replied sympathetically. "Well, what are you waiting for? Try those lenses of yours on!"

Quirt scooped the lenses off the workstation and was attempting to position them onto his eyes when the laboratory doors opened.

"Ah, we have visitors!" Albeinius chirped, striding out of his chair to welcome the soldiers. "Lovely to see you two once more!"

Quirt looked at the pair, slightly bewildered at first, for all he could see was darkness. He blinked a few times and passed his gaze over each of them once more. "Commander Eldeerim! It is wonderful to see you once again!"

"It's good to see you too, Dr. Zefrityn."

"He prefers to be called Quirt," Albeinius mumbled, feigning a cough.

Rezaaran stared at the scientist with wide-eyed amazement. He had seen this person before, at the Atmari Altar. He was the mortal embodiment of Mergen. Surely the Vaux had brought the three Sentinels together.

Quirt recognized Rezaaran as the person he'd seen in the shimmering metal before Silvermire had arrived at the Meston facility. How had this young man survived a battle with that monster?

"Pleasure to meet you, Captain Rezaaran Valhara, War Mage of the Vokarii."

Rezaaran shook his hand apprehensively. "How do you know that about me?"

"It seems his lenses that connect to the interface are fully functional," Albeinius remarked with excitement that threatened to burst out of him. "It has been such a privilege to work with a famed, brilliant Thyrillian!"

"Well, Quirt is also the reason we got to you on time on Zynoo," Ashana explained to Rezaaran. "He was a scientist forced to work for the Dominion at a research facility in Meston. He saw your presence through a sample of enchanted metal and knew that Silvermire was heading to you."

"Then it seems I owe you a debt of gratitude," Rezaaran replied, flashing a warm smile and grasping Quirt's delicate hand in a firm handshake.

"Not at all," Quirt replied. "Were it not for Commander Eldeerim, I fear I may also have met my end at Meston. I feel most fortunate to help IRIS however I can."

"We're glad to have you as part of our team, Quirt," Ashana replied. "Besides, it's healthy for Albeinius to have someone other than machines to talk to. And someone who can understand him."

"You're looking a bit worse for wear," Albeinius commented bluntly, shifting his attention to Rezaaran. His amethyst eyes roved from the new scar on the War Mage's face to his tattered and scorched thermal suit. "It's only your first day back, and you've damaged a suit. I'm glad some things haven't changed!"

"Yeah, about that," Rezaaran remarked with a sheepish grin. "I had a…magic malfunction. Anyway, it appears this material will not stand up to my abilities."

"Well, you are in luck, my young friend!" Albeinius clicked his fingers excitedly and typed a series of commands onto his interface. A large tray hovered toward him containing a lustrous folded doublet.

"With a lot of assistance from Quirt, we analyzed the composition of the metal from that Arkanian droid you retrieved from Imperitus."

"The Arkanians are not simple androids with metal exoskeletons," Quirt elaborated. "While I was working at Meston, the metal sample I dealt with was taken from an Arkanian, and I found it displayed behavior akin to biological samples. It has the ability to adapt at will to electrical stimulation so that it can assume various forms."

Rezaaran remembered his duel with Itara Zelzo and how the former Guardian had transformed himself instantly to a variable arsenal.

"Quirt is a leading expert in bioadaptive technology," Albeinius continued, "and was able to reverse engineer the Arkanian metal into a lightweight structure that can be fabricated. Furthermore, the metal will incorporate and adapt to the genetic structure of the wearer."

"What does that mean?" Rezaaran asked the scientists, raising a skeptical eyebrow.

"Why not try it out, Rez?" Ashana suggested.

Rezaaran fitted the doublet over his crisped thermal suit. Despite its metal composition, it was surprisingly light. He raised his hands and conjured flames to himself once more. Instantly the armor ignited, blazing yet not distorting beneath the heat. The fire spread to his head, immolating his entire upper body, yet still the weightless armor did not melt. He abruptly extinguished the fires to a smoky whisper and transformed himself to liquid metal as Zelzo had once done.

The doublet transitioned from a dark gray to sleek silver and distorted when Rezaaran focused his mind on various forms, to which the suit instantly responded. He ended with a set of gleaming wings on his back. Regressing these once again, Rezaaran returned to his natural state, amazed that the armor had responded so easily to his magic.

"This is incredible!"

"The magic you use appears to leave residual exotic matter upon anything that is in contact with you," Quirt said. "This matter in turn also enters into your genetic structure and provides subtle alterations. The suit is able to read these changes based on the analysis of genetic material in your skin and adapts to your requirements for combat."

"The science to magic unlocked!" Albeinius exclaimed, beaming with pride at the incredible invention they had created.

"I am quite excited to see how it tests in a combat application," Quirt admitted with a chuckle.

"Just don't break it, like you did with the last one!" Albeinius quipped sternly with a finger raised to Rezaaran.

"I will try my best," the War Mage replied with a hearty laugh. "You said that you were able to fabricate the metal?"

"Yes…why?"

"I have a design in mind."

"Let's see what I can do for you."

Rezaaran followed Albeinius to his work desk. He passed Quirt's workstation, where he spotted the schematics for Muraka's war hammer on a monitor.

"Hey, before anything else," Rezaaran said once out of Ashana's and Quirt's earshot, "I am really sorry about how I treated you on Zynoo. It was repulsive of me, and not how you deserved to be spoken to."

"It is in the past, Rezaaran," Albeinius replied with a smile and a reassuring hand on his shoulder. "Xephyrus explained everything that had happened to you, and I understand that you were not completely yourself at the time. I appreciate and accept your apology. It shows you to be the better man. I know this because I would never have had the courage to admit I was wrong the way you just did."

Albeinius pulled up a glass panel for Rezaaran upon which to illustrate the design he had in mind.

"Oh, I…" Rezaaran murmured, perplexed at the device. He passed Albeinius a piece of paper, onto which he had sketched a hooded doublet with a wing pattern on the back. It was identical to the statues of the Sentinels he had seen at the Atmari Altar.

"A rather archaic method to pass a message," he mused wryly, unfurling the parchment. "Inspired design. Any preferences?"

"I'd prefer a lighter color scheme."

"Easy enough to arrange, but I meant preferences for weaponry."

"I'd prefer it to be a basic suit—no added technology. I think I need to master my combat magic before the next time I face Silvermire. Although, with that in mind, I would like a pair of gauntlets. I'm not particularly eager to have to regenerate a hand again."

"A grim and sobering affair, I am sure. Not to worry—Quirt and I will get to working on a suit for you. The fabrication process should take approximately six hours."

"That should give us enough time to prepare ourselves for the mission to Hysforth," Ashana piped up.

"If it is not too much to ask," Quirt said slowly, "I very much wish to accompany you on your mission."

Ashana looked disconcerted and shifted her gaze between the scientists and Rezaaran. "I'm not sure that is a wise idea, Quirt. You've only just recovered from your injuries."

"I could be of help during your missions. I know I am not combat trained in any manner, but I could be of assistance in other ways. Besides, I feel that I owe much to you and IRIS for this second chance I have been given."

"I think it's a great idea," Rezaaran said with a broad smile.

Ashana shot him a narrowed gaze. "Where would you stay? My ship has limited space."

"I can suggest an option," Albeinius said, his enthusiasm whittled in response to Ashana's furtive glare. "Quirt was able to enhance the teleportation technology I use within the *Metrovia* to allow for terrestrial transfer. You wouldn't need your shuttle anymore."

"I could set up a workshop in the former loading bay to help with ongoing technological development as and when it is required," Quirt said.

Ashana still seemed reluctant. She knew how dangerous the missions with Rezaaran could become and was not prepared to put a civilian like Quirt into such a dangerous situation.

"I'm going to need Quirt on the future missions, Ash," Rezaaran explained. "This new suit is going to take some getting used to, and it would be helpful to have one of its inventors available to improve the design if needed."

Quirt looked marginally offended that Rezaaran felt the suit would ever need any measure of improvement. However, he remained silent. This line of reasoning seemed to win Ashana over.

In truth, Rezaaran really needed Quirt to be a part of the mission, for he knew he possessed the Sentinel soul of Mergen. However, heeding Kashari's advice, he knew it would be some time before he could reveal this to Ashana.

"Well…all right." Ashana resigned herself to the additional crew member. "We will leave as soon as the suit is ready. Meet us in hangar 1138M."

The soldiers left the laboratory to prepare for their first mission since Zynoo.

When the doors closed, Albeinius turned to Quirt. "Are you sure this is a wise idea, my friend? You are a scientist—a brilliant one at that—but you are no soldier."

"I know that, but what use is such a vast intellect if it is not used for the benefit of all? You do incredible work here, Albeinius; you do not really need me beyond the capacity of someone against whom you can reflect ideas. I can perform that task remotely. However, out there with Rezaaran is where I feel I belong—using my gifts as a Thyrillian to make a difference, to find my atonement for whatever I have done."

Albeinius regarded his laboratory companion carefully. "I can see this is something you have thought through. I just hope you know that I will take you up on that offer to discuss ideas!"

"I shall welcome it gladly," Quirt replied with a sincere laugh. He was glad to have met Albeinius after Zynoo. In many ways, the Zenorian reminded him of Griff. "I would like to make one final request. I would like to take the heavy-duty assault suit that Rezaaran used on Zynoo and the decommissioned Arkanian on our journey."

"That old thing? And the creepy android? They're all yours. I was going to use them for spare parts around here. Why do you want them?"

"Oh…just a small project. And for some tinkering purposes."

CHAPTER FIVE

THE WOODLAND MAIDEN

"Well, that's it," Quirt said, stepping back. "The suit is fitted, and according to the feedback, it is in perfect working order. Synchronization with your genetic material is complete, and the vital-sign feedback is operational. Although, if I may provide an opinion on it, why did you opt for a hood instead of a helmet?"

"It was a design inspiration I had. I suppose it is less practical, but I think this should provide me with adequate protection—especially as it is able to adapt to my magic."

"According to Albeinius, the lighter-weight weave you chose for the design should protect you against glancing strikes and forceful impact. Furthermore, the metallurgy analysis suggests the Arkanian metal has a tendency to dissipate electrical and energy-based attacks. However, neither of us is certain how the armor will react if you are exposed to magical attacks."

"I guess we will have to adapt it together as we learn more."

"The ability to swiftly adapt is the surest sign of a high-functioning intellect," Quirt replied, seating himself at the workstation he had set up in the *Larkesian Liberator*'s loading bay. He was dressed in a black thermal suit with a green collar, signifying his role in the science division of IRIS.

"Is that a Thyrillian saying?" Rezaaran asked, testing the flexibility of the gauntlets, which Albeinius had fashioned from a denser version of the metal used to make the rest of the suit.

"It is indeed. These past few months have been intriguing in one regard: I have transitioned from being a skeptic about magic to knowing that it exists and now to being interested in studying it further. Alas, it is a Thyrillian custom to live curiously, and there is little we do not seek to learn more about. So, if it is not too much trouble, could I ask for your tutelage in magical practice?"

"Well, I am still learning myself, but I will teach you what I can. You and Xephyrus really should speak sometime; it would be interesting to hear the conversation that would arise."

"I imagine I could learn quite a lot from the Elder Mage; however, I am sure you are more likely referring to my genteel manner. Once more, this is simply part of Thyrillian culture."

"Your culture sounds rather interesting."

"As does your own, Rezaaran. When I spoke to Xephyrus, he referred me to a library of ancient texts that detail the history of magic and the various kingdoms of Zenor. The religions of many civilizations, like yours, are steeped in the practice of magic. However, what was interesting was that various sects of the Zenorian population tended to practice magic differently. Two that emerged as the most renowned include the Vokarii and the Silver Saints."

"What do you mean?" Rezaaran asked.

"Well, according to the texts I had available, the two major magical orders on Zenor were fundamentally different in their philosophies, which in turn affected their use of magic. The Silver Saints were the older of the orders, and their belief was that magic was a means to attain enlightenment through introspection. Because of this philosophy, their magic tends to center on the caster. This resulted in fields of elemental manipulation that began around themselves and spread outward. The Vokarii, on the other hand, existed as a group of magical warriors to serve and protect the kingdoms. Their primary use of magic was for defensive or offensive spells to this end. As this was their focus, their training overlooked the nuances into which the Silver Saints delved. Their key philosophy was discipline and focus so that the mages would always remain calm and in control amid battles."

For a non-Zenorian, remarked Rezaaran's fastidious mentor, who sounded genuinely impressed, *he certainly knows our history well. He is entirely correct.*

"Over time, eventually these two differing cultures merged, and there is, of course, overlap between the magic used by current-day

Zenorian mages. It is quite fascinating that within a single world could exist such varied cultures that developed due to different philosophies. Through different religious ideals, even."

"Didn't you have that on Thyrillia?"

"Not at all. Our culture is entirely atheistic. We believe that all answers await discovery through logic and reason. Consequently, religion and philosophy never developed a central role in our culture as it did in other civilizations. As a planet, we shared a common goal of working to eradicate problems together, and ours was one of the few worlds ever to be truly at peace. When we integrated into intergalactic governance, we for the most part offered assistance with technology and applied-scientific fields. That used to be my occupation: a scientific advisor to the Galactic Governance. It was also how I met my wife."

"You were married?" Rezaaran asked, pleasantly surprised that Quirt had willingly opened up to him.

"Indeed," Quirt replied with a smile. "Jeena was all that made my world right. My life with her and our children, Frintly and Kitrina, was the happiest time I had ever known. In our exile, after the loss of Thyrillia, we settled on a remote backwater world, where we worked as simple mechanics for appliances. It was very different from the glory days of the Thyrillian Scientific and Advanced Research Academy or the Galactic Governance. But we never cared—we were happy as a family."

"What happened?" Rezaaran asked, his heart growing heavy. He knew how this tale would end. He could see that behind Quirt's amicable persona was a soul laden with guilt and sorrow. Despite his vast intellect, Quirt was broken beyond any means he could find to repair himself. Rezaaran knew that feeling all too well—and knew what must have happened to the Thyrillian.

"There is only, so far, one may escape from the world before the world reaches out to consume you. The Dominion found us. I do not know how, but they did. Silvermire and Luferikas, a Demokarva and his most trusted general, personally came to see to our departure. I recognized Luferikas from the Galactic Governance, and he recalled Jeena and me. Silvermire performed a spell that penetrated my mind.

I felt excruciating pain, as though he had forced my brain open to peruse at his leisure."

Rezaaran recalled a similar feeling when Thaedis had attempted to read his mind on Zynoo.

"He decided to spare my life, but he would not show the same mercy to my family. He slit their throats before me—first the children and then Jeena. I lost everything that day."

The War Mage looked away as Quirt choked on his words. Tears welled in the scientist's brown eyes, and he raised a hand to stifle his sob.

"However, Silvermire needed them for leverage over me. I do not understand how he did it, but he held my family's souls in suspended animation and used the threat of their destruction to torment me." He closed his eyes and took a moment to compose himself.

"That's a terrible ordeal for anyone to experience." Rezaaran spoke softly, his hand resting comfortingly on Quirt's shoulder. "Silvermire has taken a lot from many people in the galaxy. He killed my father when I was a child. His soldiers murdered my mother. I know the pain this loss caused you, Quirt. You're not alone, though. You have Ashana and me here for you. I know we can never replace your family, but if you ever feel you need someone to lean on, we are always here."

"Thank you, Rezaaran," Quirt replied with a sincere smile and a dash of joy in his bloodshot eyes. "You, Ashana, IRIS…everyone has been so kind to me since I arrived. I did not think there were any good people left, but I am so glad to have been mistaken. However, I do not wish you to feel that I have joined in pursuit of vengeance. I know it is irrational to hold on to anger and hatred. It will do me no good, and I have never been a man to seek vengeance. However, there is something I wish to seek in joining your company."

"And what is that?" Rezaaran asked. Telepathically, he saw that Quirt had started on the concepts for a project he had wished to keep to himself.

"I seek atonement for the crimes I have abetted against the galaxy. While in captivity, I was coerced to create technological advancements in warfare that could further the goals of the

Dominion. I may not have been on the front lines detonating the weapons, but I am as culpable as the rest of the Dominion."

Rezaaran was about to respond when Quirt lifted his hand to stop the War Mage from pardoning his guilt.

"Nothing can be said that will change my mind, Rezaaran. When I lay dying from my injuries in the vault at Meston, I found a sliver of peace knowing that I was free of the Dominion and would find comfort with my family once more. The irony that such a thought crossed the mind of an atheist does not elude me. However, Ashana and IRIS saved me. No rational reason exists that I was given a second chance at life."

"Perhaps it was simply not your fate to die that day?"

"I would agree, except that I do not subscribe to the belief in fate. I believe I have this second chance to atone for my misdemeanors. I ought to have been more resilient, resisted the Dominion, and faced death with my integrity. Instead, I succumbed. I was weak when I needed to be stronger, and that will not happen again. As I have said, I do not seek vengeance, only the chance to do some good and repent for all the evil acts in which I may have aided the Dominion. I am not a warrior or a mage like you, but I will contribute my assistance and expertise wherever possible so that we can reach a goal of peace and justice."

"I understand your motives, Quirt. I too am in pursuit of redemption. Perhaps it is a journey we can steer each other through?"

"I would not object to that," Quirt replied with a smile, accepting Rezaaran's handshake.

"Well, I had better get ready for our mission down on Hysforth. Do you know much about the planet?"

"Only that it is an uncharted arboreal world inhabited by countless exotic creatures. It drew the Dominion's interest because of the potential to add spliced genetic material to the Kalaran soldiers to further improve them."

"What do you mean 'spliced genetic material'?"

"It is common knowledge that the Kalarans are a genetic hybrid," Quirt replied, surprised that Rezaaran found this to be news. "They were a primitive reptilian race on which the Dominion experimented early in their rise to tyranny. What intrigued scientists was that the creatures reached maturity rapidly and could adapt readily to changing environments within the span of two generations. On further investigation, they realized this was because their genetic material was relatively unstable, likely due to an infection that caused its degradation. They theorized that due to this unstable genetic structure, the Kalarans would be perfect to experiment with for genetic splicing. After numerous failed attempts, they created the first generation of robust but primitive Kalarans, the predecessors of the current soldiers."

"The Dominion has had the Kalarans for years. Why look to enhance them now?"

"Perhaps it was a response to the growing threat of IRIS? Or perhaps the Harbingers and Silvermire grew weary of the countless errors in judgment made by the regular Kalarans. Regardless of the reasoning, when I was in Meston, Silvermire ordered some of my peers to create a mechanized suit that could fit onto a Kalaran soldier. None of us thought a Kalaran could operate any type of mechanical suit—which led us to the unnerving suspicion that the Dominion was seeking to develop cyborg Kalarans."

"Great," Rezaaran muttered. "Well, if that is true, then having less advanced Kalarans under the cybernetic armor will be a small but necessary help to our soldiers."

"Perhaps. If it is permissible, I could operate a surveillance for you and Ashana while you undertake your mission."

"That works for me! Actually, since you will be with the ship..." Rezaaran adjusted the Badge of Kings inset in his blade and carefully removed the relic. "Could you run diagnostics on this badge for me and see what you find? I retrieved that artifact from Zenor last year. It contains a red dust that enhanced my magical abilities and reconfigured the appearance of my sword. However, I suspect that other secrets are locked within it."

Curious, Quirt flipped the badge through his fingers at eye level while the scanners in his lenses analyzed its structure and composition. "I will see how I can help you with this."

The thicket parted beneath Ashana's probing bow as the two Zenorian soldiers ventured through the undergrowth. Hysforth was a dense arboreal realm similar to Artherikas; however, it was far more humid and lively than the eerily deserted domain of Sarganium. The frequent bursts of midday birdsong from the canopy were interspersed with sporadic shrieks of creatures that leaped through the bushes around them amid the buzzing of insects that covertly navigated the underbrush and evaded the lurking eyes of predators.

"According to the scanners, there is no shortage of life down there," Quirt remarked over the communications channels. "However, the density of the forest is proving difficult for the scanners to penetrate. I have yet to identify any structures consistent with a building or any heat signatures to suggest technological activity."

"Thanks, Quirt," Ashana replied. "Not to worry—I have ground-based surveillance covered. Set a lock on our position, and let us know of any movement approaching us."

"I will indeed, Ashana."

The archer activated a seeker droid and dispatched the dainty, mechanized butterfly to scout the undergrowth.

"That's odd," Rezaaran murmured, coming to a halt. "I sense something nearby."

"I do not see anything near your vicinity," Quirt remarked.

Suddenly something ensnared Rezaaran's ankle and yanked him skyward. A gentle patter sounded beside Ashana as the War Mage dangled in midair, strung up from a tree.

"You really should pay attention to where you step, you know?" Ashana chided him.

The air beside her shimmered, and a soldier wearing a cream suit with a dark-blue visor emerged from the shadows. Rezaaran focused his attention on the soldier and recognized the echo as Leta. She offered a curt nod of acknowledgment and abruptly released Rezaaran to the ground.

Their communicators pinged alive this time with a message from Stryker Branderhart. "Greetings, Ashana and Rezaaran. Our time is brief, so I'll keep this short. We arrived a few hours earlier and have identified where the Dominion forces are located. There seem to be predominantly scientific teams along with a dispatch of Kalaran guards. They don't seem to have a base of operations yet and have been roving across the jungle. Leta was dispatched to locate the two of you a while ago."

"We have made contact with her, Commander Branderhart," Ashana informed the cavalry commander.

"Excellent. She will bring you to our position. Over."

Several minutes later, the three soldiers arrived on the bank of a wide river, where Moraya, Stryker, and several elite troopers met them. Rezaaran identified most of the elites as Stryker's battalion by the sabersteed engraved alongside the IRIS insignia. The remaining two wore blue suits that matched Moraya's.

"Moraya," Ashana exclaimed as she grasped the naval commander's martial handshake. "Quite a small turnout to have to travel through such a vast forest, don't you think?"

"Not at all," Moraya replied with a contemptuous snort. "I have allocated my soldiers to search along the rivers for enemies that *actually* exist, not these fairy tales you two seem to subscribe to."

Stryker offered a derisive clearing of his throat.

"However, I have been ordered by General Libranth to assist in this mission, so my battalion and I are happy to be of service."

Despite the cordial lip service she offered, Moraya's rolling eyes suggested she was anything but happy about their coercion into this mission.

"According to the information we have gathered thus far," Stryker continued, his stern voice the only sign of his opinion of Moraya's juvenile antics, "the Dominion's forces are navigating on foot and along the water's edge. Moraya, your ship can serve as a means to intercept their next stop. In the meantime, we will have to follow on foot to track them and try to predict where that will be. Rezaaran, how do you suggest we proceed?"

While the leaders deliberated their plan of action, Moraya's elites peeled away from the group and stepped toward the riverside.

"I'm hungry," grumbled one of the soldiers.

"Yeah? Well, what else is new?"

"Hey, that wouldn't be the case if they hadn't cut our rations on this trip. Besides, I want something more than that powdered trash we eat every day. I want *meat*."

"You're sounding as simpleminded as a Kalaran."

"Don't you know better than to insult a hungry man?" growled the first soldier.

"Well, if you're desperate, maybe *that* could better your temperament." The second soldier indicated a small reptilian creature perched atop a log, foraging through the wood for insects. His partner looked back cautiously at the other soldiers, who were still finalizing their plans.

"Don't worry about them," the second soldier said. "We'll be quick about it, and you can roast that critter back on the ship. I'm sure Moraya will let you return to the ship. She has no love for that idiot or his ridiculous mission."

"Yeah, well...I guess you're right," replied the first soldier. With a greedy smile, he unsheathed his knife.

The two soldiers stealthily edged their way toward their quarry, which remained oblivious that it was now prey.

Stryker looked up at the sound of a scuffed shuffle and sighted Moraya's soldiers stalking a krogoan on a nearby log. He had expected such poor discipline from her soldiers, since she displayed such a capricious attitude toward leading them.

"What in the name of the spirits do you two think you are doing?"

His shout of condemnation startled the krogoan, which darted from the log into the nearby bush. Moraya's soldiers ignored Stryker's disapproval and sprinted after the creature.

"Moraya," Stryker snarled at his fellow council member, "we will have words about this later."

Stryker led them in pursuit of their renegade companions through the brush, but Rezaaran suddenly saw something that made him stop. The entire party came to an abrupt halt.

"*That* is not disturbing in the least," he murmured, staring.

Quirt's voice came over the communicator. "Rezaaran, I have successfully calculated a means to bypass most of the vegetation interference with the scanners, and they appear to be showing a large structure at your location. Is that the Dominion building?"

"No, Quirt," Rezaaran replied. "This is something else."

In front of the group, nestled among the thick bushes, was a colossal skull that dwarfed the soldiers. Rezaaran estimated it to be bigger than the Arkanian Sarganium had controlled.

"It's definitely organic," Stryker remarked grimly. "We need to find those two—and quickly. I have a bad feeling about this forest."

They set off with renewed haste. However, when the soldiers had left the skull behind them, a vine unfurled from the eye of the bony behemoth and touched a bulb growing above the nasal ridges. The bulb exploded, dispersing red spores into the wind. Leaves rustled as more of the vines writhed.

Rezaaran led the group into a clearing, where they found that Moraya's soldiers had cornered the krogoan. However, they did not intend to attack the diminutive reptile.

The creature turned to face the soldiers and chirped threateningly.

Rezaaran sensed the fear in Moraya's soldiers, understanding immediately that it was not due to the krogoan. There was a foreboding in the clearing. The trees groaned beneath the constricting vines, and the leaves rustled. They were not alone.

The soldiers drew their weapons—except Rezaaran. The War Mage cautiously touched his fingers to Harkenathor. Although he sensed inbound life-forms, he also sensed a presence around the clearing.

Behind the hopping krogoan, the vines intertwined and took the form of a face. "Who dares enter my domain?"

"What the..." Moraya appeared startled by the apparition, and Rezaaran sensed that her fear eclipsed that of her soldiers.

Three hulking reptilian creatures crashed through the bush and surrounded the soldiers, towering over the IRIS troops. Each held a rudimentary club constructed of stone and wood.

"It's going to be all right," Stryker reassured the group in a whisper. "Everyone slowly lower your weapons. These creatures are guards of some sort. They will not attack without provocation."

"They are just beasts," Moraya hissed. "Whether we provoke them or not, they will attack. We have superior firepower. We should wipe them out!"

"No!" Stryker seethed in a hushed voice so as not to startle the beasts around them. "If we act in violence, they will respond in kind, and we may lose soldiers in a pointless skirmish. I am issuing you and your soldiers a direct order. You will obey!"

Several more of the forest's denizens crept from the undergrowth into the clearing. Five murine creatures appeared at the ankles of the primitive, club-wielding guards. The tawny rodents sported several rows of symbiotic yellow bulbs flowering along their backs.

Eight smooth-skinned serpentine creatures slithered between the others and added to the growing crowd. Despite their lack of limbs, these slimy animals sported impressive wispy tendrils on their faces that were comparable in length to their bodies.

Moraya and her soldiers grew more uneasy at the arrival of these new beasts. They could see the animals outnumbered them and knew that Stryker was being foolish to choose a pacifist approach. The naval commander offered a subtle nod to her soldiers.

The hunter whose knife was drawn raised his arm as he surveyed the clearing, deciding which enemy to dispatch first. However, one of the lumbering reptilian guards took the rising weapon as a provocation and bellowed in rage. At the behest of the guard, a serpent flicked a tendril, which struck the soldier on the arm. The strike discharged an electrical current into the armor and seized the machinery in the arm. The knife dropped to the ground.

Moraya and her soldiers began to panic. What would they do now?

The remaining serpentine creatures attacked the other soldiers. They struck at the neck plates of their armor and forcibly retracted the helmets. The mousy animals squeaked anxiously. The bulbs on their backs burst, dispersing a haze of spores that rendered every soldier unconscious.

Ashana's eyelids lifted ever so slightly before closing once more. She felt the coldness of sand against her cheek and, when she drew up herself to sit, heard the shuffle of her cloak against the dirt.

She gazed around her, struggling to orient herself. Her attention shifted sharply to her side, but she heaved a sigh of relief when she realized the low grumbling she heard was Stryker's snore.

The archer's eyes adjusted to the dim blue light emanating from the surrounding rocks. They appeared to be in a cave. She edged warily toward Rezaaran's form, taking care not to draw the attention of whatever else was in this cave with them. The War Mage began to rouse.

"Hey, Rez," she whispered between glances that probed the cave, "are you OK?"

"I think so," he replied groggily, rubbing his eyes. "What's wrong? You seem anxious."

"I seem anxious?" she hissed. "Yes! Because being drugged by a group of animals and awakening in a cave is completely normal!"

"Fair point. Where are we?"

"Some sort of cave—and I don't think we're alone. I need you to use your animusense to see what's with us."

"Can't you use your future sight?"

"It's not working," she mumbled, grateful that the dimness of the cave hid her flushed cheeks. "Those creatures released some sort of hypnotic toxin. I can't seem to use my powers."

Rezaaran furrowed his brow in concentration. He too found it difficult to utilize his abilities. However, with greater concentration, he perceived the echoes of the soldiers in their company. Clarity overcame his mind, and his perceptive field expanded. His eyes flashed open with a gasp.

I felt it too, my friend, Kashari said within his mind.

It has us surrounded. And that power...it feels familiar. Almost like the echo of the Archlords.

It is indeed familiar, but I do not believe this echo to be that of an Archlord. I have sensed this presence before, but the memory of when eludes me. What does your heart tell you?

That this is an echo of one bound to the Light.

"There's something in here with us," Rezaaran said softly. His hand slowly reached for Harkenathor's hilt. Evidently whatever had commanded the creatures to bring them here had overlooked disarming the unconscious soldiers. "I can sense its echo all around us—and it seems to be coming from..."

Rezaaran turned his attention to the luminescent streaks glowing blue in the rocks overhead.

The other soldiers began to wake and stumbled to their feet. Stryker remained the most composed of the group, taking in his surroundings with the air of the seasoned commander he was. Moraya, on the other hand, despite her bravado toward the others, fooled neither Stryker nor Rezaaran. She was, in reality, terrified. And as with all matters, Leta remained silent.

The War Mage's head swiveled at the sound of crunching gravel. He looked toward the blue streak he'd seen earlier and noted that it had shifted.

"Soldiers, ready yourselves—but hold your fire," Stryker commanded the company.

Do you raise your weapons when you enter any other's home?

The ethereal voice spoke into the minds of every soldier.

"Did you hear that?" Moraya shrieked. Her feet shuffled in the sand, and she raised her rifle toward the cave roof. "What by the spirits *is* that thing?"

"That's not creepy in the least," a soldier beside Stryker murmured.

I feel your deserved fear. You come to this world and seek to kill as a first instinct. It never crosses your mind that all life deserves to live. Or is only yours sacred because you hold a weapon? Have you anything to say for yourselves?

"If we have offended you in some way," Stryker said calmly, "then we apologize. But perhaps we may discuss this face to face."

You have no right to make demands!

Several soldiers clutched their heads as the telepathic voice thundered to induce a dull aching.

I have seen your kind before: sentient species who walk this world with the self-imposed authority that they are superior because of their technology. They come to a peaceful world. Yet instead of respect and admiration, they ravage it with their need to burn and destroy. But life endures. This world may have once been vulnerable, but no more. I am its judgment, and I will not tolerate such brazen disrespect from the mortals who have no foresight to appreciate that life exists of its own accord. This realm precedes your fleeting existence and shall exist when all mortals perish into the cold voids of time.

"This reminds me a lot of Sephiron," Ashana whispered to Rezaaran, edging closer to him.

"Except this isn't an Archlord, Ash. There's something more powerful at work here."

You! The mage! What do you know of the Archlords? Speak!

"Great," Moraya snorted, feigning her typical smug demeanor. "Another fanatic believing in this Archlord and Guardian mythological nonsense. If you're going to eat us or whatever you beasts do, then just get on with it."

A colossal eyeless head erupted from the depths of the cave and unleashed an enraged screech, bathing the soldiers in the blue light emanating from its toothless mouth.

Rezaaran rushed between the annelidian behemoth and the startled soldiers. "Wait! We aren't here to fight."

Then tell them to lower their weapons!

I know this voice, Kashari murmured to Rezaaran.

"Get out of the way, kid!" Moraya shouted, aiming her collapsible harpoon at the head of the cave-dwelling worm before them. "I am not going to listen to some mindless creature that will kill us all!"

The glowing worm hissed at Moraya and edged toward her. However, it stopped its advance when Rezaaran caught its attention once more. It turned its head to the diminutive soldier in the robes.

Rezaaran looked at its head and saw that the luminescent cells sat in an unusual pattern: a circumscribed, multipointed star between two slanted spires.

Rezaaran—kneel! Kashari said sharply.

The War Mage followed Kashari's order without question. "I did not come to this planet with the intent to harm or destroy anyone," he said. "I am here to free Hysforth from a common enemy. To that end, can we count you as our ally, Lady Luminara?"

The cave worm turned its attention solely to Rezaaran, regarding him carefully. *Who are you? What is that sword that you bear?*

"My name is Rezaaran Valhara, the last War Mage of the Vokarii Order. This weapon bears the name Harkenathor."

*Loradún...*This time Luminara spoke solely to Rezaaran. Her voice grew softer, free of her initial resentment and bitterness. *You took your time getting here.*

The soldiers secured the entrances to the cave and left Rezaaran, Ashana, Stryker, and Leta to speak with Luminara. Afraid that Moraya's petulant nature would hinder their cause, Stryker commanded her to oversee the soldiers securing the perimeter.

"Lady Luminara," Stryker said slowly, bowing before the cave worm, "it is indeed an honor to be graced by your presence."

An honor? Or merely the insincere servile words of one who seeks my aid?

"The archives of Zenor hold the Anmorian Guardians in the highest regard, my lady."

If that is true, how do you explain the denunciation of our existence by your comrade?

"Youth often fails to embrace tradition until it gains the wisdom to heed its value."

Or perhaps she is right to disregard our existence, Luminara lamented. *Time has advanced, and this current circumstance of Anmor is the culmination of our failings.*

"How did you come to this form?" Rezaaran asked.

It was Thaedis Silvermire, the exiled Guardian.

"Is he really the one who is leading the Dominion? After all this time?"

In your heart, you know the truth, Rezaaran. You have faced him—and another disciple of Nethriziin. I see the scars upon your face and soul. We underestimated how far he has strayed from the Light. When he allied himself with Nethriziin, he found a way to endure the ages of his exile. In that darkness, his soul transcended death. Then, somehow, he returned to life and power. But both are a perversion of the Vaux. He sought to destroy the Aetherealm and with his dark touch drove us against one another. He weakened us so that Nethriziin's disciples, his Edarians, could possess us and turn us into these Archlords. However, he spared Tyrel Salvidawn and myself. Initially, in any case.

"Why did he do that?" Ashana asked woefully.

His true target has always been Tyrel. However, his vengeance drove him to seek Tyrel's destruction, not merely his death. When he attacked the Aetherealm, I held the defense around the sanctuary while Tyrel secured Anmor's future and shielded the Maelinthian, the mortal realm, from the threat of Nethriziin.

She turned to Rezaaran and offered her next thought privately. *I trust that by now you know of what I speak, Loradún.*

Rezaaran offered a surreptitious nod, which caught Ashana's notice. However, the archer decided to let the matter be for now.

I was able to hold the line for some time; however, the legion of Edarians Thaedis unleashed on our home overwhelmed me. As I have said, his true goal was to crush Tyrel, and to this end, he remained merciless. He ripped my soul from my body and bound it to the form of a larval creature. My corporeal form with my Guardian powers became the vessel of an Edarian. Thus, the Archlord with my abilities came to be upon this world. I was destined to exist beneath her rule.

"How have you survived this long?" Ashana asked with concern.

"More importantly, why have you not tried to contest this Archlord?" Stryker asked. Receiving stern glares from Ashana and Rezaaran, he added, "with no disrespect, of course, my lady."

To answer your first question, it appears that a lifetime in the presence of the Aetherealm's Valinthian stone bound my soul closer to the Vaux. I believe this magic has helped me endure as long as I have. However, there was something else. When I reached this cave, I felt a power emanating from within the caverns beyond. In its presence, some of my primal abilities resurfaced despite my being in this body. I connected with the animals around me. I communicated without a spoken word in a manner they understood. I never sought to dominate their world, only to serve alongside them in creating a safe haven away from the conflict overhead. In time, I learned telepathy and connected through the planet's life force. That experience reminded me of my home world, Skylark. This cave is one of the vital nodes for Hysforth's life force, a point where the Vaux flows strongest through the planet. I think the prolonged exposure led me to obtain this larger-than-normal form.

Luminara turned her glowing, eyeless head to face Stryker.

As for your question, in this form, I lack any real power to contest the Archlord. I may be able to rally these creatures to my side, but the Archlord has the ability to dominate their will. She can force them to engage us at her command, willingly sacrificing their lives to further her cause. Even with my full powers, I would never drop to that level. I am sure that is a sentiment you can understand, Commander Branderhart.

"Indeed, my lady," Stryker replied with a bow of his head.

I am grateful in some measure for being gifted this experience.

"In what way could this experience have been a gift?" Ashana asked exasperatedly. Sometimes the philosophical views of mages and their like were beyond her comprehension.

Every instance of our lives is a gift, for we gain the grace to be a part of that ephemeral moment. My time on Hysforth allowed me solitude and moments of introspection. I gained time to connect with nature once more, to become part of a planet's life force again. Hysforth proved to me that despite the conflict and strife around us, life always finds a means to endure. Alas, as civilizations progressed, they neglected to heed the pleas of worlds that buckle beneath the burgeoning strain of advancement. This has been a haunting reminder of my failures. It was my duty to preserve the natural order. Yet now the Maelinthian only holds civilizations that see the remnants of creation in the spectral ores and wonder what price they may fetch. People no longer walk through forests to listen to the tales held within the trees; they pay no heed to the lives of creatures within those sacred woods. So many civilizations stake their claim as the dominant life-form on their world yet know nothing of how to commune with their planet's life force. And slowly these worlds are falling to ruin.

Rezaaran's eyes passed around the cave in amazement, for as Luminara spoke, several of the flowers that lined the rocky chamber unfurled. Their petals glowed with a soft yellow hue and signaled a pathway deeper into the caves.

What people seem to forget is that there is no supreme or dominant species. We are all connected; each of us is merely another node in the intricate web of existence spun by the Vaux. None can exist without the next.

"There are some civilizations," Ashana said firmly, "who remember the lessons of which you speak. Sylvoria on Zenor is such a kingdom."

Indeed, there may be some. However, that Thaedis's Dominion was able to seize such a foothold within the Maelinthian is an indication that that number may be too few. That being said, I am convinced that this group of soldiers before me is committed to preservation of life and peace. Together we can defeat the Archlord and drive the Dominion from this planet. However, we will need some help. Follow me.

Luminara slithered down the passageway lit by the luminescent plants. With each step the soldiers took in her wake, more of the flowers unfurled to light their way forward as they ventured into a vast cavern while Moraya and her soldiers brought up the rear of the company. Crevices in the roof provided entry for water from the surface to cascade into the subterranean rivers, which in turn nurtured the thriving cavernous forest.

Scattered throughout the subterranean forest, members of a herd of large, horned animals grazed within the slivers of sunlight. Some of the parents nursed their young and watched fondly as they took their first steps out of their nests. These affections resonated within the hearts of every soldier, and they felt an echo of memories from their family lives on Zenor.

Stryker wandered off from the group and approached the largest of the hulking horned herbivores. To any other, this beast would have been terrifying for its sheer size. However, this exquisite creature did not deter Stryker; after all, he rode a proud and mighty sabersteed into battle.

The cavalry commander approached the wary behemoth and knelt before its fearsome gaze. He offered a supplicating hand and slowly raised his head to meet the animal's dauntless eyes. It approached him with a bowed head and allowed Stryker to mount its neck.

Astonishing! Luminara remarked. *Berjiin are renowned as wary and territorial creatures that resist interaction with any other species outside their herd. Yet you are able to win the trust of the matriarch so swiftly.*

The berjiin matriarch looked back at her herd and gestured toward the other Zenorians with her horn. The herd lumbered forward, each thunderous stride shaking the cavern walls as the creatures approached the visitors at the behest of their herd mother. Stryker's elites followed their commander's lead, and each mounted one of the berjiin.

Despite drawing the immediate interest of the soldiers, the burly berjiin were not the only creatures in the cavern. Dwarfed by the colossal beasts, the other denizens of this cavern sought to escape the initial attention of the visitors. However, when Stryker and his elites had won the trust of the berjiin, the other creatures took this as an invitation to come and inspect the Zenorians.

A pack of shaggy canine creatures leaped through the thick shrubs along the river. Intermittently they appeared, their heads cocked and tongues lolling, to curiously survey the soldiers before they dove back into the foliage. The tall reptilian creatures that had surrounded them in the clearing now entered the cavern through a hidden passageway. Despite the passing snarl with which the beasts regarded the travelers, the guards did not engage them, as they were in the presence of Lady Luminara. Instead, they laid down their clubs and wandered off to their families.

"What is this place?" Rezaaran asked in awe, pivoting to take in the full expanse of the cavern.

When I arrived on Hysforth, Luminara explained, *this cavern resounded with a powerful but ancient echo. Within these walls, I found a place of solitude but also of respite from the ongoing conflict. It has since stood open to all creatures that sought to escape the Archlord's war.*

The electrical serpents that had deactivated their armor slithered from the river's edge. They ignored the Zenorians and hastily encircled Luminara. An army of purple amphibians hopped along behind the serpents, one of which tumbled over on itself and landed on Moraya's boot. Its large black eyes looked at her longingly.

"Ah, well…aren't you the cutest," she said, leaning down to pet the amphibian, whose back began to darken.

Leta seized her hand and lifted it high.

"Hey! Let go!" Moraya said.

The mute soldier said nothing but offered a subtle inclination of her head toward the amphibian. Moraya looked back at the critter she had been about to pet and saw that its back was laden with serrated quills.

Be careful, Luminara warned. *Their quills contain a toxin that could knock one of the berjiin out. Oh, and do not startle him. They can also spray their quills in self-defense.*

"Well, I take that back about you," Moraya mumbled as she stood and slowly paced away from the creature. The naval commander turned her attention to the river once more, drawn by the bubbling water. A fever of aquatic creatures with large membranous wings surfaced. Their wings treaded the water while their four tails edged them closer to the river's edge.

Luminara slithered to a towering tree at the center of the cavern. Its thick boughs bore no leaves but steadfastly held the vault intact. The roots sank deeply into the ground, ran through the river, and burrowed into the walls of the cave.

Rezaaran caught the sheen of light emanating from the pools at the base of the tree. On closer inspection, he realized that they were Valinthian crystals filled with magical energy.

"Hey, lady," Moraya piped up, turning from the river to face Luminara. "You spoke a lot about my soldiers' disrespect for life on this planet. What have you been feeding on all this time?"

Stryker glared at Moraya from the back of the berjiin while Leta covered her eyes with her hand, unable to comprehend Moraya's endless and brash stupidity.

Although Luminara's head was eyeless and otherwise expressionless, Rezaaran was certain she regarded Moraya with the utmost disdain.

This is the shlarpiri tree, one of the vital nodes for Hysforth's life force. Its roots are deep and strong, wrapping around an enormous cache of Valinthian crystals. The tree in turn incorporates the Valinthicite into itself and bears it in its fruit and sap. I sustained my larval self with those products and ventured on to other vegetation as I grew. I am no hypocrite, if that is what you seek to imply.

"Only a crazy lady in the body of a worm speaking to trees," Moraya muttered to herself. "That tree sap must give one hell of a trip."

"Why are we here, Lady Luminara?" Ashana asked quickly.

The life force I speak of operates throughout the planet as a hive mind. If accessed through the vital nodes, one can tell what the planet thinks and says.

Luminara placed her head against the tree. The Guardian insignia on her head pulsed with a steady blue light as she listened to the whisperings of Hysforth's heart. A soft, melodic hum escaped her mouth. It soothed the creatures of the cavern and resounded with the planet's life force. Several vines crept from the ground and touched Luminara, while the crystals beneath the tree flared brighter.

A series of fungi glowed alive and illuminated a passageway that led onward from the cave.

The Dominion facility that you seek is this way. The creatures that are with us have agreed to aid us in this battle. They will respond to the commands of those who ride them forward. Choose your steeds, and we can move on.

"My men and I can lead the charge with the berjiin," Stryker replied, and his cavalry unit came to the vanguard. "Their strength should help break any resistance we may encounter."

A sound strategy.

"Your guards can augment our infantry," Ashana suggested. "The two smaller creatures that are here, the shrub jumpers and the amphibians—what are they called?"

The ginkwara and memuvar, respectively.

"They can be our ambush utilities."

If you wish to incorporate stealth and subterfuge into your battle plans, then I suggest you include the bhacara in your ranks. They are masters of natural stealth.

"Very well. Where are they?"

Luminara gestured toward the upper branches of the shlarpiri tree with a soft hiss. Thirty creatures instantly dropped to the ground and surrounded the soldiers.

"I'm sold," Rezaaran exclaimed, amazed at how well these animals had remained hidden.

Each stood at approximately the height of the Zenorians. They were ungainly creatures in their strides because their long arms impeded their gait. However, their hands were large and tipped with thickened nails and knuckles, which they used to break open tree bark for food. To augment their disguise, they incorporated broken twigs and leaves as well as moss into their fur. Yet despite their bizarre and awkward appearance, they were surprisingly nimble when among the trees.

Ashana turned to Moraya. "We'll need you and your elites to provide naval support. Take your soldiers, and track down the rest of your crew. Meet us at the location on your interface. We'll ping it when we arrive."

Moraya reluctantly saluted. She was not entirely pleased with Ashana issuing orders to her but could not deny that her plan was comprehensive.

Ashana tapped on her interface and adjusted her earpiece. "Quirt…Quirt, come in…"

"I think the cave may be disrupting our transmissions," Rezaaran suggested.

"Never mind, we can relate our plans to Quirt once we're on the move, and he can offer aerial support from the *Liberator*'s battery assault cannons."

Leta stepped forward. Although silent, her demeanor expressed her intent to be at the core of the cohort.

"Leta, you will join Rez and me, following in with the guards."

A hasty scratching sounded across the cavern, and a flock of red birds careered toward the soldiers. Flaring their wings, they skidded to a stop, curiously surveying the three soldiers who stood among Luminara's guards.

Ah, perfect! It seems Hysforth is glad of our presence and seeks to aid our cause. These are safrin. They are flightless birds who have adapted extreme speed to compensate for being land bound.

Rezaaran approached the large bird that stood just slightly taller than he did. Its majestic red-and-gold plumage held a lustrous sheen. The creature's yellow eyes would appear threatening to any who found themselves prey to its sharply curved beak. However, the safrin regarded Rezaaran and the others with mild curiosity. It twisted its head to each side to obtain a better view of these new visitors. Three of the flock stepped forward and offered themselves as steeds to the remaining soldiers.

It appears that all is in order. It is time for us to move forth!

"Wait…us?" Moraya asked suspiciously. "I thought you were opposed to violence."

I am opposed to senseless aggression. We, however, are fighting for an ideal, for freedom from an oppressive force. To that end, aggression is a necessary means.

"With no disrespect, my lady," Stryker said calmly, extending a blade from his prosthetic arm, "I believe we have stood on ceremony long enough. Let us take the battle to the Dominion!"

The defenders of Hysforth charged along the cave passageway in the thundering wake of the berjiin. Rezaaran held tightly to the feathers of the safrin that carried him. Although Ashana's plan was sound, he had an ominous feeling that it would pan out differently. After all, when it came to the Archlords, best-laid plans often went awry.

The charge came to an abrupt stop when the berjiin unceremoniously halted. Rezaaran's safrin skidded to a standstill, and a loud squawking erupted from the rest of the flock. Their cacophony was a terrified response to the throng of ferocious beasts interspersed with a battalion of Kalarans and security guards that had surrounded the cave's entrance.

Rezaaran glanced across the plethora of enemies around them. He was not entirely surprised that Moraya and her soldiers were missing, but perhaps their absence could be an asset if they reached their vessel.

"You did not really expect to succeed in a surprise attack on me?"

The soldiers looked around, trying to locate the source of the saccharine, sultry feminine voice that had spoken out.

She is here, Luminara murmured. Her thoughts bristled with indignation.

"I know that we trapped you in the body of a worm, but we did not expect your mind to warp into a mire of irrationality. Have you forgotten, Luminara, that I am the one true ruler of this world? Your place is beneath my feet as the insufferable maggot you Guardians always were."

An olive-skinned woman casually stepped through the army of enemies. Her long black hair lifted in the breeze that billowed her tattered red-and-black robes. With each step, a silver medallion of a wolf's head that hung around her neck swayed. Rezaaran felt Luminara's ire deepen at the sight of the medallion and this imposter who paraded her unkempt form as a tarnished prize.

The Edarian who possessed Luminara's body stood before them. The darkly ringed blue eyes that surveyed the soldiers may once have known benevolence, but now they found comfort only in malice and cruelty.

"You would do well to bow before me. I shall show mercy for those who do so. You cannot hope to defeat my army with the rabble you have assembled. That worm may speak to the trees, but this planet's life force answers to *me*!"

No one being can command any planet's life force. The planet belongs to itself. Nature is a sovereign entity and incorruptible by one as yourself.

"Rich for you to say!" the Edarian spat. "The Guardians stormed Torementhias and subjugated my kind to an eternity of watching souls pass through the maze. You denied us our right to feed on those wretches."

Yet we never slew a single Edarian. We let your kind exist peacefully alongside us.

"A mistake that you lived to regret. At least Thaedis knew and respected us for what we are destined to be. We are the gods that Anmor was created to bow before. It is as our lord has predicted!"

You are no god. The Edarians were aberrations of creation. You were born of dark magic to spread war and suffering for your bloodthirsty and devious Lord Nethriziin.

"Silence!" the Edarian roared. "That is enough of your heresy. We have lived beneath your judgment long enough! Thaedis and I showed you mercy in sparing your pointless life. It is time to correct that mistake!"

The crowd of Kalarans parted, and a group of cadaverous creatures came forward and dumped their helpless quarry before the Edarian. It was the remainder of Moraya's crew.

"This usurpation of my divine rule has failed," she seethed. "And your failure begins with their death!"

A chilling screech filled the forest, and a flock of hideous, eyeless monsters grabbed Moraya's soldiers with their talons, hoisting them skyward.

Ashana closed her eyes briefly and stole a glimpse of the future. She drew her electrical arrows and fired at the winged creatures that had seized her comrades. Each arrow stunned the beasts, causing them to release the soldiers. However, their plummeting screams ended as the ginkwara leaped to catch the falling soldiers and cushioned their descent in the brush. The soldiers emerged several minutes later, and their rifles fired furiously into the crowd of Kalarans.

The Kalarans retaliated and emptied their cartridges upon Moraya's elites, but their focus broke when a stampede of berjiin tore through their ranks. Stryker leaped from the back of the matriarch, and his blade found the throat of a Kalaran commander as he landed. Rolling aside, he retracted the blade into his arm and opted for a mounted gun instead to assault the Dominion army.

The cavalry soldiers remained atop the berjiin, slashing at the enemies with heated pikes and firing intermittently from their pistols. The reptilian guards' hefty clubs swept Kalarans aside with ease. But the fervor of battle saw them hurl their clubs into the crowd and brawl with their counterparts. Their powerful jaws ripped through armor, severing limbs and sinew with ease.

"The three of us need to focus on taking that Edarian down," Rezaaran said to Leta and Ashana as their army locked with the Dominion. "Leta, get in close to her!"

The silent soldier nodded simply and then faded into darkness, disappearing from sight.

Luminara swung her heavy tail and cleared a safe zone around Rezaaran and Ashana. Her Guardian crest flared brightly. Vines ensnared several Kalarans and yanked them into the undergrowth, where the forest stifled their surprised roars.

The Edarian sneered. Her blue eyes darkened and she ensnared the minds of more creatures to rally to the battle. Her hatred for the Guardians simmered, and her breathing hastened, her fingernails transformed into talons, and her teeth sharpened. Her vengeful glare fixated on the enormous cave worm at the center of this rebellion.

One of Moraya's elites flung a punch at her face, but the Edarian caught the soldier's armored hand and crushed every bone. Just then, an arrow flew through her wrist and paralysed the muscles of her hand. Ripping the arrow from her flesh, she snarled at the archer. If they dared strike her, she would return the favor. Her face distorted into an unnatural grimace, and a growl escaped her lips.

A stampede of heavily armored ursine beasts tore through the Kalarans. Their blood rage did not care for allegiance—all they sought was carnage. The beasts charged toward Rezaaran and Ashana, one of them closing the distance rapidly and raising a paw to slash at Ashana. The archer did not react, for she foresaw no need. A bhacara appeared before her and absorbed the furious swipe into the thick bark upon its back. The ungainly creature turned to face the growling adversary, slunk beneath its swipes, and unleashed a series of punches to the midriff. Its heavy hands broke several ribs with each strike, reducing the creature to a whimpering state. However, the Edarian's dark magic strengthened at the sight of the beast's weakness. Despite the angst on its face, the fell magic raised the creature to stand tall and bite into the bhacara's arm. The tree dweller howled in agony before a kinsmen rallied to his aid and yanked the jaws of the predator apart. Ashana sank a pair of arrows into the frenzied predator's heart.

"Rez, that Archlord's magic can will them to fight through anything. We cannot harm these creatures in any way that will slow them as long as her magic continues to flog them through battle. We need to take her out!"

"I'm on it! Cover me!"

Rezaaran and Ashana. Luminara spoke into their minds while she burrowed underground to launch several more Kalarans into the trees, where the bhacaras disposed of them. *I understand and agree with the need to destroy the Archlord. However, her vessel is my body, and we can return my soul to it if it remains intact.*

Ashana passed Rezaaran a querying glance. How could he destroy the Archlord *and* keep the body intact?

"I'll try to find a way," he said.

Rezaaran blasted his way through the crowd of soldiers with a series of spectral blasts. Harkenathor sang as it leaped from its sheath to taste battle once more, its edge sinking through the armor of Kalarans and opposing beasts alike. Rezaaran dodged a flying beast that sought to capture him.

The winged menace pivoted in midair and was preparing to make a return when two barbed chains darted forth and embedded themselves into its flesh. Leta hoisted herself through the air onto the back of the creature and used the chains to control its flight. From her vantage point, she peppered the battlefield with smoke bombs and fletchets into the horde of Kalarans.

Amid the chaos Leta wrought, Rezaaran saw an opening and ran toward the Archlord with Harkenathor faithfully at his side. However, as he closed the distance, the Edarian conjured a swarm of insects that savagely devoured Rezaaran's flesh.

Ashana fired an explosive arrow at the War Mage. The detonation incinerated the swarm instantly and immolated him. The Archlord cackled in triumph. However, when the smoke cleared, her laughter subsided. Within moments, the charred face of Rezaaran and his armor regenerated with a green shine to their original state.

Enraged, the Archlord released another insect plague upon Rezaaran. The War Mage purged the swarm with a fireball and whirled to find the Archlord kneeling on the ground. Her robes transformed into fur, and her teeth were now fangs. She slammed her hands into the ground and scorched a black branching burn into the barren earth.

Fissures raced along the ground from her feet toward the Zenorians. Serpentine creatures with scythed forelimbs and numerous venom-laden fangs slithered their way toward the soldiers. Two of the creatures coiled their tails around Rezaaran's ankles and brought him to ground with a thud. Their heads moved toward Rezaaran's face, fangs bared and ready to strike. But Harkenathor flew into the War Mage's hand and sliced one serpent's head while a throwing star found its mark on the other's neck. Rezaaran shrugged off the laxed coils and acknowledged his appreciation to Leta as she made yet another sweep atop her new steed.

Rezaaran leaped up, casting about for the Edarian, but could not locate her. With all the activity in this forest, his animusense would be nearly useless.

Ashana had shouldered her bow in favor of her rapid-firing crossbows. She picked off the Kalarans with the aid of the safrin, which had significantly thinned their ranks. Although several safrin had fallen, the flock persisted in ravaging the Dominion soldiers. A few of the Kalarans decided to rout. One of them darted away from the archer, but the clawed hand of a new feral beast seized the deserter.

Rezaaran spun around. He had felt a massive echo near Ashana.

"What in Novanior's mercy *is* that thing?" Ashana murmured, raising both crossbows at the terrifying creature that held the Kalaran by its throat.

No...she is transforming! Luminara's thoughts sounded aghast. *She has perverted the Vaux with my abilities to create life and enhanced herself into an amalgamation of all the creatures she has encountered on this planet.*

"That's the Archlord?" Stryker asked suspiciously.

The creature clutching the Kalaran grew ever larger, rivaling Luminara's height. A snarling visage with serrated teeth and black eyes had replaced the beautiful face, and the heavily muscled arms ended with sharp claws and electrified tendrils that delivered the death stroke to the Kalaran's three hearts. She glowered at the Zenorians beneath her and ripped the dead Kalaran in half.

Just as the possibility of victory seemed to escape the grasp of the Zenorians, another behemoth clawed its way out of the fissured ground. It was the creature whose skull they had passed during the chase after Moraya's soldiers.

"Does anyone on our side have any fantastic surprises they would like to share?" Stryker asked.

The subterranean monstrosity slammed its fists onto two of Luminara's guards, crushing them instantly. Its roar crippled the soldiers, who fell to the ground, covering their ears in agony.

Kill her for me, my pet, the Archlord ordered as she glared at Luminara. *Make that worm writhe in agony!*

The beast nodded in agreement and lumbered toward Luminara. It seized her at the neck and dragged her toward the lake. Despite her thrashes and screeches, Luminara was defenseless against this colossal foe.

Rezaaran's ears bled out, and he struggled to find his footing. He took aim at the beast but could not be certain he would not hit Luminara as well.

The gargantuan monster raised Luminara high and was about to plunge her into the lake when a leviathan broke the surface and sank its fangs into the beast's neck. Riding atop the head of this many-finned and spiked drake stood a proud Moraya.

"Sorry, beasty, but this worm lady is with us. Looks like today I get to be the hero!" Moraya launched herself onto the creature's face, and Leta landed smartly beside her comrade. Together they drew their weapons and plunged them into the eyes of the monster. Moraya leaped off the creature's head into the lake while Leta fired her grappling chains at a nearby tree. While the stealthy warrior made her departure, she swiveled in midair and hurled a handful of exploding shurikens at the belly of the beast.

Luminara sank beneath the surface of the lake. The mass of her cave-worm form made it impossible to create any propulsion through the water. This, however, was not necessary, as Rezaaran telekinetically raised Luminara from beneath the water and returned her safely to land.

"That was easy," he said quietly as he set her upon the ground.

Well, that is the point of training, is it not? Kashari remarked tartly.

At that moment, a series of heavy-ordnance rounds pelted the staggering beast, leaving only its smoldering remains.

The communications channel crackled sharply. "Did that hit the target?" Quirt asked anxiously.

"Perfect timing, my friend!" Rezaaran said, beaming.

"The scanners indicate there is another large hostile in your region. I can have the cannons ready to fire in a few moments."

"No!" Rezaaran blurted out.

"What do you mean?" Moraya asked furiously.

"That is the Archlord," Rezaaran explained, "but she controls Luminara's body. We can return her soul to her body if we find a way to drive the Edarian out."

"Wow, lady," Moraya said, looking up at Luminara, "you sure don't make this easy."

"Quirt, I need an idea on how to subdue this creature without injuring and destroying it."

"Give me a moment. I fixed the long-range scanners, so I just need to analyze the biological functioning."

Meanwhile, the Archlord seized the soldier whose arm she had crushed earlier and raised him to her face. *There is an overpowering bloodlust to this form. I have never experienced anything quite like it in my existence. I wonder if the taste of Zenorian flesh shall sate it.*

"Quirt, hurry up with a plan!"

"Just give me a few minutes."

"We don't *have* a few minutes!"

"It's fine," said Ashana as she rapidly formulated a countermeasure plan with the aid of her future sight. "Rez, try to keep her in stasis with your telekinesis. Moraya hit her with a focused screech to lower her resistance to Rez's stasis. Luminara, summon as many memuvar as possible. And I'll need you as a failsafe if Rez is unable to hold her in stasis. Quirt, get back to us with a plan as soon as possible."

"Will do, Ash. I am running a scan of the Archlord's brain activity."

"I don't need the specifics," Ashana replied sternly, loading her bow with tranquilizer-tipped arrows. "I need a final plan. Get back to me when we have one, Quirt."

Ashana unleashed a flurry of tranquilizer arrows, but the Archlord merely stumbled, showing no real sign of hindrance.

Strike me again, you insufferable archer, and your friend here will see how long he can survive with only half a body!

"Moraya, hit her now!"

The naval commander unleashed a focused sonic blast at the Archlord's head. Despite the Archlord's attempts to disguise the agony, the shrill ringing had a noticeable effect. She stumbled forward, desperately trying to retain her composure.

Enraged, the Archlord moved to grab her quarry's midriff between her two hands. But a grappling chain wrapped around her free wrist and snared her to a tree. Leta immobilized her for a moment before the Archlord ripped free, disregarding the burning as she sliced through her own flesh and tendon.

Rezaaran then seized her in a spectral snare and held her fast. Despite her greatest efforts, she could not free herself of these invisible restraints. Moraya's sonic assault further hindered her attempts and rendered her immobile.

You think this is a victory, mortals? This is a farce, a stalemate! You cannot know true victory unless you destroy this vessel. Only then can you know true power, Rezaaran!

Stirred by the mention of power, a darkness rose in the War Mage's heart. It was the familiar call of ambition.

No, Rezaaran thought. I will not go down this path again. I am better than that. There has to be another way.

You are indeed better than you once were, Kashari said softly in his mind. *I am immensely proud of your growth. There is always a better way; it will reveal itself in time.*

"Bioscans of that Archlord's brain are complete," Quirt said into their communicators. "According to the data, her brain activity is extraordinarily enhanced, with rapid firing at regions indicating increased N-methyl/D-aspartate receptor activity. However, that can easily be countered by high doses of CI581 and use of electroshock therapy."

"What in Baharim's name did I just hear?" Moraya roared, still concentrating on restraining the Archlord with her sonic attack.

"Quirt, I said give us a *final* plan," Ashana retorted, "not the science behind it!"

"Very well," Quirt replied, marginally affronted. "You need to inject her with a high dose of a sedating compound and issue a high-voltage electrocution to her nervous system. The Colonial Guild database indicates there is a creature on this planet known as a memuvar that holds a neurochemical in its spines that is chemically identical to CI581. Based on her size, I estimate you will require more than ten times the dose needed to neutralize the berjiin."

Ashana looked behind her at the many purple amphibians that had crawled from the cave to surround Luminara. She remembered her words from the cavern.

"Luminara," she commanded the former Guardian, "have the memuvar fire a volley of their spikes. Rezaaran, get ready!"

The army of diminutive amphibians turned their backs upon the Archlord and showered her with every spike upon their backs. Rezaaran released his hold over the Archlord, and Luminara coiled herself tightly against her nemesis. The War Mage telekinetically gathered the cloud of poisoned spikes and marshaled them to hover behind him as he ran along Luminara's body to the Archlord's shoulder. His position achieved, he unleashed the volley of spikes upon her face and her exposed wrist, the few areas not covered by the dense fur her mutated form had assumed.

The War Mage rested his hands on the Archlord's temple. A spark formed on his electropads. "Luminara—release! Moraya, keep her still!"

Rezaaran released a massive three-second surge of electricity into the head of the Archlord before discontinuing his attack and using a vine to swing to the ground. The Archlord staggered one last time and then crashed to the ground. Her monstrous form reversed, each mutation regressing, and she returned to the simple form of the beautiful but disheveled Woodland Maiden.

Finally, shrunken to her original size, the Archlord lay panting on the ground. In her fleeting moments of consciousness, her bleary eyes sought Rezaaran's.

"You think you've won?" she asked between agonal breaths. "You can't gain these powers without destroying this body. Just do it! Why pass on such an opportunity to be better than what you are? End me!"

"This is me being better," Rezaaran said quietly as he knelt beside his fallen foe. "I am no mere warrior. I am a Zenorian, a Vokarii—and that means I fight with honor. I give my word…and mean it."

"You simple fool." She regarded him wearily through her twitching eyes. "If I go, so does this body. Luminara will never leave that meager form. Either way, you lose!"

"You're wrong," Rezaaran replied firmly, drawing Harkenathor.

He took aim at the Archlord and drew on Kashari's strength to ensnare her dark presence, as he had done with Tolbetrius in the Nuhremorn. He felt the burning rage of the Edarian lash at him, stronger than the darkness of the basilisk fighters he had contested. Yet he endured.

A dark, smoky cloud appeared above the tremulous Woodland Maiden. The Zenorian soldiers watched the spectacle in horror. Amid the smoke, the visage of the monster they had contested emerged and disappeared. From the smoke emerged a new horror: the snarling face of a horned creature that evoked terror with its malevolent glare. Coalescing into a humanoid form, it sought to draw itself whole in pursuit of a new host.

Just in time, Rezaaran extracted the last remnants of the Edarian's presence and purged her instantly in a blast of fire. An eerie roar echoed through the forest as the Edarian dispersed into oblivion.

"By the holy spirits," Moraya murmured. Her collapsible harpoon slipped from her laxed fingers. "What in the name of Baharim's royal balls have I just seen?"

The War Mage quietly gathered his thoughts and crouched to scoop up the limp body of the Woodland Maiden.

"Is it true?" Moraya asked. "You could have gained incredible powers if you'd killed that Archlord?"

Luminara lowered her head toward Rezaaran. She sincerely hoped that Tyrel's conviction about this young mage had not been amiss.

"Whether what she said is true or not is irrelevant. I gave my word to Luminara, and I intend to see my vow through to completion." Rezaaran marched off from the group toward the cave with the shlarpiri tree, Ashana at his side and Luminara's limp body in his arms.

Rezaaran waded waist deep into the still, cold lake at the roots of the shlarpiri tree. The other IRIS soldiers stood along the riverbank with those animals who had survived the battle.

Upon their return to the cavern, the anguished cries of the survivors who mourned their fallen family resounded in the hearts of every soldier. Even if Moraya cared not to admit it, she too had shed a tear at the sight of the battle-scarred matriarch comforting the newly orphaned berjiin. Despite the vast expanse across the evolutionary wilderness that separated them, their poignant cries and low groans of heartache were feelings the soldiers knew all too well. The aftermath of the battle served as a somber reminder of Luminara's words about their shared commonality.

However, everyone's attention shifted from thoughts of loss to those of hope when Rezaaran entered the lake.

"So...how exactly does this work?" Rezaaran asked Luminara. Despite his solemn expression, he found holding her limp, lifeless body while talking to her disembodied soul a trifle eerie.

I will connect to the planet's life force and command the magic of this lake to augment your powers as you transfer my essence from this vessel to my body.

I will need your help, my friend, Rezaaran said privately to Kashari.

Whenever you need my aid, I will be there. However, in this instance, both Luminara and Hysforth can assist you better. But I shall guide you as best I can. Remember the spell you cast on Tolbetrius to siphon his essence into me? This is no different.

Rezaaran thought back to his battle in the Nuhremorn and allowed himself to relax. He could do this.

Releasing his hold on Luminara's corpse, he placed one hand on her submerged face and the other on the cave worm's glowing head. With Kashari's guidance, he grasped Luminara's soul and drew her home.

A warm shroud embraced the War Mage, and he felt Luminara's soul pass through him. When he had channeled Tolbetrius to help Kashari, Rezaaran had felt only insatiable rage and hatred. However, when Luminara's soul passed through him, it was a surreal experience. Great love nestled within her every thought—an emotion so pure and yet unspecific. Although strongest on thoughts of Tyrel, it spread to all she had ever met in her lifetime. Every being who had encountered this phenomenal woman had known kindness through her actions.

During this moment, Rezaaran felt a surge race through his body, and a rush of gratitude flooded his heart with light and warmth. It was the appreciation of an entire planet when Luminara had selflessly sacrificed herself to save her home world, Skylark.

Rezaaran focused and directed Luminara's soul to its rightful resting place. The shroud of warmth passed through him toward his hand like an ephemeral summer breeze.

Luminara's eyes flew open. Bubbles escaped her lips, and her body briefly convulsed beneath the water. Breaking the surface, she gasped for breath—and saw the world for the first time in a century. Her fingers touched her face disbelievingly. She was back to herself once more.

The Woodland Maiden gazed around the cavern. Looks of astonishment adorned the faces of every Zenorian soldier and creature alike. Her lungs burned as she took her first free breaths. She was alive!

"It worked," Rezaaran murmured in disbelief.

"You have my deepest gratitude, Rezaaran," Luminara replied, placing her hand on his shoulder. She smiled as she realized this was the first time she had uttered a spoken word.

Luminara approached the cave worm and reached for its head. The creature offered a low groan and bowed before her.

"I will forever remember your kindness in allowing me to have a home when I was lost. For any injury I may have caused you, I am dearly sorry. I pray that you find peace, my friend." She gently kissed the creature's head, and a yellow glow appeared where the Guardian crest had once been.

It has been my honor, Lady Luminara.

"It can use telepathy now?" Ashana asked in amazement.

"One of my abilities as Guardian," Luminara explained, "was conveying sentience upon primitive creatures so that they could advance their world. It is the least I can do for all he has done for me." She winced and reached for her wrist. The euphoria of regaining her body abated as she felt the pain of the injuries her body had sustained during the battle. "Well, we definitely did not hold back. I can feel it now."

"Don't worry," Ashana replied cheerfully, offering Luminara her hand. Rezaaran did likewise, and they helped Luminara step out of the lake. "We'll bring you aboard our ship and get you patched up."

"I must admit, I am intrigued by such a prospect. Despite all my years, I have never traveled upon a space vessel. Besides, I believe I am needed in your mission. It is the will of the Vaux." She stood upon the shore of the lake and regarded the Zenorians fondly. "Each of you has my sincere appreciation for the part you played in returning me to my entirety and for saving this beautiful world."

"Well, we still have to destroy that complex," Moraya replied, regarding the Woodland Maiden shrewdly. "You're definitely much easier on the eye now than before."

"Indeed, there is much that still needs doing," Luminara replied, her cheeks slightly flushed from Moraya's compliment. "However, before we part ways, there is the matter of a promise to fulfill."

Streams of red Valinthicite flowed from Luminara's palms and materialized as the dark crystals to which Rezaaran was accustomed. The War Mage clutched the shard and felt power infuse his being. Shortly after the last fragment of the crystal was bound within him, he began to transform.

Rezaaran's entire body shuddered and grew bulkier. His face extended to a snout with sharp, ragged teeth. The friendly and comforting smile of the War Mage disappeared into the growling maw of this new beast. Spines of steel ripped through his back and shoulders. Metal claws extended from his fingers, and his flaming eyes hungrily surveyed the room.

"Luminara," Ashana said, finally wresting her voice from the terror rising in her throat. "What is happening to him?"

"My transformation power was corrupted by the Archlord," Luminara replied, aghast. "That, coupled with all the other abilities Rezaaran has gained, has mutated him into this feral beast. Like Rezaaran, this creature can transform and adapt to any situation to become truly invulnerable."

"That does not sound good," Stryker remarked grimly.

Rezaaran snarled and turned on his comrades. He then charged through Luminara's guards with a savage roar, his heavy paws swatting them aside with ease before he came to rest near the shlarpiri tree. He gouged his claws into the ground and issued another ferocious roar that antagonized the berjiin.

Sensing that they were poised to charge, Stryker intervened and placated the mighty matriarch. However, he doubted he could achieve the same result with Rezaaran.

Moraya fired a sonic blast at Rezaaran, but this only further stoked his feral rage. Metal plates rose from his shoulders and formed protective earpieces to shield him from the attack.

"Well, that makes it a bit more complicated," she muttered. She unsheathed her harpoon.

Rezaaran set his blazing eyes upon the naval commander, snapped his jaws menacingly, and stomped his feet in preparation for another charge.

Leta fired a grappling line at him. But despite its form, this creature retained Rezaaran's enhanced conditioning. It grabbed the barbed line in midflight and used it to slam Leta into the shlarpiri tree. In an instant, Rezaaran was upon her. His strong grip closed around her neck, and he hoisted her against the tree, into which the metal claws gouged. His choke hold tightened.

Suddenly he dropped her to the ground and howled in agony. Rezaaran yanked Moraya's harpoon from his back with a sneer and contemplated using the weapon to skewer Leta. He unleashed another furious roar upon the mute assassin.

"Stop this madness—*now*!"

Rezaaran lowered his gaze and saw Ashana positioned between himself and Leta. Her outstretched arms kept both soldiers from attacking one another again.

"This is not who you are, Rezaaran," she pleaded. She refused to lose him once again.

The feral War Mage slowly lowered his arms and stood before Ashana with a quietness he had not displayed since his transformation. In the background, Luminara commanded forth the army of memuvar while Stryker readied a tranquilizer dart from his weaponized arm. Neither of them was certain that anything could subdue him.

Rezaaran raised a hand to Ashana and ever so carefully touched her face. He took the greatest care not to injure her with his claws. Something about her reached deep within him, far beneath the animalistic layers.

An unusual sound left the creature's lips, almost a whimper yet vaguely comprehensible. It made the sound again but remained indistinguishable.

"Ashana," he finally murmured.

"Yes, Rez," she said, smiling in relief. "It's me, and I'm always going to be here to bring you back home."

The transformation regressed, step by painful step, until Rezaaran's usual form stood before them. He looked around, bewildered. "What just happened?"

"Like you don't know!" Moraya seethed, shoving him aside on her way to help her injured friend.

Rezaaran's disorientation turned to horror when he saw Leta slouched in pain against the tree. Moraya helped her to her feet, and she gingerly walked forward.

"Leta, I'm so sorry! I—"

"Save it!" Moraya snapped. "Just get off this world with your girlfriend and that witch so we can get on with our mission. You all have stalled us long enough. This is why I don't trust you mages. Now leave—before I decide to sonically shatter your skull, you monster!"

CHAPTER SIX

TEMPLES IN THE CLOUDS

Rezaaran sat upon the edge of a bench in Quirt's workshop. His teeth chattered incessantly, and his clammy hands twitched between repeated failed attempts to hold them still. The War Mage's ashen face stared into the distance as he futilely tried to expunge the fleeting images of his last moments on Hysforth. The sheer terror he'd sensed in the minds of his comrades. What he'd felt in Ashana's heart before she stopped him. He remembered the blood rage and the overwhelming strength with which it had urged him to kill Leta.

Rezaaran closed his eyes and hoped to escape these images, even block them temporarily for a few moments of peace. However, in the darkness, he heard the growling of the beast grow stronger and saw its menacing glare. Moraya's words about his nature haunted him, and the growls grew louder.

His eyes flashed open, and he shuddered when he felt someone approach. A weary sigh escaped his lips when he saw it was Ashana with a blanket for him.

"Maybe she was right, Ash," he murmured between his trembling lips. "Maybe I *am* just a monster. After everything I did last year, maybe what we saw on Hysforth is really who I am."

Ashana slapped him across the face, glowering. "Don't you *dare* start pitying yourself, Rezaaran Valhara! Yes, you did terrible things. And yes, Thaedis committed horrible acts as a direct result of that. But the universe is still in existence. We have not yet met our end days, and there is time to make amends. But none of that can happen unless you get your head out of the past and into the present."

If only she could see my ardent affirmation, Kashari mused. *She is quite right. You are placing far too much time on thoughts of what may have been. That manner of thinking will not aid you. All you can do now is move forward.*

"You're right, Ash," Rezaaran murmured. "I just need to figure out what's happening to me and get it sorted out."

"Well, Quirt is working on that now," she replied more gently. "Hopefully this helps as well." She handed him a long flask of a steaming herbal infusion.

"What's this?" he asked, taking a whiff of the floral aromas.

"I kept a cache of herbs from various places I visited while on missions with Legion Ninety-Nine. This was from a mission to Akero. The locals' name for it roughly translates to 'angel's whisper.'"

"Well, I'd like to have some, but I don't think I can hold anything with all this shaking."

Ashana pointed a finger at him with a stern face.

"Please don't slap me again."

"Don't tempt me!"

"Ahem." Quirt cleared his throat, interrupting the lovers' quarrel. "I may have something to help with the jitters *and* your desire to avert further injuries to your pride. I will just need your shoulder."

Rezaaran lowered his thermal suit's neckline to expose his shoulder. Quirt administered a sharp prick into his muscle, and a few seconds later, the shivering abated.

"What was that?" Rezaaran asked, adjusting his suit.

"That was a mild sedative to control the withdrawal following the catecholamine torrent that flooded your body during your transformation," he said. The soldiers looked at him blankly. "Ah. My apologies. I was rambling again."

Ashana slowly nodded, raising an eyebrow.

"When I requested to join this mission, I asked Albeinius for all the information related to you and your previous missions. As I read through the data, I learned you had been injected with a host of nanobots before your first mission to Aquaridor."

"I'd forgotten about those," Rezaaran murmured and subconsciously scratched the site where Orin had injected him last year.

"Well, beyond their primary function of recording your location, they also capture information about your biological functioning. During your transformation, your body underwent a tremendous surge in adrenaline and other stress-mediated hormones. That sedative should help return your physiology to a relaxed state. However, those nanobots could help construct a complete picture of the changes your body undergoes when you channel your magic. I would like to request an additional parameter, if I may."

"Does this mean you'll have to inject me again?"

Quirt held a small silver disc up to Rezaaran's face. "Not at all. This device will be placed behind your ear to record your brain activity during future missions. I believe it will also allow me to understand the changes made to your body following your use of the badge you asked me to analyze. I was able to retrieve data from your first admission to the medical bay when you arrived at IRIS. For someone with regenerative abilities, you do tend to frequent the infirmary extraordinarily often."

"Yeah, I've noticed that too."

"If I may, Rezaaran," Luminara said, gingerly walking toward the young mage.

The battle for Hysforth had evidently caused more injuries to her body than the Archlord had led them to believe. On his initial assessment, Quirt noted several contusions across Luminara's body. In addition to her latest wounds caused by Leta and Ashana, it appeared the Archlord had incurred a number of other injuries during her impersonation of Luminara. Several had become septic, and the Archlord's magic had been the only force keeping Luminara's body active. Were it not for her Guardian powers and eternal soul, she would have succumbed to the overwhelming infection. While aboard the *Liberator*, Quirt treated these old wounds and, through several of his devices, was able to heal her rapidly.

The Woodland Maiden gently placed her hand on Rezaaran's head and felt the raging bestial spirit within his heart. Her serene presence acted as a balm to soothe the savagery in his nature.

"I am able to quell the rage rising from this power. In turn, this will allow you to harness the power of the transformation without its enslaving you. However, I sense that something else is troubling you, Rezaaran. In that regard, alas, the answer lies within yourself."

"That part feels like it's going to need some time," he murmured, taking a sip from his flask.

Ashana's interface beeped alive with an inbound message. "It's from Xephyrus," she remarked with mild surprise. A projection of the Elder Mage appeared above her interface.

"Greetings, everyone. Lady Luminara, it is indeed an honor to have you aiding us in our efforts."

Although Xephyrus addressed her formally and in his usual crisp manner, Rezaaran knew he was struggling to contain his elation at the chance to commune with a Guardian in his lifetime.

"It is my honor to serve with those who selflessly protect Anmor in our stead," Luminara said.

"IRIS has recently received a call for aid from a splinter faction on the planet Halsyn. Primarily composed of acolytes of their magical order, this resistance seeks to be free of the Dominion presence that has blockaded their world at the behest of Halsyn's political leaders. Thus, the mission to ally with said acolytes is delicate, to say the least. They have also notified us that the planetary blockade has stranded a platoon of Space Rangers upon their world. If this is true, perhaps we may get a rare opportunity to negotiate an alliance with an established intergalactic justice force. Such an allegiance would be greatly advantageous in our current circumstances. Rezaaran, per Commander Moraya's reports, I am aware that the mission to Hysforth has crippled you significantly. Needless to say, I speak euphemistically; her report was...more colorful in its description. Will you be able to undertake the mission to Halsyn?"

"I am ready to serve IRIS," Rezaaran said with renewed fire in his heart.

"I am glad to hear that. Gerrin and I will meet you at Halsyn in due course. Our Halsyn informant has requested a meeting at the Temple of Hunsu. The coordinates will follow this message."

Luminara looked out the view panel at the forest planet they still orbited. Her mind meandered in reminiscence as she watched the clouds roll through the atmosphere.

"Are you all right?" Rezaaran asked.

"Alas, I am far from being all right, my young friend. Physically, I am complete, yet I inhabit a body so wrought with injury that every step is steeped in agony. Despite the kindness and advanced medical technology Dr. Zefrityn has utilized on me, I fear these injuries will take some time to heal. However, I feel adrift about the news of trouble on Halsyn. I fear an old friend of mine may have returned home."

"Who is it?"

"Her name was Nish Ira. You may recall another Guardian you encountered named Itara Zelzo. Well, before the Edarian corrupted him, Zelzo was once the valiant leader of a rebel unit of Arkanian assassin androids. Zelzo inspired others to forgo their programmed imperative to kill and instead to use violence as a means of defense. However, many Arkanians viewed his violation of their prime directive as heresy against their creators, the Arcara. The Arcara are a reclusive but sophisticated race who live on a remote, outer world. They advanced their technology at such an exponential rate that they were already space faring when the Thyrillians had barely grasped the concept of using the stars to navigate their own world."

Quirt looked down, his cheeks flushed. Despite how advanced the Thyrillians were, they always fared second best to the Arcara.

"However, unlike the Thyrillians, the Arcara sought to use their technology to conquer less advanced worlds. To this end, they specialized in military technological advances. The Arkanians were their greatest invention in this regard. One of the conquering parties that ventured across the Maelinthian many millennia ago found their way to Skylark. Their leader was Nish Ira. She was fierce and ruthless. Fortunately, she lost her greatest advantage when she crashed into our planet after her ship sustained significant damage from a solar storm. Regardless, she was intent on conquering my home world and establishing communications with her people. Once more to her misfortune, Skylark was perhaps the most technologically removed world at the time. Her raiding party wandered deep into the jungle and became lost, entirely at the mercy of the forest and its magic. Battered and bruised, she arrived at my village, looking the worse for wear. In that state, she held little of her conqueror's pride and humbled herself to ask for aid. During the next few months, she and I became grudging friends."

"How did Zelzo fit into her story?"

"Zelzo was the Arkanian war chief assigned to protect Nish Ira. When she crashed, he traveled to her last known location and tracked her down. His initial drive was to slay everyone in our village. However, Nish Ira reprogrammed him and spared our lives." Luminara wiped a tear from her eye, recollecting memories of her youth on Skylark. "Together with Zelzo, she was able to repair her ship. She left our world and established a colony with her crew on the planet of Halsyn. Unlike her kinsmen, Nish Ira dedicated the rest of her life and resources to finding peace within herself and the Vaux. Her colony became a sanctuary amid the raging wars around her for any who desired peace."

"Couldn't Rez redeem her soul the way he did with you?" Ashana asked. Witnessing Luminara's tears over the inevitable outcome awaiting her friend saddened her.

"Alas, nothing can be done for Nish Ira. When Thaedis unleashed his Edarians upon us, only I was spared their corruption. The others have been lost to the Edarians who possessed them. Nish Ira's fate, as with the rest of my friends, is sealed. That is perhaps what saddens me most."

Luminara slowly rose to her feet and lightly held her side. "Is there perhaps somewhere I may rest?" she asked the soldiers. "Besides the emotional conflict I feel about contesting Nish Ira, I am in no physical state to assist you in your quest as yet."

"Of course," said Ashana gently. "Follow me. I'll show you to your chambers."

"Thank you, my dear."

The doors whispered shut behind Luminara, and she sat down on the floor. Breath escaped her lips, and her mind attempted to find the sanctuary offered by the Vaux.

Cold, cackling laughter filled her mind—sultry yet undoubtedly wicked in nature. "I love how you lie so easily to them."

Luminara turned sharply. Her eyes darted across the chamber. She was alone. Maybe the infected wounds and fatigue were tricking her mind.

"Oh no, my precious dear, I am no hallucination."

"What is this?" she asked. Now she recognized that sickly saccharine voice.

Luminara looked in the mirror and saw her reflection morph into the face that Darzuka masqueraded in when in possession of her body. "You! I thought Rezaaran destroyed you!"

"That whelp has much to learn, yet you place your faith in him. Your rebellion against my lord truly is doomed! No, I forced him into a decision: either await my full removal from your vessel or destroy most of me before I inhabited another of his pathetic friends. Heroes. They're so predictable."

"I will find a way to exorcise your presence from my mind," Luminara said. "I am a Guardian; defeating Edarians is my sworn duty."

Darzuka appeared in her Edarian form as a smoky apparition before Luminara, her sharp teeth locked in a malignant grin. "Yet for all your posturing, you could not save the one you loved. At first, I thought it would be difficult to appear before you with the little that remained of me in this vessel. However, your vanity made the task far easier than I'd anticipated. Your soul is a cesspit of darkness…as with all you hypocritical Guardians."

"There is no vanity!" Luminara shot back before she regained her composure. "I will not fall foul to your venom, Darzuka."

"Did it tug at your precious soul," the Edarian asked with a sneer, "to speak my Torementhian name?"

Luminara ignored her and turned away from the mirror to resume her meditation.

"Ignore me if you wish, my sweet Luminara," Darzuka said with a smirk, laying her claws on Luminara's shoulders, "but you cannot deny what is in your heart. Those mortals may believe your lies about Nish Ira—that her fate is sealed in darkness—but I know the truth. You wish her dead so that you alone may be the sole Guardian. You relish the divine awe with which these mortals revere you. Yet more than vanity—there is also envy. You crave the romance the Zenorians have. You yearn to reclaim what you lost. And despite what you may tell yourself, deep down in you lurks a hope that theirs should fail. After all, why should others have the happiness you could not?"

"That happiness was snatched from me by you!" Luminara spat. When she realized what was happening, she composed herself and spoke calmly. "I will not entertain this perversion. I will find a way to be free of you and your vile words."

"Oh, my dear." Darzuka spoke sweetly despite the menace of her Edarian visage. "No matter what you do, I will always be a part of you."

Steam rolled around the ankles of the two soldiers as they cautiously walked along the streets of this new alien world. Although their attention was piqued, they attempted to blend into the crowd to avert the notice of the patrolling soldiers.

"Well, at least Quirt placed us near enough to mix with the locals," Rezaaran said.

"I can't believe he was able to teleport us from such a distance," Ashana remarked with mild amazement. "Docked on a moon one planet away, he manages to place us right next to a building. For a moment I was worried we'd end up outside the habitat!"

"What would have been so wrong with that?"

"Oh yes, I forgot—you don't read," Ashana remarked with a mocking grin as they parted to allow a local to pass between them. "The Cartographer's Guild reports Halsyn as an anomalous planet. The upper atmosphere exists as a thick layer of toxic clouds, while the surface is a barren wasteland populated by an assortment of fierce creatures. However, what truly makes this planet bizarre is that the surface is littered with what the locals call time pools. These are essentially wormholes through time and space that for some reason are able to exist on this planet. Luminara says that during the creation of the Maelinthian, some of the largest shards of the Valinthian stone found their way to the surface of Halsyn, and this accounts for the time pools."

"I guess only a Guardian would know that," Rezaaran remarked with a shrug. "Hey, did she seem a little odd to you?"

"Not really. Why?"

"I'm not sure. She just seemed withdrawn when we left."

"Well, I don't think it's easy for her to see us leave, knowing that you will possibly have to kill her friend."

"Perhaps," he replied. "She also said Nish Ira and her crew were responsible for creating the habitats on Halsyn. Did she mean this city?"

"According to the archive files on Halsyn, when the first colonists arrived on the planet, they realized they would not be able to sustain themselves on the surface. Part of what makes Halsyn so unusual is that the gravity levels differ in different regions of the planet. At this level of the atmosphere, gravity's pull is incredibly weak and allows the jira to float through the air. The jira are enormous native animals. On any other planet, they would rightly belong in the sea, because their weight is too immense to be supported. What is interesting is that they survive off the toxic gas clouds that circulate at this level of the atmosphere, and their waste product is oxygen."

"Well, that was a lucky find. So how did they get the oxygen from these creatures into the habitats?"

"They built the habitats onto their backs."

"What?" Rezaaran asked incredulously. "So…we're standing on the back of an animal?"

"See? This is why you should read before we come to a planet. The locals care for the jira, who in turn sustain their habitats by providing them with oxygen. It's a perfect symbiotic partnership."

Several of the occupants of the street turned to face the Zenorians.

"Well, it seems your startled response has drawn more attention than we would have liked," Ashana remarked, surreptitiously reaching for her earpiece. "Quirt, we are approaching the location. I need an update about our friends as soon as possible."

A few moments later, the Zenorians arrived at a patrol blockade. Several cyborg Kalarans barred the entrance to the Temple of Hunsu.

"This road is off limits to civilians and off-world visitors," the commander informed them in a detached digital voice. "This is the directive of Sekian Yakura, eighth of his dynasty. Necessary force will be exercised if you disobey."

Well, this upgrade already seems a lot more intelligent, Kashari mused.

"Commander," one of the soldiers said as he gazed over the Zenorians, "facial recognition does not register these two as visitors, according to the port records before the lockdown."

The cyborg soldiers closed the distance on the interlopers. "Are you stowaways?"

Ashana slowly slipped her hand beneath her cloak and closed around her crossbow's handle.

"Commander, they are IRIS soldiers!"

"Seize them!"

The soldiers rushed forward, intent on trapping the Zenorians. Rezaaran repelled them with a telekinetic blast while Ashana drew her crossbow and fired a flurry of electrified bolts. The commander activated a red button on the side of his face, and a shrill ringing filled the air.

"That's not good," Rezaaran murmured as a garrison of troopers headed toward them. He knew he could easily clear his way through the soldiers, but given their location atop the back of a jira, he felt uncomfortable casting any form of offensive magic.

The cyborg Kalarans surrounded the Zenorians and aimed their guns at their heads. Just then, a white quarterstaff flew through the air and struck one of the Kalarans on the head. The Dominion soldiers turned in the direction the staff had come from, and many fell to a powerful gust that crippled them.

Charging toward the garrison with no trace of fear in her sparkling blue eyes was the fiercest teenage girl Rezaaran had ever seen. She slipped beneath the heavy swing of the first Kalaran, slicing his abdomen open with the edge of her sword as she skidded past him. Then rose to her feet in the thick of the garrison and surveyed them unflinchingly. Her sword sang and zipped through the air toward her midline. Spinning rapidly about her heels, she generated a powerful vortex.

Despite their efforts to resist, several of the Kalarans flew toward her. Suddenly her spinning stopped and unleashed a gale that scattered the Kalarans around the road. The Halsynian caught her breath and fixed her eyes on the Zenorians.

"Are you two going to stand and gawk, or will you actually do something with those fancy weapons?"

"Oh, I like her already," Ashana quipped with a smile as she drew her second crossbow while regarding the Halsynian. She reminded Ashana very much of her younger self.

The Halsynian girl swayed to the rhythm of an unheard song, her sword gracefully twirling about her wrist. Dust from the ground rose around her. In a burst, a powerful squall rushed through the street and surged into her. She spun the sword one last time and charged her adversaries with speed comparable to Xephyrus's. She leaped between the soldiers, slicing as she cartwheeled and dodged their shots. Each acrobatic movement generated blasts of wind that rebuffed any enemies who approached her.

"Well, I'll be damned," Rezaaran murmured as he watched the young girl dismantle the cyborg Kalaran garrison. He and Ashana joined the fray to offer her aid but sincerely felt they really did not need to.

The War Mage seized two Kalarans who had set their rocket launchers upon her and smashed them together telekinetically. Ashana's electric bolts fried the circuits on a Kalaran, who issued a distress call to their command station. Her attention shifted at the sound of a battle cry from the Halsynian, who knocked a Kalaran to the ground with the momentum of her movement. She raced toward a wall and with a backflip sliced through three more soldiers before landing smartly beside Rezaaran, who dispatched the remnants of the Dominion soldiers.

The Zenorians looked at the girl with amazement while she struggled to catch her breath. A blue portal rippled in the air beside them, and Gerrin and Xephyrus strode forth.

"Well, it appears we have missed the entertainment," Xephyrus mused. "However, I would prefer that we do not engage that incoming garrison. A full skirmish would be dangerous for the locals."

"I agree with Gray Hair here," the girl said. "Most of our people are not soldiers. We can avoid this unnecessary fight. Follow me."

The Zenorians followed the girl along an alleyway and down a stairwell to a decommissioned construction passage.

"They won't be able to find us here," she informed them as she sealed the door behind Xephyrus. "This will lead us right beneath the temple and through Master Suya's hidden room."

"How did you know to come find us?" Rezaaran asked as he regarded the young warrior beneath the dim lights of the tunnel. Her bald head and the ornate, concentric tattoo on her forehead added to the mysticism of her simple white robes.

"My master told me some days ago that he had reached out for help from a group called IRIS. He intended to meet you outside the Temple of Hunsu. When I saw the soldiers not allowing you to pass and that you were offworlders, I knew you were from IRIS."

"So where is this master of yours?" Gerrin asked impatiently. "Why could he not come meet us himself instead of sending a child?"

"I am not a child," the girl growled. "I am fourteen years old and an acolyte of Nish Ira!"

"Great—another arrogant brat," Gerrin murmured. "Well, take us to this master and your cult, if you please."

The girl reached for her sword, but Xephyrus placated her. "I apologize for my associate's blunt nature," he said. "We are here to help, truly. What is your name?"

She glowered at Gerrin for a moment. For a reason she could not explain, the gray-haired man seemed to calm her. He had a natural presence that reminded her of Master Suya.

"My name is Ikso Poe," she replied firmly, sheathing her weapon. Her piercing blue eyes locked on Gerrin's, daring him to laugh at her name.

"It is a pleasure to meet you, Ikso," the Elder Mage said gently. "I am Xephyrus, a fleet commander for IRIS. I believe you have already met Rezaaran and Ashana."

Ikso offered a simple nod of acknowledgment to the Zenorians she had met in the street.

"And, of course, my colleague Gerrin," Xephyrus concluded with a stern glare at his fellow council member. "Can you tell us what happened to Master Suya?"

The young girl released a weary sigh, and Rezaaran saw her warrior nature falter.

"He disappeared three days ago. Nobody has heard from him since. I went to his home today and found everything in a mess. Master Suya always keeps his things in order, though. I knew that he had arranged to meet you today, so I grabbed his sword and rushed to do so in his place. I do not know where he is. Recently, when people disappear like this, they're never heard from again."

Ikso seemed to retreat into her thoughts for a moment. "I think he knew his time was nearing. He had been behaving very strangely these past few months. He was spending more time alone and down here. I think he found something that troubled him deeply about the Order and the Sekian. I will show you his hidden room."

They walked for some time before arriving at a solid-steel vault door. Ikso worked on each of the seven rotary locks and then swung open the door to her master's chamber.

The inside of the chamber had an aged scent, much like Mokshar's rooms. However, unlike the deceased Zenorian Elder Mage, Master Suya was not averse to using technology. A large desk filled the back wall of the vault, and it housed numerous monitors that relayed the feeds from security cameras across the habitat. Pages containing Master Suya's scrawls plastered the walls. Some of the notes were in Galtic, but a fair proportion was scribed in the Halsynian language. Interspersed with the notes were pictures of various Halsynians.

"This is fascinating," Xephyrus said softly, studying the wall.

"How is that supposed to help us?"

"Gerrin, there is more to our efforts than storming bases and waging frontline battles. As a council member, I really should not have to remind you of the value of reconnaissance. This Master Suya has conducted a full investigation of the misdemeanors of his leader."

"Do you think that's what got him into trouble?" Ashana asked. She activated her helmet to capture the entirety of Suya's investigation with her camera and then relayed the information to Quirt.

"I would postulate such an outcome as the most probable explanation," Quirt said over their communicators. "The translation software is still busy deciphering the Halsynian notes. However, this is quite a conspiracy."

"It appears the Sekians are a recent addition to your history—is that correct, my dear?"

"That is what Master Suya said. He said that since the first days of Nish Ira, our people existed without leaders and without divisions in society. However, when travelers began to arrive, they brought the prospect of wealth and trade. The Order forbade its members to partake in the trading. The Elders said that riches deviated us from our true purpose."

Gerrin smirked but said nothing. Although he fought the honorable fight most of the time, he was not averse to acquiring money. Only after living through poverty could one preach about the triviality of money. He sincerely doubted anyone would.

"The short version is that the most prominent traders were the Yakura family. In time, they assumed enough prestige among those living outside the Order and established a dynasty upon this and several other habitats."

"How many habitats are there, exactly?" Ashana asked.

"I can't say for sure. Master Suya says there are at least fifty thousand."

"I'm sorry, what?" Gerrin asked sharply, turning to face Ikso.

"Well, that complicates things quite substantially," Xephyrus said with a sigh. How would they be able to liberate such a vast number of scattered cities located atop the backs of giant flying creatures?

"I don't understand—why don't the people overthrow these Sekians?" Rezaaran asked Ikso.

"I can answer that." Xephyrus approached the wall and touched a sketch of a jira. "This planet has an atmosphere rich in chemicals that serve a multitude of industrial functions. Ordinarily these chemicals would be toxic. However, the jira appear to take in the toxins and exhale oxygen and carbon dioxide. The chemicals also form a breeding ground for their prey and are used by the locals to synthesize everything they need within the habitats."

His finger moved over to a list that started with Sekian Yakura, eighth of his dynasty.

"The Sekians have colluded with the Colonial Guild for exclusive sale of all environmental products of interest. In exchange, the Dominion provides them with a functional military to assert their rule. Furthermore, the influx of travelers allowed a thriving tourism business that saw an escalation of alcohol, narcotics, and other indulgences never experienced before on Halsyn. I believe the Order sought to preserve its legacy and forbade members from such indulgences. A standing agreement also exists that Halsyn will provide the Dominion with any graduating acolytes to serve as soldiers."

"Master Suya never could understand how the Elders willingly sold our culture to these offworlders."

Luminara said that Nish Ira would be on this world, Rezaaran told Xephyrus privately. He did not wish to upset Ikso with what she may view as heresy. *Maybe they used the Archlord to manipulate the Elders' faith and bend the Order to the needs of the Dominion?*

Xephyrus nodded his acknowledgment of Rezaaran's theory. It seemed highly likely that the Dominion would use such means to gain control of this world. However, the fact they were enlisting magically trained soldiers was far more ominous.

"Hold on a moment," Ashana said with a furrowed brow. "If the Colonial Guild siphons off the gases that form the bulk of the ferrying zone from the atmosphere, then the jira will have nothing to convert to breathable air, and their food stocks will dwindle."

"Ira's bow!" Ikso gasped. "That means we will all die! How could the Sekians agree to this? They'll die too!"

"No, they won't," Xephyrus remarked grimly, tapping a note. "In exchange for their loyal service, the Dominion has granted them free and secure passage from Halsyn before the planet reaches the critical point."

"Is this plan occurring only on this habitat?" Rezaaran asked.

"The Sekians on every habitat have sold their people to the Dominion," Quirt informed them.

"This is beyond our capacity to handle," Xephyrus said. "The four of us cannot covertly subvert this plan across fifty thousand habitats. At the same time, an assault strike would be a disaster. The risk that we may inadvertently shoot down the habitats is too high."

"I have an alternative plan," Ashana said slowly, considering the nature of the battle. "Rezaaran and I came to this habitat using the teleportation technology Quirt devised. Gerrin was able to bring the two of you here. If we could outfit the citadels with a mass teleporter, we could instantly send through enough troops to fight at street level while the citadels engage the orbiting Dominion vessels. That way they cannot shoot down the habitats."

"That will take some time to achieve," Quirt interjected. "The transporter I installed on the *Larkesian Liberator* is a prototype. However, a more advanced model will be required to transport the numbers necessary to fulfill your plan."

"I am confident that Albeinius and you can handle that," Xephyrus said simply. "What would help, though, is having allies on the ground aiding us in overthrowing the Sekians and their Dominion soldiers."

"Master Suya believed so as well," Ikso replied. She skipped over to the desk and accessed three of the monitors. "He felt that we could not in good faith ask others to sacrifice for our freedom yet not be part of the struggle. He secretly started a group devoted to upholding the teachings of Nish Ira. We are called the Tayko."

The Zenorians watched the screen, where a group of warriors dressed in the same attire as Ikso performed a synchronized martial arts routine.

"Are the Elders aware of this rebel faction?" Xephyrus asked with a raised eyebrow.

"No, not at all," Ikso stated firmly. "Master Suya grew to distrust most of our Elders. He built the Tayko mostly of new recruits he felt he could trust, as well as some of his older students. Working with the friends he had, he was able to coordinate smaller groups on the other habitats. However, with his disappearance, there is a concern that the Elders may discover our plans to defy them and the Sekians."

"That explains why he would have reached out to the Rangers."

"I agree, Ashana," Xephyrus said. "Perhaps our efforts for now should be limited to an assessment of what resources are available for a successful future mission. Ikso, will we be able to meet the Tayko group that has been established at the Temple of Hunsu?"

Ikso thought a moment. "I don't think that will be possible, Xephyrus. The Elders have many loyalists within the temple. Also, the Order strictly forbids offworlders entry into the temple. Trespassing carries the death penalty."

"Then this is a lost cause."

"Don't be so hasty, Gerrin," Rezaaran chastised the council member. "Ikso, I get a sense that you have some people you trust within your Order. Have any of Master Suya's older students been designated as next in command in the event of his disappearance?"

"Master Suya did not say who would be in charge if this happened to him, but my older sister may be able to help us. There's a secret entrance to my room from these passageways. Come with me!"

A few moments later, they emerged from a trapdoor beneath a rug in Ikso's chamber. Although simple, the girl's abode had a homely spirit. There were no pictures of family or her past, for the Order condemned attachment to the past or fear of the future. Instead, scrolls of Halsynian scripts detailing the tenets of Nish Ira's philosophies decorated the walls.

"I just want to leave my weapons here, and then we can—"

"Someone is coming," Rezaaran said sharply as he detected incoming echoes of magic users. "Five people, to be precise."

"It will be all right, Ikso," Ashana said gently. "This is not the place for a fight, but if they see us, that is exactly what will happen. I'm going to leave this tracer on you. If you're in danger, we will be there instantly to help."

"Thank you for coming to help us. I know Master Suya would appreciate that you have taken our cause as your own. Will I see you all again?"

"Sooner than you know it," Xephyrus replied with a kind smile.

Ashana attached the tracer beneath the back collar of Ikso's robes, and Gerrin opened a portal to transport the Zenorians back to the vault they had left.

Moments later, the door opened, and a young woman in a purple tunic, flanked by four red-robed warriors, entered the room.

"Who were you talking to?" the young woman demanded. "We heard voices in here. Tell us the truth, Ikso!"

"There were no voices—only my own, Moya."

"Please do not be difficult," Moya sighed. "You've really done it this time. The High Master has asked us to bring you to him. I'm here to make sure these guys don't mishandle you. As much trouble as you cause, you're still my sister."

"Nice to know that you care," Ikso muttered.

The red-robed warriors strode forward and removed Ikso's quarterstaves.

"That serious, huh?" she said mockingly, reluctantly passing on her rune-inscribed staves.

One of the warriors reached for Master Suya's sword and promptly received Ikso's elbow to his face. The other guards snarled and channeled wind magic in their hands, but Moya placated them.

"That's really not necessary, you know."

"He's trying to take something that doesn't belong to him!"

"Neither is it yours," Moya shot back.

"Maybe not originally, but Master Suya is gone now. This is all I have of him, and I will not forget his teachings. Neither should you!"

Moya bristled at her sister's fiery nature. More than being agitated that Ikso was being difficult as usual, she was morbidly embarrassed that she was being so petulant in the presence of senior acolytes.

"That's enough!" Moya raised a hand and incarcerated Ikso with invisible bindings.

The red-robed warriors shoved Ikso before the High Master, who was perched atop a stone chair elevated above the chamber. Ikso straightened up and smoothed out her tunic. Her stormy blue eyes looked straight at High Master Cheyi.

"You are brought before me with very serious allegations," boomed his drawling voice throughout the chamber. "How do you plead your case?"

Ikso remained unabashed. Master Suya had always disdained the High Master. He held Cheyi responsible for the perversion of the Order and viewed him as more avaricious than virtuous.

"I am innocent," she said firmly. "I tread upon the path of Nish Ira's teachings."

"You would dare stand there and lie to me? Well, have it your way, then!" High Master Cheyi waved his hand, and a projection filled the wall behind him. Moya reluctantly turned her eyes to the image, afraid of what she would see.

The footage of Ikso's entanglement with the Kalarans appeared before the chamber. Cheyi sneered when he saw Moya squirm. He had longed to rid his temple of this troublesome youngster, but Suya had protected her incessantly. Now that the old fool was no more, he could free himself of her nuisance.

"There it is," he declared. "Undeniable proof! You attacked the guards of Sekian Yokura, eighth of his dynasty. You aided offworlders who are sworn enemies of the Sekians and brandished the weapon of a master despite your rank as an acolyte! All crimes worthy of expulsion from the Order. However, I have something more interesting for you."

Moya apprehensively looked from the High Master to her sister and back again. She wanted her to learn a lesson, but she did not like Cheyi's ominous tone.

"For your acts of treason and rebellion, I sentence you to exile upon the surface. Oh, and you will not be on the acolyte's path. No, you have forced my hand and warrant exile to the Yaban Plains."

Moya's eyes widened. The Yaban Plains were far from any charted paths and plagued by an assortment of savage creatures. To prevent the possibility of stowaway outcasts, any shuttles that reached the Yaban Plains never touched land. This was a death sentence!

"If there are any objections, I will not entertain them. To defy the Sekians and our Order is to defy the goddess Nish Ira. To defy me is to defy our divinity. Get her ready for transport!"

The red-robed warriors seized Ikso and dragged her from the chamber. Her eyes desperately sought Moya's, but her older sister averted her gaze. What could she do now? The High Master had spoken, and his word was law.

"This is an absolute waste of time."

"Well, of course you would say that, Gerrin," Ashana remarked roughly and adjusted the settings on her interface to hear what happened to Ikso.

"Why should we be concerned with what happens to that girl?"

Xephyrus spoke with his back to the group as he pored over the documents Suya had left scattered across his table. "Being concerned with the happenings of the people we seek to liberate is the cornerstone of every one of our mission efforts."

Gerrin bristled. "She's just a rebellious teenager, Xephyrus!"

"Perhaps," the Elder Mage responded, turning to face his comrades, his arms crossed behind his back. "Yet each of us once was a teenager like her. Despite her age, she possesses the wisdom to understand that the political interferences of the Dominion do not bode well for her people. I believe this insight is what led Master Suya to entrust her as his second-in-command."

Gerrin seemed to need a better argument to change his mind on the matter.

"I thought helping those in need was what we *do*," Rezaaran said as he watched the monitors showing the training acolytes.

"Well, of course *you* would think that," Gerrin replied. "Always eager to be the hero."

"In any case," Rezaaran continued, ignoring Gerrin's jeer, "Ikso has valuable intel about the situation on Halsyn and her influence can sway the acolytes."

"I'm not so sure about the influence part," Ashana murmured as she overheard the conversation between Ikso and her sister. She adjusted the volume on her interface so that everyone could hear.

"Great. So her own sister thinks she is a menace. Yet we persist in following her lead."

"Patience, Gerrin," Xephyrus said, obviously straining his own patience to tolerate his colleague.

"Sorry to disturb you all," Quirt said into their ears, "but I have located the quarantined Space Rangers. I will upload their last known locale to your interfaces."

"A little busy at the moment, Quirt," Ashana replied. "I'll link you into the tracer with Ikso, and you can gain us surveillance."

"I will do what I can."

Silence fell upon the vault, and they listened intently to Ikso's sentencing.

"They're banishing her for helping us," Ashana whispered.

"Quirt, get us information on the Yaban Plains," Rezaaran ordered.

"This High Master Cheyi," Xephyrus said slowly. "He is mentioned often in Suya's notes. According to the information he gathered, he frequented the Sekian's palace fourteen times a week."

"Maybe they had leadership meetings," Gerrin suggested.

"That is a euphemism if ever I heard one," Xephyrus said. "According to Suya's notes, the founding people of Halsyn established their laws in accordance with the teachings of Nish Ira."

"She later went on to become an Anmorian Guardian," Rezaaran added.

"Under those laws, it was prohibited for members of the Order to seek to govern or rule the habitats. They were to coexist as equals."

"Implying there were no leaders within the Order," Ashana said, following Xephyrus's line of thought. "So the teachers would instruct and raise the members through the Order to reach the same level."

"In a manner of speaking. It seems that originally there was no discerning between members of the Order concerning level of experience. That was a new addition to the Order instated by the Sekians. Through their leadership, they fundamentally changed the Order and created the need for a High Master."

"So they could have someone to control the Order in a way that aligned with their interests."

"Precisely, Rezaaran. I postulate that they offered monetary incentives, but the High Masters had no need for money within the

Order—only power to retain their position. In his spying on Cheyi, Suya found evidence that implicates him in corrupting the Order to serve the Sekian. I believe he also discovered the identities of the high-ranking officials in the Dominion who frequented the Sekians' palace."

"If only we could retrieve his memories," Gerrin remarked grimly.

"Ikso is that solution," Xephyrus said emphatically. "She was privy to all that Suya learned, and she mentioned the resistance movement he started within the Order. Only with her help can we win their trust to turn this battle in our favor."

"Sorry to interrupt," Quirt said, "but this information on the Yaban Plains does not hold well for your young friend. It is a wild and uncharted wasteland containing an assortment of vicious creatures. According to the docks' manifest, a shuttle is scheduled to depart soon. I am uploading the coordinates to your interfaces now."

"Rezaaran, you and Gerrin need to get Ikso before she reaches the surface," Xephyrus said. "She is the only hope IRIS may have to overturn this corrupted governance on Halsyn."

"I still think this is a waste of time," Gerrin said firmly. "But orders are orders, right?" He clasped Rezaaran's shoulders, and they disappeared through a blue portal.

"Ashana, we have some friends to meet."

The acolytes and Elders gathered diffidently behind the billowing black cloak of High Master Cheyi. He had been adamant about using Ikso's exile as a forewarning to any other would-be traitors within the Order.

Ikso calmly stepped onto the platform. She had shed her tears in private, but here, at the moment of her banishment from her home, she refused to give Cheyi the satisfaction of knowing he had eroded her spirit by pitting her sister against her. She had already forgiven Moya. She understood the difficult situation she was in and did not begrudge her for looking after herself. Ikso would never be able to find peace knowing she had jeopardized her sister's life.

"Since this is the last we shall be seeing of you, I will be gracious and afford you a last good-bye to your sister. Understand that I only offer this because you are a child. Contrary to what you may think, I am not a complete monster."

Moya apprehensively approached Ikso upon the platform, but the red-robed warriors formed a barricade with their arms to prevent their touching.

"I will not allow you to be that close to your sister, Ikso. I do not want your treacherous spirit to stain her good soul."

Ikso glowered at Cheyi but said nothing. Anger was a wasteful emotion: such was the teaching of Nish Ira, the teachings that Master Suya would want her to continue living until her very end.

"You were always the best mentor and friend I could have asked for, Moya. I was blessed to have you as my sister. You were always someone I could look up to."

"Then why did you do this, you fool?"

"There are times when we must act beyond ourselves. I want you to know that I forgive you, and I need you to know that I am innocent. Remember how we started. I will always be with you."

Two red-robed warriors strode forward and bustled Ikso into the waiting shuttle. Moya watched with tearful eyes. "Good-bye, you idiot," she murmured, struggling to keep her expression neutral. "I love you. I'm sorry I wasn't strong enough for you."

The doors of the shuttle closed, and the airlock separated the platform from Ikso's lonely cabin. Electricity buzzed alive and formed the conveying pathway to the Yaban Plains. Ikso watched with some sadness as her home disappeared from view and in mild amazement as she passed the eye of the jira upon which she had lived.

However, clearing her mind, she knelt to meditate. Nish Ira had taught that emotion was fleeting and that the path of the Onsei dictated faith that a course greater than what was apparent would in time be revealed. She had to keep her faith, especially when all else felt hopeless.

A blue light shimmered beside her, startling Ikso from her meditation. Gerrin and Rezaaran stepped through and looked around the shuttle as though they anticipated a threat.

"Don't worry—we're here to rescue you."

"Could we drop the clichés and just finish the mission?" Gerrin asked, rolling his eyes.

"Can we ever have a conversation where you do *not* get confrontational?"

"OK, look—what's the plan?" Ikso interjected and stepped between the Zenorians. She could not believe they were supposed to be the adults.

"Quirt, get a lock on our position, and establish an uplink to the terminal Ashana sent you the details for."

"You know, I could teleport us out of here faster than that scientist can tinker with his equipment," Gerrin said.

"You see? This is exactly what I'm talking about! Could you just not do that?"

"Are you guys really the heroes?" Ikso asked. "How your organization does anything with this much disagreement is a miracle! I really don't understand why Master Suya reached out to you."

"Stay out of this, child!" Gerrin said.

"Hey! I am not a child!"

Suddenly the shuttle burst apart. The glass and steel shattered as the three occupants were hurled through the air in different directions.

Rezaaran regained his orientation first and looked around, desperately seeking Ikso. He spotted her falling some distance away from him. Gerrin prepared to open a portal, and Rezaaran knew the commander meant to make his way toward him.

Save the girl first, Rezaaran said. *I will be fine.* Sensing Gerrin's resistance to the order, he added, *Just do it!*

Telekinetically, Rezaaran moved Ikso toward Gerrin as they plummeted through the air. The War Mage saw the soldier grab the teenager and disappear through the portal. He himself fell farther through the clouds.

In the distance, an archer lowered her bow with a sneer. It was all too easy. Her white-and-gray robes fluttered in the wind, and she approached the site where she had struck the ferry craft. The kazera upon which she flew was a colossal magical creature composed entirely of wind-bound magic in the shape of a bird.

Her blue eyes pierced the dense clouds, seeking evidence of her quarry, but perhaps she could not see them because the gravity wells had drawn them down too rapidly.

A screeching pierced the skies, startling her. Amid crackling electricity, another avian apparition appeared. She recognized the form as the symbol Tyrel Salvidawn had passed to the Zenorians. Simarata.

Riding atop the creature's back was the young War Mage she had sensed, his sword readied as if any possibility existed of his contesting her on this planet. Nish Ira readied her bow and unleashed a flurry of enchanted wind arrows upon the Zenorian warrior. However, Simarata effortlessly wove between the whistling blasts of air and closed the distance to her kazera. Her eyes narrowed, and she dispersed her bow into the clouds. She was not afraid to meet him in battle.

The two magical birds careered toward one another and locked talons in a deafening blast of power. As they tussled, Rezaaran scrambled along Simarata's back and leaped toward Nish Ira. Landing substantially short of his target, he attempted to stand but felt every inch of his body dragged down.

"You honestly expected to come to my vessel's home world and defeat me?" Nish Ira jeered. "I would have expected more from the one Salvidawn chose to oppose us."

"What did you do to me?"

"I have not done a thing…yet," she snorted.

"Rezaaran, according to the nanobots within you," Quirt piped in his ear, "your body is undertaking gravitational strain because of the time pools on the surface. It appears they create fluctuating gravitational wells similar to thermals."

"Great," the War Mage muttered. He focused on drawing himself up to stand tall and thought of the spell he'd used to spar with Atomauran. The Vaux streamed to his body and infused him with greater strength to resist Halsyn's gravitational paradox. He held

Harkenathor at his side and fixed a narrow gaze upon the Edarian masquerading as Nish Ira.

"Intriguing," the Archlord murmured. "Perhaps you are not as utterly useless as I first assumed."

"So, should I call you by your true name, Edarian?"

"You have been awakened to the truth, I see," she mused. "Indeed, my true name is Rizthna. However, these meek-minded fools see this body I possess and believe their goddess has returned. They have no idea that I am not their savior but rather the omen of their end times. The Obsidious rises, and soon Nethriziin shall walk this realm."

"I made a promise to a friend that I would save Nish Ira no matter the cost."

"Then your friend will be disappointed. These people will bow to whatever I tell their leaders, for I am their goddess. Nish Ira is nothing more than a hollowed vessel."

Rezaaran pursed his lips. He sensed the vague flicker of Nish Ira's echo rouse at the presence of a challenger to this pretender. Luminara had asked, and he would do his best to save whatever fragment of Nish Ira existed beneath this Edarian's evil. He charged toward Rizthna, Harkenathor's edge singing out as it cut the air, narrowly missing her.

A shudder beneath his feet briefly diverted Rezaaran's attention from the Edarian. Channeling a gale of wind to her hand, she punched Rezaaran in his midriff and knocked him off the kazera.

Harkenathor flashed through the air and sank into the beast's hide. Somewhere beneath the shifting clouds of its exterior was solid tissue, for the blade embedded and held fast. Rezaaran drew himself to his feet and sheathed Harkenathor.

Any suggestions would be welcome.

Well, considering your experience, Kashari chided, *your first attempt was rather lackluster.*

How exactly is that helpful?

Fair point.

Rizthna took aim at Rezaaran and unleashed a hurricane-force series of blasts. The War Mage dispersed each with a spectral blast but felt his footing shift with every attack he dissipated. Arcs of electricity seared the air as he hurled bolts of lightning toward his adversary. Yet she remained unperturbed and easily evaded each bolt.

Suddenly the battlefield tilted. Simarata had gained an advantage in the battle against the kazera. However, as Simarata overpowered the beast, the adversaries skidded toward one another. Rezaaran leaped at Rizthna with sparking fists, yet she effortlessly evaded each strike and retaliated with a swift strike to his chest.

Air rushed from Rezaaran's lungs, and he crumpled. He lost focus on the augmentation spell and could not rise against the added gravity. The War Mage took a moment to compose his thoughts and then rose to his feet and immolated his body. He hurled an arc of flame at his enemy, to no avail. She calmly siphoned the air surrounding the arc and absorbed the Valinthicite into her hands.

"The people of this planet call it the Onsei; yours know it as the Vaux. Whatever you primitive beings choose to call it, know that we are the true masters of its power."

Kashari...any time now...

You cannot contest her at range. Force her into a mistake in close quarters.

Winds flowed along Rizthna's arms and converged at her fingertips to form lengthy whistling blades. A vortex swirled at her feet, and she drew the magical energy of the kazera into herself. The mystical beast upon which they stood disappeared.

Without the kazera beneath his feet, Rezaaran plummeted in a free fall toward the surface. His eyes sought the crackling electric form of Simarata, but the legendary Zenorian creature had also disappeared.

We really need to learn how to control that conjuration.

Perhaps this is not the opportune moment for such thoughts! Watch out!

Rezaaran spluttered blood from his mouth, and pools of crimson expanded across the white of his armor. A cruel smile split Rizthna's face. She flitted about the War Mage, her fleeting movements no more than a whistling gust in his ear, yet each time, she sliced into his flesh with her pneumatic blades, carving him apart to sate her Edarian bloodlust.

Rezaaran focused his eyes through the tears but could not find his sadistic adversary.

You need to put an end to this!

How am I supposed to do that? I can't see her!

Stop searching with your eyes!

The War Mage closed his eyes and heeded the advice. Rizthna's echo appeared clearly. This was exactly like his training with Leta. He felt the Edarian's echo shift around him. Nestled in her darkness was the sliver of Nish Ira.

I know exactly what you are planning, my friend. You need not ask.

Rezaaran reached into a reverie of concentration and ignored the burning gashes in his back, his attention locked onto Rizthna's echo. Electricity surged about his fist, crackling and spitting furiously. He swiveled sharply and punched the Archlord in the jaw.

Rizthna fell from her aerosynchronus state, startled that the Zenorian had reached her and paralyzed from his electrical attack. Temporarily disconnected from the winds around her, she careered toward the gravity well.

The War Mage streamlined his body and plummeted toward her, rapidly firing blasts of electricity from his hands as he neared her. However, Rizthna had recovered her senses enough to counter his attacks with more wind arrows. He wove between the arrows until he was close enough to drive Harkenathor through Rizthna. Her eyes widened, and red blood spattered onto her white robes.

Rezaaran looked at his chest, noting the pneumatic blade embedded beside his heart. He felt the pain, but his resolve drove him to seek an end to this battle in spite of it.

Wisps of black smoke curled around Nish Ira's listless frame, and in their haze, Rezaaran glimpsed the malevolent face of Rizthna. He felt Kashari guiding his actions. His hand reached out and scoured the Edarian in a burst of bright light.

Nish Ira's hand drew away from his chest and allowed the gaping wound to heal. She touched Rezaaran's face with a sad smile. She had never seen this boy before, yet there was a familiarity to his features. He had an aura about him. He had been in the presence of Luminara. She was the friend of whom he had spoken.

"I'm sorry I couldn't save you," Rezaaran said, cradling the dying Arcarian in his arms through their descent to the surface.

"You already have," she replied kindly. "Tell Luminara not to despair. He is not lost."

With those words, she closed her eyes and dispersed into the winds. Her powers infused into Rezaaran moments before he crashed through a cobalt-silver pool.

Trees groaned at the roots and crashed to the ground despite their protests. Hordes of Kalaran soldiers swarmed the forest. Their energy weapons felled any creature that passed their crosshairs.

Rezaaran's perplexed eyes scanned the forest frantically from beneath his cover in the undergrowth. He turned his attention to the leaves of the bush in which he hid. It was such a familiar fragrance. The War Mage sniffed the pale-green foliage and remembered the baked dishes his mother used to make on their holidays. His eyes widened with realization.

"I'm home," he whispered. "I don't understand."

A moment ago, he had been on Halsyn, and now he was on Zenor. How could this be Zenor? He had been home last year, and Sephiron had scorched the entire planet. Furthermore, why was the Dominion deploying regular Kalarans instead of the upgraded cyborgs?

"Unless…no, that's impossible!"

There are far stranger things than this, my friend.

"This is good, Kashari!" he said excitedly. "However it happened, I think this was meant to be. I can make a change!"

I would strongly advise against this, Rezaaran.

"I can save them both!"

Rezaaran was working his way through the undergrowth when the sound of shattering glass and a woman's scream broke the ominous silence. His blood froze, just as it had almost a century ago.

"No…no, not again!"

A hollowness grew in his heart, yet this spurred him onward at a faster pace until he faced the balcony of his family home. Black smoke coalesced in the air beside his father, who struggled to his feet.

"This is it," he whispered. A chill swept through the air. He was just in time. He may not have been able to save his mother's life, but he could preserve the sanctity of both their souls.

Rezaaran rose, intent on charging toward his house, when a strong grasp on his forearm held him fast. The War Mage swiveled on his feet sharply, holding a pulsing fireball in his free hand.

Gerrin offered him a solemn look.

"Let me go this instant!" Rezaaran snarled.

"I cannot allow you to do this. I understand your pain, but you cannot change history."

"You understand nothing!"

Rezaaran wrenched his arm free and focused on the balcony. The Vaux flowed to him in a powerful gust, and his eyes turned white. "I will not let him die again!"

"You cannot intervene," Gerrin repeated. This time his words carried an uncharacteristic gentleness. "It will create a rippling paradox that nobody can predict."

"I don't care! I can't stand by and watch my father die again—not when I have the power to prevent it! I won't!"

"Wait! Look over there."

Rezaaran released his siphoning of the Vaux and followed the direction of Gerrin's spear. Thaedis's shadowy form paused in his strides toward the wounded Zaran. The tyrant's attention had shifted when he sensed a Vaux surge in the forest. However, his swiveling head told Rezaaran that he alone had not distracted the Exiled.

A burst of light exploded on the balcony where, moments earlier, the Kalaran commander had roughly hauled away the younger Rezaaran. From the blinding light emerged a regal figure in gold-and-white armor. His blond hair glowed with an ethereal power.

"Lord Salvidawn," Rezaaran whispered in awe and confusion. "What's *he* doing here?"

In a flash, the Anmorian Guardian King summoned a hefty glowing sword to his hand and leveled his weapon at the Exiled. "Your rampage has lasted long enough, Thaedis." He spoke calmly yet with imposing authority. "Let us end this the way we should have so long ago."

Salvidawn looked pityingly at the man who gasped for breath beside him. He had survived a gunshot and then Thaedis's brief torture.

"This man has done you no harm. *I* deserve your vengeance. If any part remains of the man I once called my friend, then show your honor and spare this man's life from this dark magic."

The hooded head dropped as he considered Tyrel's words.

"You killed that man a long time ago."

In a burst of smoke and cinder, Thaedis appeared beside Zaran. He grabbed his victim by the neck and in the next instant stood upon the railing, ready to drop the despair-wracked man to the forest floor.

"Why does your heart bleed for this worthless filth while you thought nothing of betraying the one who sheltered you at your weakest? Without my father, you would never have become that pious hypocrite."

"I am done asking your forgiveness or trying to explain the truth to you. Nethriziin has poisoned your mind to reason."

"I don't want to hear another of your lies!" Thaedis flung Zaran across the balcony and ravaged his body with red lightning. When his assault ceased, Zaran struggled to draw his last breaths.

"Every soul in Anmor shall burn in Obsidian fire! And you will always remember that it was your fault, Tyrel."

"I know that."

Thaedis threw a jet of Obsidian fire at Zaran, but the shot struck the blinding light shield formed by Lord Salvidawn's enormous wings that surrounded the dying man.

Tyrel's head turned toward the forest. His gaze met Rezaaran's, and he offered the slightest nod of acknowledgment. The Guardian King strained beneath Thaedis's relentless onslaught of Obsidian magic, yet his wings held strong. With all his might, he resisted the pain that ravaged him to ensure that Zaran's soul passed into the Light of the Aetherealm.

An awestruck Rezaaran watched Zaran's soul leave his body and hold hands with the soul of his wife. Together they transcended the simplistic dichotomy mortals understood as life and death and merged with the Vaux in a manner the Vokarii could only dream to behold.

Tyrel Salvidawn looked at Rezaaran one last time and smiled. He wanted the young War Mage to know it had been complete. The mighty warrior lowered his defenses and absorbed all the hatred that his fallen friend had held for him.

Obsidian fire ruptured through the gleaming breastplate, and Salvidawn crumpled to his knees. Yet the sight did not sate Thaedis. The vengeful Exiled bombarded his former mentor with repeated waves of dark magic. But in his brief pause to relish the revenge he had long pursued, Tyrel escaped in a flash of light.

Thaedis roared in fury. Amid a burst of cinder, he pursued Tyrel one last time.

Rezaaran knew that the Guardian King had retreated to the Aetherealm. Yet he also knew that the gallant warrior had not flown as an act of cowardice but rather as a distraction to avert Thaedis's gaze from finding the younger Rezaaran.

"He risked everything to save me," the War Mage whispered.

Salvidawn always believed in your ability to end the war that he could not. He believed in the strength of your spirit. As do I.

"I don't understand," Rezaaran murmured, slumping to the ground. "He looked straight at me before he sacrificed himself. He knew I would be here." He looked at Gerrin, not because he needed confirmation but because there was nobody else with whom to share his realization. "That means in every version of time, I always returned here."

Your presence in this forest is the affirmation Salvidawn needed in order to know that the sacrifices he and Luminara made were not in vain. You survived—and with you, hope survives.

"He saved my parents' souls. Thaedis never corrupted them."

Gerrin shifted uncomfortably. "I'm sorry, Rezaaran. That couldn't have been easy to watch again. I know there are a great many more things I have done that warrant apologies too."

"I appreciate that, Gerrin, but there is no need. I have seen the truth today, and I know my purpose. I cannot afford to squander more time in doubt and regret. I have only one favor to ask."

"Anything you need."

"Take us back to Halsyn. We have a war to win."

"Aye. That I can do, kid."

CHAPTER SEVEN

A HUNTER OF THE DARK

The door to the bar slid open with a hiss, and the soldiers crossed the threshold. Biological scanners passed over them and scoured any infectious agents that clung to their outfits. After they had taken a few more paces, an android approached them.

"Welcome to Sheroko," the usher droid said in an unusually friendly tone. "Our scanners indicate you have weapons on your person. Our management would humbly request that you leave them with me. You can be assured they will remain safe, and you can collect them when leaving if you present me with this tag."

"I'd feel a lot safer with these on me," Ashana muttered as she reluctantly placed her quiver, bow, crossbows, and daggers into the steel crate offered to her.

"I suppose the establishment has reasons for such security," Xephyrus replied, placing his daggers into the same crate. "Bloodshed within these walls would be bad for business. Besides, if the situation seems amiss, you always have your wits and your fists."

"Small comfort," she said wryly.

A second frosted-glass door parted to reveal the bar within. Styled more as a lounge, this bar was far more elegant than the Zamtian one she had visited with Rezaaran. Granted, that bar had served as a front for the spy network operating within the building.

Dark-glass counters topped with silver panels spanned the walls of the bar. Levitating frosted-glass chairs conveyed patrons from the bar to tables. Several floating orbs illuminated the bar in a surreal aura with slow pulses of violet and cyan.

Interspersed among the crowd of aliens were numerous androids. Some were designated to clean the counters, while others dispensed drinks ordered via cerebral circlets worn by the guests.

"It appears Suya was right," Xephyrus remarked grimly. He glanced across several inebriated customers lying slumped upon the tables toward a large glass-walled room where others rebreathed each other's narcotic fumes. "Narcotics and alcohol are readily available—most likely permitted to subdue potential uprisings against the Sekians. Let us make swift work and be gone from here. I can feel the rot of this place encroaching upon me."

"There they are," Ashana said to Xephyrus, identifying the Space Rangers by their signature brown coats and metal-braced black boots. However, even out of uniform, their sporadic glances and terse behavior marked them as soldiers in an uncomfortable environment.

The Rangers shifted uneasily when the Zenorians approached.

"Greetings, friends," Ashana said with a genial smile. "Mind if I take a seat?"

"Sure," said a humanoid Ranger with thinning black hair. "Besides leaving the planet, you can do whatever you feel down here."

"Well, it's great to meet you all. My name is Ashana."

The Rangers remained silent, regarding the newcomer and her accomplice warily.

"Don't all jump in excitement at once," she murmured to herself, grateful the ambient music had obscured her glib remark.

"Perhaps I can expedite this process," Xephyrus said. He took a seat beside Ashana and reached for the edge of his cloak.

Instinctively the Rangers reached for their holsters to retrieve their sidearms. But their faces turned ashen as they realized they had checked their weapons at the entrance, as per the rules of the establishment.

"At ease, Rangers," Xephyrus said, his gray eyes passing among the company of six. "Well, no need for surprise—your outfits are renowned, as is your reputation. Furthermore, we had reliable intel that a cohort had been caught planetside in the quarantine."

Xephyrus leaned in closer to ensure that potential spies of the Sekians would not overhear whatever exchange happened next. Lowering his cloak, he revealed the IRIS insignia upon his war suit.

"My name is Xephyrus Grievior," he said in his calm, inspiring voice. "Ashana Eldeerim you are already acquainted with. We are both commanders within IRIS, sent to scout Halsyn before we commit our forces to a liberation mission."

His forthcoming nature reached out to the Rangers and garnered their trust. The thin-haired man seemed to hold some authority over the others. A simple nod was the sole necessary signal for the other soldiers to speak.

"Any mission to this planet," a green-skinned, amphibious Ranger said, "will have to be built on guerrilla tactics. For obvious reasons, aerial assaults will not work. However, with the blockade, landing troops in the habitats is impossible. Of course, we are at hand if needed, but our numbers are far too few. We too arrived to assess the situation and make a decision with headquarters."

"Fortunately, some of the locals are rebelling." A portly, gray-bearded soldier now took over the conversation. He eyed the crowd around the bar, wrinkling his beefy nose. "None of this rabble, though—their minds have been ailed by all the booze, drugs, and whores. No, that lot in the temples—they know something is wrong. One of them is the reason we came 'ere in the first place."

"Those warriors are..." The amphibious Ranger paused for a moment, searching for the right word.

"Brave?" Ashana offered.

"Odd," he finally said. "Very unusual in manner. But for the most part, they seem honest. However, the corrupted rulers do not have only the Dominion at their disposal. There is something evil on this world. Out on the streets at night, you feel its presence around you. It lurks in the shadows. The locals call it the Towari. The soul's end."

"Whatever it is," said a feline Ranger with a neck frill folded beneath his coat, "it scares the locals senseless. Within this district—and especially in these bars—they are safe. But if they walk the streets, they believe the Towari will drag them away, never to be seen again."

"Sounds like a folktale," Ashana muttered, trying to ignore the bumps rising across her skin.

"I would not be so hasty to dismiss such an anomaly," Xephyrus remarked sagely. "The Dominion has many unusual allies within their ranks."

"Is there any tangible evidence that this Towari exists?"

"Aye, there is, miss." The portly Ranger spoke again. "Folks here have been abuzz about people that go missing in the night. Our informant was one. We believe the Sekians are using a bounty hunter to remove any opposition to their empire."

"Admittedly, though, we do have a selfish interest in this," said the thin-haired man. "Several days ago, a group of Rangers left to patrol the streets and investigate the situation."

The other Rangers shifted uncomfortably in their glass chairs.

"They're still out there," said a younger female Ranger. "We have to believe they are."

"I wish I could, Nerdosa."

"Perhaps we could help you locate this missing patrol," Ashana suggested. "You said this bounty hunter typically attacks under the cover of night. Well, there's a few more hours of light left. If we leave now, we may find some clues."

Nerdosa squealed with delight and clapped her hands. "Come, Sharaf! We have to try to find our friends!"

The thin-haired Ranger futilely attempted to resist a smile, but Nerdosa's energy was contagious. "Well, I would love to go and find what we can, but ultimately our patrol leader or captain has to issue an order."

"Why haven't they already?" Ashana asked, raising an eyebrow.

"They've been preoccupied with the leisures of this fine place!"

"Orach!" Sharaf snarled.

The portly, gray-bearded man blushed, his whole face taking on the color of his nose.

"You can find the patrol leader over there," the amphibious Ranger said, with a subtle gesture of his head indicating the bar behind Ashana.

"May I request an audience with your captain?" Xephyrus asked, rising to his feet.

"Of course," Sharaf replied. "Asora will lead you to his rooms and help you pass the clearance to have a meeting."

"Excellent! I will leave the rescue of your comrades in Ashana's capable hands. Perhaps she may be able to persuade your patrol leader to join in."

"I wouldn't hold my breath," Orach mumbled, earning a fiery glower from Sharaf.

The amphibious Ranger escorted Xephyrus through the bar. They passed a room where several female aliens danced sensually among the drunken guests. Xephyrus felt his skin crawl with disgust, and his pace quickened. The sooner they left this accursed bar, the sooner he would be at ease. This was no place for any self-respecting person.

Asora gestured with two fingers over his left breast to the Rangers standing guard, and they opened the door to the plush penthouse room. The Elder Mage entered, his thinly veiled disdain evident upon his face. Slouched on a red velvet couch was the person he assumed to be the Rangers' captain—although were it not for the foreknowledge that he was to meet their leader, he would never have thought it. Beyond his lax posture, this man was clad in neither the usual modest attire of the Rangers nor their signature coat. Instead, he wore fitted black-leather pants and a richly detailed metal vest that was unfastened to expose his athletic torso. His fingers lazily twirled a goblet containing a purple liquid while his hungry eyes surveyed the bar below.

Xephyrus was uncertain if this young man was intoxicated or if he simply chose to make him wait to assert his authority. Both options vexed the Elder Mage.

"It's marvelous, don't you think?" the captain finally asked in a smooth voice that almost purred. "Amid all the conflict and turmoil throughout the galaxy, there exists this retreat of leisure. Even when the war arrived, it forced me to remain in this oasis. Fate, it seems, continues to smile upon me."

As the captain sipped his liquor, his attention roved to a scantily clad dancer who had taken the stage to perform her alluring song.

"So why have my men allowed you in?" he asked abruptly, turning to face Xephyrus with his dazzling blue eyes. "You obviously require the assistance of the Rangers, but I would like to know why."

"Thank you for affording me this audience," Xephyrus said, uneasily lowering himself onto a velvet recliner that reeked of alcohol and smoke. "My name is Xephyrus Grievior, a commander with IRIS.

I am sure you are aware of our organization's activities throughout the galaxy."

The captain drew a long sip and kept his eyes fixated on the Elder Mage. "It seems fate continues to shine warmly upon me. My name is Varathis Kalamdor, captain of Detail H258."

Xephyrus's eyes widened in disbelief. "You are more than a captain," he whispered. "You're the Prince of Kel-Ardimus, last heir to the thrones of Zenor."

A scowl crossed the handsome features of Varathis. "What do you know of Zenor?"

The Elder Mage pulled back his sleeves to reveal the electropads on his wrists. "IRIS was founded by the last survivors of Zenor. To know that another of the royals survived will boost morale tremendously. That is something needed more than words can express."

Varathis shifted in his chair and smirked at what he had heard. His return to a life of power and influence was finally here. "You said *another* royal? Tell me more, Commander Grievior. It seems there is much for me to learn."

Ashana drew back a floating glass chair and perched herself at the bar beside a gray-scaled, burly reptilian soldier. She estimated he was at least as broad as Muraka. Chipped, fractured, dark-gray crystals ran along his head in a ridge, and smaller crystals capped the knuckles of his strong hands. Yet for now, his hand seemed content firmly clasping a glass of amber liquid while the other stubbed out a rolled log of what smelled like illicit spice.

His coat was more grizzled than his peers' were, but there was no mistaking he was a Space Ranger—although he did not subscribe to the same etiquette as the small party with whom she had just spoken.

"Want something, miss?" he asked in a gravelly voice, his eyes still locked on the drink in his hand.

"My name is Ashana Eldeerim," she replied, offering her hand.

The soldier downed his drink and passed his yellow eyes from her outstretched hand to her concerned face. "Not interested," he muttered and signaled the bartender for a refill.

"You're not interested in what, exactly?"

"Whatever it is you're selling."

The wiry Halsynian bartender regarded the Ranger with a furrowed brow. "You haven't paid for the last five days."

"Just bill it to the pretty boy upstairs," he growled and dismissed the bartender with a wave of the glass.

The barman slammed the glass on the counter and left a new bottle of Yasu whiskey. "Well, if he gets the bill, why not take the bottle and serve yourself? That way, at least I will be free of drowning you for the next few hours until my shift ends."

"You think this will last a few hours? See you in fifteen minutes!"

The barkeeper grumbled and whisked himself along the counter to gain some distance from this drunk malcontent, who had been a permanent fixture to the bar of late.

The Ranger swallowed a glass of whiskey without flinching at the burn in his throat and patted his coat down for another stick of spice. He looked up and was surprised to see that the woman was still beside him. "Thought I told you to scram."

"Your patrol sent me over to speak to you."

"Is that so?" he said, shifting his gaze to the other Rangers, who were engaged in conversation. "I guess there's no other way to get rid of you?"

"So it would seem."

"Well, get to it, then. I have other things to do."

"Like what?" Ashana asked with half a laugh.

The Ranger turned his yellow eyes to fix a stern glare at the woman who had interrupted his solitude.

"I'm sorry," she offered hastily. "Look, I'm just here to help. Your friends back there—"

"We're just members of the same patrol. Nothing more."

"Yeah, well…" Ashana tried to hide her surprise at his callous attitude. "They're worried about the patrol that went missing and wanted to investigate the disappearance, but they need your permission to do so."

"They're free to do what they want," he remarked idly. "Maybe that patrol dispersed into the civilians to make a life for themselves outside the war. Can you really blame them?"

"We cannot assume such a thing," she replied. "You owe it to them to at least discover their fate!"

The Ranger shrugged her concern away. Ashana followed his eyes to a stage at the center of the bar. A green alien woman wearing nothing more than black leather strips that reached around her body and barely preserved her modesty held the attention of the intoxicated crowd. Her hips swayed slowly in rhythm to the music of her band, which remained obscured by the shadows. Bioluminescent tendrils unfurled from her back, imbuing her with the appearance of a sultry butterfly. Her large eyes surveyed the bar, and her tendrils adapted to the shades of the lighting orbs. Then she sang. Her voice reached into the recesses of every drugged and drunken soul in the amphitheater around the stage.

Several droids buzzed around the patrons and offered them an assortment of narcotics while other droids extracted the fumes from the air. When the singer began her piece, every guest drew a deep breath and grew mesmerized by the light show upon her back and her sensual movements.

For reasons she could not explain, Ashana felt herself drawn to this woman. A haze clouded her mind and smothered thoughts of everything else beyond the walls of Sheroko. She could not understand a word of the alien woman's song, but she grew enraptured by her ethereal voice.

As if sensing this, the woman focused her gaze on Ashana. Her foreign lyrics purred from between her black lips, slowing the archer's heartbeat.

"It's so beautiful," Ashana whispered. Then thoughts of the missing patrol crawled through the mist of her attention to root her back in the present, and she emerged from the spell. "What in the name of Veritius Star was that about?" she muttered, rubbing away the dull throb in her temples.

"That is the mystical intrigue of Legaya," the burly Ranger informed her as he gulped another glass of whiskey. Roughly seizing a pack of spice sticks from a passing droid's tray, he lit one. "She's a Terinian siren, one of the best in this quadrant."

"So you'd rather spend your day in here, lost in alcohol, drugs, and her songs. If anyone can even understand her. I've never heard that language before."

"Not many have," he said, drawing deeply on his spice stick. "What I do is my business. Besides, I find her songs pleasant." He pointed toward Legaya with the smoldering spice stick. "Beyond the musical ability to effortlessly glide between octaves, she's the best current singer of her kind."

"So you're a musical expert and not just a drunk?" Ashana retorted.

"I guess you could say that," the Ranger replied with a distant reminiscence. "But what I am drawn to are her words. She captures the beauty of despair and a life that escaped but remains tethered by the barest of threads. In these times of death and angst, she utters the ugly truths in the most pleasant of ways—if you have the ability to hear her words."

Ashana's eyes passed over the Ranger with pity. This was a broken man whose scars ran deeper than mortal wounds. "There are people out there that you can help. It's your duty as a Ranger to do so. By the spirits, they're not even my comrades, and *I* am willing to help!"

"Nobody asked you to be a fool, miss. Go out and look for them. Maybe they're doing as I said they were. Or maybe they've met a violent end, which may very well await you too. Now isn't that a waste of life?"

"Not nearly as much as the slow death you're dealing yourself here."

"Yeah, well, I got darker things in me that need killing," he growled, pouring himself another drink. "I don't know you, and even if I did, I don't give a jira's flabby shithole what your judgment of me is. You wanna find that patrol? Then get on with it. I've given you my answer: the others are free to follow you. Now scram, and leave me alone!"

With that, the Ranger roughly turned away and continued to watch Legaya's performance. Ashana sighed in dismay but left the counter to gather the Rangers and head into the city to search for the missing patrol.

The grizzled Ranger raised the glass to his lips and for the first time that week hesitated to gulp down his whiskey. He did not care what she had said; words had stopped afflicting him a long time ago. No. There was something uncanny about that girl—a strange familiarity that he could not understand. He had never met her before. Despite how drunk he was, he was certain this had been their first interaction.

He gulped the shot down and then grabbed the whiskey bottle, stuffed it into an inner pocket of his coat, and headed off to follow the girl. He insisted in his mind that this was for no reason other than to satisfy his irritating curiosity.

Xephyrus followed Prince Varathis through a doorway onto the roof of the Sheroko Lounge. The city below teemed with civilians making their way home after a day of revelry. Some of them opted to find new locations to spend the night. However, Xephyrus also noted that despite the number of people wandering the streets, their ranks outdoors thinned quickly. A palpable fear rose in the air. Perhaps there was some truth to the whisperings of the Towari.

His interface beeped with a message from Ashana. She had set off with the other Rangers to investigate the disappearance of the patrol, but she had been unsuccessful in convincing the patrol leader to accompany them. The Elder Mage muted his screen in disappointment, but he was not entirely surprised. The patrol leader's disinterest stemmed from his captain's apathy toward the lower ranks. He had always mused that leadership was akin to a flowing river. If those upstream were stagnant, how would those lower down ever move?

His brief interaction with Varathis thus far had disheartened him, but he reconciled himself with the belief that perhaps due to his time adrift in the war as an orphan, with no ties to his people or any adequate training, Varathis had grown less regal. He seemed to be a young man more interested in the idea of ruling than being a ruler. However, Xephyrus felt that perhaps it would be better to bring him before Orin. After all, the general was the best judge of character he had ever known. He would surely know the right course of action. In any event, their heritage decreed respect for the king, and Xephyrus was not going to be the Zenorian who disregarded their sacred laws.

Besides, not all hope was lost. The Zenorians would take heart in knowing the Prince of Kel-Ardimus had survived, and his training with Orin would help shape him into a leader that would inspire hope the way that Rezaaran's bravery and Ashana's compassion did.

"I hope you do not mind the change of scenery," Varathis said in his casual drawl. His arms swept out to display the rooftop. "I fear that several of these establishments are crawling with Sekian spies. Knowing their close ties to the Dominion, I would not wish to endanger the life of other IRIS soldiers or the other royal you have mentioned."

Xephyrus smiled a little to himself. Perhaps he had misjudged the prince. After all, he was no Orin. "A wise move, my liege. The other royal of whom I spoke is Ashana Binarjiin, heir to the throne of Sylvoria. She has accompanied me today to meet your cohort of Rangers."

"She is here?" Varathis's excitement heightened the tone of his voice. "When can I meet her? I can only imagine how much we will need to catch up on!"

"Alas, that will be some time from now. She has left with the detachment of your Rangers to investigate the disappearance of a patrol."

"Is that not beneath her role?" he asked with a raised eyebrow, taking a seat on a glass chair. "Plus it's dangerous. The locals have rumors about this thing called a Towari. Shouldn't she have some sort of security escorting her?"

"She has a company of Rangers at her side," Xephyrus replied. "Besides, Ashana is a competent soldier herself and a fine commander in IRIS. She has never shied away from helping those she can in any capacity and always involves herself with their cause."

The Elder Mage could see the gears turning in Varathis's head as he weighed this against his own sentiments.

"I suppose I understand her actions," he finally said. "After all, I am a Ranger myself, hopefully to make a difference and retain some vestiges of order in these times of chaos."

Suddenly a blue portal opened upon the roof. Varathis leaped off the chair and readied himself for a fight as his guards rallied to his side. Two men emerged from the portal, confused by their new surroundings.

"Identify yourselves!" one of the guards barked.

"At ease, Rangers." Xephyrus spoke calmly to placate Varathis and his guards. "These are my friends. May I introduce Captain Rezaaran Valhara, last Vokarii War Mage, and Commander Gerrin Mordakai."

"I thought I told you never to say my surname," Gerrin grumbled.

Oblivious to Gerrin, Xephyrus continued. "This is Varathis Kalamdor, Prince of Kel-Ardimus."

"You two are Zenorians? Then why do you not bow before your king?"

"Listen, kid, we've just been through all sorts of craziness, and we aren't in the mood to be bossed around."

"I am—"

"Yeah, I know who you are. My hearing is still good. You want respect? Start by showing some to people who deserve it, like your War Mage. If it weren't for his courage and resilience, we wouldn't be gaining ground against the Dominion."

Xephyrus allowed himself a small smile. Gerrin's change of heart was a pleasant surprise.

"Thanks, Gerrin," Rezaaran said sincerely.

Varathis sulked but turned his attention to Rezaaran, regarding his unusual white cloak and the large sword strapped to his side. "So...what exactly can the last Vokarii War Mage do?"

"How do I even begin to answer that?" Rezaaran asked, raising an eyebrow. Suddenly he turned his head sharply toward the streets.

"I felt it too, Rezaaran," Xephyrus said slowly.

There is much fury and power in this being, Kashari remarked.

I've never felt anything like this before. It reminds me of Thaedis, but this doesn't feel entirely like him. I feel like I've encountered this before.

His eyes widened suddenly. "It's nearing Ash! I have to get to her!"

"I would advise caution with this," Xephyrus said, gently grasping Rezaaran's arm.

"Xephyrus, I've faced far worse things than whatever *this* is."

"What are you two talking about?" Varathis asked.

"Your Majesty," Xephyrus explained calmly, releasing Rezaaran's arm, "those who are magic users are able to perceive the presence of other mages. We call it their echo. Out in the city, a powerful sorcerer is approaching your patrol."

"Is this the Towari?" Varathis asked anxiously.

"I would strongly suspect so, Your Majesty."

"You can't go after this monster!" Varathis pleaded with Rezaaran. "You could die!"

"That is a risk I am willing to take," Rezaaran replied sternly. "A Vokarii's life is about honor to the end." He set off at a run toward the edge of the roof.

Are you sure about this? You have never tried this before.

Always a first for everything, Kashari. Here we go!

Rezaaran leaped from the roof and free-fell toward the street. Wind whipped his eyes and howled in his ears. Despite the throb in his temples and the thunderous hammering of his heart, Rezaaran sought to retain his focus. Exhaling deeply, he saw shimmering columns rise around him from the streets below. The Vaux rushed toward the War Mage, wrapped him in streams of its power, and lifted him into the air to soar upon a thermal.

He focused his attention on reaching Ashana before the approaching dark echo and rocketed over the Halsynian streets.

Ashana walked quickly along the streets of the Halsynian habitat. Her rapid pace was born not of trepidation but rather a haste to see this mission completed. She was sure that by now Rezaaran and Gerrin had successfully rescued Ikso, and they would need to prepare for extraction. However, she could not in good conscience abandon this missing patrol—even if the same conscience did not move the patrol leader to assist her. She could not shake her irritation at how rude he had been toward her in the bar. But meeting people like him, jaded from the war, was not entirely surprising.

In any case, she hoped his initial simple assessment of the situation would be true. She knew such a hope was juvenile—after all, how could there be a happy outcome for anyone when the Dominion was involved? However, she could not bear to see sadness mar Nerdosa's rambunctious nature.

Asora mentioned that the Rangers had trackers inserted into their suits that allowed the crew aboard the ship to track them. With Quirt's help, Ashana had linked their ship's tracker to her interface and had located the current position of the patrol. The mission could possibly reach a swift conclusion.

Despite not having a superstitious nature, she felt a presence skulking upon the edges of their perception. Adding to her frustration was that for some inexplicable reason, she could not glimpse the future.

They arrived at an alleyway between two large buildings containing restaurants and housing complexes. Along the ground were numerous pipes and ventilator grills that hissed steam into the alley, obscuring the end of the path. This was where the trackers placed the missing patrol.

"Keep sharp," she said to the Rangers. "I have a bad feeling about this place."

She loaded her bow with an electrical discharge arrow and waited until each Ranger had his or her weapon poised and ready before she advanced cautiously through the thick steam to investigate the alley.

When they reached the middle of the path without sighting anyone, Ashana rechecked her interface. "That's odd," she murmured. "According to this, they should be right here. Could the trackers have malfunctioned?"

"Unlikely," replied Sharaf. "Those trackers are rigorously combat-tested to resist interference and malfunction."

A soft spattering on the lapel of her coat drew Nerdosa's attention. Her mouth curled in disgust as she followed the direction of the blood drops. Struggling to find her breath or words, she resorted to tugging at Asora's sleeve.

"Barang's mercy," he whispered. "What demon would do this?"

The others followed Asora's gaze and were struck by terror. Above them were suspended the mangled remains of the missing patrol—eight mutilated and dismembered bodies strung against the walls high above the street. Several corpses had had their chests ripped open and their hearts removed.

"Stay sharp, and keep strong," Ashana said firmly to the group. "We need to find out what happened here."

"Cordon off the area," Sharaf ordered the Rangers. "We need to gather whatever evidence we can."

"Excuse me, miss—I have to ask yer to leave here," Orach said. He approached a slender woman dressed in a black cowl that merged into a cloak wrapping around her black-and-red leather suit. A red mouth guard obscured her face, but her piercing blue eyes swept a hostile look over them from beneath her black curtain of hair.

"Miss, I'm going to repeat this one last time," Orach said, taking a stance in front of the woman. "You have to leave this area. This is an active Ranger investigation."

"I smell your fear, Ranger," the woman said in a cold voice with a thick accent. "I feel your anger, your desire for vengeance. You want to hurt the one who did this. Well…here I am!"

"Murderous whore!" Orach spat. He drew a stun baton and lunged for the woman, but she easily evaded his wild swing. Grasping his wrist, she sharply twisted it and delivered a severe strike to his arm that shattered his bones. Orach howled in agony, his arm hanging limp and disfigured at his side. The hooded assailant then leaned down and drew a knife from beneath her cloak. She pressed the blade to his neck and with a flick of her wrist inflicted a nonlethal wound.

A cold sweat embraced Orach, and his heart hammered against his chest. He turned around frantically, oblivious to the agony in his flailing arm. All around him, the ground caved into molten lava.

Where he had last seen his friends now stood a horde of smoky, demonic creatures. A scream of terror escaped his quivering mouth, and he edged away from the woman.

She spread her arms wide, savoring the scent of his fear, and turned her attention to the remaining soldiers. Her eyes grew paler, and Ashana had the distinct feeling that this attacker could see into her soul.

"Fire at will!" she ordered the Rangers. She released the first electrified arrow ahead of the energy-round volley. The woman appeared to dodge most of the shots. Despite several finding their mark upon her torso, however, she remained undeterred in her approach toward them. Sharaf signaled for the Rangers to advance while they continued their barrage of energy rounds.

Ashana's brow wrinkled. Why could she not see into the future?

Suddenly their attacker leaped off a wall and struck the feline Ranger with the side of her fist. The disoriented soldier staggered briefly and was too slow to fend off the dagger that impaled his arm. He roared in agony, the roar becoming a whimper seconds later at the sight of feral beasts all around him. Setting his sights on an injured beast, he charged.

A blue-scaled Ranger lowered his rifle in horror when he saw his feline friend leap upon and maul Orach, ravaging the portly man with claws and teeth. Pausing for a brief moment to savor his rising fear, the woman seized him by the neck and flung him toward his hallucinating comrades. Then she turned her now-white eyes to the remaining four soldiers and charged once again. This time her pace seemed far quicker. Each round from the soldiers found its mark but could not hold her. She leaped up and landed a sharp punch on Asora's neck, cracking his larynx, and then followed with a hefty strike that snapped his spine. The amphibious Ranger crumpled to the ground. His legs lay paralyzed, and green blood spluttered from his mouth. Defeated, the Ranger reached out to his adversary and begged for mercy. But she neither knew nor cared for such a pathetic gesture. Her foot snapped his wrist, and she turned her attention to the last three victims.

Nerdosa lowered her gun. Her lips trembled, and tears streamed from her eyes. "We can't stop her," she whispered. "She's the Towari. She's too strong for us!"

"Don't give in to fear!" Ashana yelled.

Another electrified arrow flew toward the rampaging cowled woman. She caught the arrow in midair, reached into her cloak, and withdrew a similar black-tailed arrow.

"How did you get that?" Ashana whispered. "You've been following us from the bar!"

The woman charged at a speed that would have left Xephyrus flatfooted and skewered the two arrows into Nerdosa's torso.

"No!"

Nerdosa fell to the ground. The corrosive toxin from the arrow stolen from Ashana immediately set to work from within while the electrical current stopped her heartbeat.

In an instant, the woman sped toward Sharaf, her fist tore through his chest and ripped his heart from its confines. Lowering her red mouth guard, she squeezed his blood into her mouth as the Ranger fell to the ground. Her wounds healed immediately.

"Now it is only you, my dear," she said, exposing her bloodied teeth in a cruel smile. "There is no one to save you now."

"Who says I need saving?"

Ashana fired a blue-tailed arrow into the woman's shoulder. The woman seemed surprised that her speed had faltered and then realized that this last soldier was not afraid of her.

The Zenorian archer ran toward her enemy, slammed her bow into the attacker's chest, and pivoted to land a follow-up kick. Immediately she drew a red-tailed arrow and fired at her adversary's feet. The explosion flung the cowled woman down the alley.

The woman laughed darkly, trying her best to mask her astonishment that this last victim should be so dauntless. She squeezed the last drops of blood from Sharaf's heart, healing her wounds and renewing her strength.

"Well, this is going to be fun," she said with a smirk. "It will give me great pleasure to kill you, Dilisin."

Ashana was not sure why, but the name this woman addressed her by stirred something deep within her. "You've got the wrong person," she snarled. "Call me whatever you want, but you won't be leaving here! Not after what you did to these people! They were good, honest men and women, you monster!"

"Ah, you and your bleeding heart. I look forward to savoring its taste when I squeeze it dry!"

A wave of heat rose from the ground before her and spread rapidly toward Ashana. Sensing the imminent danger by intuition rather than through her abilities, the archer started the armoring sequence. Dark fire and cinder scoured the road, passing between the woman and Ashana in the wake of the heat wave. The Zenorian raised her arms and closed her eyes, bracing for impact.

Suddenly a pair of arms wrapped around her, and a roar of agony filled her ears. Opening her eyes, she saw Rezaaran embracing her tightly, shielding her from the dark fire that should have killed her. Tears streamed from his red face.

"Are you OK, Ash?"

"Don't worry about me! Are you?"

"I...I don't know," he murmured. The sorcerer's attack had scorched his armor, and his wounds were healing far too slowly.

What's happening, Kashari?

I do not know, my friend, she replied. Her voice seemed distant.

"So, you have chosen to join us, Loradún," the woman shouted with a cackle. "You escaped me on Mar-Karatheer, but you cannot outrun destiny forever!"

The woman was generating dark fire in her hands once more when a bulky Levira crashed into her and pinned her against a wall. Amid the thick billows of black smoke, the Rangers' patrol leader whom Ashana had seen at the bar dismounted the bike. He placed a spice stick between his lips and searched for a lighter, looking idly around. A snarl crossed his face, triggered by the sight of his murdered comrades and the mutilated corpses.

"You've got a lot of answering to do," he said gruffly as he walked over to the woman, who was slowly rising to her feet. "By the authority vested in me as a Ranger...ah, just give me your damn hands!"

"You have no authority here," she spat and shoved the Levira aside. From closer range, she fired a ball of dark fire at the Ranger. But her malevolent smirk evaporated when she saw the reptilian creature stand tall, his crystal spikes pulsing with a lava-orange hue. He looked at her with a maniacal grin. Whatever she had done had supercharged him.

"Someone's cruising for a bruising!" he yelled. The Ranger slammed his fist into the cowled woman, knocking her back a hundred yards.

Drawing on the terror of the whimpering feline Ranger, the woman straightened and drew her breath. How could this primitive, hideous creature resist her?

"I see it now," she said slowly, peering deeply into the soul contained within this drunken creature. "You are here too, Morak."

"You're confused, lady. According to the law, I need to arrest you, but you do not deserve the mercy of justice."

"I *am* justice!" she proclaimed with a sneer. "My name is Diothur, and by my hand the Sentinels shall fall!"

"You're not going to hurt anyone again," the Ranger said firmly. "Have your last drink." He threw a bottle of whiskey toward Diothur and withdrew his modified blast cannon from his cloak. The five chambers fired with a loud crack, exploding the bottle in her face.

The Ranger smiled smugly to himself and turned to face the Zenorian soldiers. "Are you two all right?"

The young man who had shielded the girl from the dark-fire blast began to heal his flesh and clothing.

"I knew a boy who could heal like that once," the Ranger said idly as he lit his spice stick. "His name was—"

He fumbled his light when he caught a glimpse of the young Zenorian's face.

"Rezaaran Valhara!"

"Jet Bal Sara," the War Mage replied with a kind smile and turned to face his old friend.

"You haven't aged a day. It's as though...oh, I don't feel so good."

Both Rezaaran and Jet buckled and collapsed to the ground. Ashana rushed over to the two soldiers. They were still breathing but unresponsive.

"Quirt, I need you to extract us immediately! Get Xephyrus to meet us on the *Liberator*! It's an emergency!"

"I'm preparing the teleporter now, Ashana," Quirt replied. "According to the scanner, there is also a Levira in the alleyway that has a transmitter linked to the city watch."

Ashana rushed over to the bike and activated the distress call, informing the city watch of the fallen Rangers in the alley. "Transport that bike with us."

"Stand by, Ashana."

Moments after Jet and the Zenorians teleported away, Diothur's fingers flickered. Slowly she turned her head to look around and crawled toward the whimpering feline Ranger. She roughly pulled the Ranger down, slit his throat, and drank his gushing blood.

With her strength replenished, Diothur rose to her feet. The burns across her snarling face healed, and she fixed her gaze skyward.

"This is far from over, Sentinels. I will relish this hunt!"

CHAPTER EIGHT

THE UNLIKELY HERO

"What happened to him?" Xephyrus asked sternly. His blue eyes crackled with the intensity of a storm moments from eruption. Rezaaran convulsed vigorously on the table in the medical bay of the *Liberator*.

"We went to look for the missing patrol," Ashana explained, gulping back her rising panic, "when this woman calling herself Diothur attacked us. She struck Rez with dark fire, and after that, he collapsed. Can you help him, Xephyrus?"

"I will try my best," he replied grimly. Because of his mission, Rezaaran invariably encountered powerful magic; healing from it often proved beyond Xephyrus's capability. Nevertheless, he would not abandon his friend. If there were anything he could do to help him, then he surely would try.

The Elder Mage placed his hands beside Rezaaran's temples, and a warm glow passed from his hands across the younger mage's head. Rezaaran's convulsions subsided, and he eased into a rested state but remained unconscious.

"Is he going to be all right?" Ashana asked. Her concern raised the pitch of her voice. She could not bear the thought of him lying in a coma again.

"I think he should be," Xephyrus replied. "This feels different to his last incident on Zynoo. I only wish I knew what had happened to him."

"He's suffering from Toremanthian blight," Luminara explained. "It's a side effect of being exposed to high quantities of Obsidian magic."

"We would say that it is an improvement," Darzuka said with a smirk as she slunk between the Zenorians gathered over Rezaaran's slow-breathing frame. "These mortals are broken, weakened, by the presence of Valinthicite within them. A little bit of our darkness is what makes them fun. Although it baffles me that you should love them so dearly and yet despise us so vehemently. More of the Guardians' hypocrisy, I suppose."

Luminara ignored the apparition. Evidently she was a hallucination, as none of the others seemed to hear her words. "Those affected," she continued, "are typically mortals and beings who contain Valinthicite within them."

"What is the course of this affliction, my lady?" Xephyrus asked.

"It differs for each, but the common point is a disconnection between their souls and minds for a variable period of time."

"Well, if he's stabilized," Ashana said with a sigh of relief, "then all we can do is wait for him to wake up. In the meantime, Xephyrus, can you try to help this Ranger as well?"

The Elder Mage nodded and proceeded to survey the unconscious Jet, who entered on a levitating examination bed. "This is the patrol leader from Halsyn!"

"Yes, it is. He followed us to the alley when we went searching for the patrol."

Xephyrus repeated the healing spell he'd used on Rezaaran but frowned when the glowing light of his powers did not manifest. "I do not understand why it is not working."

"It's because he is an Erebonian," Luminara said, barely concealing her loathing. "They're creatures of darkness, impervious to light magic. Get him off this ship!"

"We will do no such thing," Ashana said, glowering at her. "This man risked his life to save ours, and he barely knew us. I will not cast him aside. And I am surprised a Guardian would think *any* life does not deserve saving."

"Well, despite how this pleases me," Darzuka sniggered, "that little outburst was all on you. Oh, don't look so distressed, dear. Is it really that hard to believe that your pious mask hides a face no different than my own?"

The Edarian shimmered away and left Luminara to deal with the growing gulf of shame within her heart.

"If magic cannot stabilize him," Quirt interjected, hoping to fill the awkward void that had formed, "then perhaps science may find a way to help. I can set him up in my laboratory and see what I can do."

"Thank you, Quirt," said Ashana solemnly.

Gerrin helped the scientist move Jet's levitating bed to Quirt's workshop, where they placed Jet onto an empty table.

"This guy reeks of a brewery," Gerrin said in disgust, coughing as he caught a whiff of Jet's breath when the bed latched onto the table. "How was he able to serve with the Rangers in this state?"

"I do not have an answer for that, Commander," Quirt replied slowly as he removed some of Jet's possessions and connected various monitors to the Ranger's body. "However, I would postulate that his habits are a by-product of his misfortunes."

"You and Xephyrus would have a field day chatting to each other."

"So I have heard," Quirt replied. He raised the battered gauntlet and broken hologram chain Jet had been wearing. "This looks like a man who has been broken by the war."

Gerrin looked at the face of the young woman in the hologram. She seemed jubilant in her smile, and her shoulder-length tendrils held an echo of euphoria. He looked at Quirt, who also regarded the hologram pendant. There was the sadness of one who had recently suffered a similar loss of a loved one. Despite knowing his background, Gerrin was unsure how to console the scientist.

"Will he be all right, Dr. Zefrityn?"

"We shall know in a while. I will perform some blood tests on him to see if there is a possibility for an antidote to whatever affliction he has."

Gerrin nodded and left the scientist to his work and his thoughts. Perhaps it was better to let him be than to pry.

Quirt placed the vials of blood into his analyzer and turned his attention to the battered gauntlet. "You are a mess," he mumbled as he zoomed in with his lenses. "May as well do something useful while we wait."

Back on the bridge, Xephyrus placed a comforting hand on Ashana's shoulder. He knew this was difficult for her; they had only just gotten Rezaaran out of a similar state. However, as was always the case, Ashana showed remarkable resilience in the face of turmoil.

"It will be all right, Ashana," he said soothingly. "He is not lost from us completely. Like Lady Luminara said, he just needs time."

"I know," she replied with a warm smile that showed her appreciation for his concern. "It's just…that woman we versed back on Halsyn—I've never seen anyone like that before. She was so brutal and unhinged. I just hope that when Rezaaran wakes, we can decide on a strategy to counter her power."

"I'm sure the two of you are more than capable of doing so. Besides, you seem to be building quite a team here."

"It seems we are," she said with a chuckle. "A former Guardian, a Thyrillian scientist, and an acolyte of Nish Ira."

"Not to mention the Ranger who saved you."

"If he chooses to join us," she sighed, remembering his abrasive attitude in the bar. "He is on his own path, Xephyrus. But he seems to know Rezaaran."

"That may be enough to inspire a change. You know how he influences those around him."

"I do indeed," she replied. Her gaze shifted to Gerrin, who came to stand beside Xephyrus.

"Well, in the spirit of that influence," Xephyrus continued, "I would like to volunteer another addition to your crew, if you would permit it." He gestured for Varathis to step forward. "It is my honor to introduce to you Prince Varathis Kalamdor, last heir to the throne of Kel-Ardimus."

Varathis approached and regarded Ashana with a charming smile. He could not believe his luck that the remaining royal was so beautiful. "It is indeed a pleasure to meet you, Ashana Binarjiin."

"Charmed," she said, passing Xephyrus an inquisitive glance.

"So, Commander Grievior, is it our moment to return to our home world and restore the rule of order?" Varathis asked.

"The time will come for the return of the monarchy," Xephyrus replied calmly. "However, our world will never be granted a chance to rise from the ashes until we seek an end to this galactic conflict. Rezaaran and Ashana are at the heart of our efforts, and IRIS would benefit from having the crown prince of Kel-Ardimus aid their endeavors."

"I hear the wisdom in your advice," Varathis replied with a slight bow of his head. "I agree. It would be remiss of me to neglect my duty toward my people and not aid in this conflict. If you would permit me, Ashana, I am a capable pilot. Could I assist in our course?"

Gunner growled at the prince, but Ashana stroked his head and placated the robotic hound. "I think my current copilot has some objection to that," she chuckled. But secretly she was relieved that Gunner had appeared to save her from this awkward situation. "I will have his security protocols adjusted to include the signature of your interface. You may want to swap your Ranger scanner for one of ours."

Varathis bowed his head once more and took the interface.

"We aren't going to be moving too far for now. You can move your things into the troopers' chambers at the back."

The prince thought it rather offensive that she would relegate him to a common barrack chamber and yet allowed the woman with the wild hair to have her own. However, he did not press the matter.

"Excuse me, Xephyrus," Ikso said. "If you would allow it, I would very much like to travel with you to learn more about magic. I doubt I will be welcomed home anytime soon."

"I appreciate your interest in my tutelage," Xephyrus replied. "However, I feel you would stand to learn the most if you were in the company of Rezaaran and Ashana."

Ikso bowed to indicate her agreement and was about to head to the barrack chamber when she spotted Gunner. She cautiously approached the robotic hound, which responded with a happy bark and bounded behind her to the chamber.

"Well, they seem to be getting along well," Ashana mused, thinking that Gunner probably also saw the likeness between Ikso and the younger version of herself.

"It's time for us to get going," Gerrin informed the Elder Mage. "Orin has another assignment that needs our attention."

"Farewell, Ashana," Xephyrus said with a bow.

The Zenorian soldiers parted through a portal to Gerrin's ship and left Ashana alone on the bridge. She stared out at the asteroid field where Quirt had hidden their ship and in the distance saw the swirling orange sphere of Halsyn. Luminara had said all they could do was wait for Rezaaran to wake. She just hoped it would not take another three months. Nothing was more infuriating or disempowering than having no pursuable course of action other than waiting. But she would wait for Rez.

Rezaaran's eyes opened to a dark corridor with dim lights. He looked around sharply and realized he was crouching. Although he appeared alone, he sensed he was in a hostile environment. But how he had appeared in such a situation was a conundrum in itself.

Moments earlier, he had been in a street on Halsyn, and now he was who knew where. This was just like his experience following Zynoo.

"I am not going through that again," he whispered to himself.

This is different, my friend.

Well, at least we're back together. That woman in the street...she said her name was Diothur. But I thought she was supposed to be a Sentinel.

One problem at a time, Rezaaran. Let us escape this entanglement before we venture into this mysterious new person.

Rezaaran nodded to himself and reached for Harkenathor, usually strapped to his side. His fingers grasped nothing but air. *I guess this means we aren't physically wherever we are.*

A presence approaches.

The War Mage drew himself against the wall. In the midst of an unknown environment, he was not eager to engage any enemy, especially without Harkenathor at his side. This thought stirred a realization. He rose and strode into the corridor. An ethereal spirit passed through him and continued on its path forward.

Despite your inability to see it, there is a line between bravery and recklessness.

Perhaps, but at least now we know we are safe from harm. That spirit looks a lot like how you appear in the Nuhremorn, but this is definitely not the Nuhremorn.

Rezaaran cautiously followed the floating spirit. Despite knowing that he was invisible to the inhabitants of this place, he could not shake the sense of foreboding. His skin bristled, and a chill swept over him.

Thaedis is here! His thoughts carried a higher pitch, for he was thunderstruck by another realization. *We're on his ship!*

As the spirit turned into a side chamber, Rezaaran continued along the main corridor. At the end of his path, he spied an open door—and within the chamber stood the hooded figure of Thaedis Silvermire.

Rezaaran cautiously approached the frame leading into the chamber. Despite being invisible to the others here, Rezaaran was reluctant to be too near Thaedis, fearing the sorcerer may perceive his astral presence.

Thaedis stood at a view panel, looking out at a distant cluster of stars. Rezaaran wished he had listened to Ashana's advice about reading more in his spare time; at least then he would have an inkling as to where they were now. He cast his eyes quickly around the chamber. It was mostly bare except for a large table in the center spread with an opened series of star charts that mapped the galaxy.

The Exiled held his hand out to his side and summoned a dark-fire portal to the Obsidious. The flames framed the face of an ominous creature bearing a striking resemblance to Tolbetrius yet more heavily set in his features.

"Hidar," Thaedis said in his frigid tone, "what is the progress on my blade?"

"The soul has set and binds well, my lord," the Edarian replied in a low rumble. "I worked the metal as you ordered, and the Soulforge is now ready for your next task. Narak believes he has found a solution."

"Excellent. I do not need to remind you the price Tolbetrius paid for his failure."

"I will not fail, my lord," the Edarian growled. Despite his obedience, there seemed to be great animosity between Hidar and Thaedis.

The portal closed, leaving Thaedis to his thoughts once more.

"I need to find that damnable box," he muttered. "Tyrel, you devious bastard, even in your death you continue to vex me. Without the Ark of Torementhias, I will always be a pawn to Nethriziin. The Ark, coupled with this new blade, will seal his fate."

Thaedis raised his hand beneath his hood, most likely massaging his temples, Rezaaran assumed.

"On the one hand, I could draw the memories of its location from your stasis mind. Although knowing your manner of strategy, you no doubt would have expunged that memory—even going as far as hiding it within the Ark itself."

Stasis mind? Does that mean Salvidawn is still alive?

It is difficult to tell in what state of life he would exist. Thaedis is known for his hatred of Lord Salvidawn. I doubt he would spare his life.

"Alternatively, there is always 'Sahar's Requiem.'"

What is "Sahar's Requiem"?

Patience.

"'By strife it shall enclose,'" Thaedis murmured to himself, "'never to reopen. The bonds strengthen, until purer spirits rise awoken.' Why are these prophecies so frustratingly cryptic?"

Suddenly the chamber Rezaaran was standing in fell away. He looked down at the ground rising to meet his face and in an instant was standing on a hillside.

A furious battle spanned as far as he could see. Tanks and soldiers, both IRIS and Dominion, clashed against one another, tearing apart the terrain between rounds of artillery fire. However, beneath the presence of a large shadow, the fighting ceased. A red glow burst forth from the center of the shadow and washed over the land.

Rezaaran roused slowly and massaged away the throbbing pain in his temples. Luminara sat beside him, pensive and silent.

"Glad to have you with us once again," she said with a smile when she realized he had awoken.

"How long have I been out?"

"About two hours, I believe. How do you feel?"

"Relieved. At least it hasn't been three months. What happened to me?"

"You were attacked by Obsidian magic and as a result suffered Torementhian blight, an illness that afflicts magic users who have a high concentration of Valinthicite and are then subjected to Torementhicite, the substance that powers Obsidian magic."

"That woman in the alley," Rezaaran said, recalling his last memories of Halsyn. "The one who attacked me with Obsidian magic. She said her name was Diothur."

"The Sentinel of Justice," Luminara replied grimly. "The situation is indeed dire if Thaedis has corrupted her soul. If he found her, perhaps he knows about the Sentinels."

"Thaedis! I saw him…in a vision. He was searching for something called the Ark of Torementhias."

Luminara's face darkened, and her expression grew solemn.

"He also mentioned something called 'Sahar's Requiem.' Luminara, do you know what these things are?"

"I do indeed," she replied slowly. "However, for now you must rest. There will be time to investigate these occurrences. We can discuss it when you and your friend have recovered."

Rezaaran clapped a hand to his head. He had forgotten about the person who had saved him on Halsyn. "How is Jet doing? Was he also affected by Torementhian blight?"

"He is stable in Quirt's laboratory. The scientist is looking after him. Personally, I do not trust him. He is an Erebonian. They are creatures of darkness and known to readily betray others for personal gain."

"Jet is a good person," Rezaaran replied, closing his eyes to rest. "Besides, if he was affected by Torementhian blight, then there is more Valinthicite within him—so he can't be all that bad now."

"I suppose you are right," Luminara replied. Her cheeks flushed, knowing her prejudice had surfaced again. Perhaps there was more truth to Darzuka's taunts than she cared to admit.

Dark clouds gathered over the barren plains. Lightning coursed through them against a thunderous backdrop and reddened their charcoal mass.

Jet surveyed the crumbling stone-wall remnants of a fortress that surrounded him. Despite their efforts, they had weathered beneath the ravages of time. Several broken areas revealed the desolate and dusty gray wasteland beyond the confines of this solitary building. He was certain Halsyn did not look like this on its surface, which begged the question: where was he?

"Well, this is one crazy trip," he said to himself, adjusting his cloak. He patted himself down and noticed that his gun and mechanized gauntlet were missing. At least he still had a few spice sticks. "Now, if only I could find a light."

A red pulsation caught his attention. Behind him stood a towering crystal that beat in time with the lightning overhead. He could not explain it, but Jet felt a power flowing from this crystal, and it intrigued him. His clawed hand reached out to the pulsing red rock, drawn by the power emanating from within its core.

"Hold!"

Jet turned sharply to the creature that had shouted. It strode toward him with great purpose, its bony armor taut over its leathery red hide. The creature looked at him with eyeless sockets and a malicious smile that revealed its pointed teeth.

"Ah…another soul has entered our realm!"

"Uh…yeah," Jet replied. Surely he could not still be on Halsyn. There were no known sentient creatures on the surface—and certainly none that looked like this. "Do you have a light for me?"

"There is no light to be found in Torementhias! Beneath our dark skies, we serve Lord Nethriziin, who has kept the scourge of the Light from our lands for eons beyond count. I am Revarthin, gatekeeper of the maze. All who enter from the great stone must walk the maze."

"About that," Jet growled and placed his spice stick into his coat, realizing this creature would not indulge him. "I'm not walking anywhere unless it's to a bar."

"You must walk the maze and face my brothers!"

"I don't have to do a damn thing," Jet retorted.

"It is the law of Lord Nethriziin!"

Jet connected a right uppercut to the gatekeeper's jaw that knocked him off the ground and rendered him unconscious.

"Boring conversation, anyway," Jet mumbled.

In the distance, he heard what sounded like chanting. Crouching, he cautiously worked his way through the maze. When this was over, he vowed, he needed to have a word with Sheroko's management about selling such potent spice.

Revarthin had said he was in Torementhias, but surely that could not be true. Torementhias was a fable, a bedtime story used to scare children on Erebon.

Jet continued through the maze, heading toward where the chanting seemed loudest. He hid behind a half-broken wall and surveyed the rabble of creatures that looked similar to Revarthin. They were gathered around what looked like an altar. Five of the locals were forcing a cyborg Kalaran to his knees in front of a taller native. Based on the reverence they showed him, Jet assumed this was their leader.

The leader had a spiked, slate-gray bony armor that covered his gray flesh. His helmet was fashioned to resemble a crown, and his large wings folded behind his back to create the impression of a regal robe. He approached the bowed Kalaran and with a flaming palm sundered the reptile's soul from its body. The leader then summoned one of his disciples forward. Another disciple passed him a fragment of a black crystal similar to the crystals on Jet's head.

The kingly creature rammed the crystal into the Kalaran's heart and then placed one hand onto the reptile's head and the other on the head of his disciple. The chants intensified, and a burst of light from the large crystal Jet had passed earlier surged into the sky. A bolt of red lightning struck the crown of the leader. His disciple gasped and disintegrated. Seconds later, the Kalaran roared loudly and rose to his feet. A guttural roar of approval erupted from the crowd, and their leader appeared pleased.

The Kalaran turned his attention toward Jet and pointed out the Erebonian's location. Every head of the crowd swiveled to face him, their agitated growls giving Jet a clear idea of their feelings.

"No need to stand up," he said gruffly to the crowd as it rose. "I can show myself out."

At the order of its leader, the crowd charged. Jet sprinted through the maze. He could not let them catch him and make him the subject of whatever twisted ritual they had performed on that Kalaran.

The maze was alive with the gnashing of teeth, screeches, and howls of the locals that pursued him through the maze. One of the creatures leaped from the wall onto his back, but Jet slammed its head into the wall and continued on to where he had seen the towering red crystal. Then he skidded to a halt, feeling a hammering in his chest. Barring his way was the tall, crowned leader.

Who are you?

"OK, those were some powerful drugs," Jet said, wide-eyed. "I'm hearing voices in my head now!"

I asked you a question!

The creature was on him in an instant, placing his large taloned hand onto Jet's head. A torrent of memories flooded Jet's mind. Every person he had seen or interacted with passed through his consciousness, along with every experience he had ever endured. Whatever this creature was, it seemed to fixate on the memories of Jet's kills.

Perhaps there is a purpose for you yet. My master will be most pleased to know that you endured. Now, await my summons.

Jet felt his mind return to his control. He shook his head sharply and looked into the slit eyes that sneered at him.

"Nobody summons me!"

He slammed a right hook to the king's midriff, knocked him aside, and sprinted forward to touch the red crystal.

Jet leaped off the worktable, startled but unsteady. He struggled to find his footing.

"Where am I? What happened to me? Who are you?"

"Calm down," a red-haired scientist said to him. "You are safe here. My name is Quirt Zefrityn. I am a scientist."

"Don't tell me to calm down! I've seen your kind before! You want to study me…like I'm some kind of animal!"

"No, that is not true. I only want to help you."

"Yeah," Jet growled, baring his sharp canines. "I've seen your kind of help, and I don't want it!" Grabbing a nearby blade, he held it threateningly toward the scientist, who immediately raised his arms.

"I do not wish to fight you," Quirt said.

"Well, at least you're smart!" Jet snarled as he backed out of the laboratory. He wandered into a corridor made of marble with golden floral patterns along the roof, staggering as he tried to run away from the scientist.

Relax, Jet. It will be all right. There is no need for alarm. You are safe.

"Get out of my head!"

I am your friend, Jet. You know my voice—even in thought.

"Rezaaran," he whispered. He felt a soothing aura overcome his mind, and his breathing slowed.

Take the first door on your left.

Jet hesitantly sheathed the blade under the belt of his pants and followed the telepathic instructions. The doors slid apart, and he saw Rezaaran seated at a table with the girl he had met at the bar.

"Glad you two survived," he muttered as he walked into the galley, slightly mortified that he was wearing only his Ranger-issued beige pants with the metal utility belt.

"Well, that was thanks to you," Ashana replied with a smile.

"If you want to thank me," he grumbled, taking a seat next to Rezaaran, "get me something for this horrible headache, will you?"

Ashana nodded and walked across to the storage cabinet in the galley to retrieve an analgesic tincture.

"What happened to me at Halsyn?" Jet asked.

"Well, both of us were struck by Obsidian fire," Rezaaran explained. "It caused us to experience something called Torementhian blight."

Jet gulped down the medication Ashana handed him. He closed his eyes and waited for the pain to subside.

The doors to the galley opened again and admitted a young Halsynian girl in white robes, a middle-aged woman wearing red-and-black robes, and a person Jet wished he would never have had to see again.

"This Torementhian blight you mentioned," Jet said, ignoring Varathis's smug face. "That means Torementhias is real?"

"Unfortunately," responded the woman with the red-and-black dress, scowling.

"I don't know how," he continued, recalling what he had hoped was a bad trip, "but after I passed out on Halsyn, I found myself in Torementhias."

"What did you see?" the woman asked. Her gaze was so intent that it seemed to look into Jet's very soul.

"There was a group of creatures…I've never seen anything like them before. They gathered around this altar, and a leader of theirs performed a ritual on a Kalaran soldier. He seemed to force the soul of one of the creatures into the Kalaran."

The woman's eyes widened, and she looked at him with a grave expression. "Are you sure that was what you saw?"

"Look, lady," he growled, meeting her gaze, "I told you what I saw. Why would I not be sure?"

"OK, let's all take a breath here," Ashana said in an attempt to dissipate the growing tension in the galley. "Jet, this is Luminara, one of the Anmorian Guardians."

"I don't care *who* she is! If she wants respect, she should show some!"

Luminara seemed affronted that the Erebonian had spoken to her in such a manner.

"Show you respect?" Varathis asked with a hearty laugh. "You run from any responsibility and couldn't even hold your rank as captain because you're a washed-out drunk. Now you have the gall to demand respect?" The prince leaned over Jet. "We don't need you on this ship. Your only loyalty is to whatever is in a bottle and nothing else."

Jet leaped to his feet and glowered at the Zenorian prince who had become his captain. "You want to repeat that, you little punk? At least *I* have the courage to help another. I'm loyal to my duty. You run from the first sign of trouble to save your own ass and then parade yourself like a prison whore!"

"That's enough!" Ashana shouted and stepped between the former Rangers. "Jet saved Rezaaran's life and mine on Halsyn. Now, I don't care what his history was in the Rangers, but this is *my* ship—and he is staying!"

Varathis looked at Ashana pityingly. "Oh, my dear sweetheart," he said mockingly. "You forget that I am the future king of Zenor. Your whims of pity are touching, but it is *my* authority that will count, not that of a queen."

Ashana threw a furious jab to Varathis's face.

"You dare hit your king?" he yelped, clutching his bleeding nose. "Oh, I get it! You're just playing hard to get!"

Luminara sighed in exasperation and clicked her fingers. Varathis's voice instantly transformed to a singing bird.

"Much better," she mumbled.

"Ikso, take him to the barracks and sort his face out," Ashana said irritably. On further thought, she ordered Gunner to stand watch over the obnoxious prince.

"As much as it irks me," Luminara said slowly, "I am inclined to agree with the braggart. There is no need for an Erebonian as part of this team. They are renowned for turning their backs on allies."

Jet glowered at her. "I want no part of any team if you'd rather judge me by *what* I am than *who* I am! You don't know a damn thing about me!" He stormed out of the galley.

Rezaaran fixed Luminara with an exasperated look and followed Jet. A few moments later, he found him seated on the floor of the cargo hold, shivering. Rezaaran passed him his Ranger's coat. Jet snatched it and lit one of his spice sticks.

"She's not entirely wrong about me," Jet muttered, following the slowly rising curls of smoke. He held the stick idly but for once was reluctant to put it to his lips. "I fight this inner conflict every day of my life, keeping this darkness in my soul at rest."

"There was no darkness in the friend who saved me numerous times on Mar-Karatheer."

Jet snorted. He thought back to his time in slavery and lost himself again in the smoldering orange glow of his spice stick. "I only got to that forsaken planet because my people are the scum of this galaxy. My father sold me to a slaver to pay off gambling debts. What parent does that to his child?"

Rezaaran remained silent. There were no words to ease what afflicted Jet's heart.

"Erebonians have a bad reputation," Jet continued. "It's no secret, but as with all races, that is a gross generalization. Most of us are the very dregs of civilization, but I wanted more. When I left Mar-Karatheer, I wandered for a long time with a raging fire in my soul. I hated what my parents had done to me. I hated that I was alone, that the one person I had befriended chose not to join me." He turned his yellow eyes to Rezaaran.

"I'm sorry, Jet."

"Yeah, well, it's in the past now, isn't it? In any case, my fortunes changed when I met Hera. She was a beautiful Terinian siren. She brought out the beauty in the world for me to see. We performed across the galaxy as a couple act called the Black Kiss." He smiled slightly as he quietly reminisced. "We got married and were planning a life together. But you can't escape the darkness. I don't know how, but the Dominion ambushed us at a hotel while we were on tour. They killed Hera in front of my eyes and took me prisoner for their experiments."

Jet's eyes closed, and his fists tightened as the painful memories of his imprisonment flooded his mind. "The world never changes. *We* never change. I thought love had the power to change my world. I let go of my darkness with Hera because she made me think I could be a better man. Then they ripped her away from me. I joined the Rangers. I felt that with them, I could find a way to use my darker nature to stop the Dominion. But the truth is they cannot be stopped. The darkness cannot be stopped."

"They *can* be stopped, Jet," Rezaaran said firmly, placing his hand on his friend's shoulder. "We can stop them—together. You're part of a team on this ship. Whatever challenges you feel lie before you, you don't have to face them alone. We can help you get justice for Hera's murder."

"Justice?" Jet asked with a sorrowful shadow in his eyes. "How can there be justice when I am responsible for her death? I brought darkness into the life of the most beautiful woman I ever knew. Luminara is right. I will bring darkness to this team. I cannot escape what I am."

The Erebonian turned away from Rezaaran. The War Mage took his cue and left the cargo hold. Jet looked at his smoldering spice stick and stubbed it out on the steel decking. Closing his eyes, he retreated to his memories of Hera.

Rezaaran walked into the galley lost in thought. He knew it was a ridiculous notion, yet he could not help but feel guilty for abandoning his friend when he had desperately needed him.

"How's he doing?"

"He's a bit unsettled and angry," Rezaaran said with a sigh, taking a seat beside Ashana. "Honestly, Luminara, you're being too hard on him. I don't care what Erebonians have done. I know Jet, and I want him on this team."

"What conceivable reason could there be to have him here?"

"Well, besides that he is my friend," Rezaaran replied with frustration, "he is a Sentinel!"

Luminara seemed stunned by this revelation.

"We need all the help we can get if we are going to stop Thaedis from reaching the Ark," Rezaaran said.

"What are the two of you talking about?" Ashana asked.

Luminara took a deep breath and drew up a chair for herself. "When we became the Anmorian Guardians, our first decision was to take the battle to the Edarians and Nethriziin, denizens of the Obsidious who directly threatened the stability of Anmor. Thaedis and Tyrel entered the fortress of Torementhias on a scouting mission, during which they discovered the Ark. It is a stone casket made by the first mages of Torementhias, who unwittingly released Nethriziin. Most of their kin revered him as a divine being. However, some grew suspicious and planned to lock him deep within the Obsidious. Unfortunately, he wiped out their race before they could imprison him. When Tyrel and Thaedis looked into the Ark, they found a poem called 'Sahar's Requiem.' Hidden in the poem was a detailed plan on how to trap Nethriziin within the darkness of the Obsidious and craft a magical prison that could hold him for the ages."

"'By strife it shall enclose,'" Rezaaran said, reciting the words he'd overheard Thaedis say, "'never to reopen. The bonds strengthen, until purer spirits rise awoken.'"

"Conflict strengthened the magical bindings that locked the Ark. After the genocide Nethriziin committed in Torementhias, there was no longer any war, and this caused the magic to weaken so that we could open it. After we imprisoned Nethriziin and subjugated the Edarians, we moved the Ark to the Aetherealm, where it served as a storage vessel for our various records and relics."

"Wait…let's take a step back here," Ashana said. "What is Torementhias, and who are Nethriziin and the Edarians?"

"Torementhias," Luminara explained, "was a great fortress that stood in the realm of the Obsidious, but it now lies in ruins as a maze surrounding the Torementhian stone. The Obsidious is a realm of darkness inhabited by Edarians, creatures crafted by Nethriziin. All souls banished to the Obsidious must pass through the maze where they face the Tormentors, powerful Edarians with unique abilities. The Tormentors oversaw the atonement process and navigated cleansed souls to Hidar, the smith. He would reforge the souls at the Soulforge, which rebirthed them into the Maelinthian."

"That is a lot to take in," Ashana whispered. She felt like her mind was about to explode with this new knowledge. Every mythical story she had heard as a child was true. Yet how could any of this be real?

"Nethriziin is the Scion of Darkness," Rezaaran continued. "He is the ruler of the Obsidious and is Thaedis Silvermire's master. I think he has some leverage over Thaedis, and the contents of the Ark would help Thaedis free himself."

"Well, look at you being the archivist for once," Ashana teased.

Rezaaran chuckled lightly at this. "You mentioned Hidar," he said to Luminara. "In my vision, I saw Thaedis speak to him about a weapon of sorts that he had made at the Soulforge. Hidar said that the forge was ready and that Narak believed it would work."

"Narak is the most powerful of the Edarians, and their leader," Luminara explained. "He passes judgment over souls that have completed the maze. It appears that despite his exile, Thaedis still holds influence over the Edarians, perhaps at the order of Nethriziin."

"Jet mentioned that he saw them bind the soul of a creature to a Kalaran," Ashana said slowly. "Could that be why they are using the Soulforge?"

"That may explain it," Luminara replied darkly. "He has found a way to bring the Edarians into this realm. If he succeeds, then Nethriziin will walk the Maelinthian, and his conquest of Anmor will be complete."

"And if Thaedis has the Ark and its contents, then he controls—"

"The greatest force of destruction ever known," Luminara said. "We need to reach that Ark first."

"Well, it may be a good idea," Ashana said, "if we knew where to look. Any thoughts on where we can find it?"

"Even if we find the Ark," Rezaaran countered, "we still have to defeat Thaedis, Diothur, and potentially an army of Kalarans possessed by Edarians. None of us can win this fight alone. I definitely cannot; neither can IRIS, and not even you, Luminara. We need to work together. Lord Salvidawn created us and went to great lengths in doing so. This is what we were born to do." He met Ashana's eyes. "It's time we talk about the Sentinels together."

Jet ambled toward the loading bay. He hoped that Ashana had brought his Levira with him. Maybe some maintenance work would help take his mind off his current troubles. The doors parted, and he found the scientist tinkering with his bike.

"You slimy, ishtharian, shithole-licking maggot!" he shouted. "Get away from that!"

Quirt immediately backed away from the Levira and shied away from the Erebonian.

"Don't worry, I'm not going to eat you," Jet growled.

"To be honest, I am more worried that you may try to stab me again."

"Yeah, sorry about that," he said sincerely. "I've had bad experiences with scientists in the past."

"Clearly."

Jet fixed a stern glare at Quirt, but the corner of the Erebonian's mouth curled slightly upward. "Rez says you're the one who fixed me up after that scrap at Halsyn."

"I stabilized your condition," the scientist replied. "Rezaaran and Ashana said you were a friend, and they are good people, so I trust their assessment of you."

Jet looked at the scientist, unsure what to say. It had been a long time since he had been with people who viewed him as more than just a curiosity. He looked at his Levira and realized the scientist had completed most of the maintenance Jet had been neglecting for several months.

"I came here thinking I'd have a smoke and fix my Levira," Jet grunted. "Turns out my Levira is already fixed, and I don't crave spice anymore."

"I may have had something to do with that," Quirt replied slowly. "While stabilizing your condition, I noticed that your serology showed high levels of the narcotics you have used. I neutralized their effect with an antidote to return you to a conscious state sooner. It appears to have also cured your addiction."

"Great," Jet grumbled, throwing his spice sticks away. "Have you seen my gauntlet?"

Quirt reached to a shelf behind him and retrieved a heavily chromed arm-length device. Set into the metal at the back of the hand was the glowing blue hologram of Jet's wife. The Erebonian turned the upgraded gauntlet over in his hand. "You tinkered with this too?"

"I prefer to think I gave it a much-needed upgrade," Quirt replied sternly. "I have incorporated IRIS's interface so that you are connected to its archive and network. I also added microfission blasters to improve the striking power with the redesigned plate for close-quarter combat. The gauntlet now uses a neuroreceptive interlink so that it reacts to thoughts for function toggle. There are other functions in there as well that we can go over if you are interested."

Jet did not seem to care much for the scientist's technical ramblings. The hologram disc of his wife, which had been restored and preserved perfectly, held his attention.

"I know how important it is to hold on to the memories of the loved ones that we lose," Quirt said.

"Look, I'm not into the whole holding hands and feelings things."

"Yes, of course," Quirt said softly.

An awkward silence reigned between the two as Jet continued looking at the image of Hera. "Thanks for fixing her hologram," he finally said, giving Quirt a small smile. He attached the gauntlet and marveled at the flexibility. "I still don't understand why you would want to help me, though."

"Like I said before, you are a friend to Rezaaran and Ashana. I saw you risk your life for them. You are a hero. Plus the fact that you seem to irk that brat Varathis is a bonus."

Jet laughed loudly at this. Quirt looked at him, perplexed.

"Well, if I can do anything to repay this kindness, let me know."

"Now that you mention it, there *is* a favor I would like to ask," Quirt replied.

"Hey, I may have been single for a long time, but I'm not into other guys. If that's your thing, it's cool, but I'd be the wrong guy for you."

"What?" Quirt asked, confused. Suddenly realizing what Jet had meant, he blushed. "No, no—not that. I want you to train me to fight."

The Erebonian regarded Quirt carefully, and a smile crept across his reptilian face. "Aye. That I can do!"

CHAPTER NINE

THE SENTINELS

Quirt adjusted his thermal suit and stretched his arms. He looked around his workshop expectantly, but the only people who kept him company were Ikso and Gunner. A few moments later, though, Quirt felt he should have appreciated their presence more as Varathis slunk into the loading bay, sulking.

"Do all these missions involve sitting around and doing nothing?" Varathis grumbled to the room in general.

"Doing nothing seems to be your usual action," Ikso quipped as she held Gunner's front paws and danced with him. "Although you also don't need a particular reason to complain."

Varathis glared at her, although his strapped, fractured nose attenuated the menace of his stare. Not that Ikso paid any mind to his attempt to intimidate her.

"We are stationed until we receive orders from IRIS," Quirt said.

"What do you normally do between missions?"

"Rezaaran says this time is perfect for further training."

Prince Kalamdor sneered. Only those who were inept needed further training.

"Training?" Ikso asked, her interest piqued, and her eyes twinkled. "When can we start?"

The door to the workshop creaked open, and a yawning Jet entered.

"Did you just wake up?" Quirt asked, raising an eyebrow.

"Yeah, just now," Jet replied. He removed his gauntlet and looked fondly at the hologram. In truth, he'd hardly slept through the night. The antidote Quirt had administered had removed his cravings for spice and alcohol and provided him with a clarity of thought he had not experienced in a long time. Throughout the night, he had been transfixed on the hologram of Hera, enjoying the nostalgia of their adventures throughout the galaxy while on tour.

Jet cracked his knuckles and walked toward Quirt. "Are you ready?"

"What—now?" the scientist asked in alarm. "Do we not need to warm up first?"

The Erebonian offered a nonchalant shrug. "We're training, so it will be light," he replied. "Here, take these."

He offered Quirt two short wooden staves, and the pair assumed a starting stance opposite one another. "We're going to practice a basic countersequence," Jet explained. "Move toward me, and I will show you."

Quirt cautiously approached Jet with a meek swing of his staff toward the Erebonian's head. The former Ranger met the strike with a solid block and a swift counterstrike that stopped shy of Quirt's neck.

"What was that?" Jet asked with a raised eyebrow. "You need to have some drive and aggression in your action. Let's try something else."

Jet positioned himself closer, a foot away from Quirt. "You're a Thyrillian, right?"

"I am indeed," Quirt replied slowly. "What does that have to do with our training, though?"

"During my travels," Jet explained, "I heard several tales about the Thyrillians being brilliant scientists, but they were renowned as a civilization with no warfare, crime, or violence. If there is no threat, then you never learn how to react with instincts."

To illustrate his point, Jet swiftly brought his staff to rest on Quirt's cheek but took care not to injure him. The scientist startled and backed away a few steps.

"You are talking about the flight-or-fight response," Quirt said between his rapid breaths.

"Exactly. Your instinct is to run. We need to train you to fight."

Jet patiently worked Quirt through an alternating series of high and low blocks to improve his responsiveness. Ikso looked on with interest, while Varathis silently polished the red crystal blades of his long swords.

"Great! You're getting the hang of this," Jet finally said with delight.

"Perhaps…but my arms are burning."

"That's because you've never used your muscles before. Let's pick up the pace."

Quirt struggled to match his trainer's increasingly faster measured attacks with the required blocks.

"Don't look at my hands. Stay focused on my eyes."

The scientist acknowledged the advice with a nod and resisted the burn in his arms.

"Use that incredible brain, and follow the flow of the battle."

"There should be a pattern you can discern," Quirt repeated to himself, beginning to analyze the moves of his instructor as they subtly became more complex.

Suddenly, Jet pulled his student's foot aside with his leg and caught Quirt before he fell to the floor. "Which is why you need some spontaneity," Jet said with a chuckle, helping the scientist to his feet. "The trick is to act faster than your opponents but not to let them know your next move. That is where the aggression comes in for a sudden burst."

"Rage alone, though, is not enough," Ikso said as she rose to her feet to join the pair. "May I have a chance to train with Master Bal Sara?"

"Sure thing," replied Quirt, relieved at the opportunity to rest. His attention drifted to a beeping coming from the monitors on his desk.

"I'm no master," Jet said to Ikso. His gravelly voice carried a softer touch with the Halsynian. "As for you, Quirt, in our next session, we need to get you to focus. If you're distracted, even for a moment, it may mean the difference between life and death. Focus on the here and now."

"Aren't you always about the here and now?" Varathis mumbled beneath his breath. To his annoyance, everyone ignored his jab at Jet. When he'd been with the Rangers, he'd always had a cohort that enjoyed his barbed remarks toward the disgraced captain.

"This is fascinating," Quirt remarked to himself. The readings of the badge were remarkable, defying belief. He informed Rezaaran about the discovery over his interface and turned to watch Jet instruct Ikso, hoping to passively glean more skills.

"You are quite right about mindfulness," Ikso said. "When you submit to the present moment, you find the Onsei will reach out to you and direct you on the best possible course."

Jet and Ikso stood before one another, ready to practice the same reflex training he had demonstrated with Quirt. However, Ikso elected to use her Halsynian staves instead of the regular wooden ones the scientist had used.

Unlike Quirt, Ikso was not apprehensive. Rather, there was an aura of tranquillity about her. She fixed her pale-blue eyes on Jet and matched his progressively faster strikes with deft yet graceful blocks.

"We learn to treat battle as a conversation," Ikso explained. She found a gap in Jet's defenses and tapped him squarely on the chest. "The conversation is like a dialogue."

"A conversation with your opponent?" Jet asked as he repositioned himself for a second round with his swift adversary. "That could be a costly delay in a fight."

"The Order of Nish Ira teaches us that freedom from passion leads to clarity of mind. In the end, the dialogue is not between you and adversary but between you and the goddess. The more we submit..."

With a gust of wind, Ikso swept Jet to the floor but caught hold of his leather vest before he made impact.

"The greater the extent of power she grants us."

She helped her astonished teacher to his feet. The Erebonian laughed heartily.

"There is a greater wisdom to you than your years," he said, fondly clapping his hand upon her shoulder. "There is merit to what you say. A lighter heart allows a fighter to move faster."

"Well, it does not take much to off-foot a blithering oaf such as yourself," muttered Varathis.

Jet released an exasperated sigh. "If you have so much to say, why not test yourself against her?"

"Gladly," Varathis said with a smirk. "In truth, the only thing that matters in a fight is precision and merciless skill."

The Zenorian prince grabbed the training staves from Jet and positioned himself opposite the young Halsynian. "This is training, but do not forget that in a real fight, you will face an opponent wanting to kill you. You need to fight for your life!"

Varathis leaped toward Ikso, feigning an attack to her head and following through with a swift strike to her torso. Yet he did not deter the Halsynian acolyte. She deftly blocked his initial strike and met each initiation with a confident block.

The prince heightened the tempo of his attacks yet frustratingly found that the young girl was able to match every new attack he threw at her with an unwavering serenity to her actions.

"They're perfectly matched," Quirt exclaimed with astonishment. How could this lithe young girl be so fast and hold her own against a battle-hardened warrior such as Varathis?

Incensed by the scientist's observation, Varathis unleashed a flurry of strikes at his young adversary. Yet once again, he failed to break through her guard.

The Halsynian girl locked her short staves together into a single weapon and surrendered herself to the will of the goddess. She moved toward Varathis with an unnatural alacrity. Spinning her staff, she placed her adversary on the defensive, with each of her strikes forcing him to step back. Her attacks moved unpredictably from his head to his leg and alternated as erratically from left to right.

Despite being able to defend himself, Varathis found it surprisingly difficult, only managing to block by the merest of moments. Suddenly Ikso struck him squarely in the chest with an open palm that broke his defense and knocked him across the loading bay. Varathis gasped for air, his mind reeling. How had this little girl gotten the better of him?

Ikso approached her adversary, respectfully bowed, and offered her hand to help him to his feet. Varathis snarled and knocked her hand away.

"Varathis, stand down," Jet growled, reaching for his gauntlet.

The prince ignored the threat and attacked Ikso in a savage rage. Taken by the surprise of his vicious assault, the Halsynian hastily raised her staves but received a strike across the face.

Varathis smirked at her astonishment. At least she had learned her place as second best to him. However, his smirk evaporated when he saw white energy ribbons flowing toward her, and a gust of wind erupted from her joined staff. The prince braced himself and swiftly countered by sweeping Ikso's feet from beneath her. He pounced at her, his red crystal sword drawn—but the blade stopped in the air behind his head.

"That's enough!" Jet shouted. "What the hell is wrong with you?"

Varathis drew his sword out of Jet's gauntlet, sheathed his weapon, and straightened himself. "I was teaching her not to be too confident in her abilities. Overconfidence could get her killed."

Ikso stood slowly and wiped the trickle of blood from her lip. "It was an enlightening experience," she said with a scowl.

Varathis regarded her with a smug smile.

"What's going on here?"

Ashana, Rezaaran, and Luminara stood at the entrance to the loading bay. Their eyes warily passed between Varathis and Ikso.

"Nothing to see," Jet grumbled. "Just a training exercise."

Rezaaran saw in his friend's mind exactly what had happened but decided it was best to let the matter rest. "Quirt, you said you had found something about the badge."

"Ah, yes," the scientist replied. "Over the course of these past few weeks, I studied that badge you gave me while monitoring the data from the nanobots in your body, as well as performing an analysis of your sword. During this time, I charted a direct correlation between the red dust within the badge, your body, and your weapon. They all resonate with the same vibrational frequency and share similar energy-output readings that are linked."

Realizing the scientist's excitement was bound to precede a lengthy explanation, Luminara and Ashana took a seat on some nearby metal crates.

"The nanobots within your body detected the presence and activity that this dust displays during your periods of meditation.

Based on the data I retrieved from the nanobots, it appears that this dust facilitates a dissociation between your mind and your body. During this dissociation, your centers for memory and higher functioning display usage far surpassing any other sentients during their waking hours."

Do not let this get to your head, now, Kashari said wryly.

"When you leave your meditation state," Quirt continued, "your functioning appears to return to normal. Yet interestingly, the dust, you, and your sword all display a heightened attraction for exotic matter and unquantified energies that you are able to manipulate as magic. Even more intriguing is that whatever magical energy you interact with leaves an imprint within the dust. I theorize that I may be able to extract data from the badge that can detail Rezaaran's entire magical experience since joining IRIS."

"Wait—extract data?" Ashana interrupted. "Like accessing a computer?"

"Precisely!" Quirt beamed. "The inescapable conclusion is that what is within this badge is not dust at all but rather a highly sophisticated form of nanotechnology that appears to display a level of sentience."

"I don't understand," Rezaaran said, wrinkling his brow. "How could an ancient artifact contain such technology?"

"I may be able to shine some light on the matter," Luminara interjected. "About one hundred years ago, we completed our work on creating the Sentinels. We charged Zelzo with the duty of creating a method to unite and activate their latent powers. He decided on the idea of using nanites to hardwire the genetics of the Sentinels. Zelzo handed the badge to Tyrel to keep the information hidden. He feared that if anyone found it, our efforts would be in vain. Tyrel in turn had the idea to hide the contents of the badge in mythology and so delivered it to the Vokarii on Zenor three thousand years in the past."

"Time travel is real," Quirt whispered excitedly to himself.

He planned this all along, Rezaaran remarked to his mentor.

You and the other Sentinels are Salvidawn's last hope for peace.

Even more reason that we cannot fail.

"Well, this is all rather fascinating," Varathis remarked with a yawn. "But I have outgrown fables and fairy tales, so I'm going to get some rest until there is something real to be done."

Ashana scowled. Via her interface, she ordered Gunner to follow Varathis closely.

"As much as I detest that smug punk," Jet said slowly, "he does have a point. This does seem a little farfetched, Rez."

"And can we finally find out more about the Sentinels?"

"Of course, Ash," Rezaaran replied. "However, I think this may be easier if we can do the explaining at the altar. Quirt, would you be able to pass the nanites from the badge into each of us?"

"Whoa, wait a minute!" Ashana exclaimed, stumbling off the crate. "You want us to use that badge? Don't you remember what that thing did to you? We don't all share your healing ability!"

"If I may," Quirt said tentatively, "I have been able to stabilize the nanites within the badge into a serum that is able to perform the necessary functions without the adverse reactions Rezaaran experienced upon his initial inoculation. Personally, I am intrigued to learn more about what this technology is able to unlock."

Ashana sighed and reluctantly agreed. Perhaps through this she could find answers to the unusual connection she shared with the people around her.

"Well, I've injected all manner of junk into myself before," Jet remarked. "What's one more to the tally?"

Ikso approached them, eager to participate in the magical journey on which they were preparing to embark. However, Rezaaran curtailed such thoughts.

"We'll need you to keep an eye on things in this realm while we are in our meditative state. If anything happens that seems it may threaten us, wake me first."

The young acolyte nodded with some disappointment and took a seat on a crate behind Rezaaran.

Luminara positioned them in a circle and stepped into the center to place an ignited incense stick on the metal floor. She then turned to Jet and offered a respectful bow.

"Before we continue," she said softly, "I owe you an apology for the deep disrespect I have shown you since our first meeting. You deserve a chance to prove yourself, and taking into account your actions, I know there is more to you than the harsh words with which I judged you."

"I appreciate that," Jet replied with a small smile. Subtly he bowed his head toward her.

Quirt moved between the Sentinels and carefully injected each of them with his synthesized serum. Once he had administered his own, he resumed his place in the circle around the slow-burning incense.

"If you could all close your eyes, please," Luminara said softly. "Concentrate only on the sound of my voice."

The Sentinels followed her instruction as Ikso watched with growing fascination.

"Relax your body from your shoulders, through your torso, and down to your extremities. Surrender your thoughts to the sound of my voice. Breathe deeply. Experience the air passing from your nose through to your chest and returning its same course. With each passing breath, release your worries and fears. Feel the computers in the background pass beyond the reach of your mind. Ignore their alarms and sounds. Let the cold metal beneath you drift to the edge of your senses. Experience the serenity of the moment washing over you, cresting over your fear. Follow me forward, my friends."

Rezaaran felt himself reach his deep meditative state. Luminara's soothing voice made the transition far easier than usual.

Ashana felt the soft rustling of a breeze in her ears and across her skin. Her consciousness passed beyond the loading bay. She saw the *Liberator* nestled on an asteroid in a field of its kin. She wandered onward, passing through the nebulae and star fields, traversing the galaxy to the shining mass of light at its center, and then speeding along the axis into a white oblivion.

Ashana squinted as she stared into a white emptiness. Luminara's soothing voice still echoed in her mind. A few moments later, Jet materialized beside her, and finally Quirt appeared.

"What is happening to us?" Quirt asked tentatively.

Release your fears, Dr. Zefrityn.

The white void thinned, and the trio stood in a stone courtyard overlooking a dense forest with a gray sky expanding overhead. They stepped forward and looked over the ramparts at the world beyond the boundaries of the ancient citadel.

"Well, this is interesting," Jet murmured to himself.

"Interesting?" Quirt asked wryly. "How did we get here? More importantly, where are we?"

"Welcome to the Nuhremorn," Rezaaran called out from behind them.

They turned and saw the War Mage flanked by Luminara and an ethereal woman with flowing white hair. "This is Kashari Alda-Fyre," he said. "She is a former Elder Mage of the Vokarii Order and the spirit bound within my sword."

"So...you mean to say that we are now inside your sword?" Jet asked with a raised eyebrow.

"Not exactly. The sword acts as a conduit to transfer my consciousness to this realm. You can think of it as an alternate dimension."

This intrigued Quirt, who sought to take in every detail of the world around him. However, it sparked a revelation for Ashana.

"This is where you do your training?"

"It is indeed, Ash—and now it is the place where the Sentinels begin their journey together."

"You still need to explain that, you know."

Rezaaran nodded, and at his mere thought, their setting changed to the Atmari Altar.

"How did we get here so fast?" Quirt asked in alarm.

"The Nuhremorn is shaped by the thoughts of beings with a strong connection to the Vaux. Within this realm, we are able to alter the world around us. This monument behind me is the Atmari Altar, the resting place for the souls of the Sentinels. Each of us holds a powerful soul crafted by the Guardians to be the last defenders of Anmor. This war against the Dominion is for more than merely freedom—it's a war for the existence of life."

The three friends looked at him skeptically. Knowing how this would sound to a non–Vaux user, Rezaaran could understand their disbelief and knew they would need proof. He directed each of them to the statues around the altar. Each of the Sentinels touched their respective marble figures and instantly saw their lifetimes' experiences ripple through the water beneath their shrines.

"This all just seems so impossible," Jet murmured as he watched the memories of himself and Hera in the water.

"Who is that for?" Quirt asked, indicating the solitary statue.

"That's Diothur's shrine."

"The bounty hunter that tried to kill us on Halsyn?" Ashana whispered.

"Individually the Sentinels are capable of more than any mortal," Luminara explained. "However, defeating Thaedis Silvermire will require your combined strength. I believe he has learned of your existence, though perhaps not yet your identities—but he knows there are those who can oppose him. He tracked down Diothur and corrupted her essence in order to have someone trained to hunt down the remaining Sentinels and remove the obstructions to his goal."

She cast her gaze over the four Sentinels still allied with the Light and realized that Rezaaran was right. The only way to win this war against the forces of Torementhias was to fight together. This was their time, their purpose.

"We can train in this realm," Rezaaran said, returning them all to the stone courtyard. "Within the Nuhremorn, time passes differently than in our realm, giving us the advantage."

"Well, what are we waiting for, then?" Jet said, cracking his knuckles.

Kashari drifted through the corridors of the citadel with Quirt at her side, guided by a glowing orb that hovered above her hand. Despite his best efforts, he could not hide his thoughts from the spirit.

"You seem troubled, Dr. Zefrityn," she said gently.

"Please, call me Quirt," he replied with flushed cheeks. "You're telepathic, I assume?"

"Indeed I am. Yet I do not have to use my abilities to understand the troubles that weigh upon your heart."

"Being here in an alternate realm…oh! It defies belief. It defies the very reality I have come to understand through science. Even communing with the spirits of people long passed stretches what I know to be real."

"Everything we now know was once beyond comprehension. We utilize magic in combat, yet you understand the science behind the spells we cast. To you, what we can do is extraordinary, yet it is still explainable in the realms of science and therefore reason. However, understanding on reason alone explains only a fraction of existence. Many mysteries cannot yet be explained. Perhaps that may change in years to come; perhaps it may not. Either way, these forces continue to exist within the world we inhabit. Only by submitting yourself to the knowledge that there is a world beyond your understanding can you hope to understand such a realm."

"That is a perplexing conundrum," Quirt said, wrinkling his brow.

With a wave of her hands, Kashari opened a large double door and led the scientist into a vast library filled with ancient tomes and scrolls. "This library was granted to me by Lord Salvidawn when he bound me to the Nuhremorn. You may not possess any innate magical abilities like the other Sentinels, but I know what you seek to accomplish."

The Thyrillian looked at the ancient specter with raised eyebrows. "Does Rezaaran also know about it?"

Kashari simply nodded. "Each of the others displays his or her quintessential qualities differently. You possess an incredible mind, and among the Sentinels, you will always be their necessary voice of reason. A mind such as yours can easily find the answers you seek for your quest within these walls."

"How can I learn everything in here? Even with the relative time drift due to the dimensional change, this is a lot to get through."

"You were the youngest entrant ever into the Thyrillian Advanced Scientific Research Academy; I doubt this will be a challenge for you."

"How do you know about TSARA?"

Kashari offered him a knowing smile and left Quirt alone to the myriad of books that awaited his ravenous thirst for knowledge.

The dull-purple comma-shaped figure stared at the ground with vacant black eyes, its edges constantly shifting in a haze of darkness.

Jet walked around the creature and examined its every aspect. It was unlike anything he had ever seen. "What *is* this thing?"

"To be honest, I am not entirely sure," Luminara admitted.

"Well, that's not comforting," he mumbled. "I thought you knew all things related to magic."

"Despite my years, there are a great many things I still have to learn."

Kashari drifted into the courtyard to join the two visitors to Antarika. "This is an eidolon left behind by Tolbetrius, an Edarian who captured the citadel. He created this Obsidian construct with the sole intention of hunting me down."

Jet looked at the eidolon with renewed interest and apprehension. "What happened to this Tolbetrius?"

"Rezaaran defeated him," Kashari replied simply.

"So...why not destroy it?"

"In truth, we only found it recently. Rezaaran felt it may be useful for training the Sentinels."

"The intriguing thing about Erebonians," Luminara said, "is that your bodies contain a substance identical to Torementhicite. The highest concentration is in the crystals along your head."

Jet looked at her outstretched hand quizzically and then sighed. He cracked off a small piece of a crystal and handed it to Luminara.

"Kashari, if you would be so kind as to hold this for me," Luminara said.

The Elder Mage nodded and telekinetically suspended the crystal fragment in the air. Luminara placed her hand on the eidolon's head and activated the dormant construct. Fixing its glowing orange eyes on the crystal fragment, it fired a stream of dark fire. The crystal flared with a lava-orange hue and shuddered steadily.

"The substance contained in these crystals and your body," Luminara explained, "makes you immune to arcane and light magic.

However, they confer on you the ability to absorb and harness Obsidian magic. Effectively, you can redirect the power from spells used against you to counter the caster."

"What exactly will I be able to do with this power I absorb?"

"That is what we are going to find out while we are here."

Suddenly the crystal shattered, spraying fragments across the courtyard.

"Well, it appears," Luminara remarked wryly, "there is a limit to how much power can be absorbed. We will have to determine your limit through our training."

"Let's get started, then," Jet said grimly. The thought of him exploding like that crystal was unsettling, but he was eager to determine the range of abilities he could gain.

Ashana looked out the window of a stone outpost along the citadel's ramparts, her gaze wandering beyond the veiled gray sky. A set of footsteps drew her attention back to the present, and she saw that Luminara had sought her out.

"Is there ever any sunlight here?"

"Unfortunately not. Like Rezaaran said, the Nuhremorn exists beyond the mortal realm. This world is a collection of magical energies flowing between the Aetherealm and the Maelinthian. The only souls able to wield the power flowing through here are beings of other realms and the Sentinels."

Ashana chuckled lightly. "A few hours ago, I never would have imagined I was on the same path as Rezaaran. Since he joined IRIS, he has been this inspiring magical warrior, able to conjure elements to his side and fight all sorts of enemies. I'm good with my weapons and do well as a strategist, but magic? I can't imagine how my ability to see glimpses of the future is going to help stop the war."

Luminara smiled at her kindly. "When we created the Sentinels, we unwittingly added an element of ourselves to each of you. Rezaaran is similar to Tyrel, just as Quirt is similar to Zelzo. In a manner, you and I share a likeness. You care deeply for people, regardless of how long you may know them. Your empathy is what drives your power."

The Guardian passed Ashana a fragment of the crystal that had shattered while training with Jet in the courtyard. The archer held the dull-gray piece up to her curious eyes. In an instant, with a gush of wind past her, she saw herself upon a battlefield. Her view fixed behind Jet, who was smashing his way through several Kalarans. Her vision rippled to a cold and dark stone room. Once more, Jet was the focus of her vision, but this time he was absorbing a blast of Obsidian fire and pulsed with an orange glow. He unleashed a roar of rage and tightened his grasp around Rezaaran, whom he was shielding.

Returning to the present moment, Ashana looked at Luminara in alarm. "What was that? Are they going to die?"

"What you saw was a possible future, events that may yet transpire. Your ability allows you to see the unknown, seeing the potential in everyone. Mine offers me glimpses of the past of any item I may hold. However, unlike the past, the future is ever changing."

"The battle I saw Jet fighting," Ashana said softly, "I've seen it before. It's been haunting Rezaaran since his Torementhian blight. He can't sleep at night, and when I'm awake, I can see what he dreams."

She looked through a window at the side of the tower and saw Rezaaran seated in the courtyard, guiding Jet through a meditation session. Another vision filled her mind. This time Rezaaran embraced her against the background of a thousand blazing suns in a marigold sky. Although they spoke no words, she felt every emotion in that moment as though it were real.

Again her mind returned to the present beside Luminara. The Guardian passed her a poignant look.

"The drawback of having the power to see beyond the present is that we realize how fleeting these moments are. All the more reason to cherish them."

"You miss Lord Salvidawn, don't you?"

"Every day," Luminara replied. Her gaze wandered beyond the Nuhremorn. "Our last moments together were at the Sanctum. I defended us against the horde of Edarians while Tyrel traveled through time to save Rezaaran. Before he left, he begged me to leave the Aetherealm, to find a place of safety for myself, but I could not leave him to fight alone."

"You sacrificed yourself for him," Ashana whispered, taking Luminara's hand in her own.

"Love is sacrifice," Luminara explained with a grateful smile. "To truly love someone is to be willing to sacrifice everything to keep them safe and happy. I gladly sacrificed my existence to give Tyrel the chance to save Anmor. Our sacrifices were made as an act of love for Anmor."

"Will you see him again?"

"When this is over, I hope to join Tyrel as an aspect of the Vaux in the Aetherealm. However, for some reason I am unable to feel his presence within the Vaux. Perhaps the war is clouding my connection."

Secretly, Luminara wondered if Darzuka's remnant within her consciousness was responsible for weakening her connection to the Vaux. The alternative—and frankly the more ominous—possibility was that perhaps Thaedis had trapped Tyrel in the Obsidious. However, she could not allow herself to dwell on such probabilities when so much was at stake.

She turned her attention to Ashana, who was watching Rezaaran in the courtyard below.

"I know that you love him and that he feels that same love for you. The bond between the two of you was not something Tyrel and I could ever have foreseen. That the four of you should have interacted without our intervention is evidence that it was the will of the Vaux. For all we have learned of magic through the years, love remains the greatest power of all. The love you have shown Rezaaran, despite the difficulties you have endured, has released the Light within him. Love has touched his heart after countless years of cruelty. In turn, he exudes light and hope because his heart swells with love toward you."

"What about the vision I had?"

"That was a possible future. None of us can predict the course time will take us through. Despite all my powers and a lifetime of studying the Vaux, I cannot reclaim those lost years with Tyrel. Enjoy whatever time you have."

The War Mage looked over the ramparts of the Antarika Citadel, his arms raised before him. He closed his eyes and attempted to still his mind in a hopeful attempt to summon the Vaux to his fingertips. However, nothing more than a few puffs of smoke materialized at his command. He clutched the stone bricks in a white-knuckled grasp. Why could he not get this one spell to work?

Luminara and Kashari arrived at his side.

"How are the others doing?" Rezaaran asked.

"Their training seems to be going quite well," Kashari replied, beaming. "It is wonderful to have students to teach after all these years. Not that I do not enjoy our lessons, but as an avorion must always take to the sky, I will always be driven to teach."

"Well, I'm glad everyone is making progress," he replied with a half smile. "We're going to need all of them at their best in the coming months."

"They will be ready, my friend," she replied. "However, I sense that you are not entirely at ease yourself. What troubles you?"

Rezaaran shot her a fleeting glance but said nothing.

"I understand," Kashari said.

"Care to enlighten me?" Luminara asked with a raised eyebrow.

"Despite his best attempts," Kashari explained, "he cannot summon Simarata's spirit at will."

"Ah, Simarata," Luminara replied with a nostalgic smile. "We learned of the threat of Thaedis's return through the rise of a sorcerer calling himself Lord Aeron nearly three thousand years ago. We recognized that Aeron used magic far beyond the understanding or limits of any mortal at the time and knew that Thaedis aided him during his exile. However, our Guardian laws forbade us from direct involvement. Thus, Tyrel came upon the idea of providing a spirit Guardian to the people of the time. He drew upon the Vaux and crafted its power into the form of a havaka, the aerial apex predator of Zenor at the time and symbol of Kel-Ardimus. He named his creation Simarata, Emperor of the Sky, and bestowed the powerful Guardian to protect the Zenorians in their darkest hour. However, to wield such a conjuration required a powerful mage with a pure heart." She nodded subtly toward Kashari.

"You were the mage to first summon Simarata?" Rezaaran asked with awe and heightened reverence toward his teacher.

Luminara placed her index finger on Kashari's forehead and awakened the dormant memories of her life before Rezaaran had retrieved Harkenathor. Tears slowly rolled from Kashari's eyes.

"I tried so hard to forget the Great War," she said sadly, wiping the tears away. "We lost so many promising mages. I lost Mehara without having the chance to tell him how I felt about him. Why should I have to relive these memories?"

Luminara embraced Kashari and consoled her gently. "I am sorry, my friend," she said. "However, you needed to remember that you were the first to summon Simarata. That was because the Vaux chose you to hold such power."

The Guardian turned her attention to Rezaaran. "Simarata is no mere conjuration," Luminara explained. "You cannot summon him upon command the way you do with other spells. In every instance that you have drawn him from the Vaux, what was the circumstance in which you found yourself?"

Rezaaran thought about this for a moment.

"The first time since the Great War," Kashari said softly when she had regained her composure, "was when you retrieved Harkenathor."

"It was when I was willing to risk my safety to save Cosmonox," Rezaaran corrected her. "Then again when I saved the boy on Zeema-Tamius…and again when saving Ikso." He looked at Luminara with dawning realization.

"Simarata only appears to a soul who would use the power to save another," she said, confirming Rezaaran's suspicion, "and not seek to use such power for conquest." She positioned Rezaaran and Kashari opposite one another. "The bond between you formed because of the heroic and noble spirits you share. Within that bond lies the secret to calling upon Simarata. Clear your minds, and fill them only with the thoughts of the ones you love."

"The Vokarii of old were taught to act beyond emotion," Kashari said with a wrinkled brow. "Emotion clouds action and keeps you from performing your duty to the Order and to your people."

"During my years as a Guardian, the one thing in short supply throughout the galaxy was a capacity for love. Yes, love does open your heart to vulnerability, and it is through that ensuing hurt and need for attachment to others that we make rash and harmful decisions. Love itself is the purest emotion, and there is far too little of it in these times. A soul that knows love and shows love with no limitation is one that knows the truest power. Now, close your eyes."

The Zenorians closed their eyes. Rezaaran remembered his night with Ashana in the forest of Artherikas beneath the stars. He remembered the love and joy she had greeted him with when he awoke after his coma. An aura of warmth surrounded him, and when he opened his eyes, he saw a channel of energy streaming between himself and his mentor. The power within the channel intensified, and particles of Valinthicite appeared in the colored streams of energy. A column of the particles rose skyward from the channel, and electricity crackled across its surface.

Suddenly, a piercing screech filled the air, and the wings of an enormous bird erupted from the top of the column. The mages turned their eyes skyward and saw Simarata's electrically charged wings looming over them. The spirit protector passed to the Zenorians so many years ago separated himself from the column that had birthed him and circled the courtyard. His high-pitched screeches drew the other Sentinels from their training.

With a dull thud, Simarata landed upon the stone pavement of the courtyard behind Rezaaran and Kashari. Particles of Valinthicite rushed from the air around the Zenorian mages and cloaked the magnificent beast in gleaming gold-and-white plumage. His vacant white eyes surveyed the souls to which he had bound himself, and he held his four wings open to display why he alone was the lord of the skies. Yet despite his ostentatious mannerisms, he bowed his head before Rezaaran.

The War Mage tentatively approached the powerful friend, the force of nature that had intervened on numerous occasions to save him and others he cared for. Placing his hand on Simarata's face, he felt the warmth of a creature yet the sparking power of magic beneath his touch. Rezaaran steadied his hand and leaped onto Simarata's neck.

Simarata dipped his head once more to acknowledge Kashari and leaped high into the air, lifted by the tremendous gusts generated by his four wings. Each powerful flap pushed Antarika farther from sight, and they reached higher toward the Nuhremorn's firmament.

"Well, that's something you don't see every day," Jet said as he watched Rezaaran circle the citadel on the back of a mythical bird.

"Or something you hear every day," Ashana whispered.

Simarata's screeches awakened the dormant souls. Their chorus echoed in unison around Antarika and resounded throughout the Nuhremorn.

"It is beautiful," Quirt said with a broad smile. "I have never heard anything like it before, yet I feel that it speaks to something within me that I have always known."

"It's a song of hope," Jet said, a grin drawing across his face.

Vaguely they heard Rezaaran's whoop of exhilaration as he soared through the skies, and the chorus of souls rallied at his return.

CHAPTER TEN

LADY JUSTICE

A flickering star pulsed one last time and faded into darkness as a growing shadow seeped into the star field and consumed its light. The agony of its death mirrored the waning patience of the being at the helm of the ghastly vessel.

Thaedis's leather-gloved hands tightened around the frame of the console he stood over, and his pale eyes narrowed. It had been three weeks of poring over every star map he could find, and his nerves were frayed. Not from a lack of sleep; a side effect of the accursed second life given to him by Nethriziin led him to not require sleep for sustenance. Using his insomnia, Thaedis had scoured every available star map at his disposal, but he was no closer to discovering a single planet that could possibly contain the Ark.

He last remembered that he and Tyrel had moved the Ark from Torementhias to the Aetherealm after imprisoning Nethriziin. Then the traitor had banished him as the Exiled. However, Tyrel was not stupid. He would not hide the Ark in the Aetherealm where the horde of Edarians would find it.

"'By strife it shall enclose,'" Thaedis said, reciting "Sahar's Requiem" yet another time, "'never to reopen. The bonds strengthen, until purer spirits rise awoken.'"

Thaedis looked over the star maps the Colonial Guild had gathered. By its nature, the Ark required conflict for the magical seals to lock—which meant that the only place able to hold the Ark was a planet in the Maelinthian. Yet despite his tireless research, he could not isolate a planet on which he might recover the Ark. Every planet in this forsaken realm had been embroiled in conflict over the eons.

None of his scientists could find the Ark based on the Valinthicite output it should be displaying, nor could his archivists retrieve information on any artifact resembling it.

Overcome by frustration, he felt compelled to incinerate every star map. But he knew that such an outburst would draw the unwelcome attention of Nethriziin to his pursuit.

The doors parted behind him, and a near-silent set of footsteps approached. He turned to the intruder, and his eyes narrowed.

"For your sake," he said coldly, "I hope you bring good news."

Diothur bowed her head and deliberated whether what she had to say was actually good news. "I encountered the Sentinels on Halsyn," she said crisply.

Thaedis regarded her sternly. "Is the situation handled?"

The cowled woman lowered her gaze to avoid direct contact with her master's pale-eyed glare. "They have united," she said slowly. "They overwhelmed me."

Thaedis's wrath simmered once more. The last thing he needed was the Sentinels working together to curtail his plans for freedom.

"There is something else," Diothur said, undaunted. "While recovering after the battle, I sensed the fourth Sentinel and a powerful echo. I believe it is the Guardian you said you would deal with: Luminara. It seems we both underestimated our adversaries."

Thaedis's eyes narrowed. Ordinarily he would severely punish a subordinate for such a brazen statement. However, Diothur was no mere soldier in his army. She was his personal prize in his conquest over Tyrel Salvidawn. She was the Sentinel he had corrupted.

"It seems you are right," he said finally. "We cannot allow them to remain unchecked. What do you think we should do, Yustina?"

The cowled woman looked at him blankly. "That is not my name."

"It was once," he replied coolly. "You were Yustina Ivanova, a soldier who came to my attention when we invaded Earth. You had an innate strength about you that caught the attention of my Harbingers and a sense of justice that remains indomitable. I passed you through the maze of Torementhias for Narak to appraise you. He found that in your heart, you know this galaxy is unjust and needs to be saved from itself."

"Indeed, my lord," she replied firmly. "That was the day I accepted my true self as being Diothur, the person I had spent my entire life hiding from. Yustina was a weak human. She lacked the strength to do what is necessary to preserve justice."

"These Sentinels and Luminara," Thaedis explained, "they directly threaten the stability we are creating through our Dominion. The Sentinels have allied themselves with IRIS, a rebel organization that believes the people should have the right to govern themselves. What do you think about such an ideal?"

"Such a notion is foolish. On Earth, we had an entire planet of people who had freedom and free will, yet they chose to use such a luxury to commit further crimes and flout justice. Justice cannot prevail with freedom. The two are directly opposed."

"We are very close to our goal of a peaceful galaxy. They cannot interfere with our progress."

"They will not. This victory occurred because they caught me by surprise. It will not happen again."

"I am glad to hear that," Thaedis replied, turning to face his star maps once more. "I am seeking an artifact that will end the Sentinels, and no doubt they will try to subvert my attempts."

"There was something I noticed," Diothur said, recalling her fight on Halsyn. "Loradún, the one calling himself Rezaaran—he is susceptible to Torementhicite. It slows his healing."

This piqued Thaedis's interest. As he pondered this new piece of information, he noticed the liquid-metal pool at the center of the chamber begin to congeal. The ferrous fluid rose to form the face of an Edarian with a spiked crown atop his head.

"Lord Silvermire," said Narak with a bow of his head. "I am pleased to inform you that our experiments with the Soulforge have yielded success. We have bound the soul of an Edarian to the body of a Kalaran bearing Torementhicite. Furthermore, the Edarian is still able to use Obsidian magic within the Kalaran vessel."

"Excellent," Thaedis replied. Combined with what Diothur had divulged about Rezaaran's susceptibility to Torementhicite, this was finally a change of fortune. A legion of Kalarans immune to

Rezaaran's magic and able to exploit his weakness would serve well in the coming battles.

"There is something else, Lord Silvermire," Narak said with a smirk. "A creature passed through the maze earlier—the one from whom your scientists cultivated these crystals."

"Where is he now?"

"He escaped. However, before he did, I gazed into his soul, and I believe there may be a means to tear his company apart. He is allied now with the young mage who opposes you."

"Thank you, Narak, for bringing this to my attention. I will deal with it in due course."

Narak bowed his head once more, and the ferrous fluid returned to the pool that had birthed it.

Thaedis thought about the creature he had seen last year, the one whom Narak had encountered in the maze, and he recalled the angst and rage within the beast. If Narak was right and they could turn him to their cause, the Sentinels would scatter more easily. He typed into a keypad on his console, and Luferikas's face filled the view panel.

"How may I serve my lord?" the Demokarva asked.

"Luferikas, I require your assistance in locating a test subject we used last year in our study on Torementhian crystals."

Luferikas thought about this for a moment. "As you wish, my lord. I shall investigate the subjects used for the experiments and provide you with a current location."

"No, not quite," Thaedis said, smirking. "I need you to persuade this individual to ally with the Dominion. It should not be too difficult. He is driven by basic desires."

"I shall see it done, my lord. I wish also to inform you that the Harbingers are in agreement with your plans for aggressive actions against IRIS."

"Luferikas, you have been my trusted ally throughout this conflict. Upon my authority, you may handle the future war effort as you see best, for you are now my Grand Harbinger."

"You do me a great honor, my lord," Luferikas replied with genuine surprise but immense satisfaction.

The transmission ended, and the screen darkened.

"If this business is concluded," Diothur said crisply, "then I wish to continue my hunt for these criminals."

"Before you go..." Thaedis began. Reaching under his cloak, he withdrew a sheathed dagger. "Take this."

Diothur drew the blade from its scabbard and marveled at the black crystalline edge.

"It's a blade made of Torementhicite," Thaedis explained. "Rezaaran is the heart of the Sentinels' rebellion. Kill him, and you will shatter their resolve. Only then can we ensure that justice is maintained."

"I shall bring you his head," Diothur replied coldly.

"You are my best hunter. Do not disappoint me again."

CHAPTER ELEVEN

A ROCKY ALLIANCE

Jet relaxed in his chair and surveyed the aftermath of his meal. He had recently learned that the *Liberator*'s galley was fitted with a reconstitutor that from powdered substrates could create any recipe in the IRIS archive. After several years with the Rangers, during which he'd survived off tavern swill, this was a feast. He pushed aside his plate holding the remains of two cleared rib racks. They joined the stack of dirty dishes he had accumulated on his own. Jet's eyes roved across the table, and for the first time in a long while, he felt happy.

All around the table, the team sat and chatted happily, ravished by the training and enjoying one another's company. Gunner quietly sat at Ashana's ankles, his tail wagging as he followed the conversation, glad the *Liberator* had cheer once more. Even Quirt seemed less reclusive and was currently deep in discussion with Luminara. Varathis sat quietly at the end of the table, sulking over his meal, but he received little attention from anyone else.

Jet felt at peace and content with the sheer simplicity of being able to enjoy a superb meal in the company of people who accepted him as a friend. Leaning back in his chair, he belched loudly.

"That's really nice, Jet," Ashana said wryly. "Very charming."

Ikso attempted to copy him but released only a splutter.

"Great. See what you've done?" Ashana asked in exasperation.

"Well, I want to get myself some water," Jet replied with a chuckle and pushed his chair back.

"I can refill you there," Rezaaran chimed in. Blue streams of Valinthicite flowed to his hand and passed into Jet's goblet, refilling it with clear water.

Jet looked at the goblet with apprehension. "You know that's disgusting, right?" he asked, furrowing his brow.

The group laughed as he tentatively tried the water. However, a shrill beep from the bridge interrupted their festive cheer. Gunner barked loudly and sat at attention beside Ashana.

"What is it, boy?"

Gunner's eyes brightened, and he projected an equation onto the galley wall. Quirt left his seat to look more closely at the message. His eyes widened.

"This is a mathematical cryptogram," he said with astonishment. "It is quite complex, but I should be able to—"

The projection abruptly changed to a numerical matrix accompanied by a narration in a solemn voice that spoke a language none of them recognized.

"What is this?" Rezaaran asked Ashana.

"I don't know," she replied, checking her interface. "The signal barely makes the range of our scanners, and they have not indicated their position."

Once more, the projection changed. It now showed a series of dots interspersed across lines.

"I am not entirely sure if this is also a code," Quirt said with some confusion. "There seems to be a pattern, but I cannot be sure what the sequence reveals."

"I know what it is," Jet murmured. "Give me a few minutes." He left the room and returned moments later with an eight-stringed instrument. He took a seat beside Gunner.

"What are you doing, Jet?" Ashana asked.

"That sequence is a series of musical notes," he explained and proceeded to play the tune captured in the message.

Gunner barked excitedly and displayed a separate panel that identified the tune Jet had played.

Rezaaran read the song title on the panel. "'The Traveler's Plea.' What is that?"

"It's an old tavern favorite at the ports of Magnar," Jet explained, setting his instrument aside. "The ports were a neutral ground during the war and a sanctuary for wanderers displaced by the conflict. The song tells the story of a traveler begging for help finding his way home."

"So...basically, this is a distress call?" Luminara asked.

"Or this could very well be a group of bandits," Varathis suggested.

"It is possible," Jet said, "but that would seem unlikely. Using three coded messages to request help, as well as a voice recording in their own language, is a lengthy ploy to attract victims. Although bandits have used stranger methods in the past."

"Well, if this is indeed a distress call," Rezaaran said firmly, "then we should offer our aid. Can we find the source of the signal?"

"I believe I have," Quirt said, slowly looking back at the group. "That cryptogram equation and the numerical matrix provided their coordinates. I will enter the answers into the navigation system."

"I still feel this is a bad idea," Varathis said solemnly. "These people are transmitting a request, but they do so with music and equations? Why would they not send a distress call in Galtic? This smells of a trap."

"Even if it is," Rezaaran countered, "together we are more than capable of handling a rabble of bandits. Our duty is to rescue anyone calling for aid." He could see that Varathis was not convinced. "We should put this to a vote. All in favor of following through on this transmission, raise your hand."

Everyone in the galley did so—except Varathis.

"Very well," Rezaaran said. "Quirt, plot our course."

Several hours later, the group teleported onto the barren plain of the planet from which they had received the transmission. In the distance, through the umber haze of dust, they glimpsed the ruins of a city. Quirt pulled the shawls around his head tighter to guard against the stinging sands that rasped his face, and he adjusted his breathing mask to improve the seal.

"The transmission is coming from this direction." The Thyrillian pointed toward a long flight of stairs that led up from the sandy field.

Quirt guided the group with the aid of his interface. Along the way, they passed the scorched carcasses of toppled motor vehicles and the shattered remains of buildings that flanked the lengthy staircase. Desiccated wall-crawling plants festooned the ruins, and barren trees broke the uniformity of the razed buildings. Squalls of dust blew across the deserted settlement, offering the only disturbance to the travelers' ascent of the seventy-five granite steps.

"What was this place?" Ashana asked, sorrow tinging her voice.

The few walls that remained bore the scorch marks of artillery shells. Evidently the war had ravaged this planet before IRIS had been able to provide any relief to their plight.

"Maybe it was a temple?" Ikso suggested, looking at the chipped and cracked pillars that formed the façade of a large hall beyond them.

"It's a bit large for a temple," Jet replied. "Especially when you consider that massive field we just walked up from."

"Well, those stairs were certainly a test of faith," Varathis said, trying to catch his breath.

"Are you feeling tired, Princess?" Jet asked mockingly.

"Guys," Rezaaran chided, "can we focus on why we are here?"

"Luminara, do the scanners show any nearby hostiles?" Ashana asked the Guardian, who had requested to remain on the ship to continue her recovery.

After a lengthy pause, she replied, "It appears you are alone. I apologize, but operating this vessel is difficult."

"Don't worry," Ashana said, "I've programmed Gunner with emergency protocols in case of any trouble."

"This architecture seems more fitting for a place of education," Quirt commented, thinking that it held similarities to the Thyrillian academies. "Although it was built along the slopes of this great mountain, I imagine it must once have been rather scenic. The signal is coming from behind this hall."

The band of travelers wandered to the right of the grand hall and cautiously walked through a dusty passageway strewn with overturned tables and stools toward a double glass door that had remained intact. Several metal letters littered the floor, covered by years of sand blown into the passage by the howling winds. Quirt tried the door's handle and crossed the threshold, quickly closing the door behind Ikso, who entered last.

"The air in here is breathable," he informed the others after reading the report on his interface.

"Well, it seems you were correct," Ikso said to Quirt as she took in the full extent of the massive library. All around them, numerous shelves were stocked with a vast array of books and several large screens that remained offline. Several chairs and shelves lay toppled onto the blue-carpeted floors.

"Stay alert," Ashana warned. "I don't think we are alone here."

"Spread out, and report anything you find," Rezaaran ordered.

The group dispersed across the library floor, carefully inspecting every shelf to locate the source of the distress signal.

Ikso bumped into a large black-metal box beside an oaken desk and spun around with a start. A large circle in the center of the library floor glowed alive with a blue haze, and a hologram of a curly-haired man appeared. A strange digital warbling escaped his mouth, but Ikso could not understand what he said.

The rest of the team arrived a few minutes later and curiously examined the hologram.

"Does anyone understand what he is saying?" Ikso asked.

"No idea," Jet admitted gruffly. He doubted this hologram had sent the transmission. How could it possibly know about "The Travelers Plea"?

Quirt walked over to the desk Ikso had passed and connected a cable from his interface to the metal box. The hologram flickered for a few moments and then looked at them genially.

"Wamkelekile," he said with a smile, folding his arms.

"I don't recognize this language," Jet murmured to himself.

"I would not expect you to," the hologram replied. "It means welcome in isiXhosa, the vernacular of this province."

"Wait...you can speak Galtic!" Ikso yelped.

"What is Galtic?" the hologram asked.

"It is the galactically accepted language for trade and interstellar communication," Quirt said with fascination in his eyes as he approached the hologram.

"Ah, a man such as yourself must no doubt be a scholar," the hologram proclaimed.

"You have no idea," Jet mumbled.

"Well, on this planet, we call the language English," he explained. "You are on the planet Earth, on the continent of Africa, in the country South Africa, in the city of Cape Town. According to our calendars, it is the year 2029, and the time is one thirty-four in the afternoon."

"Who are you?" Ashana asked.

"My name is ADAM," he said proudly. "It is an acronym that stands for Automated Digital Assimilated Media. I am the artificial-intelligence assistant for the library. Although I know that none of you are of this planet, you all look remarkably humanlike. Except you, of course."

"Yeah, I know," Jet grumbled. "I'm probably the first alien you've ever seen, right?"

"Hardly," ADAM said. "This planet was once filled with sentient life-forms. However, war and conflict plagued their history. Following a terrible war involving every nation of the planet, we received our first alien contact, and it was not friendly. An invasion force ravaged Earth. Legions of reptilian creatures razed the cities and slaughtered the people. The humans' ideological differences had divided them. They could not unite and act against their common enemy. The invaders swiftly crushed all resistance, and those that survived were enslaved."

ADAM took a moment to reflect on the stream of clips playing through his computer systems, showing the days during the invasion.

"After the war, I lay in a dormant state, but I was activated recently by another group of three aliens."

"These aliens," Rezaaran said, "where are they?"

"You can find them on the next level," ADAM replied. "Those stairs will lead you to them."

"I'm going to download ADAM to my interface," Quirt said to Rezaaran.

"Meet us when you're done," Rezaaran replied with a nod.

The group cautiously climbed the stairs led by Ashana, her bow drawn at the ready. Jet brought up the rear. Everyone remained sharply alert for any sign of the people who may have contacted them.

"Hey, what's that over there?" whispered Ikso.

They approached a small fusion heater perched atop a pile of books. However, their sweep found them entirely alone.

"What is your business here?" a deep voice suddenly boomed from behind them.

The soldiers spun around and found a towering warrior covered in heavy gold-and-black armor with a large war hammer in his right hand. His violet skin creased at the forehead, and his amethyst eyes narrowed.

As he raised his left hand to the group, the small book chained around his waist snapped open. A runic symbol on the page came to life with a purple glow and lifted off the aged paper to float before his hand.

"I will not ask again," he bellowed. His grasp tightened around the shaft of the hammer. "Identify yourselves!"

"Look, buddy," Jet said calmly, stepping forward to placate the guard. "We aren't here to harm you."

The rune flared from the warrior's hand and instantly locked the group of intruders in place.

"I can't move my body," Jet grunted with great effort to Rezaaran.

"Me neither," Rezaaran replied.

"Brother, what are you doing?" shouted another warrior. Although more slight in build than his burly sibling, the second warrior was no less intimidating. His heavy armor, dual morning stars, and maniacal energy deferred any notion that he would be easier to overwhelm.

"The job *you* should be doing," his brother growled.

"Always so serious," remarked the slimmer warrior with a sigh. "Well, it seems you have them incapacitated for now. What should we do with them?"

"Release them immediately," called a third voice.

The two warriors spun around and immediately knelt. A slim alien draped in tattered brown garments sauntered between them.

His skin was a deep royal blue, yet his face seemed far kinder than those of the warriors, his simple dress a stark contrast to their heavy black-and-gold armor. Besides the garb that covered his body, he wore brown leather boots and an equally bland headscarf.

"Blayloch, please...could you release them?" he said to the bulkier warrior. "How can we expect aid when we are reluctant to trust the people who come to help us?"

"With due respect, Tetros," Blayloch replied, "how do we know they do not come to harm you? Why do they bear weapons?"

"You carry a weapon, yet you mean me no harm," the simply dressed man replied.

Blayloch nodded and released his stasis spell. The warriors stumbled slightly before they regained their footing.

"I apologize that this is your first impression of us," the man said with sincerity. "However, we did not find ourselves here under the best of circumstances, and it has heightened my guards' apprehension."

"It is understandable," Rezaaran said. He then bowed before the man who seemed to lead the trio. "I am Captain Rezaaran Valhara, and this is Commander Ashana Binarjiin of IRIS. My friends here are from the Space Rangers: Jet Bal Sara and Prince Varathis Kalamdor, who is also the crown prince of Zenor. Finally, this is Ikso Poe of the Order of Nish Ira from Halsyn. We have another friend who is downstairs handling the library's computer system, Dr. Quirt Zefrityn, who is also a part of IRIS."

The slimmer warrior bristled slightly at the mention of Varathis being the Prince of Zenor but remained silent. However, Rezaaran noticed the uneasiness that overcame his stoic brother and their leader.

"So...you three are Zenorians, am I correct?" the leader asked, eyeing the soldiers in question.

"That is correct," Varathis proclaimed proudly.

"And you are the last heir to the Zenorian throne?"

"I am indeed," he shouted and puffed his chest, glad that someone had finally recognized the magnitude of his royal title.

"Then it would seem we owe the crown a great debt of gratitude," he replied with a respectful bow to Varathis. Blayloch and his brother followed suit, albeit reluctantly.

"Well, I doubt there is much a pauper with two armed guards could offer to settle such a debt," Varathis replied with a sneer.

Jet slugged him in the ribs. "That was not necessary!" he snarled.

Blayloch's face pulsed with rage, and he rose to his feet, hammer at the ready. "How dare you?" he roared at Varathis. "This is Tetros Reikon, third of his name and last leader of the Dorassi! How dare you insult him in my presence?"

"The Dorassi!" Varathis seethed. His anger numbed the pain of Jet's strike. He charged forward with his swords drawn, but Rezaaran and Jet restrained him. Similarly, Reikon placated his warriors with a hand over their breastplates and sternly reprimanded them.

"I am Reikon the Third," he said. "We are Dorassi, that is true. These are Blayloch and Tarsik Aurelius, my Enchiridion knights. I know our people have a long history of animosity, but it is built on a lie and manipulation by one of your own."

"Liar!" Varathis spat. "Your people raided our world and slaughtered countless Zenorians! You deserve neither help nor mercy!"

Kashari, is Varathis correct about this? Rezaaran asked his mentor.

As much as it pains me to admit, she replied, *he is correct. During the Great Mage War, when I led the Order, an army of Dorassi led by a man named Lord Aeron invaded Zenor. However, those warriors were not of the living world and unlike these three before you.*

Tarsik drew his morning stars and swiveled them about his wrist. He looked eager to smash them into Varathis's head for disrespecting his leader. However, Reikon passed him a solemn look, and the rambunctious warrior reluctantly returned the weapons to the holsters on his back.

"Lord Aeron came to our world from Zenor," Reikon explained calmly to Rezaaran. "He razed several of our smaller towns with dark fire and resurrected the fallen souls before our eyes. He subjugated our planet and used our fallen people to further his cause across his home world. The entire war between our people and yours was because of his evil intentions. The Dorassi mean no harm to the Zenorians."

"Everything he says is true, Rezaaran," Luminara said over the communication channel. "Thaedis chose Aeron to test if Obsidian magic could work through a mortal in the Maelinthian. He in turn used the Dorassi to raid Zenor, sparking a war that lasted generations—until the Dorassi lost their home world through a cruel strike by an overzealous General Braldon. Since then, they have been a nomadic people."

"Your armies used the portal Aeron created to decimate our civilization," Reikon explained. "Alas, Zenor showed us no compassion after the wise Elder Mage Kashari Alda-Fyre passed."

Ashana looked at Rezaaran from the corner of her eye.

"What do you mean?" the War Mage asked, discomfort rising in his throat.

"Elder Mage Kashari Alda-Fyre gave her word to our leader at the time," Reikon explained, "that the Zenorians understood the armies that attacked your world through the portal were corrupted souls of fallen Dorassi. She promised to keep the portal open so that Zenor could help us rebuild our civilization after all that Aeron had wrought upon us."

I remember this, Kashari said. *I urged King Regarius that we could not stand idly by when others needed our assistance after what a Zenorian had done to them. We needed to show them that we were better than Aeron. Together we brokered peace between our worlds. Shortly after that, I vowed my service to Lord Salvidawn and was bound to Harkenathor.*

"What happened to the truce?" Ashana asked.

"Several months after the Elder Mage gave us her word, a contingent of Zenorian soldiers passed through the portal and ravaged our last cities. They did not kill all of us, though. They spared some of our ancestors to spread the word not to trifle with Zenor. The soldiers marched us onto transport vessels and ensured that we left our planet before they disappeared through the portal."

General Braldon was always a stoic man, but he was not callous.

Perhaps the Obsidian influence corrupted him to set Thaedis's plan in motion. With the Dorassi scattered, it would be one less magical adversary to contest.

It does seem to be so, Kashari said sadly and regressed to her own thoughts about the war.

"How did you come to be on this planet?" Ikso asked Reikon.

"The Aurelius family has been friends with mine for generations. Despite being adrift amid the stars, some of our people remained together in small bands. Our culture, armor, magic, and heritage passed through the generations in these small communities. The three of us were on a voyage for an unoccupied planet to establish a colony where all our people could come to call home."

"Wait…the three of you are on a discovery mission?" Ashana asked in astonishment. "Surely you need more men?"

"Our culture dictates," Blayloch explained, "that the Tetros must lead his people to a new kingdom if he is to be worthy of his title."

"Even then," Jet said, releasing Varathis from his grasp, "surely if you are the leader, the others would rally behind you on a journey to a new planet."

Blayloch bowed his head to avoid eye contact with them.

"The truth is," Tarsik confessed uncomfortably, "not everyone believes that Tetros Reikon is truly the Tetros of our era."

"What do you mean they don't recognize you?" Varathis asked with narrowed eyes. "It is your birthright to be a ruler like your ancestors."

"The title of Tetros," Reikon explained, "does not pass from one generation to the next. It is bestowed by the grace of our ancestors, who choose one to lead the people in every era."

"Great!" Varathis exclaimed with exasperation. "So we are helping the sworn enemy of our people and the dregs of their civilization. A delusional peasant with his two equally deranged cronies."

Jet wrestled Varathis away from the Dorassi, certain that if he did not, Blayloch and Tarsik would break every bone in the prince's body.

Reikon's face was solemn. He knew that generations of hate existed between their people, but he had hoped in his hour of need to be met by a leader with vision.

“Do not pay him any attention,” Ashana said soothingly to the humiliated Dorassi travelers.

“None of us do,” Ikso snorted with a slight giggle.

“You still haven’t told us how you ended up here, though.”

“Ah yes. Of course, Captain Valhara,” Reikon replied, pleased that this entire group did not resent them as much as Varathis did. “During our approach to a planet, bandits ambushed us and attempted to board our ship. We escaped into a Torus tunnel, but the significant engine damage to our craft caused us to crash onto this planet. The remains of our ship are farther along the road to the south of this building. We sent out an encrypted distress signal and hoped it would reach a Dorassi ship. Unfortunately, to get the strength needed for such a long-range signal, we used our auxiliary power reserves and are now trapped here.”

“Well, we’re here to help you out,” Rezaaran replied cheerfully.

“What?” Varathis barked. “We will do *no such thing*! I forbid it!”

Reikon looked crestfallen but resigned himself that his fate would be to wait upon this barren planet until death took him.

“For what reason should we not help them?” Rezaaran asked calmly.

“They are enemies to your crown!” Varathis spat.

“Perhaps,” he replied, “but they are not enemies to us. The Dorassi invaded our world nearly three thousand years ago. None of us who live today experienced that war, and we are not affected by its impact. You heard what happened to their people. If anything, we deserve their hatred for what Zenorians have done to them. Thousands of years of hatred can be undone by moments of kindness. Today—this right here—is our moment to show kindness and to begin to atone for the terrible things we did to a people who never deserved what became of them.”

Reikon’s eyes glistened at Rezaaran’s words. This Zenorian dared oppose his monarch’s order for their cause. Perhaps there was hope for his people. Perhaps there was hope for peace.

“We’re with Rez on this,” Jet said, standing beside his friend with Ashana and Ikso. “This war is bigger than any race, and everyone needs to be saved against what is to come.”

"That's settled, then," Rezaaran said, ignoring the disgruntled mumbles of Varathis. "Ashana, please transmit a message to Orin requesting a rescue convoy to retrieve our new friends and assist them with their repairs."

Reikon clasped Rezaaran's hands between his and beamed at the young War Mage. "My people owe a great debt of gratitude to you, Captain Valhara, for showing my friends and me mercy. I hope you understand that we bear no grudge against the Zenorians, for we know what befell us was due to the actions of people acting alone."

At that moment, a powerful tremor shook the library and after a few moments subsided. The group looked around warily.

"Those tremors are starting to occur more often," Blayloch remarked.

Rezaaran's head turned sharply to the corner of the library.

"What is it, Rez?" Ashana asked.

"I sense an Archlord here," he replied softly. "We need to get the three of you to our ship to keep you safe."

"With no disrespect, Captain," Tarsik said with a grin, drawing his dual morning stars once more, "we won't be running!"

"Please, do us the favor," Reikon said, "of allowing us to fight for our honor once more."

"I know those two will be all right," Jet said, indicating the Dorassi brothers with a nod. "What about you? Do you have any weapons?"

Reikon drew a long metal staff from behind his back and locked a fiercely determined gaze at their new allies.

Jet whistled. "Well…OK then."

"Quirt, where are you?" Rezaaran asked over their communicator.

"I had just completed the download of ADAM onto my interface when I felt the tremors. What is going on? Is everyone all right?"

"Everyone here is fine. We've made contact with the Dorassi. I believe these tremors are the result of an Archlord on this planet. Get back to safety on the ship."

"Will do," Quirt replied. He immediately headed to the hall, readying the teleporter via his interface.

Meanwhile, the other warriors used a side escape to leave the library, following Rezaaran's lead to where he sensed the Archlord.

Rezaaran and the others arrived at a monument along the slopes of the hill, where the War Mage's animusense placed the Archlord. A green statue of a rider mounted upon a beast, his gaze locked on the desolate horizon, guarded the foot of a staircase, along with eight green feline creatures. At the top of the gray and weathered stairs stood a series of chipped columns identical to those of the hall behind them.

"What is this place?" Jet asked, running his hand over the cold granite pedestal beneath the rider statue.

"According to ADAM," Quirt informed them, "this was a monument named Rhodes Memorial. The locals built it to commemorate a colonizer of this country, but in time it became a contested historic landmark. According to the feedback from Rezaaran's nanobots, this is where the tremors are originating."

"That's really weird," Jet murmured.

"What is?" Rezaaran asked.

"I can feel a presence here," he explained. "Not something I can see, but I just know that someone else is here."

"That would be the nanites we injected ourselves with," Quirt said.

"Luminara, do you have any suspicions about whom we may face?"

"Based on what you have told me, Rezaaran," she replied, "I believe you will encounter the Edarian possessing Gebtah. He was never one for conflict but was adept at craftsmanship and stealth."

Another tremor rocked the ground amid a squall of dust, disrupting their communication channel.

"Luminara?" Rezaaran called, reaching for his earpiece. "Quirt? Hello? Can you hear me?"

"Maybe the sandstorm is interfering with the transmission?" Reikon suggested.

"This no ordinary sandstorm," Rezaaran said.

The dusty squall circled a defaced bust at the top of the staircase, and its glowing red eyes fixed their attention on the intruders. Then, quite unexpectedly, the green statue yawned.

"Who dares disturb my rest?" the statue demanded of the group.

"I'm here to end your claim to this world!" Rezaaran yelled.

A howling gust swept across the platform upon which the warriors stood and encompassed them in a blinding haze of sand. The debris drew together and, at the base of the rider's pedestal, formed a bald humanoid wearing a simple robe. His glowing red eyes were riveted on Rezaaran and his allies.

"Yet I did not lay claim to this world," he said. "I was simply tasked to secure the world for the Dominion, for Thaedis. Not that it needed securing. This world was on the verge of collapse after its last war. The people were too outmatched to contest our forces. I have lain dormant since then."

There was an unusual distance and depth to this Archlord that Rezaaran had never encountered before. He felt the conflict within him.

"This vessel I control," the Archlord explained, "was once called Gebtah, the Guardian of Sands. My name is Avisi. I was—am an Edarian. Alas, our form does not change despite how we wish it could."

"You're an Edarian?" Jet snarled, recalling his encounter with Narak and his followers in the maze. "Give us a reason not to slay you right here and now!"

The Archlord's smoldering eyes seared into the Erebonian. "You have encountered my kind before, I can tell. I recognize that rage and fear in your heart. All too often, I was the cause of it myself. However, you, Jet Bal Sara, more than the others, should appreciate what it means to want to be different from the rest of your kind."

Jet looked at Avisi apprehensively.

"I know who you are because Edarians see the soul of all creatures," he said, answering Jet's unasked question. "We hunger for souls. My reason for avoiding conflict with you is that I wish to explain my story to you."

"What?" Ashana asked. They had never yet met an Archlord who did not wish harm upon them.

Despite my reservations about him, I do believe he truly means no harm upon you. For now, in any case.

Rezaaran agreed with Kashari's assessment, for he could feel that this Archlord was very different from the others. No rage or hatred brewed in his heart. Instead, he seemed fatigued.

"Edarians were created by Nethriziin," Avisi explained, "to wage his war against the progenitors of the Obsidious. We were to relish the kill—created with a bloodlust for any soul with Valinthicite. My brothers and sisters seemed to have no problem with this. If they did, they never made it known. I felt that fire in me from the moment the Soulforge birthed me."

The Archlord lost himself to his thoughts and reflections. Streams of sand flowed around him and formed a small sculpture of his tale.

"We wreaked havoc upon the Obsidian people, slaying anyone who resisted our superior might. I remember that first kill. It should have made me feel complete. I should have been hungrier for more blood. Instead, all I felt was a void. My first victim was a child. I regret nothing. Why should I? After all, I did as my lord commanded. Yet each life I took in that conquest of the Obsidious further carved the walls of that void."

Blayloch's jaw tightened. Why were they allowing this confessed child murderer to speak? However, since Reikon made no move to attack, he would contain his outrage for now.

"I suspect my brothers knew I was flawed," Avisi said softly. "They brought me before Nethriziin, who thought me a failure of his creation, an indictment to his supreme power. He ordered Hidar to reforge my soul. Yet remnants of that disobedience resurfaced in my next incarnation. Despite Hidar's smelting the darker qualities from my imperfect soul, I retained memories of questioning the need to have blind faith in Nethriziin's belligerent plans. However, I kept my concerns to myself behind a better-crafted mask. This time, I was birthed to be the Edarian that would control a Guardian."

He chuckled lightly to himself. "What a coincidence, then, that one such as I should be fated to share the vessel of Gebtah, the most pacifist Guardian! It was Thaedis's great idea that we be bound to the darkness in the Guardian's hearts, their fundamental weaknesses. Gebtah had feared that his beliefs painted him a coward among his peers. However, what Thaedis did not know was that to share a vessel with another soul means a conflict. An eternal struggle wages within each of us who possessed a Guardian. Their souls imprint upon us as much as ours did upon them."

Avisi watched as a stream of sand flowed from his hand onto his foot and was reabsorbed as part of his body. "Every world I traveled to in fulfilling Thaedis's quest and commands gave me a greater glimpse of the universe he and Nethriziin seek to build. Every time I manifest upon a world, I draw on its soil, and from that, I learn the planet's history. There is no world within Anmor that has been without conflict. Yet this planet..."

He paused for a moment and considered the sandstorm raging across the abandoned, dilapidated city. "By all accounts, these people may have been primitive, yet they could not stop killing one another. Despite the number of terrible wars fought, they just never learned. When I arrived on this world, they were so fractured that I barely needed to do anything more than summon the occasional sandstorm to appease Thaedis. Then they left me here, and for the first time...I have known peace."

His smoldering eyes turned to the Dorassi. "Then along you came and issued that distress call. It was clever of you, Tetros Reikon, to encrypt the message; however, I knew that someone would arrive in response to your plea. To my surprise, it was you lot. The group Thaedis fears most."

"What do you mean he fears us?" Jet asked with narrowed eyes.

"He has become aware of a group of mortals with far greater echoes than any other in the Maelinthian. When he arrived on this planet, he found another before you could. He took her into his ranks and worked to break her will to his own means."

"Diothur," Ashana whispered, remembering the cowled woman she had encountered on Halsyn.

"Indeed," Avisi replied with a slow nod. "Although on this planet she was known as Yustina Ivanova. She served as a soldier to the nation called Russia and was part of a few factions that sought to oppose the Dominion invasion. However, their attempts were doomed to fail."

"Why are you telling us all this?" Rezaaran asked suspiciously.

"I am tired, Rezaaran," he replied. "I am tired of the war, the killing, and the senselessness of it all. I do not believe in Thaedis's or Nethriziin's lofty crusades. However, just like this planet, I too am doomed. You were the first to decode the message, but you certainly will not be the only ones. In time, Dominion forces will come to this planet. If I do not present you before Thaedis's Harbingers, then he will personally scorch me from existence."

"What do you mean by that?" Ikso asked.

"It means, Ikso Poe," he said with a solemn face, "that my soul will pass into oblivion. Thaedis holds the power to burn the souls of any who have high Torementhicite concentrations." Avisi closed his eyes and abated the sandstorm. "On the other hand, if I allow myself to be slain at your hands, I shall come before Hidar's gaze, and he will know exactly what transpired. My brother will surrender me to the will of our lord, who would torment me for eons beyond recollection. Neither of these are fates I would wish upon my greatest enemy. That is why I am asking…can you help me?"

"What?" asked Ashana.

"You came to this planet to answer a distress call. Can you answer another and help me find a means to escape these confines?"

The group members looked at one another, unsure how to proceed. Was this a genuine plea for help? Or was this an elaborate ruse to ensnare them for Thaedis?

Varathis drew his pistol and fired a bolt through Avisi's head. "On a day I find myself beside my sworn enemies," he growled at the slow-falling body, "I have been forced to surround myself by liars. Not anymore. There's your solution!"

To his surprise, Avisi's body disintegrated into sand, dispersing into a large cloud that flowed along the passing winds. The dust touched every statue and scattered across the memorial monument.

A few moments later, the statues rumbled to life. The lions leaped from their resting spots and prowled toward the intruders.

Meanwhile, the rider rallied his steed, and the eyes of both flared red. In the distance sounded the thunder of a stampede, and a legion of stone warriors stormed across the mountain toward their position. Rocks flew into the air around them and formed over a hundred golems.

Avisi formed again, taking his place at the head of the army he had summoned for himself. "I had hoped to avoid conflict," he said sadly. "However, it seems you would rather fight than find peace, and I will not go quietly into a suffering worse than death. So…conflict is the inevitable outcome."

Quirt looked up at the beeping computers in his workshop. The folder containing ADAM was cleared of any malicious software and had been deemed safe for connecting to the IRIS network.

"Welcome to IRIS," he chirped with a smile and activated ADAM once again.

The blue face of the hologram he had met in the library now appeared in a window on the terminal. Quirt downloaded him directly to his interface and plugged the various programs into the artificial intelligence.

"There is so much knowledge here," ADAM exclaimed with scarcely contained excitement. "These archives explain so much about everything. It is a rush to gain hold of this!"

"Have you read through the entire archive already?" Quirt asked, almost falling out of his chair.

"Ah yes, my friend. My primary function was the processing of data. Despite the complexity and volume, it is still essentially data. It will take me time to understand what is contained in the archives, but for now I can instantly access any file upon request."

"The difference between knowing and understanding," Quirt mused to himself, paraphrasing his father's favorite piece of wisdom.

"Well, this is very interesting," ADAM said to himself.

"Hey!" Quirt yelped. Switching to a whisper, he added, "I am not sure browsing through the military files of IRIS is the best idea—you were only just uploaded to its system!"

"I believe it is permissible. That is what Commander Albeinius Grievior has informed me."

"Well, that changes things, then," Quirt replied with a relieved sigh.

"I am intrigued by this project of yours," ADAM murmured as he swiftly browsed through the files stored on Quirt's workshop computer.

"How did you get access to that?"

"Quirt, I need some assistance," Luminara said, walking into the workshop and startling the scientist.

"What can I do?"

"I seem to have lost contact with Rezaaran and the others."

The Thyrillian scientist checked his computer and accessed the feedback from his friends' interfaces. "According to the telemetry from their interfaces, a particulate interference is causing a disturbance to the transmission. Most likely a sandstorm." Quirt turned in his chair and looked at Luminara with a sliver of apprehension. "Yet this situation perplexes me. I can feel the sand against my skin. I feel their confusion listening to the Archlord. And—no!"

"What is it?" Luminara asked.

"That is bizarre," ADAM murmured. "I still have access to the network I originated from on Earth. According to this, there was an unauthorized access to an exhibition at the waterfront."

"What exhibition?" Luminara asked.

"There was a display of the Terra-Cotta Army. It's a historic collection of clay sculptures crafted as armed soldiers."

"I can see them," Quirt whispered. "They are outnumbered!"

Luminara crouched beside him and gently held his hand. "You are all connected by the nanites you shared," she explained soothingly.

"They cannot fight off so many, Luminara," he said, trembling.

"They will not be fighting alone," she said as she rose to her feet.

"What can I do there?" he asked with an ashen face.

"Sticks in a bundle are unbreakable," ADAM said sagely.

Quirt nodded slowly. The others had repeatedly sacrificed and risked much for him. Now it was his turn. He would not shy away and cower in safety. What was the point of his training if he was always going to stay out of the fights? The Sentinels were more than a team. They were his family.

The Thyrillian walked to a workbench covered with a white sheet.

"There is no shame in wanting to take action," ADAM said softly. "You can walk this path."

Quirt pulled aside the sheet, and a smile edged across Luminara's face.

A leaping stone golem shattered beneath Blayloch's maul. The heavily armored knight snarled and plowed his arm into the face of another creature and then swung it into the path of Tarsik's spinning morning stars.

The older brother turned sharply and to his dismay saw Tetros Reikon leaping between the golems. "Tarsik!" he bellowed. "We need to protect him!"

His younger brother looked around and clapped a hand to his face. "Well, he doesn't make it easy," he grumbled.

The brothers summoned a green rune from their tomes and conjured a swirling green electric shield around themselves. Rallying to the side of their leader, they buffered him against the endless stone golems while Reikon's iron staff swatted aside their enemies.

Meanwhile, the three Sentinels, Varathis, and Ikso found their rhythm quickly in the heat of the battle. Ashana acrobatically wove her way between stone golems and clay soldiers alike, loosing an explosive arrow on any stray targets. Rezaaran telekinetically smashed any of Avisi's warriors who drew too near to the archer. In turn, Jet covered the War Mage and alternated between his blast cannon and the newly improved gauntlet. Now in the midst of a fight, though, Jet wished he had taken Quirt up on the offer to walk through the gauntlet's function. Besides using the augmented punching power to crush his opponents, he accidentally discovered that the gauntlet had a built-in deflector shield and a high-powered laser. However, this was definitely not the environment to discover its full functionality.

Jet shoulder-barged a golem that was storming toward Rezaaran and blasted a clay soldier to pieces. Then he looked for Varathis. Unsurprisingly, he was absorbed in his own personal crusade. The Zenorian prince loudly counted out the targets he felled with his pistol but paid no attention to Ikso, who fervently covered him. Her empowered staves swished gracefully through the air as she summoned stronger wind currents around her to knock back her foes.

Suddenly, beyond her field of vision, one of the animated lions leaped at her, its claws and teeth bared. Ikso heard the roar and called on the Onsei and her goddess's grace to her quarterstaves. Her eyes fixed on her adversary without fear.

A sharp whistling cut the air. A free-falling object slammed into the airborne lion and pummeled it to the ground in a thick cloud of sand. Squinting, Ikso locked her staves together. Rapidly spinning her staff in a figure eight, she summoned a gust of wind to clear the sand clouds.

Crouched within the ruptured metal carcass of the lion, its fist lodged in the stone landing, was a dark-gray armored suit with a red visor. The new warrior rose to his feet and looked toward Ikso. The young Halsynian spun her staff to the side and readied herself to defend against this new threat. However, to her surprise, the new warrior simply bowed and extended a hand to his side, indicating where Luminara had teleported.

Rezaaran allowed himself a smile, pleased that Quirt and Luminara had joined them.

The Thyrillian scientist fixed his sights on the large contingent of the Terra-Cotta Army. He bolted at supersonic speed through them, shattering those he struck while his sonic boom knocked aside those beyond his damaging momentum. Unable to halt his destructive sprint, Quirt smashed through a stone wall and skidded to a dusty stop. Beyond his position, he saw an army of every statue from the city and more of Avisi's stone constructs stampeding toward them.

Luminara held an arm out toward the incoming army, and a pale-green glow surrounded her. As the glow dispersed into the air, thousands of ethereal beasts rose from the ground to engage the incoming army of stone golems and statues.

"What are those?" Ikso asked, watching Luminara's army of ghostly beasts fight back the Archlord's forces.

"They are the resurrected souls of fallen creatures," Tarsik replied. "But that's impossible. Unless...no!"

"What is it, brother?"

"Their friend is a Guardian!" he said, gasping.

Ikso was so fixated on watching Luminara command the legion of spirit animals that she did not notice the approaching shadow overhead.

Propelled by the rocket thrusters in his suit, Quirt leaped at the incoming stone dragon. His added momentum was just enough to knock the dragon's grasp away from Ikso, and it seized a golem instead. The Thyrillian wrapped an arm around the leg of the dragon as its stone wings carried them higher. With his free hand, he quickly typed a series of commands into his interface and pulled the stones apart, dismantling the construct with his hands. He scaled the beast's limb, tore his way through its chest, and ripped off one of the wings. Taking aim upon a group of golems approaching the position the other Sentinels held around Luminara, the Thyrillian powered his rockets to their maximum thrust with the idea of thinning the enemies. But suddenly, his thrusters spluttered and died out, leaving him in free fall.

Rezaaran telekinetically caught the rock and flung it into the approaching golems while Jet leaped off the shoulder of a golem to catch Quirt in midair. The Erebonian set his friend upon the ground and placed a hand on his shoulder.

"Are you all right?"

Quirt simply nodded. The sandstorm interference prevented him from speaking to Jet via his communicator. He lifted his hands to his face, wondering why the suit had malfunctioned, and electricity sparked from the fingertips. The Thyrillian tapped on his interface, but it too did not respond.

"Well, if your suit is not working," Jet said grimly, raising his blaster cannon in preparation for the approaching enemies, "then you'll just have to do what we practiced. Remember—be spontaneous."

Quirt nodded once more and curled his fists. Having Jet beside him helped quell his fear; although the Erebonian did not say it, Quirt knew he had someone to back him in this fight.

The pair charged forward, grappling with the stone golems and showing no fear. Jet's gauntlet smashed through the stone exteriors while his cannon blasted apart those that escaped Quirt's reach. He was proud to see the scientist resist his fear and fight valiantly beside him. Together they bolstered Ikso and the Dorassi knights to protect Reikon and Luminara.

The Zenorian warriors drew closer to their allies. Despite their brave defense, they were not making ground against Avisi's army. The enemies' ranks seemed endless.

The only path to end this conflict is at its source.

Rezaaran knew his mentor was right. He took a moment to compose himself before telepathically issuing the plan to the team. Each of them nodded in acknowledgment.

Ikso spun her staff overhead to summon the Onsei to her grasp and then split the weapon in half, infusing herself with the power. Racing around the monument with an alacrity that would make Xephyrus proud, her dual staves spun vigorously and generated a wall of wind that contained Avisi's dispersed form. Meanwhile, Ashana covered the Halsynian acolyte from harm while Luminara's army of spirit animals encircled the warriors to fend off Avisi's constructs.

Seeing the young girl tiring, Tarsik summoned a rune from his tome and, using a variant of the stasis spell, bound Avisi to his solid form. Ikso stumbled to an abrupt stop and gasped for breath. Quirt and Reikon rushed forward and brought her into the protection of the group under the fierce gaze of Luminara's ethereal conjurations.

"Fire everything!" Rezaaran bellowed.

Blayloch unleashed a powerful surge of lightning from a summoned rune to augment the barrage of electricity that flowed from Rezaaran's hands toward Avisi. Ashana emptied the cartridges of her crossbows and added to the storm over the Archlord, who did little to resist the onslaught. Instead, he spread his arms wide, welcoming his end as the high-voltage assault transformed his body to glass.

The warriors ceased their attack at Rezaaran's command. The War Mage thought he saw the faintest flicker of a smile cross Avisi's face before the glass shattered and the stream of Valinthicite flew forward to infuse into him. All around them, the magic disappeared from the constructs, and they returned to their lifeless forms.

"It's over," Ikso wheezed, clutching the stitch in her side.

"Yes, it is," Rezaaran replied with a serene smile. He sheathed Harkenathor and turned to find Reikon standing near him with an outstretched arm.

"Thank you for allowing us to regain our honor," the Tetros said proudly. "I will ensure the Dorassi remember what you did today."

Varathis sullenly holstered his pistols and turned away from them, unable to make eye contact with the Dorassi leader. Yet despite his sulking, he thought it best to remain silent.

"Well, we still have to get you back to safety," Ashana replied with a grin, holstering her crossbows.

"If I may, Commander Eldeerim," Blayloch said sternly but with a deepening mulberry hue to his cheeks. "Could we do that *after* we eat?"

"Now that's a plan I'm definitely behind!" Jet shouted gleefully. "Put it there, big man!"

Blayloch tentatively hit a curled hand against the Erebonian's outstretched fist. The group laughed at the sight of Jet's exuberant nature and growling belly unsettling the stoic knight.

CHAPTER TWELVE

ELUSIVE

The *Liberator* docked on the grassy plains of an uninhabited moon. According to ADAM, scientists on Earth had named the star Ran, and AEgir was assigned to the enormous red gas giant around which their chosen moon orbited. When he learned that the IRIS archive had no recorded name for the system, he whooped with delight and updated the entry. The AI system fondly observed his addition to the database, which appeared on all interfaces instantaneously. The essence of life truly was a spirit of adventure, and until meeting these travelers, he had been unaware of how direly he craved it.

Rezaaran disembarked with his friends and their new Dorassi allies. Together they strode across the dark-blue plains of grass beneath an orange midday sun.

"Why exactly are we here?" Blayloch asked, sweeping his gaze across the empty alien grassland.

"General Libranth sent us these coordinates," Ashana replied. "He should be here any—"

Suddenly Orin, Atomauran, and Krayzar appeared before them.

"Moment now," Ashana said, completing her sentence.

"That is quite spectacular," Reikon exclaimed with delight. "An instantaneous teleportation device. How marvelous!"

Varathis rolled his eyes, but Rezaaran was grateful he did not voice the hateful thoughts upon his mind.

"General Libranth," Rezaaran said in a crisp, formal tone. "Allow me to introduce to you Tetros Reikon the Third, last Tetros of the Dorassi people, and his Enchiridion knights, Blayloch and Tarsik Auerelius."

Orin nodded slowly. He sensed there was more of this story to tell. Krayzar and his brother exchanged a solemn look. For a fleeting moment, Blayloch and Tarsik thought these two might show the Dorassi the same bigoted reception as their prince had. However, to their utter surprise, the Zenorian brothers flashed them a cordial grin and quietly awaited their general's orders.

"Thank you for this audience, General Libranth," Reikon said and showed great respect with a bow to the blinded IRIS leader, which his knights mirrored. "Our ship sustained severe damage following a battle with bandits, and we crashed onto Earth. Your soldiers responded swiftly to our distress call. I fear were it not for their presence, we might have perished."

"Well, there is more to tell than that," Ashana said, chuckling. "The Dorassi were instrumental in helping us defeat the Archlord. We could not have won that battle without their assistance."

"You do us a great honor, Commander Binarjiin," Blayloch bellowed and rested a heavy hand upon her shoulder.

"I know there is a deeply held distrust between our races," Rezaaran continued. "However, the reasons we begrudge them are the result of Thaedis Silvermire's actions. Due to his cruelty, our galaxy now stands poised upon the edge of collapse once more. Whatever our differences may have been, we have to stand together against Thaedis."

"Captain Valhara speaks with great wisdom," Reikon said. "It would be the honor of the Dorassi to serve alongside IRIS and stand for a path of justice. We seek to redeem ourselves and rekindle the friendship that once existed between our worlds."

"Captain Valhara and Commander Binarjiin are among my most trusted soldiers," Orin said proudly. "I agree with their assessments, and we would be honored to rebuild our alliance with the Dorassi. However, I believe that before we begin such discussions, it would be best to help you and your men with some medical care and rest."

"You have my deepest gratitude for your kindness, General Libranth," Reikon replied, offering a sincere smile and a bow.

Atomauran prepared the teleportation sequence on his interface.

"Awesome spikes, my man," Krayzar yelled out at Jet moments before he disappeared through the teleporter.

"Well...OK, then," muttered a bewildered Jet. "Anyone else hungry?"

"You just ate a whole meal with Blayloch," Ikso replied in exasperation. "How can you *still* be hungry?"

"There's never a time when it's not good to eat," he bellowed with laughter.

"Hey, where's Quirt?" Ashana asked.

"Maybe he's making a start on dessert?" Jet suggested.

"I doubt it," Rezaaran replied with half a laugh. "But I could do with something to eat again."

"See what I mean!" Jet exclaimed.

Quirt gingerly lowered himself into a chair at the terminals of his workshop and winced when his ribs touched the backrest. Adjusting the ice pack on his shoulder, he called up the footage of the battle on Earth. His attention lingered on his involvement in the fight, and he repeated the segment several times.

"I do not understand," he lamented to himself. "Why did the suit not work?"

He opened the files containing the designs and reviewed the layout of the interconnected relay system that linked to the Valinthian crystal cortex he had constructed to fill the torso of the suit. All his specifications seemed perfect. After all, the combination core had powered the suit adequately, albeit fleetingly.

"What did I do wrong here?" he mumbled, running his fingers through his rusty hair.

"May I offer a suggestion?"

Quirt jumped in alarm and then groaned at the sudden dull ache in his side.

"My apologies," ADAM said softly. "I believe I may have a theory as to why your first model failed to meet your expectations."

"I welcome any suggestions that could make this suit functional."

"Perhaps the problem lies in its complexity."

"How so?"

"Well, your combined crystal core is meant to power the suit and facilitate its emulation of selected magical abilities by manipulating exotic matter. However, Albeinius designed the suit for a Zenorian's physiology. They naturally produce a heightened electrical field that the suit draws on for basic functioning. More specifically, he constructed this suit's frame for Rezaaran, who produces a far higher output than the average Zenorian soldier does. Basic functioning alone places a considerable resource demand on the core you installed."

"Leaving little reserve power to sustain the augmentation functions," Quirt murmured as he followed ADAM's train of thought. "That, coupled with the auxiliary functions such as flight, means that the core will be prone to a short circuit."

"Precisely. It is too much strain for the suit to be able to run all functions simultaneously."

"Well, I could reassign the basic utility and auxiliary functions to a separate power unit similar to the one used to power the Arkanian. That should sustain the suit for years to come. What if I change the core from a combination to separate cores for specific functions?"

"I believe that could work."

"There is not enough space in the chassis to hold numerous cores."

"With what you have in mind for this suit, most of the ordnance weapons would be obsolete."

"You are right," Quirt remarked with mounting excitement. His fingers flashed across the keyboard and his tablet. He removed the extra weaponry Albeinius had added to the suit, which left a considerable amount of space. "I could repurpose these empty slots into controlled vents that draw the required energies in to the respective crystals depending on the situation. However, that brings us to another problem."

"What is it?"

"Having multiple cores for individual functions means that I will have to transition between cores during combat. Changing through the interface or a computer system will be laborious. I need the changes to be instantaneous."

"Well, you don't need a computer for that. IRIS experimented and perfected a cerebral interfacing system adapted from Commander Cosmonox Shazal's functioning. You have a mind far faster than any processor that exists for weapons technology."

"This could actually work!" Quirt exclaimed, beaming.

"I believe so," ADAM replied, feeling chuffed with the theoretical project they had constructed together. "Have you thought of a name for the suit?"

"Why would I name the suit?"

"Well, you can't just keep calling it suit," ADAM remarked wryly. "Besides, something this innovative deserves a name."

"I suppose I could call it the versatile emergency response, intervention, and tactical-assault suit," the Thyrillian replied in a deadpan manner.

To Quirt's surprise, ADAM chuckled about this.

"Why is that amusing?"

"Well, the acronym for that spells out VERITAS."

ADAM opened a small panel on Quirt's terminal that provided information about a mythological figure from Earth's history.

"Veritas was a goddess to the ancient Romans," ADAM explained. "They revered her as the deity of truth who was always elusive, for such is the nature of her virtue. It eludes us all, but it is for the wise to always seek the truth in all matters."

Quirt thought about this quietly, remembering his first journey to the Atmari Altar.

"Well, VERITAS it is, then," he said finally. "Let us get started. There is quite a bit to do."

A few hours later, Quirt stepped into the center of his workshop wearing his completed VERITAS. With the power disabled, the suit was quite heavy, and he could barely move a step forward.

"Well, here goes," he murmured as he activated the central crystal core via his interface.

The motors throughout the suit hummed alive, and he instantly felt the weight relieved from his frame. The display within his helmet indicated the suit was currently operating off the central core at 20 percent capacity. A circlet formed around his head, and the suit connected to him as an extension of his body. He took a few paces with surprising ease.

"Well, that is a bit bizarre," he mumbled.

He thought about doing a backflip. The microthrusters in his back activated automatically and somersaulted him through the air, landing him in a crouch. Quirt rose to his feet with a light chuckle. However, it was time to put the purpose of the suit to the test. He turned his attention toward the loading door. In a fraction of a second, he sprinted across the workshop. He looked toward his feet and saw the vents along the greaves opened and released a blue glow. The display indicated the speed core was operational and functioning within safe parameters to create a tachyonic field around the VERITAS that was sustained while Quirt retained focus on the speed core.

"It works!" he shouted.

"Incredible!" ADAM exclaimed with pride. "Try flying next?"

"I took the thrusters out to make room for the speed core," Quirt admitted, but then he realized something. "The strength core could substitute for that function. The core streams gravitons to create an artificial gravitational field."

Quirt focused his mind on levitating off the workshop floor. The vents in his arms opened and released a blue glow as the VERITAS hovered in midair.

Setting himself back upon the ground, the Thyrillian threw an ecstatic punch into the air. The new design worked perfectly. The transitions were seamless, and the resource demand on the core was far less.

"We need to test this in a real combat situation," he said to ADAM.

"Well, we don't exactly have enemies lining up to be smacked around," the artificial intelligence replied.

Quirt looked around his workshop and had an idea. He sprinted to the table where the VERITAS had lain and then to his terminal, with the decommissioned Arkanian droid at his side.

"What are you going to do with that?" ADAM asked warily.

"I am going to upload you to the Arkanian's body," Quirt replied fervently, his fingers flashing across the keyboard.

"Oh, wonderful!" ADAM cheered. "I get to be the heart of the tin man without a trip down the yellow brick road!"

"What?" Quirt asked, looking in bewilderment at the screen showing ADAM.

"Never mind, let's just do this!"

The doors to the workshop hissed open. "Hey, Quirt, I just came to check if—what, by the spirits?"

The Thyrillian turned sharply and saw Rezaaran standing at the doorway with Harkenathor drawn, enraged as he saw the Arkanian rise to its feet.

"No…wait," Quirt spluttered. "It's not what you think!"

"Greetings, Rezaaran Valhara." The Arkanian spoke with a familiar voice, and its red eyes flickered to a pale blue.

"ADAM, is that you?" the War Mage asked tentatively. He lowered Harkenathor and approached the Arkanian.

"Indeed it is," ADAM replied proudly. "Although this body could use some serious maintenance."

"I may have had something to do with that," Rezaaran replied sheepishly, sheathing his blade.

Ashana wandered into the workshop with the rest of the crew a few moments later. "What's going on in here?" she asked.

"I felt the suit needed some improvements after our mission on Earth," Quirt admitted, "so ADAM and I worked on it and created VERITAS. We were just about to test its combat abilities."

"VERITAS," Jet repeated. "What is that?"

"A mythological figure of Earth embodying the virtue of truth," Ikso answered before Quirt could reply. In response to the curious looks she received, she indicated the open panel on the terminal.

"Well, if you want to combat test," Jet said with a hearty laugh, "you can't leave your favorite teacher out."

"And if there is training, I want to be included too!" Ikso cried.

"OK, everyone, just calm down!" Ashana shouted. "Nobody is having a giant brawl on my ship. Let's take this outside."

ADAM took his first steps as a physical being onto the dark-blue grass of AEgir Five. It was a momentous occasion for the newly empowered artificial intelligence. He looked at the distant orange sun as the atmosphere of AEgir came into view.

"It's all so beautiful," he whispered. "There is perfection in every instance of life around us."

"Welcome to the world of the living," Jet quipped, clapping ADAM on the shoulder. "How's that new body working so far?"

"Well, some repairs will need to be done. I have so far managed to override the old command and combat matrices with my programming, so no need to worry about hostility resurfacing."

"Always good to hear that," Ashana murmured, adjusting her quiver around her shoulder.

"So, Quirt," Rezaaran said, "what exactly can VERITAS do?"

"May I offer a point of concern?" ADAM asked.

"Of course, ADAM."

"While we are eager to determine the full extent of the suit's abilities, we should exercise caution for the sake of Quirt's safety."

"I think ADAM is afraid he may lose any contest," the Thyrillian shot back as he connected his interface to the display ports for VERITAS.

The android looked at him with narrowed eyes. "Oh, it's on now! We're gonna go at this full power!"

ADAM attempted to race across the plains but faltered at his first step and crumpled to the ground. "OK, maybe I need to recharge first," he said sheepishly to the backdrop of Ikso's exuberant laughter.

Varathis grumbled to himself and stormed past Luminara back into the ship. The others paid him no attention.

After they connected ADAM to a portable generator, the Sentinels and Ikso walked away from the ship, while Luminara and Gunner sat at the bottom of the loading ramp.

"So what exactly can your suit do, Quirt?" Ashana asked.

"We could test the speed abilities," he suggested. "Fire an arrow at me."

Reluctantly, Ashana loosed an electric discharge arrow. The Thyrillian dashed forward and grasped the arrow out of the air. Ikso applauded with astonishment, noticing the opened vents along Quirt's greaves.

"How does it work?" she asked.

"VERITAS uses a system of Valinthian crystal cores for different functions. The speed cores create a time dilation field around me so that I experience events at a far slower rate than reality, but to you it would appear that I am moving much faster than normal. It's an application of relativity."

Ikso looked at him blankly.

"Hey, you asked for it," Jet said, laughing at her confusion.

"So, basically, you can move really fast?" she asked.

"An oversimplification," Quirt replied with a frown, "but essentially yes."

"Well, let's see *how* fast," Ikso said with a grin, drawing her staves. "Isn't that the point of this?"

"Indeed it is," Quirt replied and activated the speed core once more.

The Halsynian charged forward with the celerity of a hurricane. However, to her amazement, Quirt parried every strike with effortless ease. He bolted away from her, a blur of gray across the plains. Not willing to submit, Ikso siphoned the winds swirling around her staves into herself and pursued the scientist. Initially she moved with the same speed as his VERITAS, but before long, she screeched to a halt and gasped. A flash of gray seated her beside Luminara to catch her breath. Quirt gave her a brief salute and turned to face the other Sentinels.

"That's impossible," Ikso panted.

"Well, this should be interesting," Rezaaran said with an eager smile. He reached into the Vaux and raced Quirt across the plains for three miles. They returned to the ship with a gust of wind that knocked the others back.

"That was incredible!" Quirt shrieked, his frame trembling. "That took just under fifteen seconds. We almost broke the sound barrier!"

"Yeah, we felt that," Jet moaned and rose to his feet.

"Very impressive," ADAM said and disconnected himself from the generator. He too was eager to pit himself against Quirt's VERITAS. "How is the power-consumption issue?"

"Nonexistent," the Thyrillian replied proudly. "All systems are performing with optimal efficiency!"

"Well, what's next?" Jet asked with a crack of his knuckles.

"Strength mode," Quirt exclaimed. He fell into a battle stance, ready to tackle his sparring partner. The vents along Quirt's arms opened, and he created an altered gravitational field around himself. He easily grasped Jet's gauntlet and overpowered the brutish strength of the Erebonian even with the gauntlet's thruster augmentation. Wresting control of the struggle, he brought Jet to his knees.

"OK, I am impressed," Jet admitted as he grasped Quirt's arm in a friendly handshake.

"There's more," Quirt said proudly. He then altered the gravitational field around him that allowed him to levitate high above the *Liberator.*

"Now that's just showing off!" yelled an exasperated Jet.

Rezaaran drew on the powers he had acquired from Halsyn and joined Quirt in the air, where they continued to spar. ADAM joined in, having had his share of being an observer.

Luminara looked on proudly. She could see the bond between the Sentinels growing as they trained together late into the evening. She was glad for this moment of good fortune. The sacrifices she and Tyrel had made had not been in vain.

Varathis looked at the monitor in the barracks and snarled. Throwing his empty bottle aside, he reached for his fifth Magnarian ale.

"Look at them out there," he muttered. "Prancing and parading on this backwater world. They're nothing more than children! The lot of them! And I must learn leadership from *them*?"

He hiccuped and drew a circle around Ashana. "So beautiful...yet you may be stupider than that black lizard. We should be together. We are royalty. Yet you choose that clown. You openly insult and undermine my authority as king." Lewdly he traced the outline of her figure on the screen. "I allowed you these whims, my dear, because of your beauty. Well, no more. You belong to me—in every manner. I am the king!"

His eyes narrowed as he watched Rezaaran take flight. "And you," he sneered, his lips curled in rage, "the wizard. You think you're so grand because of your fancy magic. Take that away, and you're just a lowly peasant. Yet everyone regards you with such respect. You think your magic entitles you to be the one Zenor looks to for leadership. Well, you are wrong. You are nothing! I am their king! Zenor is mine!" Varathis leaned closer to the screen. "Ashana is mine!"

The prince turned away from the monitor and gulped the rest of the bottle without pausing to breathe. His throat burned, but he did not care. The pain numbed the harsh reality that no matter what he said or thought, he could never compete with the War Mage's power. Varathis had witnessed his abilities on Earth and realized then that despite his royal birthright, he would never be as powerful as Rezaaran. For his claim to the throne to have any meaning, he had to get rid of the War Mage. But how could he ever hope to defeat him?

His anger swelled within him, and he flung the bottle to the corner of the barracks room.

"The barracks," he snorted. "Who would imagine a prince being forced to occupy a barracks?" To vent his frustration, he kicked a pile of junk and collapsed into his bed. However, his attention shifted to a blinking light coming from the mound of objects he had disturbed.

Rolling over, Varathis fished the item from the heap. He recognized it as Jet's Ranger band. It was flashing a new message that Jet had not seen. According to the time stamp, it had been delivered over a week ago.

Intrigued, Varathis lay back in bed and opened the message. It was from a Harbinger named Luferikas. His eyes raced through the words. Despite the drunken haze that sporadically tilted the room, Varathis had sense enough to realize an opportunity had fallen into his hands.

"Lady Fate has not abandoned me yet," he said with a hearty laugh.

Chapter Thirteen

Darkest Before the Dawn

Rezaaran took a deep sip of Angel's Whisper and wandered through thoughts on his recurring dream. Once again, he was on a battlefield, the likes of which he had never seen before. Amid the explosions, he held Ashana close as a shadow crept over the land. Then everything disappeared into a void, and he awoke.

He knew these ought to be dreams, yet he could not shake the feeling that there was something more to them. They felt like visions echoing from the Vaux. What if this was the trace of Ashana's power he had acquired on Inyas?

"That explains why they're so frustratingly cryptic," he grumbled, taking another sip of his brew.

Just then, the doors to the galley parted, and a bleary-eyed Ashana wandered in to join him. "Are you OK?" she asked between stifled yawns. "I woke up, and you weren't there. Hey, is that Angel's Whisper?"

"Yes, it is," he replied and took another sip. "It really helps."

Ashana held Rezaaran's hand and instantly saw the dreams that plagued him—the same dreams that woke him most nights. Yet she hid her realization. She knew that if Rezaaran knew, he would worry about her and not do what was necessary.

The doors parted once more, and this time Luminara walked in. "Glad I am not the only one struggling to fall asleep," she remarked wryly, taking a seat beside the Zenorians.

Ashana handed her a mug of Angel's Whisper as well. "What's troubling you?" she asked as she reclaimed her seat.

Luminara silently watched the steam curl above her mug, mulling over the question and how best to narrate what haunted her.

"I have experienced a Vaux evocation," she said. "Aware of it or not, everyone is connected to the Vaux. In turn, any memories they experience become a part of the Vaux. And powerful memories are able to find their way to those with whom their owner shared a bond."

"Like Lord Salvidawn's memories," Ashana whispered, wide-eyed.

"What did you see?" Rezaaran asked, leaning closer to the Guardian.

Luminara took a few moments to collect her thoughts and closed her eyes to relive the vivid dream. "After Tyrel barely escaped his encounter with Thaedis on Zenor," she explained, "he returned to the Aetherealm Sanctum, hoping that beneath the light of the Valinthian stone, he would heal. However, the Edarians had already overwhelmed us and taken me captive. Instead of returning to safety, he returned to an army of Edarians that overran the Sanctum. Tyrel's battle with Thaedis left him critically wounded, and he struggled to hold his ground against the Edarians. They subdued him easily and passed him through a portal into the Maelinthian, where Thaedis stood waiting."

Tears rolled down her cheeks, and she fought back sobs. Ashana placed an arm around her and drew her close, allowing her to cry onto her shoulder.

"Thaedis murdered him," Luminara sobbed. "Tyrel loved him like a brother, but Thaedis killed him without a second thought. He could not even do him the honor of a good death. Thaedis ran Tyrel through his back. Like a coward! Then he gloated about how satisfying it had been to kill him. Tyrel showed Thaedis mercy. He did not deserve this fate."

Rezaaran looked at Ashana, unsure what they could say to ease Luminara's pain. The Guardian dried her eyes and composed herself.

"Does anybody sleep on this ship?"

They turned their attention to the doorway, where Quirt was standing.

"Why are you awake?" Rezaaran asked with a raised eyebrow.

"I actually fell asleep in my workshop," Quirt admitted with flushed cheeks, hurrying across to the reconstitutor. "I was working on improving ADAM so that he can be combat ready for our next mission. I fell asleep waiting for the data feedback of the native algorithms. So I just came to make myself a cup of coffee, which ADAM says is very good for concentrating through tiredness. You all seem very deep in thought. Anything I may help with?"

Rezaaran and Ashana explained Luminara's dream to Quirt while he pensively sipped on his coffee.

"Well, I feel the solution is fairly straightforward," he said, setting his mug on the table. "We need to find where Tyrel died."

"Why?"

"Ashana, I lost my entire family when the Dominion coerced me into their service. Thaedis killed my wife, son, and daughter in front of my eyes but kept their souls in stasis to ensure my cooperation. Prior to this experience, I had never believed in the concept of a soul—it was simply not the Thyrillian way. However, knowing that a fragment of them lingered filled me with questions about whether they were truly lost. Those questions found an answer the day you found me on Zynoo."

"What do you mean?"

"Prior to your arrival, Thaedis cast my family's souls into the depths of his dark magic. Even though it was horrific, and their screams at that moment still haunt me, in my mind there is a finality to their fate, and I have no lingering questions."

"She needs closure," Rezaaran surmised.

"Precisely. Regardless of the outcome of the fate, we can only move forward when we know there is a finality. We all need an answer to grant us the strength to move on. I know how important that closure is, Luminara, and I am willing to go wherever we must for you to obtain that."

"Thank you so much, Quirt," she replied with a kind smile.

"Do you recall where the scene unfolded?"

Luminara frowned, recalling the vision. "After killing Tyrel, Thaedis entombed him in a sepulcher made of the blue crystal on the planet's surface."

"A blue crystal surface," Ashana murmured to herself.

"Then a gigantic skeletal dragon appeared over the tomb, and the planet, which had been radiating such a beautiful light, darkened, and a deep, inky cloud escaped its crust."

Rezaaran gasped.

"What is it?"

"I know that planet," he said. "Rexion mentioned it during a debriefing last year. His vessel was approaching Aardii-Atia when something opened fire and decimated his crew."

"Why would they open fire on him?"

"That skeletal dragon," Quirt replied grimly. "It must be guarding something important to Thaedis. Why else would he construct it to look over the tomb unless he'd hidden something of importance there?"

"Do you think Tyrel is alive?" Ashana asked hopefully.

"I doubt it," Luminara said sadly. "His memories would not have become a Vaux evocation unless he had passed into its stream."

"Oh, are you sure about that?" Darzuka sneered. "Maybe you should venture there yourself—you can join your beloved in his cold, dark tomb!"

Luminara's jaw locked and then released when she realized Darzuka's tone had wavered during her jeer. There was something hidden in that tomb the Edarian did not want her to find.

"We have to go immediately! I need to know for sure!"

"I'll plot our course," Ashana replied with a nod and headed with Rezaaran to the bridge.

A few hours later, the warriors walked along the deserted streets of a ghost town, its derelict buildings haunting the cityscape beneath the dark sky. Their dark-blue crystalline structures twinkled beneath the light cast by Quirt's VERITAS and revealed their forgotten beauty. Now, beneath the cloak of deep despair, they lamented a bygone age of wonder.

"This place is so depressing," Varathis muttered.

"There is so much loss hanging over this city," Ikso whispered. "I can barely sense a wisp of the Onsei. There is so much death."

"Aardii-Atia was never like this before," said a forlorn Quirt. "During our early training, TSARA assigned us here to learn about their mining practices and their unique ore, which was becoming the mainstay power source for the galaxy. The most memorable thing about this world was its beautiful crystalline crust and the way the locals had carved intricate patterns into it to release the light below the surface. Aardii-Atia had no artificial light, only the glow of the subterranean lucent mantle that in its depths congealed to form the power crystals everyone sought. Yet now...this is just a shadow of that world."

Luminara's fingers brushed against the wall of a nearby building, and she saw a flash of the battle between Thaedis and Tyrel.

"Are you all right?" Ashana asked.

"I will be, my dear," she replied, quickly wiping away the tears welling at the corners of her eyes. "This is definitely the right place. I can see the memories. Follow me."

She ran her fingers along the ruined buildings and gleaned visions of the battle between the former best friends. She saw the moment the portal opened and Tyrel crashed onto this world followed by a cohort of Edarians. The Guardian King slowly rose to his feet and composed himself for his final battle. His body was too weak to attack with any conviction, but he refused to surrender without a fight.

Looking in the direction Tyrel faced in the vision, Luminara swiftly strode toward a shattered wall. As she touched the shards scattered across the ground, the vision resumed.

Tyrel cut down the first Edarian who stood before him, but the rest seized him and wrested him to his knees on the ground. One of the creatures strode forward and broke Tyrel's wrist to release his weapon. Moments later, a black flame appeared, and Thaedis stepped forth.

"What is it?" Rezaaran asked Luminara. His heart grew heavier as he watched the emotions play across her face. He could tell that being here and the visions she was witnessing broke a little bit of her at a time. Yet she fought down her despair and braved her way onward.

"I can see Tyrel's last moments," she whispered. "It is all right. I will be all right, Rezaaran. I have to be. I have to know."

She walked toward a crumbling tower and placed her hands upon the dark crystalline wall. She needed answers about Tyrel's fate.

Thaedis stormed toward Tyrel, and at the sight of his broken wrist, he incinerated the responsible Edarian with a touch of his hand. He returned his attention to his former friend and delivered a vicious cross to his jaw. Lifting him roughly off the ground, Thaedis flung him across the street and through the tower.

Tears rolled freely along Luminara's cheeks, and she walked faster through the gaping chasm in the crumbling tower. The others followed hastily but respected her situation with silence. She placed her hands on a large pile of broken pillars, where she felt the Vaux's call.

Thaedis savored his slow walk to Tyrel's crumpled figure. Pressing a foot against the Guardian King's back, he ripped off his wings and then tore away his armor. Having stripped Tyrel down to his white robes, the Exiled reached into a dark portal and withdrew a long sword. Without further ceremony, he looked along the length of the blade and ran it through Tyrel's back. The Guardian King collapsed to the ground. Thaedis seized the hood of Tyrel's robe and telekinetically summoned Dawn Shard to his grasp. He proceeded to walk down a long, column-lined corridor.

Luminara returned to the present with agony in her heart. She looked around at the group. "We need to get past this debris," she whispered. "However, I sense a weak echo, and from my previous vision, I know we are not alone, so please exercise restraint."

Rezaaran nodded his acknowledgment and telekinetically shifted the broken pillars aside. They wandered behind Luminara along the dark, bare corridors of the desolate temple. Her fingers traced the walls, and she glimpsed the final vision—which was just as well, for she doubted she could take much more of this heartache.

Thaedis unceremoniously dragged Tyrel's corpse through this once hallowed temple. He followed the glowing symbols and etched lines deep into the heart of the altar built to honor the locals' deities. This would be Tyrel's sepulcher. The Exiled turned to his left and paused at the doorway for a moment, looking down at Tyrel and Dawn Shard before entering.

Luminara's pace quickened in the wake of the Vaux evocation she was channeling. Rezaaran telekinetically cleared the rubble sealing the doorway where Luminara's vision had led her. Cautiously they entered a dark chamber. Quirt's VERITAS illuminated the room with his helmet-mounted torches.

"I am detecting movement," ADAM whispered.

"Me too," Rezaaran replied under his breath, drawing Harkenathor. "I sense an echo nearby, but it is very weak."

"Who goes there?" a weary voice called to them.

On the edge of Quirt's light field, a shadow crept into view, and a figure staggered toward them from the far reaches of the chamber. With the aid of his sword, he stood tall, and a single wing reluctantly opened.

"Hold your fire!" Luminara yelled and rushed forward to catch him. She gently cradled his head and lightly touched the battered and dusty smiling golden mask on his face. "Isiel, my old friend! What are you doing here?"

"The Edarians arrived in the Aetherealm without mercy. They destroyed everything in their path, even Alaris's dearest relics. We could not allow that, my lady. The Spektian could not allow such disrespect, such...heresy. We fought them back, but it was in vain. All my brothers have rejoined with the Vaux, but I could not abandon Lord Salvidawn. I know how much the Great Scion revered him."

"I wish it were otherwise," Luminara replied woefully, holding Isiel's hand, "but Tyrel is no longer with us."

"Begging your pardon but you are wrong, my lady," the Spektian replied firmly, despite his battered body. "When the Edarians brought him through the portal, I followed shortly after. Alas, I was too late to save him from the Exiled. However, I have done what I could to preserve his soul."

"What do you mean?" Varathis asked sharply and earned a disapproving scowl from Luminara.

"If you accompany Lady Luminara, then I shall respect you," Isiel replied tersely. "After he killed Lord Salvidawn, the Exiled summoned a protector over this world encased in the skeletal remains of a monster. That conjuration is more than a physical protector. It is the source of the dark curse upon this world. It tethers this world to the Obsidious, which is the Dark Scion's plan for all the Maelinthian. There are others too, but this world is the strongest to prevent Lord Salvidawn from returning to protect Anmor."

"How did you last this long?" Luminara asked with watery eyes. Isiel was a creature of the Light, and she knew that prolonged exposure to Obsidian magic was noxious to his essence.

"This tether encroached upon this tomb repeatedly for the last thirty years, and I have fought it back each time. There have been numerous waves of Edarian shades attempting to claim Lord Salvidawn's soul, but I would never allow their sullied hands upon our lord. However, their strength is growing, which can only mean that the Dark Scion draws closer to walking the last realm of Anmor. We cannot waste time, my lady. My fellow warriors, please help me to my feet."

Luminara obliged, supporting Isiel's arm across her shoulder despite his objections that he could not burden a Guardian.

"Is that how you lost your other wing?" Ashana asked.

"Indeed, Lady Dilisin," he replied.

"It is not a wing at all," Ikso whispered with reserved awe. She saw streams of the Onsei's energy flowing into the back of this creature named Isiel. "They're his connection to the Onsei."

"You are wise and gifted with insight, young lady," Isiel said. "Every civilization calls it a different name, but whatever the name, it is the energy that binds us and connects us with our Great Scion. It was through her breath that the Spektian came to be so that we could serve the Guardians. Now I stand prepared to serve once more."

They stood before a blue crystal casket. Telekinetically, Rezaaran removed its lid, and Luminara gasped. Within lay the body of Tyrel Salvidawn with Dawn Shard beside him. Although his once-blond hair was now mere wispy white streaks and his skin had shriveled, Isiel had succeeded in preserving him from the reach of the Obsidious.

Luminara looked at Isiel with tears in her eyes. "You cannot do this, my friend. I will not ask it of you."

"There is nothing for you to ask, my lady. Lord Salvidawn always said that doing what was necessary would never be easy, but there is nothing easier than this. I will see you in the Vaux, Lady Luminara, but for now, you must find the strength to fight for Anmor and everything dear to the Great Scion Alaris. It has been good seeing you once more."

Isiel tightened his grasp on his blade and unfurled his wing. Reaching behind his head, with a swift slice, he severed his wing and gently placed it upon Salvidawn's bloodstained white robe. The Spektian offered them a last solemn bow and then disintegrated into lucent yellow particles that disappeared into the darkness.

Salvidawn's corpse sat upright with a jolt and gasped loudly for air.

"Bayron's blistered balls!" Jet shrieked, leaping backward.

The shriveled Guardian King transformed steadily to his former regal self as Isiel's wing dissolved into him and returned him to life. His hair regained its blond luster, and he stepped out of the casket with some unsteadiness. Squinting around the tomb beneath the torchlight of the VERITAS, his eyes found Luminara, and he stumbled forward to embrace her with a tearful chuckle.

"I knew I could not have lost you, my love," she wept joyfully.

"I am glad that you are safe, my dear," he replied in a raspy voice that still carried a loving softness toward his wife. Luminara's eyes closed in serenity, and she felt a weight lift off her in the arms of her beloved. Within his embrace, the shadow of Darzuka dispersed into the choked winds of the tomb.

Tyrel released Luminara and surveyed the others who had arrived. "It worked," he whispered with relief. "The Sentinels survived." He turned to Rezaaran and gently placed a hand on his shoulders. "You have done everything and more than I hoped you would when we met on Zynoo."

"I cannot thank you enough for that, Lord Salvidawn," Rezaaran replied with a bow of his head. "However, I fear more needs to be done. I have had a vision of how Thaedis intends to fulfill Nethriziin's conquest of Anmor. He seeks the Ark of Torementhias."

Tyrel's face became solemn, and he stepped away from the War Mage in surprise.

"We need your help to find it."

"This is quite fortuitous," Tyrel replied. "I hid the Ark shortly after freeing you from Zynoo. It is on the ancient planet Tarlok, in a place known as Symphony Hills. You have to find it before Thaedis. Your spirit will yield the contents to you, Rezaaran." Tyrel cast his gaze over them all once again. "It pleases me that the Sentinels should unite and that I should witness their success in my twilight years."

"You should come with us, my love," Luminara said softly, taking his hand.

"Well, these old bones still have some fight in them," he said, chuckling and embracing her once more. He looked lovingly into her eyes and frowned when he saw shock and tears rising.

"Your hair," she whispered with a wavering voice.

Tyrel stepped away from her and looked at his shriveled hands. His hair had thinned to wispy white streaks once more. His blue eyes wandered down to his chest, where he saw the scorched imprint of a wing across his robe, and a deep-crimson patch formed beneath it.

"It appears that Isiel's magic was not strong enough to permanently restore me," he croaked. "There is a deep darkness about this place. I feel it approaching ever closer. I—"

His knees buckled, and the Guardian King fell into Luminara's arms. His kind blue eyes found hers, and his shriveled hand reached to dry her tears. "Do not despair, my darling," he whispered. "It is my time. Thank you for saving me."

"I cannot lose you," Luminara sobbed. "Not again."

"You never lost me," he replied kindly and gently held her cheek. "It has been so good to see you again after all these years. And when this is all over, I will be waiting with my arms wide open for you in eternal bliss. I love you."

Luminara kissed his head softly, and Tyrel Salvidawn disintegrated into the Vaux in a stream of lucent particles.

"I love you too," she whispered back, wiping away the tears.

Suddenly the tomb shuddered, and the roof erupted in black fire. A high-pitched screech ripped through the gravely silence.

"Luminara, we have to leave now," Rezaaran pleaded, grasping her arm.

"Wait! I have to get Dawn Shard!"

A skeletal behemoth ripped apart the walls of the tomb and began smashing its way toward them.

"There's no time!" Rezaaran yelled. He pulled her back to join the fleeing group, and they narrowly escaped the collapsing temple.

Through the smoke, they caught a glimpse of a seamless mass of Obsidian magic encased in a gargantuan skeleton. It raised its forelimbs and with another screech plowed them into the crystal surface. Pulses of red energy coursed across its body.

"What is that *thing*?" Jet asked as he aimed his blast cannon.

"According to the archives," ADAM replied, "the skeleton belongs to an emperor dragon from Kreyfor."

"Who cares what it is!" Rezaaran shouted. "Quirt, get us out of here!"

"Don't you want to stand and fight it?" Jet asked in surprise.

"We can't stand against it. That thing is tethered to the Obsidious and can summon it here in moments!"

"Rezaaran is right," ADAM piped. "We cannot contest this monster. My telemetry indicates that the gravitational field of the planet is exponentially increasing."

"That cannot be right," Quirt murmured, reading the data ADAM had seen.

"What is it now?" Ashana asked with desperation.

"It has created a singularity within the planet's core!" Quirt yelped. "I am uploading our coordinates now!"

Shards of splintered crystals flew toward them, but Rezaaran repelled them with a telekinetic field, and Quirt extended a gravity-alteration field to protect them from the strengthening pull of the planet's core. An instant later, they were aboard the *Liberator*.

"Everyone get strapped in immediately!" Ashana ordered. She leaped into the pilot seat and primed the Torus drive.

Despite its engines roaring at full thrust, the vessel strained to move.

"We are on the verge of the event horizon," Quirt informed her over the communicator. "We have only a limited time before we are drawn into the accretion disc."

"What happens then?" Ikso asked anxiously.

"There will be no escape," Quirt replied grimly.

"Well, how do we escape the pull?" Ashana asked through gritted teeth as she fought to keep Aardii-Atia from drawing the *Liberator* back to its surface.

Rezaaran watched the planet with horror. The dark-blue surface cracked and revealed the glowing white mantle beneath.

"You could eject the ordnance rounds," ADAM suggested. "If you fire them toward the planet, the singularity will consume their explosive warheads under immense pressure and generate a shock wave to repel our lighter vessel out of range."

"Firing away!" Ashana yelled.

Every missile contained on the *Liberator* blasted toward the planet. With a brilliant burst of energy, the explosion generated a massive shock wave that nudged the vessel out of the growing singularity's reach.

They escaped into a Torus tunnel and briefly caught a glimpse of Aardii-Atia imploding beneath the enormous pressure of the void formed within the core.

"Well, at least we're out of that entanglement," Ashana sighed with relief as the *Liberator* careered along the Torus tunnel.

The alarms blared across the bridge.

"Now what?" Varathis mumbled.

"There's a squadron of Dominion fighters locking onto our position," Ashana announced with wide eyes.

"How did they know where to find us?" Rezaaran asked, his brow furrowing.

"No time to figure that out," Ashana replied. "Ikso and Rezaaran, take seats at the bridge here. Jet, I need you at one of the manual turrets. ADAM, plug yourself into the ship and connect with the IRIS fleet. Varathis—"

Ashana chanced a look behind her and then swiftly returned her attention to navigating the *Liberator* under threat of enemy fire.

"When someone sees him," she said, seething, "tell him to occupy the remaining manual turret to guard the thrusters."

"Already on it, Ashana," Varathis replied over the communication network.

"Well, what are you guys waiting for? Light them up!"

The warriors marked their targets and unleashed a volley of energy rounds upon the Dominion fighters. However, the enemies responded with a barrage of missiles and ion bombs that punched holes through the *Liberator*'s shields.

"Are you guys even hitting anything there?" Ashana grumbled. "ADAM, what is our status?"

"Shields are at 65 percent capacity," he replied. "I have issued a distress call to IRIS vessels, but this Torus tunnel is creating interference."

"I need solutions, ADAM, not problems. Figure something out!"

"Yes, Commander!"

A squadron of basilisk fighters swept over the *Liberator* and sliced through the hull with concentrated laser fire. Jet fixed his sights on the fighters and pelted them with several rounds of molten rhodium slugs. His shots punctured the vessels and detonated them in flares of green. However, one escaped the range of his turret and set a course toward the *Liberator's* thrusters.

"Varathis, you've got one coming toward you," Jet barked over the communication channel, setting his targets for the shield-destroying bombers.

The *Liberator* shuddered, and the soldiers lifted out of their seats for the briefest of moments. The ship fell from the Torus tunnel and emerged into space once more.

"What the...ADAM, what just happened?" Ashana asked, her brow shining with sweat.

"It appears we lost our thrusters."

"That does not sound good," Ikso yelped.

"Do not worry," Quirt said over the communicator. "I have a plan. Ashana, there is a planet drawing us into its gravitational field. You need to pilot the *Liberator* through to land."

"What are you doing?" Ashana asked sternly.

A few moments later, they saw the VERITAS fly across their view field. The vents along his forearms flared opened, and he flew himself through several of the fighters, detonating them as he obliterated their hulls with his artificial gravity field. Once satisfied he had destroyed the enemy vessels, Quirt teleported himself back to the *Liberator*, which was making a rapid descent toward an alien world.

"Well, that's one way to deal with them," Ashana murmured. "Nice work, Quirt."

"Thank you, Ashana," he replied as he joined them on the bridge. "However, there is more to do. Rezaaran and ADAM, I need your help to slow the *Liberator*'s descent."

Rezaaran nodded and ran with Quirt toward the loading bay, where they met ADAM.

"OK, we're in the atmosphere beyond the burnout zone," Ashana informed them. "You guys are clear to go!"

Quirt activated the teleporter and then grabbed hold of Rezaaran and ADAM. A moment later, they appeared on the nose of the *Liberator* on its careering path toward the surface. The three placed their hands upon the ship, and Quirt generated a gravity-manipulation field to reduce its weight. Meanwhile, Rezaaran used his flight ability to bolster ADAM's thrusters.

Without the support of any mechanical assistance, Rezaaran felt every muscle in his arms burn beneath the strain of the enormous vessel. Looking through the view panel, though, he saw Ashana's anxiety. He could not fail. This crazy plan had to work!

Suddenly, ADAM lost his grip, and the slipstream ripped him away.

"ADAM!" Quirt yelled out. The shift in his attention caused his gravitational field to falter, and the vessel accelerated further.

"Quirt, you need to stay focused," Rezaaran said through gritted teeth. "We'll find him later. Let's just set the ship down first."

Without ADAM's thrusters, this proved harder than Rezaaran had expected. He reached deeper and drew upon the strength-fortifying spell, his telekinesis, and his flight abilities, while Quirt fought down his panic and strained his focus to maintain the graviton field.

Together they successfully slowed the descent of the *Liberator* and set the ship safely upon the ground. However, the effort had drained both Quirt and Rezaaran.

"That was incredible, guys!" Ashana squealed, looking out the view panel and seeing that they were all right.

"We have to find ADAM," Quirt wheezed.

"Don't worry," Ashana said. "His armor is strong enough to survive the impact, and his thrusters would have allowed him to regain flight. I am sure we will find him soon."

"Where are we?" the War Mage asked between gasps. That had been the most intensive use of his powers he had undertaken since his battle with Sarganium.

"Well, the good news is that our star charts are still functional," Ashana said. "We're on a planet called Turmen. Oh, no…"

"What is it?" he asked. He was not sure his heart could beat any faster than it was already pounding in his chest.

"According to this, we are on a Dominion world. Fortunately, ADAM's signal appears to have left, but that brings another problem."

"Yeah, I see it," Rezaaran replied grimly and struggled to his feet.

A large cohort of Kalaran cyborg soldiers, Arkanian assassin droids, and Kreyforian gladiators had surrounded their battered ship.

"My scanners detect over two hundred hostiles," Quirt whispered.

An Arkanian with glowing green eyes strode forward, and his four-pronged staff buzzed threateningly at the two Sentinels.

"Surrender yourself to the mercy of Harbinger Luferikas," the Arkanian ordered in a drawling digital voice. "Despite your abilities, you stand a meager 13 percent chance of victory—with an 86 percent chance of crew mortality in the process. A fight is not in your interest."

Rezaaran looked at Quirt and back at the ship. Together they slowly raised their arms and submitted themselves to the Arkanian.

CHAPTER FOURTEEN

TESTED FAITH

"Well, this is a wonderful run of luck," Jet muttered through gritted teeth, twisting his neck to gain some space against the cold steel collar that shackled his arms to his throat.

A Kreyforian gladiator smacked him hard over the back of his head and laughed at his state. Jet replied with a threatening growl and received a painful jolt in his flanks from two nearby Arkanians.

The band of warriors was now entirely at the mercy of its captors. Luminara and Rezaaran were contained within black crystalline corsets that bound their hands to their chests. The War Mage also had a crystal muzzle strapped to his face. Ikso, Ashana, Quirt, and Varathis had been dispossessed of their weapons and shackled with energin bonds that linked them together so that the Arkanian leader could easily pull them along behind him.

"What is this place?" Ikso asked as she looked at the scared faces of children, who watched as the army marched the prisoners through their settlement before they scurried back to their parents.

"What does it look like?" Varathis muttered.

"It's a slave camp," Jet replied more kindly. "Looking around here, I think we had it better on Mar-Karatheer."

"These people look awfully similar to ADAM," Quirt noted. "Besides the fact that they are not blue like his hologram."

The Kreyforian gladiator slapped Quirt over the back of the head to silence him, which further stoked Jet's fury.

"Do that again, and lose that arm," Jet growled at the Kreyforian. Their captor guffawed and slapped Quirt once again.

Jet grabbed the Kreyforian's forearm between his powerful jaws and rent his flesh with his canines before three Arkanians stunned his flank and forced him to release his grasp. Quirt watched in bewilderment as Jet fell to the ground gasping for breath and spitting the blood from his mouth. The Arkanian leader circled around to the groaning Kreyforian.

"Harbinger Luferikas was clear about his instructions in apprehending the suspects," he said coldly. "Or were such orders too difficult for you to comprehend?"

"I don't need to hear your crap!" the Kreyforian roared. "Get me a medic! I'm in pain!"

"Then allow me to ease your suffering," the Arkanian replied. From his wrist blaster, he fired a single shot between the Kreyforian's eyes. He looked over the rest of the army around him. "Are there any other objections, or may we proceed?"

The Arkanian took the silence as acknowledgment and continued the procession toward a looming fortress made of metal.

A few moments later, the captives were marched into a large chamber. The Arkanian soldiers assumed their formation behind them, ready to act if anyone sought escape. Metal chairs on the periphery of the chamber encircled the prisoners as though they were to be auctioned.

The doors to the chamber opened once more, and a procession of aliens entered the room. Ashana recognized them immediately. These representatives of the Galactic House of Governance were devoutly loyal to the Dominion. They were Thaedis's Harbingers.

A tall alien with red skin and needle-straight white hair took the central seat, granting himself the best view of his new victims.

"Well, well...here we are," he declared. "After this past year of heightened IRIS activity, we finally have the galaxy's most dangerous criminals in our grasp. I must admit, apprehending you was remarkably easy considering the devastation you have wrought upon our Dominion. Ah, but my manners escape me." He stood abruptly and walked to a slave who held a silver goblet upon a metal tray. "Is this fresh?"

"Harvested this morning, my lord," the slave responded, quivering.

"Good," the alien sneered and drank deeply of the blood in his goblet. He turned once more to his prisoners and bowed theatrically. "My name is Luferikas, Grand Harbinger to our Lord Silvermire...and head of this council." He casually strode before his prisoners and regarded them with the air of a collector. His taloned red finger caressed the face of Luminara, who pulled away in disgust.

"You must be the Guardian our master seeks," he mused. "I would have expected a being of such fabled power to have a presence about her. Alas, you are quite a disappointment."

He slowly passed to Rezaaran and regarded the War Mage with his burning yellow eyes. Luferikas chuckled at the sight of the Zenorian attempting to break free of his confines. "Oh, do not exert yourself," he chided. "Those shackles are made of Torementhicite. Your powers are useless within those bindings. The War Mage who incited IRIS's rebellion to seek greater ambition! Yet here you stand, utterly powerless." Luferikas drew his talon along Rezaaran's cheek. His sharp claw cut into the flesh, and the Demokarva relished the trickling blood he had let.

He passed his attention to the series of soldiers bound by the energin shackles. "So, we arrive at the rest of you," he said, chuckling. "Ashana Eldeerim, commander of IRIS. What a handsome bounty you have gained yourself during your escapades with Rezaaran. It will be a shame to detach such a beautiful head, but such is the fate you yourself chose in defying the Dominion."

His eyes narrowed when he reached Ikso. "I do not believe I know you," he sneered. "Are you just another cadet who sought some meaning to your insignificance? You should have chosen a better team to fight for."

"I know her," one of the Harbingers remarked. "She escaped her execution on Halsyn."

"Well, how unlucky for you that destiny brings you into the midst of these criminals, only to be executed on a different world."

"Master Cheyi of the Hunsu temple," the Harbinger continued, "has requested that she be returned to Halsyn so that she may be an example to his ranks."

Luferikas clutched Ikso's chin and then turned her head from side to side, eyeing her jugular veins. "Tell this Master Cheyi that the Dominion shall compensate him handsomely," the Demokarva replied lazily. "I have never before sampled Halsynian blood, and this is such a delectably young specimen."

The Harbinger remained quiet, hiding either his disgust or his fear of Luferikas. It was hard to say.

"So, who else do we have here?" Luferikas drawled. "An escaped scientist. No doubt we shall find some use for you in one of our labs again. And...ah yes, of course." Using a metal disc, he deactivated Varathis's energin bonds and offered the Zenorian prince a simple bow and a sly smile. "There is no need to continue the pretense. You have done a great service in bringing these criminals to justice, and the Dominion shall reward your loyalty to maintaining order."

"You backstabbing bastard!" Jet growled, struggling to lunge at Varathis despite the three Arkanians restraining him.

"What a temper you have," Luferikas remarked, cackling. "You would have made an excellent addition to our ranks."

Varathis chuckled at this and punched Jet squarely in the jaw. "I'll make sure your hide is turned into a good set of boots for me," he jeered as he shook away the stinging pain in his wrist. "At least that way your life will have some purpose."

Jet seethed at the prince with burning hate.

"How could you do this to us?" Ashana demanded.

"Is it not obvious, my love?" Varathis asked and took a stance in front of Ashana. "What future did I have with IRIS? What is a king without a kingdom to rule?"

"IRIS would have won this war!" Ashana seethed. "We would have had a home again that you could have reigned over, if that was all that mattered!"

"Oh, that *is* all that has ever mattered," Varathis replied with a smirk. "I did desire a queen, though, and you would have made an agreeable choice."

Ashana pulled away from his touch with disgust.

"Alas, you denied my affections repeatedly," he continued. "By the same measure, Zenor would never recognize me as their leader while *he* lives."

He now stood in front of Rezaaran, who was bound in the Torementhicite confines, and smugly reveled in the change of fortune he had created.

"You took everything that belonged to me!" he yelled between punches to the War Mage's midriff. "What right did you have to deny me what was mine?"

Rezaaran fell to his knees and heaved for breath.

"Look at you," Varathis spat. "Without magic, you are pathetic."

"Not as pathetic as you are!" Ikso said fiercely. "We accepted you as part of our company, and you betrayed us! Nobody will follow a king who has no loyalty!"

Varathis caught his breath and pointed a finger at Ikso. "That's enough out of you, child! I have had to tolerate your arrogance for far too long! You are mistaken if you believe that none shall follow me. Nobody will know what happened to you. I will be the sole survivor, and all that matters is my account of events."

"Orin will not believe your lies," Quirt said, emboldened by Ikso's defiance. "Nor will the council side with you."

"Either they accept the word of their king," Varathis said slyly, "or they will face extermination by the Dominion." The Zenorian prince looked toward the Arkanians. "Get this lot out of my face!"

Luferikas nodded. The Arkanians moved to action upon his command and bustled the prisoners out of the chamber. Before the doors closed, Ashana heard Varathis speak to the Grand Harbinger.

"If I may request a word with your leader, I believe I have some information he may find quite useful."

"Like I said before," Jet lamented, his arms hanging through the steel bars of their prison cell, "this is a wonderful run of luck."

"I cannot believe he sold us out," Quirt mumbled as he sat against the cold metal bars.

"You really mean that?" Jet asked incredulously. "Why would that narcissistic prick have any reason to be loyal?"

"I mean, I knew he was egomaniacal, but actual betrayal is a far reach."

"You would be surprised," the Erebonian sighed. "The reason I was demoted in the Space Rangers is that Varathis reported me to the chief commander. My direct superior was a kind man who knew of my imprisonment and losing Hera, so he overlooked my addictions. However, Varathis's report ensured my demotion—*and* my superior's removal from the Rangers due to his failure in disciplining me. Of course, that left a vacancy in the chain of command, a position for which he was all too eager to nominate himself."

"That's all well and good," Ashana said, looking out across the span of slave camps, "but it does nothing to get us out of this mess."

"Where did they take Ikso?" Luminara asked quietly.

"Luferikas probably has her being prepared for his blood ritual," Quirt replied. "He delights in gorging himself on the blood of alien species and desecrating their corpses but has created a grand ritual to make the act appear sophisticated and mask his necrophilic propensity."

Ashana's face creased in disgust. "We have to save her!"

"How are we going to do that, Ashana?" Jet asked. "I can't exactly bend these bars with my hands. Our two biggest guns are safety locked with shackles that neutralize their abilities."

"There is nothing you can do," whimpered a prisoner from a nearby overcrowded cage. "Those androids patrol down here, and they never sleep or make a mistake. You only leave when they want you to."

Jet eyed the emaciated man in his ragged clothes. Most of the prisoners in the overcrowded cells on either side of theirs looked severely malnourished and hopeless.

"We have to find a way out of here!" Jet insisted. "We cannot allow our friend to die!"

"What world are you from?" Quirt asked, approaching the prisoner.

"Is this really the time to be making friends?" Jet asked as he struggled to bend the bars of the cage.

"We are from Earth," the man replied meekly. "Most of us were taken as prisoners and brought here to work the scrapyard. We dismantled ships for parts they could reuse. Some of the debris we used to make shelters for ourselves."

"So if you were brought as slaves, why are you in cages?"

"We rebelled against them," a woman said softly, coming forward and standing beside the man. "We attempted an uprising, but they got the better of us. Many of our people died. They threw the rest of us in here."

Ashana sat beside Rezaaran and gently held his arm. The Torementhicite shackles blunted his regeneration, and despite his best attempts to mask the pain, Ashana knew better. She knew that the cowardly physical beating he had received from Varathis hurt him less than Varathis's betrayal or his own guilt over Ikso's peril. Even though Rezaaran could have done nothing that would have prevented this predicament, she knew he would still blame himself.

Suddenly the prisoners hushed one another and, to appear that they had not engaged Quirt, slunk away from the edges of the cage. The Sentinels turned to look at the cause of their fear and saw an Arkanian with glowing red eyes walking into the dungeon.

"You'd better let me out of here, tin man!" Jet growled. "If that little girl is hurt, I will strip you down to scrap metal!"

"You really should control that temper, Mr. Bal Sara," the Arkanian said.

Quirt tentatively approached the metal bars. He recognized that voice. And this Arkanian had two staves holstered at his leg instead of the typical long stun staff the others carried.

"ADAM!" he shouted. "I am so glad you survived, my friend!"

"Well, I won't be surviving much longer if you don't keep your voice down," ADAM chided him. His eyes flickered for a moment and returned to their normal blue shine. "Stand back." A blue energin blade extended from his right wrist, and he sliced through the lock of the cage.

"Am I glad to see you!" Jet exclaimed, clapping the Arkanian on the shoulder.

"We can exchange pleasantries later," ADAM said curtly. "I don't think my disguise will fool the guards for too long."

Next he sliced the shackles that bound Rezaaran and Luminara. The War Mage took in a deep breath. Now that he was free of the Torementhicite corset, his wounds healed immediately.

"We have to get to Ikso!" Rezaaran said sternly. "ADAM, free the other prisoners, and get them out of here."

"Will do, Rezaaran," the android replied with a salute. "Your weapons have been stored in a security crate in the main Arkanian's chamber. I think he's called Itara Shian."

"I recognize that name," Luminara whispered.

"We don't have time," Rezaaran interjected. "Luminara and Quirt, go with ADAM and get the prisoners free of this castle. Ashana and Jet, you come with me. We'll get the weapons and then Ikso. Jet, you can get Quirt's VERITAS back for him."

Everyone nodded in agreement with the plan and waited until ADAM had opened the last cage before turning in to the corridor leading out of the prison. However, a group of five Arkanian guards immediately barred the passage, foiling their escape.

Itara Shian entered, making his way through his cohort of guards. His glowing green eyes scanned everyone in the room. He passed over the defiant determination of the newest prisoners and the terrified faces of the emaciated humans, his gaze settling on the blue-eyed Arkanian standing among them all.

"What are you?" he asked sternly, pointing his staff at ADAM.

The android remained silent but moved to stand before Shian.

"You look like one of us, yet you do not bear the color of our ranks," Shian continued. "You are neither an itara nor a soldier. You cannot be a Zamtian—their illusions do not work on our operating matrix—and a shape shifter would yield a thermal signature So, I will ask one last time—what are you?"

"My name is ADAM," he replied fearlessly, locking eyes with the Arkanian leader. "These people are coming with me!"

Shian gazed into ADAM's eyes and sought to assess this imposter guised as one of them. "We shall see about that!" he said finally. "I invoke the sacred right of Sento Saiban."

"Very well," ADAM agreed. "If I win, these people go free."

"You have it on my honor."

"What is happening?" Ashana whispered.

"He has challenged ADAM," Luminara replied, "to a trial by combat to determine our fate."

"Great," Rezaaran muttered. "We don't have time for this! Ikso's life depends on us!" He attempted to walk toward the exit, but an Arkanian guard blocked his path with his staff.

"Once the words are spoken," Luminara explained, "none may interrupt the proceedings. We need to trust in the Vaux to keep our young friend safe."

Rezaaran gritted his teeth but stood down. He still felt Ikso's echo within the building. She was safe—for the moment, at least.

The remaining Arkanian guards stood back in respect to their leader and the sacred tradition. Shian held his staff beside him and slowly dropped into a low crouch, while ADAM circled his adversary with his quarterstaves in hand. Seizing the initiative, ADAM lunged toward Shian. He swung a quarterstaff toward his head and half stepped to follow the parried strike with a flourish to the torso. Shian pivoted, slammed his staff through ADAM's unsteady stance, and knocked the android to the floor.

"You may look like one of us, but you lack the discipline."

ADAM pulled his legs inward and flipped himself back to his feet. He struck his quarterstaves together, and the metal rods sparked alive. Focused on his enemy, he charged forward with a greater intent, shoulder-barged Shian, and followed through with a series of strikes to the torso.

Shian dropped his staff and deflected the sparking strikes with his gauntlets. He shifted his guard until he saw an opening and then rammed his knee into ADAM's chest. Leaping up, he delivered a vicious swivel kick that hurled the imposter across the room, where ADAM crashed into a steel-barred cage. Shian reached for his staff, activated the stunning prongs, and hurled the weapon through his adversary's chest. Electricity wracked ADAM's body and short-circuited his motors.

The Arkanian regarded his opponent's limp form and the dented chest plate where his weapon was still implanted. He offered a perfunctory bow of respect to signal the end of the sacred ritual and turned to issue orders to his soldiers.

Quirt looked devastated. This could not be true. He could not lose another friend like this. But his attention shifted from his grief when the scanners in his lenses detected activity.

"Is that all you've got?" ADAM called out to Shian.

Itara Shian turned to face the opponent he had thought defeated. ADAM's eyes flickered alive with a blue glow, and his fingers twitched momentarily before his movements smoothed out. Reaching to his chest, he yanked out the staff that had impaled him to the bent steel bars. He dropped the staff to the floor and drew himself up tall.

"That is impossible," Itara Shian murmured, his narrowing eyes focused on the four deep holes gouged into ADAM's chest plate, which exposed his underlying functional core.

"You cannot stop me saving these people," ADAM replied. He sprinted toward Shian and slunk beneath the charging Arkanian's swing to his head. Catching hold of the leader's leg, ADAM tossed him upward. Shian broke his fall with his gauntlets and tumbled forward. He regained his footing swiftly and charged once more.

The pair unleashed a series of blindingly fast punches at one another, yet neither found his mark as they matched their offensive speed with lithe dodges. ADAM caught hold of Shian's fist, turned into him, and flung him over his back. However, his opponent reacted immediately and, using the momentum, flipped ADAM to the ground. ADAM spun, using his legs to offset Shian's balance, and pushed himself through a backflip to land on his feet in front of his staggering opponent. ADAM dipped down and leaped skyward, spinning twice in the air and delivering three powerful kicks to Shian. The last kick found its mark on the Arkanian's head and smashed him into the metal wall.

Itara Shian slumped to the floor, disoriented and shocked by what had happened. His guards looked at his form, crumpled and still, and were unsure what course of action to pursue. ADAM walked over to the fallen Arkanian.

"How is this possible?" Shian muttered. "You are not one of us. How could you possibly defeat me?"

"I was fighting for more than myself."

"Well…get on with it, then."

"What are you talking about?"

"You're going to remove my head now, are you not?"

"What?" ADAM asked, aghast. "No. I'm not a savage." He offered Shian his hand and helped the defeated Arkanian to his feet. "Do you remember our deal?"

"Yes, of course I remember," Shian replied roughly. "You and your friends are free to leave."

"The humans are coming with us too."

"Why should you care for them?" the Arkanian leader asked. "They are weak—pathetic, even. Their kind is cruel and hateful. That is how we subjugated them so easily."

"Perhaps," ADAM replied, looking over the crowd of terrified slaves. "However, they deserve the chance to become better. It is the right of all sentient beings to find their purpose."

"Then you are far wiser than any Arkanian I have known in a while."

ADAM looked at Shian quizzically. The leader opened his chest plate and removed a glowing green orb housed within a silver tesseract frame.

"What is that?" ADAM asked, intrigued by the shifting nature of the orb.

"This is the Shirei module," Shian explained. "It confers the title of itara to an Arkanian we choose as a leader."

ADAM retained a blank expression. Shian gestured toward his damaged chest plate. ADAM unclipped the latch, and Shian removed the dysfunctional core to replace it with the Shirei module. Immediately ADAM's eyes flared green, then returned to their blue state.

"There is something very different about you," Shian admitted. "The last time I encountered an Arkanian who defied our programming was when Itara Zelzo served as our leader. That was before the Dominion corrupted his purpose and he led us down a path we had not followed in millennia. Until you put an end to that." Shian nodded toward Rezaaran. "I saw the footage of your battle with him and what he did to Zynoo. That was not the same Zelzo I knew. He was no longer my itara. After he became a Guardian, I inherited the Shirei module for our regiment. We continued serving in the manner you had taught us, Lady Luminara, when we first met on Skylark to retrieve Lady Nish Ira."

"I knew I recalled your name," Luminara replied with a smile.

"However, some time ago, Itara Zelzo returned to this realm and commanded the Arkanians to follow Thaedis. None of us could disobey his orders; he exerted an unnaturally strong influence over each of us. That was until Rezaaran Valhara destroyed him and freed us of his corrupted influence. I knew Zelzo was not at fault; he believed in peace and justice. However, we had bound ourselves to the Dominion." Shian looked back to ADAM. "Until your ship fell through the atmosphere. Then I saw an Arkanian attempt an impossible feat, and that reminded me of Zelzo. You fight with bravery and for justice. You display loyalty and honor. You are everything an itara should be. Itara ADAM, my Arkanians are now yours to command, and I will follow whatever order you give me."

Shian and the other Arkanians knelt before their new itara.

"This is a great honor," ADAM said to the Arkanians. "However, there is much to do. My friends need to find the young Halsynian girl who was with them."

"We also need to intercept Varathis," Rezaaran interjected, "before he can pass the information about the Ark to Thaedis."

"Very well," Shian said. "My fellow Arkanians and I shall escort the humans to safety until we receive further orders, Itara ADAM."

"Perfect!" the War Mage exclaimed, glad that a plan was starting to gain traction. "Luminara, Quirt, and ADAM, find out where Varathis is departing from, and intercept him. Let's get moving!"

The stone door creaked open, disturbing Ikso in her meditation. Her bright blue eyes looked up sharply, and she beamed at the sight of an apprehensive Ashana.

"I knew the goddess would send you to me!" she squealed.

"Thank the spirits you are all right," Ashana said, sighing with relief and hugging the young Halsynian.

"Now *that's* a pleasant sight," Jet exclaimed as he rubbed his heavy hand over Ikso's bald head. "How is it that you are still unharmed?"

Rezaaran cautiously entered last, satisfied the corridor was clear of any enemies. His heart unclenched at the sight of Ikso safe, and he swept his gaze across the room. Several of the cyborg Kalarans and a Kreyforian battle master lay concussed against the walls.

"What happened here?" he asked with a raised eyebrow. However, this time when he looked at Ikso, he saw thin, wispy streams of the Vaux flowing around her.

"I followed the teachings of Master Suya," she replied proudly. "I centered my fears and prayed to the goddess. She acted through the Onsei to keep me safe."

"Well, I am grateful for that," Rezaaran said. "Come on, let's get out of here and find Varathis. If this luck holds, we may be able to stop him from delivering the location of the Ark to Thaedis."

"Oh…these belong to you," Jet interjected, handing Ikso's runic staves back to her. "I get the feeling somebody's cruising for a bruising!"

The group of warriors ran from the prison and hurried through the castle in the wake of Ashana, who tracked ADAM's position on her interface. Ikso and Jet handled any adversaries that approached, while Rezaaran brought up the rear to ensure their escape remained safe.

Bursting through a steel door, they found themselves on the roof. Opposite them, ADAM flung open another door. Quirt and Luminara were at his side. In the center of the roof hovered a drop ship onto which several Kalarans were bustling a terrified Varathis. Spying the intruders, Luferikas signaled for the ship to depart hastily.

"Believe me, I would like to teach you lot some manners," Luferikas sneered at the Sentinels, his white hair blowing in the wind. "However, I will be leading the Harbingers to meet with Lord Silvermire and see the end of your pathetic rebellion."

He saluted the Sentinels mockingly and leaped off the roof. Rezaaran and his companions fought their way through the

Kreyforian battle masters and Kalarans that remained as guards and hurried to the ledge. Below them, they saw Luferikas fly away on a Levira through the cargo freighters above the expansive slave camp.

"I really hate that guy," Jet growled. "*Now* what do we do?"

"We have to get to him," Rezaaran said. "If Thaedis learns of the Ark's location, then this war will end very soon."

"How are we supposed to do that?" Ashana asked, exasperated. "Not all of us can fly."

"That's weird," ADAM mumbled. "This Shirei module allows me to experience the thoughts of every Arkanian connected to the module as though they were my own. Shian knows about a collection of Leviras in a hangar within this castle."

Rezaaran looked around sharply at the feeling of a powerful yet familiar echo. He ought to have known she would be here. Across the rooftop stood Diothur. Her cold, menacing gaze locked on the Sentinels.

"Get to those Leviras, and stop the Harbingers," Rezaaran ordered the others solemnly. "ADAM, transmit the trajectory of the drop ship, and see if an IRIS ship can intercept them."

"What about her?" Ashana asked as she nocked an arrow.

"Don't worry," he replied calmly. "I'll handle her."

The others reluctantly departed, leaving Rezaaran and Diothur alone on the rooftop.

"I am curious as to whether you believe your own lies," Diothur said with a smirk as she sauntered toward her fellow Sentinel. "In what world do you possibly believe you can handle me?"

"I do not fear you, Diothur," he replied serenely. "Or should I call you Yustina?"

"You cannot sway me from my purpose, Loradún. I know the truth. I know who I am."

"You are a Sentinel," Rezaaran replied. He stood his ground opposite her. He knew Harkenathor was at his waist, but he wished to resolve this peacefully. He had to be able to reach her. "You are one of us. We are the last hope for peace in Anmor, and with your help, we can still achieve it. Together we can defeat Thaedis and end this war. Is that not worth fighting for?"

Diothur stopped an arm's length from Rezaaran and regarded the War Mage. She allowed herself a small smile, for the fool had permitted her to close the distance and nullify the reach of his sword.

"There still is hope for peace," she said. "It lies in the death of the Sentinels!"

Viciously she slashed at Rezaaran, who adroitly sidestepped her venom-tipped dagger. The huntress swiveled her dagger about her wrist with a sharp flick. A jab flew forward and was caught between Rezaaran's gauntlets. The War Mage wrested her strike back and raised his hands to offer another attempt at a peaceful resolution.

"Yustina, search within yourself," he said calmly. "You were meant for more than this existence as a servant to the darkness."

She lunged forward once more, pivoting when she missed her target yet again. Her pale-blue eyes focused on the War Mage, and her shoulders heaved in agitation.

"You talk too much!" she snapped and leaped toward him again. The huntress unleashed a blindingly fast series of punches that Rezaaran deflected with great concentration. Ducking beneath her next powerful punch, which shattered the stone wall, he appeared behind her. She turned swiftly and threw a flurry of strikes at his face and chest. He caught her wrist, but despite his strongest attempt, he felt his grasp slipping beneath her hateful strength.

Diothur's eyes grew whiter, and she edged the blade closer to Rezaaran's neck. The War Mage reached deep into the Vaux and repelled her with a spectral blast.

Rezaaran steadied himself and noticed a sharp sting in his left wrist where Diothur's blade had nicked him. As he looked toward her, he saw the rooftop transforming to the veranda where he had witnessed the death of his father.

The War Mage steeled his mind with the Vaux, and the Zenorian veranda shimmered away. He was back on the rooftop with Diothur.

I don't understand. Why is she not tiring?

She draws her strength from the fear around her.

I am not afraid of her.

You are, however, on a planet of slaves who live in constant terror. This battle is a stalemate. You have to secure the Ark!

Rezaaran charged forward, catching Diothur by surprise. He glazed himself with Zelzo's metallic coat and effortlessly deflected the blows of her dagger. He felt her mounting frustration until finally she threw a careless punch. The War Mage caught her hand and pulled her into a choke hold, his arm around her throat. Yet she remained undaunted. Diothur leaped up and flipped Rezaaran over her back. She immediately followed through with a punch that cratered the roof as the War Mage rolled aside at the last moment. She charged at him with greater venom, and he seized her hand once more and drove her blade into her shoulder.

The huntress crashed to the ground. Her eyes widened from the fear toxin that coursed through her blood. Suddenly the rooftop shimmered to her last battle outside the Kremlin in Moscow, when several of her comrades had fallen to the ravenous Kalaran soldiers. Her temples throbbed with rage, and a savage snarl crossed her face. Through the glistening memories that warped her vision, she glimpsed the rippling form of Rezaaran, leader of the Sentinels. Were it not for them, there would have been no war, and her world, her friends and family, would have been safe. She focused on her incandescent hatred for the Sentinels and resisted the toxin's paralytic terror.

She charged yet again, this time with a bestial frenzy in her actions. Her dagger's edge sang through her fervent slashes at the War Mage, but Rezaaran evaded and parried each strike with his steel-plated arms. Reaching out to stop her punch, he expected her bones to crack against the metallic coating of his arms. However, her deep connection to the Obsidious fortified her beyond mortal capacity. Rezaaran used his remaining hand to disarm Diothur of her fear-inducing dagger and fixed a stern glare upon her.

"I do not want to hurt you," he said calmly. Flames crept along his hair and spread down his neck to embrace his shoulders. The heat flowed along his metallic arm into Diothur's fist. However, the huntress remained unyielding.

"Oh, I wouldn't worry about hurting me," she snarled. Her free hand flashed forward, and Rezaaran felt a sting in his chest. The fires across his head dispersed into smoke, and the metal coat over his arms regressed. His hands and eyes moved to the center of his chest—where Diothur had embedded a second dagger.

"It's Torementhicite," she sneered. "Unlike me, the Sentinels all have a weakness. With you out of the way, the others will soon fall. Good riddance, Loradún."

Diothur spun on her heels and delivered a powerful kick to Rezaaran's midriff that flung him over the edge of the building to plummet to the street below.

Rezaaran's brain struggled to find the focus needed to direct his hands to the blade lodged in his chest. He felt the air escaping him, and every subsequent breath grew more labored. Adding to the assault on his mind was the milieu of traffic that was zipping past him on his rapid descent to the street below.

Suddenly a strong arm snatched him from the air and pulled him onto a speeding Levira.

"Always having to save your ass, there, Rez," Jet chuckled. "Come on, snap out of it—yank that dagger out of your chest so you can heal."

Jet's gruff voice and the wind whipping his face rallied Rezaaran's mind to the present. He yanked the Torementhicite dagger from his chest and rasped as his regenerative powers returned, closing the wounds.

"There's no time for drama here," said the Erebonian. "Luferikas had a considerable lead over us and should be near the launching site by now."

"How did you know to wait for me?" Rezaaran asked as he positioned himself better on the Levira and tossed the dagger to the streets below.

"Ashana told me to wait nearby," Jet replied, dodging an autonomous barge. "Either it was her future sight, or she knows you have a knack for getting involved in things over your head."

"Perhaps it was a bit of both," she offered over the communication channel. Despite her jibe, she was relieved to hear that Rezaaran was alive. "I have a visual on Luferikas's Levira, but I don't think I can reach him before he gets to the drop ship."

"Leave him to me," Rezaaran said. He steadied himself on the back of Jet's Levira and locked eyes on the distant form of the Demokarva. "Ash, I need you to work with Ikso, ADAM, and Quirt to ground the ship with the Harbingers."

"Why do I have a feeling the two of you are going to do something monumentally stupid?"

"Well, that may be because you know us too well," Jet replied with a manic grin as he realized what Rezaaran was planning. "Ready back there?"

"Hit it!"

Jet cranked the throttle to the maximum and, after a brief sprint, suddenly braked hard. The nose of the Levira dipped while the back lifted, propelling Rezaaran, who had harnessed the Vaux to imbue him with the force of the prevailing winds. The War Mage catapulted through the air and crashed into the back of Luferikas's Levira, knocking into the Demokarva and his vessel and causing it to crash onto the roof of a building.

Luferikas leaped from his Levira and rolled across the stone roof as his vessel exploded into the wall of a nearby scrap-storage facility. The battered Grand Harbinger rose angrily and scrambled to retrieve his gun as the War Mage skidded across the rooftop.

Rezaaran fired a rapid series of spectral blasts that disarmed and subdued Luferikas and then forced him to the ground. Roughly he seized the Demokarva and looked into his glowing yellow eyes.

"Tell me where Varathis is headed," Rezaaran snarled.

"You think you can scare me?" Luferikas asked with genuine surprise. "I was trained by Lord Silvermire himself. Next to him, you are just an angry child."

"I don't have time for these games," Rezaaran grumbled.

He placed a hand on Luferikas's forehead and barged through his mind. He learned that Thaedis had tasked Luferikas with recruiting the help of one they believed would betray the Sentinels. Thaedis had believed that person to be Jet, based on what he had learned from Narak when Jet was afflicted with the Torementhian blight. However, the message intended for Jet had reached Varathis instead. Rezaaran learned that the Zenorian prince had updated the Grand Harbinger on their every move behind their backs—and that crashing on this world had been the culmination of Varathis's betrayal when he allowed the engines to be shot down at Luferikas's instruction when they had reached the coordinates. Subsequently, Varathis's ambition had driven him to seek an audience with Thaedis, who in turn dispatched Diothur to collect him in her private vessel, whose path was preprogrammed to a ghastly vessel in a distant star field.

Rezaaran felt the star coordinates burned into his memory, and he relinquished his grasp on Luferikas's head. The groggy alien turned a baleful gaze toward the War Mage.

"I hope you liked what you saw," he said, chuckling darkly. "No matter what you do now, we have won. The Dominion has won!"

Rezaaran concussed Luferikas with a spectral blast. When he looked around, he saw that the others had successfully disabled the Harbingers' escape vessel. "Guys, we need to get to the *Liberator* immediately. I know where Thaedis's ship is located."

"What about these idiots?" Jet asked.

"ADAM, have you received any response from IRIS?"

The android scanned the network and turned his glowing blue eyes to Rezaaran. "IRIS has dispatched a contingent to retrieve us. They should be arriving soon."

"They'll need at least a Citadel to free these slaves," Ashana remarked, looking over the endless fields of informal dwellings the slaves had scrapped together from spacecraft debris.

"ADAM, get some Arkanians to watch over the Harbingers until the IRIS soldiers arrive to apprehend them—and send word that a Citadel is required for a liberation mission."

"Will do," the android replied cheerfully. Then his tone abruptly changed. "Oh, no—this could be trouble."

A tall figure strode along the streets. Taking cover intermittently against the walls to avoid the notice of passing patrols, he drew his frayed hat down tighter and adjusted his long brown coat. His scanners indicated an enormous crowd of bodies all around him. Several were the upgraded cyborg Kalarans interspersed with Kreyforian battle masters. However, there was also a large contingent of slaves across this city. The commander understood now why Ashana had requested a Citadel.

Cosmonox surveyed his surroundings and climbed his way onto the overhang of a nearby building, from where he dispatched a seeker droid.

"What is going on here?" he murmured. According to the feedback of the seeker droid, an outbreak of violence was occurring across the city, the Arkanians decimating the Kalarans and Kreyforian battle masters. "I thought they were on the same team."

A series of explosions rocked the city and unsettled the cyborg commander from his perch. The feedback from the seeker droid disappeared into static. He cast a bewildered look over the cityscape at the fires that interspersed the furious battle.

Another series of tremors rocked the city, and debris from the slave dwellings flew into the air. His scanner indicated movement below his position. Casting his gaze downward, he saw two terror-struck children crying as they held onto each other. Cosmonox leaped from his position and crashed to the ground, rolled forward, and grabbed the two children in his arms. He rushed them aside, narrowly avoiding some flaming debris that flew through the air.

"You kids need to be careful," he said roughly, looking down at the awestruck children. "Where are your parents?"

The children continued to stare at him, mesmerized by his robotic green eye. Cosmonox sighed. These children had never seen a cyborg before, and like every other person who met him, they were terrified by his appearance.

"Just get to my ship there," he said, indicating the *Shazal Explorer* beyond the confines of the city. "I'll come and find you soon."

He was rising to his feet when to his astonishment the two children hugged his waist, flashing him toothy smiles.

"Thank you for saving us, mister!" squealed the young boy.

"Will you save our mummy and daddy too?" the little girl asked, looking at the cyborg earnestly with her shimmering brown eyes.

"Uh...I'll look for them," he fumbled.

The children beamed and ran off to the ship he had shown them. Cosmonox looked on, bewildered by their reaction. He eventually allowed himself a small smile, realizing that others saw him as a monster only because that was how he projected himself to the world. Yet these children saw him as something more. He was their hero.

"Why would they not revere you?"

The cyborg spun around and raised his right hand, its three barrels bared at the red-eyed Arkanian.

"I mean no harm," the android said calmly, raising both hands.

"What is going on in this city?" Cosmonox demanded. "If you've turned on your allies, then why should I trust you?"

"You make a valid point," the Arkanian admitted. "I am Shian."

"I don't care," Cosmonox replied gruffly and aimed his other hand at the Arkanian's head. "What do you want?"

"I was tasked by Itara ADAM to escort these slaves to freedom. You are Commander Cosmonox Shazal of IRIS, correct?"

The cyborg locked eyes with the android but did not lower his weapons. "How do you know that?" he asked suspiciously. ADAM was the name of an artificial intelligence that Albeinius had recently allowed to access the IRIS database.

"Itara ADAM serves with another who is allied with IRIS," Shian explained patiently. "He fights alongside Rezaaran Valhara."

"Where is he?" Cosmonox snarled. "What have you done to him?"

"We have done nothing," Shian replied. "He freed us of enslavement to the Dominion, and we rebelled against their corruption of our purpose. They are currently in pursuit of the Harbingers and tasked my regiment with escorting these prisoners to safety. I believe you just saved the children of two of these slaves."

Cosmonox slowly lowered his guns. If this Arkanian had truly interacted with Rezaaran and was carrying out the kid's orders, then he was not going to interfere.

He turned his attention and weapons to his right at the sound of a marching brigade. Several Kalarans filled the alley and aimed their guns at Cosmonox and Shian.

"Surrender now," one of the Kalarans growled, aiming his arm-mounted cannon at the cyborg. "And we'll be having your circuits, traitor!"

"Don't you have orders, soldier?" Cosmonox asked Shian gruffly.

The Arkanian cast him a concerned look. How could this cyborg contest this squadron on his own?

"Get those slaves and your regiment to my ship, and pilot it to the coordinates programmed on the bridge. It will bring you to an IRIS vessel, where Rezaaran can explain all this. Get going—I can handle this."

Shian nodded and proceeded to escort the slaves away, under the armed guard of his fellow Arkanians, toward the *Shazal Explorer*.

Cosmonox fixed a stern glare upon the Kalarans. The plates on his chest opened, and he unleashed a flurry of proton torpedoes into the crowd. Charging forward, he blasted the weapons mounted within his hands, felling every Kalaran before him as he bathed the streets in their reptilian blood. The cyborg halted his rampage in the middle of the street.

The remnants of the battalion stared at the cyborg and routed. A few moments later, one of their heads rolled along the ground.

Cosmonox looked up and saw a woman with a black cowl holding in her outstretched arm a black crystal blade dripping with blood. A larger contingent of Kalarans and Kreyforians flanked her, their weapons at the ready.

"Well, why not?" the cyborg said to himself with a smirk. "Rezaaran, give them hell for me, kid!"

Ashana led the Sentinels through the raging battle that consumed the city, using her future-sight ability to avoid the worst fighting.

"Shian has just informed me," ADAM reported to the group, "that he was able to stow the slaves we freed aboard the ship of an IRIS commander."

"That's excellent news," Rezaaran replied, glad that something had finally gone their way.

"Hey, I can see the ship!" Jet exclaimed, cranking the throttle higher on his Levira.

The *Liberator* came into view as the Sentinels exited the city. Then, just as suddenly as it had appeared, a brilliant burst of saffron engulfed the vessel, spreading heat and light across the city's edge.

"Gunner!" Ikso and Ashana cried out in alarm.

The two warriors leaped off their Levira and stared horrified at the flaming remains of the ship that held their friend. But then a sharp and joyful yapping caught their attention. To their relief, the robotic hound sauntered up and affectionately nuzzled his friends.

Despite her relief that her canine companion was safe, Ashana felt the weight of the *Liberator*'s loss within her heart. The Dominion had severed the last tether to her past. The vessel that her brother and father had constructed as a family cruiser was now a smoldering metal shell wrecked on an alien world.

Rezaaran placed a hand on her shoulder and softly kissed her head. She squeezed his hand tightly and watched the flames consume the ship she had called home.

"We have company," Jet murmured, loading his blast cannon.

A regiment of Kalaran soldiers surrounded the Sentinels, weapons readied and awaiting any sign of hostility.

"What do we do now?" the Erebonian asked.

Rezaaran drew Harkenathor, and a steely expression graced his face. "We fight!"

"Oh, I hoped you'd say that," Jet replied with a broad smile.

The ground shuddered, and a wide jet of scorching plasma seared the front line of Kalarans. The Sentinels looked back as an enormous robotic dragon crouched behind them. Its breastplate lowered to form a ramp, and at the foot of the metal platform stood a soldier in ornate orange dragon armor.

"Albeinius," Ashana whispered in disbelief.

"What are you lot waiting for?" the scientist yelled. "A damn invitation? Move it! We need to extract you—*now*!"

The Sentinels hurried toward the loading ramp, but Rezaaran stopped just inside when he sensed a familiar echo. Turning to face the inferno Albeinius had created, he saw Diothur casually stride forward. She parted the flames with a nonchalant spectral blast from her hand and tossed a frayed brown hat toward the War Mage.

He recognized it immediately and felt fury erupt from within his heart. Rezaaran attempted to charge from the platform, but Jet and ADAM restrained him as the vessel lifted off the ground. He looked around frantically, and in the sliver of light before the loading door closed, he saw Albeinius confidently stride into battle.

The scientist cast his gaze across the clearing. The cowled huntress had dispersed the flames and allowed him to assess the full magnitude of the enemies that surrounded him.

"Well, you lot are machines of some sort," he muttered. His amethyst eyes clouded to an opaque white, and his mind seized control of every Kalaran cyborg. The augmented soldiers immediately turned their weapons on Diothur. "I have you surrounded. Lay down your weapons and surrender, or face prosecution for your crimes."

"Ha! You think this lot scares me?" she asked. "All I see are the next victims for my blade. Just like that miserable cyborg. His heart was heavy with misery, so I put him down."

Albeinius's anger demanded vengeance on this monster that had killed his friend. "Then you leave me no choice," he replied. The scientist readied his searing orange plasma whips and prepared himself to seek justice for Cosmonox's murder—despite knowing that the odds towered over him.

CHAPTER FIFTEEN

THE ARK OF TORE MENTHIAS

The robotic dragon docked quietly with the *Dragonwing*, mirroring the silence within the vessel. None of the occupants knew what to say in the wake of what they had witnessed. None knew how to handle the cost of their escape.

"We have to turn around," Rezaaran said frantically.

"We can't do that," said Ashana softly.

"It appears that Albeinius locked the vessel on a preprogrammed route to his ship," Quirt informed them.

"Quirt, you and ADAM can break through the programming and return us to the surface."

The Thyrillian was about to acknowledge that he could easily achieve this, but he kept quiet following the stern glare Ashana passed him.

"Ash, we have to get to Albeinius!" Rezaaran implored her. "He stands no chance against Diothur! She's going to kill him!"

"Do you think I don't know that?" Ashana whispered darkly. "I've faced that monster just as you have. I know what she is capable of, and I know Albeinius is not a soldier. He knows that too—and he willingly sacrificed himself because he knows that this war is bigger than he is. I've known him my entire life, Rez, so don't think for a minute that this is easy for me."

Rezaaran sank into a chair and sobbed into his hands.

"I want to go back and fight beside him just as much as you do," she said more gently, wrapping her arms around Rezaaran, "but we both know where we have to be instead."

"She killed Cosmonox," he seethed as the tears freely flowed down his face. "We all know she is going to kill Albeinius. They're our family, Ash, and she's going to murder them!"

He caught his breath and attempted to still his mind. He could not submit to the rising fury in his heart that demanded vengeance.

"We'll get justice for them, Rez," Jet said, placing a heavy hand on the War Mage's shoulder. "I know this is hard, but we have to get to that Ark before Varathis tells Thaedis where it is."

Rezaaran slowly rose to his feet and composed himself. They were both right. He could not let the sacrifice of his friends be in vain. "Quirt, where is the *Dragonwing* programmed to take us?"

"According to the pilot's log," he read from the ship's monitors, "we have a course plotted to arrive at a Citadel located in system 438802, quadrant four."

"Plot the time expected for the course, and compare it against a course to Tarlok."

Quirt followed Rezaaran's orders and soon displayed a navigation course onto the main view panel. "According to the star maps, it will take the *Dragonwing* fifteen Torians to reach Tarlok, which is located in system 3989, from our current location, compared to a journey of seventy-one Torians to reach the Citadel."

"Well, that's a no-brainer," Jet muttered as he removed his blast cannon and gauntlet to take a seat.

"Check the time needed to reach Tarlok from 03.06.03.219.521," Rezaaran said with a furrowed brow, watching the navigation chart on the display panel.

Quirt read the data. "According to the computers, it should take forty-four Torians. What are those coordinates?"

"It's quite far into the outer arm of the galaxy," ADAM noted.

"That's the location of Thaedis's flagship," Rezaaran said. "When I fought Luferikas, I found the coordinates in his mind. His ship is a monstrosity—larger than anything in our fleet and crafted out of a metal that exudes darkness."

"Well, there may be some good news in that," Quirt remarked as his fingers flashed across the keyboard. "A vessel that large is unlikely to have an advanced Torus drive. Even with overwhelming raw thruster power, we could assume a standard transit time."

"How do we know," ADAM interjected, "when Varathis would make contact with Thaedis to inform him of the Ark's location?"

"According to Luferikas's memories," Rezaaran answered, "Thaedis dispatched Diothur to retrieve Varathis."

"Albeinius's sacrifice should slow her return," Ashana said.

"Factoring that in," Quirt said, quickly adjusting his calculations and displaying the updated triangulation, "if we assume that Thaedis began an advance toward Turmen to intercept Diothur, we still have a marginal advantage in reaching the Ark. However, we significantly lack the firepower to tackle the vessel you describe."

"Albeinius modified the *Dragonwing* to favor speed over offense," ADAM reported after he had connected to the ship's computer. "This vessel doesn't have much in the way of weapons, but it does contain a heavily modified Torus drive to further reduce our transit time."

"Well, what are we waiting for, then?" Jet asked with a clap.

"We need to get a report to Orin first," Rezaaran said firmly. "Ash, hail the IRIS armada."

Ashana nodded, and a few moments later, the venerable general appeared across the view field with Xephyrus beside him in the council chamber.

Rezaaran's mouth dried at the site of the Elder Mage, and a discomfort rose in his throat.

This is going to be difficult.

Yet it is something you have to do. He deserves to know the truth.

"Greetings, Orin and Xephyrus." Rezaaran spoke calmly and resisted the rising pressure in his thoughts.

"It is good to hear from you, Rezaaran," replied Orin, his relief evident in his smile. "Given that your signal is coming from the *Dragonwing*, I am assuming you have made contact with Albeinius."

"That is actually what I need to talk to you about," Rezaaran said softly, the burden of his duty weighing heavier upon his heart with each beat.

Xephyrus's face grew ashen and grave. His electric blue eyes took in Rezaaran's sorrowful expression.

"What happened?" the Elder Mage asked, his voice choked with rising emotion.

The Sentinels remained silent. The reality of the loss struck them harder now at the sight of Xephyrus.

"Rezaaran, what happened to my brother?" he asked with greater intensity and a waver in his voice. Despite his collected demeanor, his hands betrayed the slightest tremble.

"He...he sacrificed himself to save us," Rezaaran replied slowly.

There was a terse moment of silence. Orin placed a reassuring hand on Xephyrus's arm and passed him a knowing nod. The War Mage assumed the general had passed him a telepathic message, for the older Grievior brother's expression softened marginally.

"He died valiantly, then," he finally said, looking at the Sentinels with bloodshot eyes that strained to hold back their tears.

"I am sorry, Xephyrus," Ashana said softly. Her heart broke as she watched this gallant warrior wrestle with his grief.

"He died with honor," the Elder Mage continued. "We should endeavor to honor his sacrifice."

"Rezaaran," Orin said, "we shall plan our next move when you arrive at the Citadel."

"With all due respect, Orin," the War Mage countered, "we do not have the luxury of time to meet at the Citadel. I am forwarding you the coordinates for the planet Tarlok."

Orin retrieved the information on the planet from the archives and viewed it via his implants. "Rezaaran, this is a war-ravaged wilderness," he said with a furrowed brow. "Why are you looking at this world?"

"There will be time to explain this in greater detail later," Rezaaran said sharply. "However, the gist of it is that a powerful artifact called the Ark of Torementhias is located on that planet, and Thaedis Silvermire seeks it. Whoever gets to it first can end this war."

"An end to the war," Orin whispered in disbelief.

This sentiment drew Xephyrus from his melancholic brooding, and he turned his attention to the screen. "Where is Varathis?" he asked with a puzzled expression.

"He defected to the Dominion," Ashana said with determined steadiness. "However, what is more concerning is that he knows the location of the Ark and will undoubtedly pass that information to Thaedis."

"We can reach Tarlok fast enough with the *Dragonwing*," Quirt chimed in.

"I have seen Thaedis's ship in a vision," Rezaaran continued. "We do not have the firepower to contest such a monstrosity. Besides our entire fleet, we will need additional support."

"Forward us the list of transmission tags," Xephyrus said crisply.

"Quirt, get that list across to them, and prepare our Torus tunnel to Tarlok."

A few seconds later, the *Dragonwing* disappeared from the orbit of Turmen along a course toward Tarlok. Rezaaran closed his eyes and sought a reprieve from the emotional storm that strained the threshold of his resolve. Quirt's fingers flitted across the keyboard while his eyes remained fixed on the streams of data that crossed his screen. He turned his attention to the War Mage.

"They are ready when you are, Rezaaran," he said softly.

The War Mage cleared his thoughts and positioned himself before the *Dragonwing*'s bridge camera. The main view panel filled with a black screen and a revolving IRIS insignia.

"My brothers and sisters in arms, I am Captain Rezaaran Valhara of IRIS, and I come to you with a message so that you will know that you are not alone. I know the darkness is deepening and that this war has lingered far too long. I know that hope now feels like nothing more than a whisper. I know that you have all lost something to this war—and that the pain of that loss feels like it closes around you, squeezing you of breath. At the best of times, it feels like there can be no escape from this. But today is our chance to take back from the Dominion. Today we have the chance to make our stand for freedom. If you should feel as we do, if the injustices of the Dominion ignite your fervor and spark your outrage, if your courage should be fanned by their desire to oppress, enslave, and slaughter, then know that you are not alone. This is your call to arms! Rally your valor, and stand with me! Unite with us, and together we will end this war!"

Rezaaran cut the recording and exhaled deeply. Silence hung about the ship, but the air around the War Mage felt electrified after his impassioned delivery.

"What if we are leading them to their end?" Quirt asked. Despite feeling moved by Rezaaran's speech, he could not deny that the odds of their victory defied rational belief.

"'It matters not how strait the gate, how charged with punishments the scroll,'" quoted ADAM slowly. "'I am the master of my fate; I am the captain of my soul.'"

"We choose our own destiny," Ikso said with a nod, gleaning the wisdom from ADAM's utterance.

"Whatever choices people make," Jet replied, "will be of their own accord—as are the consequences. But what good is a life if there is no cause you feel is worth dying for?"

A beeping over the console drew their attention.

"There's a stream of messages reaching the general," ADAM informed them as he surveyed the network activity passing through his processors.

"Some are redirecting to us," Quirt remarked with surprise.

The screen filled with the grinning face of Tarsik Aurelius. "That was quite the inspiring speech, there, Captain," he said with a wink at Rezaaran. "It should go without saying that Tetros Reikon, my brother, and I shall be honored to fight beside you."

"I second that," Shian said, and his image appeared beside the Enchiridion knight. "We stand ready to serve you and your fellow warriors, Itara ADAM."

"Thank you," Rezaaran replied. "We shall see you soon."

The screen returned to the streaking purple flashes of the Torus tunnel as the *Dragonwing* careered toward their destination. The Sentinels sat in silence, preparing their minds for the task ahead.

The doors to the dark chamber opened, and Diothur shoved Varathis across the threshold. Despite his disdain at her disrespect, he held his tongue, for he feared this brutal woman more than he cared to admit. What was more, he was certain she could sense his fear—and she seemed to relish his terror. He had noticed the sly smirk that crossed her face when she'd ripped Albeinius's chest open through his armor and seen Varathis's horror-struck expression. She had savored the scent of his fear just as she had throughout the battle with the scientist. He knew better than to antagonize her.

The Zenorian prince stumbled briefly and drew himself tall before Thaedis Silvermire, ruler of the Obsidian Dominion. Despite the tyrant's facing away from him, Varathis felt a chill in the air, and his heart hammered in terror in the presence of this being who had laid claim to the galaxy. He cleared his throat loudly to make his presence known to Lord Silvermire, attempting to draw his attention away from the star maps.

"Do not feign bravery," Thaedis said coldly. "I can see into your soul, and I know you are a coward."

Varathis bristled. "You don't know the first thing about me!"

Thaedis turned sharply and faced the arrogant Zenorian. A purple glow encased his hand, and his eyes flared orange. Varathis felt his breath fail him. It arrested in his throat, and his wide eyes became transfixed on the glowing eyes that glared through him from beneath the black hood.

"You are Varathis Kalamdor, the last Prince of Kel-Ardimus. I never thought much of royalty. For all your pretentious ways and purported claims of power, you always paled next to those who controlled the Vaux, and so you sought to use us to defend your kingdoms. Yet I see clearer now than I did in my naïve youth. Those who do not have true power should not dictate to those who do. Your royal birth matters little to me, other than giving me a reason to loathe you further. As to your cowardice, were it not for your craven nature, why else would you be here? You falsely portray yourself as a man of valor yet thought nothing of selling your fellow travelers off to save yourself."

Thaedis released his grasp on Varathis, and the prince slumped to the floor, gasping for breath.

"Diothur, what use have I for this fool?" he asked his hunter, turning his now pale eyed glare upon her.

"I have information that is useful to you," Varathis wheezed. His fear heightened beneath Diothur's narrow gaze.

"I very much doubt that," Thaedis replied bitterly. He turned to face his star maps once more.

"Rezaaran Valhara has the aid of a former Guardian. She calls herself Luminara."

Thaedis remained silent. His lips pursed tightly, and his knuckles cracked as his grasp tightened over the console.

"There had better be a point to this," he seethed, "if you wish to still hold life in that quivering body."

"She had a vision of her husband, Salvidawn."

This held Thaedis's interest. Had Tyrel been able to reach Luminara through a Vaux evocation? That would mean he had avoided the reach of the Obsidious long enough to merge his soul into the Vaux. How was that possible? It had been thirty years since he'd killed Tyrel and summoned the Obsidious to consume his soul.

"Where did they go after this vision?" he asked. When Varathis did not answer immediately, Thaedis turned to him swiftly, grasped his throat, and lifted him into the air. Varathis screamed in agony, for his skin seared beneath the tyrant's touch. "If you think *this* hurts," Thaedis seethed, "bear in mind that I am restraining myself. Tell me what I want to know, or I will incinerate all the Torementhicite in your being!"

"We went to the tomb where you left Salvidawn," Varathis spluttered as tears poured from his eyes. "There was a creature there. He called himself Isiel. He brought Salvidawn back to life."

Thaedis tightened his grasp minimally and branded his grip into the screaming prince's flesh.

"Salvidawn told them to find the Ark on a planet that had seen countless wars."

"I want the name!"

"It's Tarlok," Varathis said, sobbing harder. "That's all I know! Please, let me go! I beg you!"

Thaedis dropped the prince to the floor. Varathis grabbed his scorched throat and gasped for air between his sobs.

"Tarlok," Thaedis murmured. His mind raced through a flurry of memories at the mention of the planet. "That was our first task as the Guardians. We ended an era of strife upon the planet, but over the years, it became a battleground for countless other conflicts. The planet is steeped in ages of bloodshed." He selected the planet and watched the slow-turning hologram with anticipation. "It is the perfect place to hide the Ark. Of course this is where Tyrel chose! Eknarl!"

The sickly spirit floated into the chamber, his head downcast, avoiding eye contact with his master. "Yes, my lord?"

"Set all thrusters to maximum power. I have set us a new course—our last course in this war!"

"Very good, my lord."

"Diothur, get word to our soldiers and all who are loyal to the Dominion to pay their tribute of warriors to our destination."

The huntress silently nodded and left the chamber to carry out her orders. Thaedis activated the portal to Torementhias, and Narak's head appeared from the black ferrous pool.

"What do you require of me, master?" the Lord of Torementhias asked solemnly.

"Today we will crush IRIS, and at last our conquest of Anmor shall be complete!"

Narak's visage broke into a cruel smile. "Our time is at last here!"

"Is your army of Edarians ready?"

"They will bathe the fields in the blood of our enemies. I shall show you how to summon them."

Thaedis followed Narak's gaze to the Zenorian prince, who staggered to his feet and stared at the Grand Edarian with terror-tinged adulation.

"What do you want?" Thaedis asked. "A man with such dubious character as yours holds self-preservation above all else. Knowing who I am, you still declined to divulge this information to my Harbingers and chose to present it directly to me. This can only mean that you desire a reward of sorts. So…what do you want?"

Varathis remained silent. His eyes roved across Narak's cruel yet well-sculpted face.

"I am by no means a patient man," Thaedis said. "Do you desire money to start your own empire within the confines of the Dominion? Or substances to dull your fetid mind further and remove yourself from the awareness of your banal existence? Or is it something as basic as carnal desires to be satisfied by a herd of whores?"

"I wish to have more power," Varathis replied darkly. Although his lips quivered, he found the resolve to stand tall before the tyrant.

This seemed to impress both Thaedis and Narak. A smirk grew across the Grand Edarian's visage, for they sensed the hatred swelling from this mortal's soul.

"I want more power!" Varathis demanded with more confidence. "I want the power to destroy Rezaaran Valhara!"

The *Dragonwing* landed with a soft hum onto the desolate, dusty plains of Tarlok a few miles beyond the walls of an enormous weathered fortress. The loading-bay door hissed open, and the Sentinels disembarked onto the surface to the sound of an eerie ethereal lament.

"Something feels off about this place," Jet remarked grimly, tightening his grasp on his blast cannon.

"There is nobody that can harm us on this planet," Luminara replied soothingly. "Not at the moment, in any case. However, those who can will be here soon, so we should make haste."

"That chorus in the distance," Ashana said softly as she listened to the disembodied voices that called to them. "It sounds like the chorus in the Nuhremorn."

"When we became the Anmorian Guardians," Luminara explained with sorrowful nostalgia, "we were drawn to this planet to quell centuries of endless conflict between the native people. However, before we could reach them, their thirst for destruction sealed their demise. Through their nuclear weaponry, they ravaged their world in an attempt to kill off their opposing nations and thereby obliterated each other. Arlen was the more intuitive of the Guardians. He believed this world was so close to the Anmorian axis that the Obsidian influence reached into their hearts and corrupted their reason."

"Tolbetrius said that he was the Emissary of Darkness," Rezaaran murmured and reflected on his battle with the Edarian. "He was able to pass between realms and spread Nethriziin's influence."

"That explains quite a bit of this war," Luminara nodded slowly. "We always suspected there was a Grand Edarian who could pass between the realms of Anmor, yet he always eluded our gaze. He would have been an invaluable asset to Nethriziin in his conquest of Anmor. Whatever else he did to the leaders of this world, he certainly led them to their end. However, their violent nature and callous disregard for life rent a deep wound upon this world."

"What do you mean?" Jet asked with a raised eyebrow.

"All worlds are connected to the Vaux," Luminara explained. "What happened on Tarlok was devastation to such an extent that the Vaux was unable to restart life upon this world, and the planet's connection to the Vaux grew ever more anemic. As with all wounds left exposed and untreated, this too festered. The Obsidious reached to this world through the axis, and the souls of those lost in conflict throughout the galaxy found refuge here. Their agony ensured that this world would always bear the brand of strife."

"'By strife it shall enclose, never to reopen.'" Rezaaran recited the words of "Sahar's Requiem," adding, "A planet seized by endless conflict and haunted by tortured souls forms the perfect magical lock over the Ark."

"Never mind that," Jet said. "Why did the Guardians turn a blind eye to this wounded planet?"

"Quite simply, it was our hubris," Luminara admitted with downcast eyes and flushed cheeks. "We were too late to save the native people and so dedicated ourselves to averting such acts on other worlds. However, in time we became elevated beyond the people. Some of us revered ourselves as new gods. Perhaps Thaedis was more right about us than we cared to admit."

"Well, we cannot let him get this Ark first," Jet said firmly. "What exactly are we looking for?"

"In our Guardian form, it is the size of a chest," she explained. "However, in the mortal realm, it would appear the size of a chamber. I believe Salvidawn concealed it within this fortress."

The Sentinels followed Luminara's lead and navigated their way through the labyrinthine corridors beneath the glare of Quirt's helmet-mounted torches. They walked for some time until Ikso drew their attention to a mural carved into the stone.

"This is an odd coincidence," Jet remarked.

"I don't think this is a coincidence at all," Ikso replied with wide-eyed wonder and a grin sprawled across her face. "This is a sign left by Lord Salvidawn! This is the Ark!"

Rezaaran's eyes roved over the mural, which seemed to depict everyone in their group. In the far right, a hooded figure knelt with his sword plunged into the ground. The War Mage drew Harkenathor from its scabbard, locked the blade into a notch at the edge of the mural's frame, and pressed its edge into the border. A loud rumble filled the silent corridors, and an eight-foot-high segment of the mural yawned open. As the Sentinels looked inside with trepidation, a buzzing field of golden light filled the doorway.

"It's an enchantment Tyrel placed upon the Ark," Luminara explained. "Only those who possess the soul of a Sentinel or a Guardian may pass the threshold."

"We'll stay here and defend the entrance," ADAM said with a bow of his head. "I expect our visitors will be arriving soon."

The Sentinels followed Luminara through the buzzing magical gate.

Despite its innocuous exterior, the interior of the Ark was a marvelous sight. The gilded walls shimmered, bathing the chamber in a warm glow.

"This place defies belief," Ashana whispered. She approached a wall that bore the weapons of every Guardian. "Are these replicas?"

"Those relics are the weapons used by each of us," Luminara replied. "They served us throughout our war against the Obsidious and aided us in bringing the first era of peace to Anmor. Whoever wields them would command the power gifted to a Guardian."

Ashana's eyes lingered for a moment on Nish Ira's bow, which still whispered with a passing gale and foretold that the thrum of its string would herald a hurricane.

Quirt and Jet walked between the numerous shelves stacked with ancient tomes and scrolls.

"Seems like this would be your paradise," Jet murmured, casually casting his eyes over the weathered spines.

"There is so much information contained in these walls," Quirt exclaimed with scarcely contained excitement. "It is a remarkable feat that it has all been stored so pristinely."

"Arlen took great pride in preserving these archives," Luminara reminisced.

The Thyrillian's attention diverted to a series of thick golden lines that led from the bookshelves to a wide pedestal at the center of the chamber. He joined Rezaaran to investigate the device.

"Do you know how this works?" Rezaaran asked the scientist.

Quirt inspected the runic markings around the device. "I believe this repository is linked to the shelves. The information in those books is scanned and uploaded to this device. If we were to place our hands on these concentric patterns, we would activate the device and be able to view the contents of the archive."

Rezaaran and Quirt positioned themselves opposite one another across the repository and activated the device simultaneously. A beam of light shone through the center of the pedestal and expanded into a projection of every event transcribed into the tomes by Arlen, including older memories left behind by Alaris of the time before Anmor existed, about how the four realms had formed and her ensuing tireless war against Nethriziin. The repository shuffled swiftly through the archive, speeding past entries on the rise and fall of every known civilization and finally settling on the Guardians' battle against the Torementhian forces that ended with the incarceration of Nethriziin.

"Wait a moment," Quirt murmured. "How did they manage to bind a primordial force of existence within the Obsidious for thousands of years?"

Immediately the repository displayed a complex series of enchantments and rites that when performed in sequence had created the nine seals of the prison that held Nethriziin.

"Does this make any sense to you, Rezaaran?"

"I believe it does," he replied quietly. The Sirantanian runes of the spell shimmered and translated to Galtic. "I think I know how to trap

Nethriziin if he returns. However, with that said, I would rather not contest him if we can avoid it. These archive accounts of him make me think the cost of such a confrontation may be higher than I am prepared to pay."

The repository swiftly passed through several more archived files that included the full version of "Sahar's Requiem," glimpses of the mythic battle that had led to Thaedis's exile, the plan to create the Sentinels as well as their identities, and a detailed theory proposed by Zelzo on how to weaponize the Vaux. Rezaaran read the last entry with great interest before he and Quirt deactivated the repository and returned to their fellow Sentinels.

"Did you find anything useful?" Ashana asked.

"I found everything we will need," Rezaaran replied. "I know how to trap Nethriziin again."

"There's so much useful information here," Jet said, looking around at the towering shelves. "Can't we download it all into ADAM or our interfaces to access later if we need it?"

Luminara passed her curious gaze across the Sentinels from afar and settled finally on Rezaaran.

"We cannot allow this to leave the Ark," Rezaaran said. "Jet, this information was in the hands of the Guardians and kept from all mortals for a reason. Knowing this much about Anmor will create more problems than it is worth. Every one of these shelves holds information on every civilization and every civilian in Anmor. That is too much power for anyone to wield."

"Despite my belief that knowledge is an endeavor worth pursuing," Quirt said softly, "I am in agreement with Rezaaran. I have seen what the Dominion did with their knowledge of the latest technologies. I unwittingly aided them throughout my lifetime. I could not have known what they would do, but I know better now. I know that such a wealth of power can turn even the best of people evil. To those who would seek it, this much information could lead to another Dominion rising in the aftermath of this war. Now that we know better, we should strive to *be* better."

Ashana had offered a slow nod of agreement throughout Quirt's oration. "I would hate to see what destruction those weapons could inflict if they ever escaped this Ark."

"Well, I guess that's settled, then," Jet said firmly. "If that is OK with you, of course, Luminara?"

Luminara looked at the Erebonian with mild surprise.

"This is the collective work of the Guardians," he elaborated. "Everything about the people that became your family lives in this…room."

"We are inside the Ark," Quirt murmured.

"I'm still not getting my head around that part," Jet grumbled and then resumed talking to Luminara. "My point is that everything here is the only link to the people you have known."

"Our souls are never bound to the material plane," Luminara replied with a smile. "I do not need the contents of this Ark to remind me of my friends, for their memories will forever live on through the Vaux. The Ark and this planet are the reminders that the Guardians failed Anmor through our arrogance. We lost sight of our sacred duty and received our penance. However, our time has long passed. Now is the time of the Sentinels and those who shall come after you. The decision of the Ark is something I entrust to you four. Although I hope that you will know and believe that I have never been more proud of you all."

"Well, let's not get all sentimental, now," Jet said with a grin and slung his blast cannon off his shoulder. "We still have to blow this Ark!"

"Whoa! Easy, there!" Ashana shouted with furrowed eyebrows. "We can't just go shooting up this place while we're inside!"

"May I suggest a more comprehensive plan?" Quirt asked. He presented a handful of red circular devices branded with a dragon's head. "These are plasma incendiary devices created by Albeinius. I found them on the *Dragonwing*. I was able to remotely link them to my interface."

A few moments later, the Sentinels stepped through the magical threshold and returned to the fortress on Tarlok.

"You're back?" Ikso asked with alarm. "How can you be back already? Did you manage to get everything you needed?"

"How long were we gone?" Jet asked, puzzled.

"Approximately three minutes and twenty-one seconds," ADAM replied.

"*That* is an approximation?" Ashana asked wryly.

"The Ark exists within a dimensional pocket," Quirt said, pondering. "I have an idea about how to destroy it."

"Well, let's do this, then," Rezaaran said.

He and Quirt passed their hands through the buzzing golden threshold field. The War Mage released a growing fireball directed toward the repository, followed by the Thyrillian's gravitational vortex. They immediately withdrew their hands to avoid the swelling wall of heat that bathed the inside of the Ark and the strengthening pull of the vortex.

The fortress rumbled around them, and the ground shuddered. Working together, the seven warriors closed the stone door to the Ark. However, the fortress's stone walls could scarcely contain the growing power within the chamber. Large fissures tore their way from the ceiling across the mural.

"Come on—let's move!"

They followed Rezaaran's lead and sprinted through the corridors. A few moments later, they emerged at the entrance to the fortress, followed by a thick cloud of dust.

Rezaaran's animusense spiked, drawing his attention away from his coughing to the legion of cyborg Kalarans that was marching toward them. The unmistakable cowled figure of Diothur led the battalion. However, a new, unrecognizable warrior walked beside her. As they grew closer, Rezaaran felt a wave of disgust creep over him at the sight of the two red-crystal-bladed swords strapped at the warrior's right hip. Despite the black metal suit that covered the figure from head to toe, the War Mage knew exactly who this warrior was, even though his echo was lost in a mire of darkness.

The pair of adversaries walked brazenly to the pathway that led to the fortress and stood their ground. Diothur signaled the garrison to halt as the warrior in the black metal suit surveyed the seven warriors who defiantly blocked his path. He reached to the side of his head and retracted his helmet.

"Is that Varathis?" Ikso whispered.

Rezaaran fixed a grim glare at the ashen face of the Zenorian prince, unable to believe the drastic transformation he had undergone. Numerous pipes connected from the armor into his bald scalp and neck, pumping liquid Torementhicite into his vessels. The black liquid engorged the veins across his cackling face, and his amber eyes darted across the faces of his former companions.

"You idiots denied me my birthright!" he shouted at the seven warriors. "Now you will face the full might of my vengeance!"

Quirt's lenses analyzed the battalion and generated a forecast of the expected outcome. "They hold a numerical advantage if we decide to engage," he whispered.

"Then we will have to split their numbers," Rezaaran muttered. He cast his gaze around the fortress and noticed ten granite wizards alongside the road leading up to them. The War Mage reached into the Vaux and whispered life into the stone constructs.

Varathis startled, and the ground shuddered as the stone wizards awoke. Heeding their summoner's call, they turned their attention to the stationary garrison of Kalarans and swung their staves into the mass of soldiers. Many attempted to dodge the incoming attack, but several of the cyborgs received the brunt of the attack and flew through the air. The other cyborgs opened fire on the stone defenders and chipped away at the constructs but did little else to deter them.

"Keep the Kalarans busy," Rezaaran ordered Quirt, Ikso, Luminara and ADAM. "Wait for us to engage Diothur and Varathis, and then make sure none of the Kalarans interfere."

The warriors nodded and held back while the three Sentinels walked along the road toward their adversaries.

"Rezaaran Valhara," Varathis sneered. "The grand and mighty War Mage who would desire to be king."

"I have never had a desire to rule Zenor," Rezaaran replied serenely. "My only desire was an end to this war. I realize I have failed the two of you. You both have fallen so far from what you once were, but I realize now that there is no returning for either of you."

The Zenorian prince's smirk evolved into a cackle. "Always the pious, naïve idiot."

"Don't feel bad, Rez," Jet said gruffly. He slung his blast cannon across his shoulder and cracked his neck. "Varathis never had very far to fall."

"Enough out of you imbeciles!" the prince snarled, drawing his two swords. "I am going to end your miserable life, Rezaaran!"

The War Mage solemnly reached for Harkenathor, but Jet placed a hand on his chest.

"He's mine," he said sternly.

With a calm confidence, Jet strode to within a few paces of his former captain, his hand and gauntlet clenched into a fist and his eyes locked with Varathis.

"I'm going to enjoy skinning that leathery hide," Varathis sneered. "Apparently the substance flowing through these tubes into me is made of the same stuff as those crystals on your body. How could you turn your back on this much power? You could have been a god. Instead, you chose to be a lowly Ranger!"

The pair circled one another while the battle against the cyborg Kalarans commenced in the distance.

"It is almost poetic," Varathis said. "You became the test subject for the Dominion's experiments, and I should reap the result of its efforts! How do you think you came to be its test subject? What else happened that day?"

Jet remained silent. He glared at Varathis and raised his fists in a guard.

"You were performing one of your horrendous music acts," Varathis spat, his eyes dancing with a malevolent spirit. "The Dominion had posted a handsome reward for your capture but was unable to track you down. But luck has always been my ally, and of all the bars I should stumble into, it was the one where you and that whore were performing."

The tension thickened between them. Each circle they completed brought them closer to one another.

"*I* told them where to find you! *I* gathered that reward—and I had the good fortune to torment your wretched ass further when you joined the Rangers. Now I stand here, empowered by the very essence that has coursed through you all this time. Wasted all this time on you, a pathetic lizard! You were too weak to be a Ranger—and too weak to save your whore of a wife!"

Jet burst forward with a half step and slammed his gauntlet into Varathis's torso. The force of the impact crumpled the metal and lifted the Zenorian off the ground. Grabbing Varathis's back, Jet flung him into the fortress's stone wall.

The Zenorian prince rose to his feet with a maniacal laugh. "Now it's my turn!" He sprinted forward and leaped at Jet, his blades held high. The red crystals sliced the air with a whistle, but the Erebonian backpedaled and narrowly evaded their edges. The blades whizzed once more in a flurry of slashes, and Jet seized a blade in his gauntlet and shattered it within his grasp. His other hand held Varathis's wrist tightly and prevented him from hacking further.

Jet flipped Varathis over his back and disarmed him. He looked at the remaining weapon with disgust and broke the blade beneath his boot. "You always favored appearance over function!"

"Well, how's *this* for function?" Varathis bolted toward Jet with a speed he had only before witnessed in Rezaaran and Ikso. The unexpected burst of acceleration off-footed the Erebonian. Varathis seized the opportunity and pummeled Jet into submission with a flurry of fists.

Quirt darted quickly between the cyborg Kalarans. Enhanced by the tachyonic field, he developed momentum that cleared the throng of soldiers and allowed him time to evade the incoming plasma blasts. ADAM acrobatically leaped between the enemies and disabled their computer systems with his electrified batons, while Ikso's blasts of wind added to the pandemonium caused by Luminara's spirit army, which disrupted the cohesion of the Kalaran legion's tactics. Following in the steps of the automated statues, the four warriors successfully contained the Kalaran army and prevented it from engaging their three allies.

Suddenly a granite wizard crashed to the ground, yanked down by a series of grappling lines. The impact knocked Ikso aside, and she skidded across the dusty ground. Her sand-stung eyes searched through the chaos for her white wooden staves and found them beneath the boot of a Kalaran cyborg who towered over her. The young girl remained fearless. She narrowed her gaze and was preparing to attack when a wind-bound kazera screamed past her and lifted the Kalaran into the air. Ikso watched with widened eyes as the mythical creature dispersed into the clouds. That was a signature skill of the Order of Nish Ira.

"Acolytes, forward charge!"

She turned to the familiar voice and was shocked to see Moya with her long white staff pointed in the direction of the Kalaran legion. Upon her command, the acolytes stormed forward and ravaged the ranks of the cyborg enemies.

"What are you doing here?" Ikso asked.

"I found my way to Master Suya's home." Moya's expression was sterm, but her face belied gentle kindness and relief at the sight of her sister. "I followed your last words, and in his house, I found the path to his hidden chamber. Not long after that, I received Captain Valhara's message and knew there was only one thing to do." As she looked at her younger sister, her cheeks flushed. "I know you discovered the truth before I did, and I should have…what I mean is that I'm…well, I'm here now, and I am sure that Cheyi will be here with those acolytes and masters loyal to him. So…are you going to just sit on your ass or actually fight for justice for our home?"

Ikso grinned, and Moya hoisted her to her feet.

Meanwhile, Rezaaran reached deep into the Vaux and connected with the bestial spirit he had encountered on Hysforth. Wrestling the raging essence into his control to bolster his strength, he sprouted thick talons from his hands. His sharpened eyesight fixed on Diothur, and the metal skin he had gained from Zelzo coated him. Ashana activated her armor and with her daggers drawn charged at Diothur. Working in tandem, they engaged the bounty hunter furiously, and she struggled to match their speed.

As Diothur fended off yet another assault by the Zenorians, she scowled. These warriors matched her every attack and counter. She held no speed or strength advantage over them. They were dauntless. Then she realized what was amiss. They had lost their weakest link.

She swiftly pushed Ashana aside and swept Rezaaran's feet out from under him to buy herself time to seek her target.

Varathis delivered a vicious cross to Jet's jaw and took a moment to savor the agonized groans of his victim. Crimson blood dripped from the Erebonian's mouth, and he heaved for breath. However, Varathis's smirk was short lived, and he shielded his eyes when a large blast of Obsidian fire struck Jet's slumped body. The prince activated the series of pumps in his suit and directed the liquid Torementhicite toward his right fist, preparing to kill Jet. His fist fired through the air, but Jet's hand caught him midpunch.

Varathis looked at his adversary with terror. Jet no longer seemed the frail and battered victim. Instead, the Erebonian rose to his feet and kept Varathis's augmented strength at bay with apparent ease. Jet slammed his gauntlet into Varathis's chest. The impact crumpled his breastplate and forced the wind from his lungs.

"How is this possible?" Varathis wheezed, staggering backward.

"Seems your new friend likes you even less than we did," Jet snarled.

Motors in Varathis's suit whirred furiously and propelled him to his feet. He charged forward and threw a series of punches at Jet's face. The Erebonian dodged the wild swings and connected a hefty cross to the Zenorian's jaw. Seizing the momentum of the fight, he grappled his opponent and hurled him into a stone column, where he slammed his fists onto Varathis's shoulders and forced him to his knees. His gauntlet ripped away the armor over the Zenorian's back, and he yanked the pipes that pumped Torementhicite to his head.

Varathis's body grew rigid. His armored body fell heavily to the ground and wept liquid Torementhicite onto the parched ground.

"Her name…is *Hera*," Jet snarled, throwing the severed pipes onto the fallen prince, "you miserable pile of shit!"

Diothur was dumbstruck by what she had just witnessed. That moron had been an utter waste of the Torementhian armor. She had known that striking the Erebonian with Obsidian fire would empower him and terrify the Zenorian prince, but she had expected Varathis to last longer so she could utilize his fear.

Seeing the opportune moment, Ashana loosed two electrical arrows into Diothur, paralyzing her. Rezaaran unleashed a fireball that flung their foe through the crowd of Kalarans into the ravine beyond.

"Well, at least that's over," Jet muttered. "Wait…what the frak?"

The liquid Torementhicite that oozed from Varathis's corpse evaporated into thick black smoke that congealed and forced its way into the prince's mouth. His rigid body rose, and his blackened eyes fixed a dead stare upon the Sentinels.

"Rezaaran Valhara!" the corpse seethed in a distant voice.

"Thaedis," the War Mage replied curtly. He had seen this trick before with Zradya, but this time he was not afraid.

"You have destroyed the only thing that could ensure my freedom!" An enormous shadow covered the land, and the loud roar of thrusters filled the air. "Now I will take everything that matters to you!"

Chapter Sixteen

The Battle of Tarlok

Streams of plasma and rounds of molten metal flew through the silent vacuum over the dusty, forgotten planet. Twenty carbon-streaked Citadels violently engaged with the Dominion capital ships that desperately sought to protect the behemothic *Sedah Destroyer* as it crawled across the backdrop of Tarlok's gray surface.

A squadron of fighters swarmed toward Thaedis's flagship to initiate a bombing run. However, their aspirations of an offensive on the tyrant disappeared in an instant as a fleet of robust Arcara warships shot out of a Torus tunnel and obliterated the squadron in bursts of nuclear detonations.

"Stay focused, everyone," Xephyrus commanded the fleet from the bridge of a Citadel. They had arrived at the coordinates Rezaaran had sent them but apparently without the element of surprise at their arrival. "Engineering crews, we need an analysis of the enemy vessels. Send the location of weak points to our fighters. Citadels will engage the capital ships and buy time for our fighters."

"Sir, what about the flagship?" one of the pilots asked Xephyrus.

"You have your orders, soldier," the Elder Mage replied sternly.

"Very well, sir."

Despite the ferocity of the battle, Xephyrus noted several of the Dominion ships slipping through and descending to the surface.

"Orin, we need our troops on the ground," he informed the general.

"I agree," the venerable leader replied. "Council members, marshal your elites and all available infantry to the transporters in the Citadel hangars. It is time to end this war!"

Meanwhile, on the surface of Tarlok, the intensity of the battle heightened further. Countless ships landed around the fortress and spilled forth swarms of enemies. Rezaaran and the Sentinels fearlessly charged to meet them head on. Harkenathor's edge sang against the cacophony of screams, roars, and artillery explosions, while the War Mage's electrified hands blasted aside any foes that evaded the swing of his blade. He knew the *Sedah Destroyer* was overhead, and that meant Thaedis would arrive soon. However, he had to keep his focus on the present. The swelling number of enemies would prove too much for the other Sentinels and the few Halsynian acolytes to handle.

Seemingly hearing his concerns, a battalion of IRIS soldiers teleported into the War Mage's wake and unleashed a hail of return fire upon the Kalaran cyborgs. Rezaaran's gaze swept around as legions of IRIS soldiers appeared across the battlefield, followed by the council members and their elites. He allowed himself a smile and then charged through the enemies ahead of the IRIS infantry. With the council members and the Sentinels, surely Thaedis would face justice today.

Ashana retracted her bow and reached for her rapid-firing crossbows. Her future sight guided her aim and allowed her to evade lethal return fire. However, despite their advancing ground, she had an uneasy feeling. Her eyes found Luminara, who commanded a herd of ethereal beasts, and she remembered her advice of staying rooted in the present. She had to keep the faith that whatever path this battle took, they would face it together.

Quirt's VERITAS made light work of the hefty Kalarans. Enshrouded in a tachyon field, the scientist sprinted across the battlefield and pummeled the brutish cyborgs with his swift punches and sheer momentum.

ADAM extended energin blades from his wrists and sliced his way through a horde of Kreyforian battle masters. Emboldened by his bravery, Shian marshaled the other Arkanians against the new itara's enemies, and together they tore through the dusty field to destroy the first drop ship.

Ikso and Moya led the Tayko acolytes into the throng of the battle, feeling no fear. They knew the goddess was with them in this just quest, for the Onsei shielded them against the Kalarans. However, their charge halted when an acolyte dropped dead as a wind arrow pierced his heart. The sisters looked in the direction of the weapon's origin and saw Cheyi atop a cliff, a smug smile on his face.

"Oh, you traitors will face your due punishment today," he sneered. "By my divine right, I sentence you to death! Kill them all!"

The acolytes and masters loyal to the dishonorable Cheyi swept forward in gusts of wind and locked staves with the Tayko. The force of their battle repelled the Kalarans, who instead opted to pick off the survivors of the Halsynian skirmish.

Ikso dodged her way between the blasts of wind magic and skidded toward Cheyi with her staves drawn. However, the cunning master sensed her approach and lifted her into the air.

"Honestly, you reprobate child," he chided. "What chance could you have when the master who trained you died at my hand?"

Her eyes widened, and she screamed in rage. The Onsei exploded from her core and knocked Cheyi to the ground. Ikso charged at him, and her short dual staves repeatedly struck the murderous Elder. She summoned the Onsei to her reach and threw a vicious strike to Cheyi's face, fracturing his nose and drawing blood from his snarling mouth.

"That is enough!" he roared, repelling Ikso with a blast of wind. He reached to his waist and ripped a narrow-bladed, single-edged sword from its scabbard. "I sentenced you to death—now I shall see it done!"

Cheyi swiveled the blade swiftly around his wrist and, with the ferocity of a hurricane, set upon the rebellious acolyte.

Ikso narrowed her gaze upon the approaching master. Locking her staves together, she raced forward to meet him head on. Ikso evaded the first strike and made to counter with a strike to his head, but Cheyi foresaw her ploy and slipped away from her staff. His blade whipped through the air and sliced into Ikso's shoulder. The young girl yelped in anguish and retreated a few paces from her adversary.

"Your skill is no match for a master," he snarled. "How can you defeat me with a set of training staves? Do you not recognize this blade?"

Ikso's hand clutched her bleeding shoulder, and her eyes wandered to the narrow blade with the glowing blue runes, recognizing it as the prophetic message the goddess had bestowed upon Master Suya.

"Surrender! You may as well be unarmed!"

"I do not stand before you unarmed," she replied serenely. Her feet shifted into a half stance, and she rested her staff behind her neck. "The fact that you do not see this shows why you dishonor that blade."

"Silence!" Cheyi roared. "I have tolerated you long enough!"

Ikso closed her dazzling blue eyes, and the battlefield slipped away from her conscious mind. Her lids lifted open slowly, and with an empowering serenity, she saw Cheyi drift toward her in a stream of white ribbons of energy.

The young acolyte burst forward. Her body moved as an extension of the Onsei. For while the mythical force flowed around Cheyi, its essence permeated Ikso's soul, attracted to her conviction. The blue runes branded into the white wood of her weapon burned alive with the same mystical power that cast their prophetic purpose. Passing right through Cheyi, she struck him deftly on the back with her staff. Master Cheyi lost his footing midway through his charge and crashed to the ground. Suya's sword slipped from his grasp.

The disgraced master dragged himself to his knees and saw Ikso standing before him, the tip of the blade at his chin.

"How is this possible?" he asked with quaking rage. "How could an insolent acolyte achieve Niharn?"

"I believed," she said simply. "As I believed, so I acted. Such were the teachings Master Suya passed on to me. The teachings of our goddess, Nish Ira. These are the teachings you swore to uphold, and yet you sold our sacred Order—for what?"

"I would not expect a child to understand such matters," he growled.

"There is nothing simpler to understand," Ikso replied solemnly. "Despite your life of violating the sacred laws of our Order, I pray the goddess shows mercy upon you."

Ikso ran the blade through Cheyi's heart. The old man's eyes widened, and blood poured from his chest.

The young acolyte quietly withdrew the weapon and turned to find her sister watching her.

"I did what was necessary," Ikso said quietly.

"I know," Moya whispered. "You avenged Master Suya. I doubt I would have had the strength to do so."

"It was not vengeance, Moya," she said, returning the weapon to its scabbard. "I acted as the goddess required me to. However, as I am the youngest of our family, this weapon is not mine to wield."

She passed the sheathed blade to Moya with a respectful bow. The elder sister reluctantly accepted the weapon and strapped it to her waist.

"Come. Our friends need our help," Moya said with a proud smile. She led her sister by the shoulder toward the other acolytes.

Meanwhile, Jet found himself locked in a duel with an Arcarian in a heavy war suit. The armor proved impervious to his blast cannon.

"Very well, then," he grunted with a snide smile. Jet slung the blast cannon over his shoulder and grappled the Arcarian. However, he had not anticipated the overwhelming power contained beneath the sleek metal plates. The warrior hoisted Jet into the air and slammed him to the ground. Jet quickly lifted his arms and caught the foot that sought his head, but the strain to resist the motors burned through his muscles.

A crackling golden spear, born of pure energy, tore through the air and pierced the Arcarian with a thunderclap. The heavy-suited warrior stumbled backward and exploded in a shower of sparks.

Jet scrambled to face the launch point of the spear. A heavyset warrior in golden runic armor swathed with burning orange energy and sparks hovered briefly before taking purposeful steps toward the Erebonian. A large four-pointed star adorned his breastplate and crested his concealing helmet.

"I am glad you are safe, Jet Bal Sara," the soldier said with a deep voice that reverberated around the Erebonian. "I hoped we had made the journey in time."

Jet eyed the new warrior suspiciously. This person spoke with the familiarity of acquaintance, yet he had never encountered a being of such stature or gravitas.

A rippling yellow portal appeared behind the warrior, and the Dorassi brothers emerged. Tarsik beamed at the sight of Jet and offered his hand to the Erebonian.

"Well, I see you've already met Tetros Reikon." Tarsik grinned, whipping out his two morning stars.

"It seems puberty caught him a bit late," Jet mumbled as he reached for his blast cannon. To his surprise, his passing remark earned a chuckle from Blaylock. "I am glad you boys could join us. Let's give them hell!"

Reikon surveyed the battlefield, oblivious to his friends' conversation. The entire landscape existed as a shimmering illusion to him, and each warrior, except those before him, stood as a shadow in the distance. However, interspersed among the carnage stood over four thousand spectral warriors adorned in the same golden suit as the one he wore. An apparition approached him and stood at attention.

Is this real?

Reality is a matter of perspective. We bestowed our blessing upon you and marked you the Tetros of this era. The ancients are yours to command so that we may uphold justice.

Then let us not stand on ceremony.

Sparks from across his armor zapped to his palm and formed a spear identical to the weapon that had destroyed the Arcarian. He focused his attention on the nearest throng of soldiers and set off at a hurried pace. Within his burning golden armor, Reikon glided across the ground as his electric spear cauterized every enemy within reach.

A rabble of Kreyforian battle masters leaped with heavy chains to restrain him. However, under the blessing of the ancients, Reikon remained protected. Five of these golden spectral warriors rallied around the new Tetros and detonated. Although the apparitions were unseen by the mortals on the battlefield, their explosion disintegrated the battle masters who laid hands on Reikon.

He turned sharply at the roar of a mighty mantharian that charged toward him with a Kreyforian battle master on its back. Reikon held his spear aside and rushed to meet the snarling steed head on. His fist, joined by the strikes of ten other apparitions, collided with the heavy jaw, hurling the beast skyward.

Reikon sensed Rezaaran's echo nearby and set forward on a charge. Several of the apparitions appeared before him and created a ramp for him to leap skyward. At the apex of his jump, Reikon spun his spear and slammed the energy bolt into the chapped ground. A powerful surge of orange electricity erupted from his weapon and disintegrated every enemy between himself and the War Mage.

He turned to look at his stunned Enchiridion knights and Jet. "We should not keep Captain Valhara waiting." Reikon's voice thundered through the air. Reforming his energy spear, he charged forward once more. In between culling the Dominion forces, Reikon marshaled the Ancients to provide protective guards to the wounded IRIS soldiers.

"Well, I guess he doesn't need our protection," Jet remarked.

"It's incredible!" Tarsik yelled. "But he can't have all the fun!"

As Rezaaran looked across the battlefield, an entire line of Kalarans disintegrated before his eyes. He traced the source of energy back to a robust warrior in mythical golden armor and recognized him instantly as Reikon. The balance of the battle had shifted in their favor. The strength of their magical onslaught augmented the IRIS troopers and proved successful in leveling the engagement. He watched in awe while the empowered Dorassi leader decimated Kalarans, Arcarians, Kreyforian battle masters, and any other foe that opposed him. The prospect of victory had once seemed unimaginable. However, now there was a chance to win.

Do you think I would just hand you victory that easily? Thaedis's voice grated against Rezaaran's mind.

The War Mage swiveled, and he scanned the vista before him, seeking the Exiled. Only in this moment did he grasp the toll the battle had taken. Their advantage had not been won without considerable loss.

I lose nothing by the legions that spill forth. However, each loss on your side wounds your company's morale. Their will to fight frays with each comrade who falls. Their fear and vengeance rise against them.

Rezaaran watched the ongoing battle with horror as artillery shells pummeled the surface. Despite their losses, the cyborg Kalarans streamed forward without end. In the distance, a drop ship reached the surface, and when its doors opened, Rezaaran's blood froze over.

Now gaze upon the devastation, and you shall know despair!

A new garrison of Kalaran cyborgs marched from the invasion vessel. Thick pipes from their armor pumped liquid Torementhicite into the organic matter of the soldiers. Their armor was also interspersed with Torementhian crystals. It was an army designed solely to resist users of magic. Yet the most terrifying aspect was that Rezaaran sensed an Edarian soul within each soldier. Thaedis had succeeded in bringing an army of Edarians to the Maelinthian—yet another seal broken in the inevitable path to Nethriziin's freedom. Against this army, Rezaaran could do little but watch in horror.

Several Halsynian acolytes, buoyed by their victories against the regular cyborg Kalarans, charged toward this new regiment. However, the first warriors to reach the soldiers were plucked from their wind-imbued charge and gutted with Torementhian blades. Enraged by the deaths of their friends, several more acolytes set upon the new enemies. But the ranged magical wind blasts dissipated upon impact.

The Edarian army halted abruptly, and a wave of chanting rose from their ranks. Their language was ancient, unknown to all within the valley, yet the malice contained within their words chilled every soul. When their chant reached a fever pitch, they swarmed forward in a frenzy. They barged through the Halsynians and slaughtered any in their reach with blades and dark fire. It did not matter to them which Halsynians stood as Tayko and which stood with the Dominion. Several acolytes were torn between Edarians, their remains sprayed across the dusty ground.

"Fall back!" Moya called out to the Halsynian cohort.

United by their panic, they forwent their clash of ideals and rushed to escape the rampaging army. However, their stampede crushed several underfoot, and the chaos only incited the Edarians further.

Moya watched her fellow acolytes scream and run for their lives to escape the reach of this new threat. They would not get far at this rate. She faced the Edarians and drew Master Suya's sword from its scabbard.

"You may be immune to magic," she muttered, her eyes flitting across the rabble of soldiers, "but you bastards must still bleed!"

She reached deep into the Onsei and made her peace with the goddess. Moya then sprinted forth, propelled by a cyclonic force of wind. She approached the first Edarian and sliced its leg cleanly off, swiveled instantly, and drove the blade through its skull. Riding her momentum, she swiftly passed to the next enemy and sliced open the exposed abdomen. Her blade found the mark on each Edarian as she drove deeper into the crowd of enemies, drawing their attention away from her fellow warriors so they could escape.

Moya leaped into the air and spiraled rapidly to create a vortex of wind around herself. She landed lightly on her feet and swiftly set out to carve her way through the garrison. She knew, though, that every step carried her closer toward a certain death. The Halsynian warrior reached the end of her sprint, depleted of the magical energy that had infused her. Reacting on instinct, she lifted the blade to her left and blocked an incoming strike from an Edarian.

"You have nowhere left to run," he snarled. "The time of mortals is at hand! Lord Nethriziin shall rise and see your kind exterminated!"

Moya's strength faltered beneath the Edarian's supernatural might. But suddenly a white quarterstaff flew through the air and struck the Edarian's head. Seizing her opportunity, Moya slipped aside and decapitated her foe. She looked down at the fortuitous staff, and recognized the runes branded into the wood. Her eyes darted across the battlefield and saw her younger sister running toward her—and stopping in her tracks, a black blade skewered through her chest.

An Edarian stood behind her, hoisted Ikso skyward on his wrist blade, and then dropped her to the ground. He had raised his weapon to decapitate her when a spear of orange electricity detonated him into a shower of sparks.

Moya ran to her sister and caught her before she hit the ground. Tears ran freely, and she cradled Ikso's face in her hands.

"No, you can't die!" she sobbed. "Not like this! Why? Why did you come back, you idiot?"

Ikso smiled weakly and reached to dry Moya's tears. "Because it's what you did for me," she whispered. "Don't be sad…I am within the Light of the goddess. This is how she wishes to receive me. I need you to promise me something."

Moya could find no words and instead hugged Ikso tightly. She was oblivious to the battle around her. She did not care, for her world was fading in her arms.

"You have to keep fighting," Ikso pleaded between coughs. "You have to free Halsyn. Promise me."

"I promise," Moya sobbed. "Stop talking; save your strength! I can run you to a healer. I am sorry. I should have protected you."

"You have always been my heroine," Ikso said with a kind smile. "I love you, sis, but it is time now."

Ikso's eyes closed, and her hand slipped from Moya's cheek.

Reikon stood a respectful distance away to offer Ikso and her sister space to share their last moments. Under his command, the ancient specters fended off the Edarians who sought to prey on the elder sister in her moment of vulnerability.

Is this truly where you wish us to be stationed? a specter asked Reikon.

The girl was a companion, he replied firmly. *She fought valiantly today and has saved me before. What value is a ruler who cannot uphold loyalty and the dignity of a fallen friend?*

I understand, the specter said with a respectful bow of his head.

Under Reikon's command, ten of the ancient spirits formed a perimeter around Moya while she grieved her sister.

Why does our magic harm these creatures, yet they remain immune to the magic of the others? he asked the spectre.

The blessing of the ancients is from a time before the magic most of them use. It is to our advantage that the Exiled has forgotten this.

Reikon searched across the battlefield until he found Rezaaran.

This new army will claim the lives of all. I can contest them.

Not on your own, you cannot! Rezaaran said. *Let me help you.*

I do not fight alone, Reikon replied calmly. *These creatures are immune to your magic, but their creator is not. You alone can end the war, Rezaaran. We each have our duties to perform.*

Tetros Reikon, Rezaaran said with a weight of emotion in his thoughts, *what has happened to Ikso?*

I am sorry, my friend, the Dorassi leader replied gently. He looked back at the elder sister, who whispered a prayer of protection for her departed sister's soul while under the safeguard of the ancients. *Ensure that justice is done for her. I will join you when I can.*

Rezaaran marshaled the Sentinels, and together they charged across the battlefield under the guard of several IRIS soldiers.

"This would be easier if we knew where we were heading," Jet shouted to the War Mage as he blasted aside a cyborg Kalaran.

"We need to get to the command post," Rezaaran yelled back, spraying a jet of fire ahead of him to scorch their enemies. "The only way we can win this is by coordinating our attacks."

No path can lead you to victory, Thaedis growled in Rezaaran's mind. *Despite your attempts, you cannot forestall my destiny.*

The Sedah Destroyer's ominous shadow rotated and bore its main cannon upon the fortress.

"That does not bode well," Quirt murmured. His scanners detected a growing surge of negative energy in the glowing cannon chamber.

Ashana risked a glimpse into the future. "It will be all right," she said. "For now, at any rate."

The Sentinels arrived at the command post beside General Libranth, who surveyed the battlefield. To the IRIS forces on the ground and those locked in the space battle, he issued his orders with a grave sternness.

"What is our status, General?" asked the War Mage.

"Our Citadels are holding back the Dominion for now," he replied, swiveling his head as he observed the conflict with his animusense. "However, if we wish to see victory today, we will need to bring the leaders to justice. Their troops are without end, Rezaaran. We are losing ground against this new breed of Kalarans. Reikon is containing them, but even with his abilities, he will be overrun if the new drop ships breach our blockade. Wait...we have just lost a Citadel. I am going to fight alongside him!"

The general reached for his dual-bladed sword and was preparing to summon the council members when a rumble rocked the heavens. A pulsing red ray struck the old stone fortress that had housed the Ark of Torementhias. Streams of energy flowed from the fortress and resurrected the slain Edarian vessels lying in Reikon's wake. Rezaaran gritted his teeth in frustration. The Dorassi leader was right: only with Thaedis's defeat could the war end.

Seemingly intercepting the War Mage's thoughts, Thaedis appeared from a burst of smoke and cinder at the entrance to the fortress. His hooded gaze took in the extent of the battle, and he savored the anarchy he had sown. The Exiled looked toward Rezaaran.

You cannot deny my purpose. It is inevitable.

Thaedis strode into the remains of the fortress, and the red blast from his ship ceased.

"We need to get to that fortress now!" Rezaaran roared. He leaped over the barricades of the command post and propelled himself through the air with his flight abilities.

Rezaaran slammed into the ground near the fortress in a roaring fireball that scorched every nearby Kalaran. At the entrance, he saw the lifeless, wide-eyed bodies of Atomauran and Krayzar. He placed his hands over their faces to close their eyes and felt an aberrant void in their echo.

What has happened to them? he asked his mentor.

This is unusual, Kashari murmured. *Their affliction appears to be similar to that of this planet. Thaedis has somehow wounded their echo...no...*

What is it?

I believe he has found a way to sunder their souls from their bodies.

"Great," Rezaaran mumbled. Flames ignited his left arm, and he clutched Harkenathor in his right hand. "Stay alert in here. Thaedis knows we are coming for him and will not submit. He will prey on your fears and rage, so focus on bringing him to justice and not on thoughts of vengeance."

A wise notion, Thaedis sneered in their minds. *It would be inspiring were it not for the hypocrisy. I taste your fear, Rezaaran!*

"I am not going to be outdone by another one of these telepathic monsters!" Moraya screamed. She charged through the stone doorway and barged past Rezaaran.

"Moraya, wait!" the War Mage shouted after her. But it was too late. The naval commander disappeared into the darkness of the ancient building.

Rezaaran, you have faced Thaedis once before, Luminara said into his mind from afar. *The Guardian I knew was a strategic mastermind and relentless in his pursuit. However, he has become a monster in his time with Nethriziin. I do not know what awaits you in that fortress, and I cannot aid you in this battle. This task is now yours alone.*

Like Reikon, I do not stand alone, the War Mage replied, and he led the Sentinels and the remaining council members into the darkness of the fortress.

Moraya crept through the ancient fortress. A deep, dark cloud embraced the stone structure, and the lamps of her helmet scarcely pierced its inky shroud. The battle outside the fortress remained obscured, and the only sound to pierce this abyss was her measured breaths. Despite the countless battles she had campaigned, this situation aroused in her a visceral fear.

She spun around sharply and released a shrill sonic blast in the direction of a threat she had perceived. A beige armored hand grasped her arm and calmed her instantly. The figure of Leta emerged from the shadows. The mute soldier held a finger to her lips.

"You have to be the creepiest person I know," Moraya muttered. "I almost sympathize with your victims. Come on, we need to find the others."

The naval commander had turned to walk away when her boot struck a heavy metal object. She looked down and saw Aloric Melias's suit of armor, his pistols out of his grasp.

A black burst of smoke appeared between them, and Thaedis emerged. He telekinetically blasted the friends apart and deepened the darkness. The Exiled then turned his attention to Leta. He grabbed her neck and lifted her into the air, his grasp burning through the armor and branding her flesh as his burning orange glare pierced her soul.

"Thus you meet the fate you have always feared: alone and never to be missed by anyone."

His blade glowed purple, and he rammed the weapon through Leta's abdomen. A pearly white projection of herself appeared separate from her body and drained into the ghastly sword. Thaedis released her corporeal husk and turned his smoldering orange eyes on the whimpering naval commander.

"You are a pitiful excuse for a soldier," he said with contempt, surveying the fear-wracked Moraya. "For all your bravado, you lack true courage and have slipped by on the valor of better people. The only thing more pathetic than you is that a person with the power of Rezaaran Valhara should willingly act in subservience to you."

He drove his sword through her chest and reaved her soul. Thaedis closed his eyes and savored the incremental augmentation to his strength. His hands reached out to touch the stone walls, and he saw a vision of Rezaaran and the Sentinels passing through this corridor. However, the memories were fading. He had to move faster if he was to gain a glimpse of what the Ark contained.

Xephyrus walked calmly through the maze of corridors. He remained steadfast, unperturbed by the darkness around him. The Vaux would guide him to his target—he remained certain of this. There would be justice for Albeinius. He sensed the wisps of an echo of the council members. Their bodies lay bereft of their souls. In the midst of their corpses stood a figure whose echo existed as a paradox.

It drew the Vaux inward instead of connecting to it. This being smoldered with an aura of unfettered rage. It was Thaedis.

The Elder Mage drew his daggers and sprinted toward his target: the man who was responsible for his brother's death. Xephyrus passed the tyrant in a blurred flurry of blades, yet every strike passed through his stationary form. Then, to Xephyrus's utter surprise, Thaedis's head turned toward him. His piercing orange gaze reached deeply into Xephyrus, but the Elder Mage's spirit refused to bow.

Thaedis reached forward and grabbed Xephyrus out of his alacritous shimmering form. "At last I meet the mortal mentor to my nemesis," the tyrant snarled, his touch burning into Xephyrus's neck. "I have to admit I am underwhelmed. Elder Mages used to be worthy of respect, but perhaps I should not have held such high hopes for a Vokarii. Your order was so similar to the Guardians, established on a value structure riddled with pietism and plagued by arrogance. You stand for justice yet seek vengeance for the death of your brother. How can you teach when your heart is so dark?"

Xephyrus's face contorted in rage, and he ignored the searing pain in his neck. He slashed at Thaedis's hooded face with his dagger, but the blade passed through the smoky figure.

"It is pointless to resist."

"Rezaaran will defeat you," Xephyrus gasped. His daggers slipped from his hands.

"He will try," Thaedis sneered, and his blade glowed purple. "But he shall meet the same fate as his teacher!"

Xephyrus's soul escaped his body and vanished into the ghastly blade amid a scream that faded to a groan. Thaedis dropped the frail husk of the Elder Mage, and his hand wandered to another stone wall. His mind filled with the image of Rezaaran and the others passing through here, but the memories faded even faster than before.

"After all these years of immortality," he grumbled, "now time is against me." He dispersed into a trail of black smoke and passed swiftly through the corridors until an echo caught his attention. He appeared in front of a soldier with dark armor interspersed with lightning bolts and fitted with golden claws.

He surveyed the warrior with mild curiosity. His eyes flared orange, and his gaze pierced the metal armor, appraising the soul within.

The commander extended his sparking claws. "You're Silvermire," he whispered, unable to grasp that he alone held the duty of apprehending the galaxy's most nefarious tyrant.

Thaedis continued his silent appraisal of the soldier.

"You are responsible for the genocide and enslavement of millions of star systems," the soldier said. "IRIS will bring you to justice for your crimes."

The Exiled remained silent.

"Do you have anything to say for yourself?"

Thaedis simply dipped his head and lifted back his hood.

Rexion gasped. Looking back at him from beneath the black robes was a face identical to his own. However, this person was paler, and his white eyes were set in a weathered face that lacked the kindness of Rexion's.

"What are you playing at?" the commander snarled.

Thaedis grabbed Rexion's faceplate and ripped it free of the helmet. His pale eyes looked over the soldier's face, and his lips curled in a sly smile. "I could ask you the same thing. How have you survived all these years?"

The pair slowly circled one another.

"I've been lucky," Rexion said.

"I doubt that is the true extent of matters."

"Enough of this! You will answer for your crimes, you monster!"

"My crimes?" Thaedis said with a smirk. "All I am guilty of is bringing order to a disorganized realm."

"How can there be order in enslavement and murder?"

"Freedom is an illusion that breeds discontentment. People are only truly at ease when they are unified under a common ruler. Every civilization has sought a single entity to lead the commoners. Kings, presidents, generals, even gods have all been conjured for this reason. They are all empty titles. I seek to unite the last realm of Anmor on the order of the one who commands me."

"You lead the Dominion," Rexion replied suspiciously.

"I merely enforce the will of Nethriziin. However, the time has come for me to reclaim my destiny. For too long now, I have allowed others to dictate my fate—a position I found myself in with the aid of your father."

"You knew my father?"

"We worked together for a period of time," Thaedis replied. "In a manner of speaking. What do you recall of your childhood?"

"I am not falling for your tricks, sorcerer!" Rexion yelled. "I am placing you under arrest to answer to the Galactic House of Governance!"

Rexion leaped forward, but Thaedis seized him by the face and forced his presence into the soldier's mind. "I asked you a question!"

The commander felt his body freeze in space and time; however, his mind disconnected and careered along a tunnel of memories that blurred past his consciousness. Finally, Rexion found himself standing in a dusty cave in the heart of a desert. Beside him stood the cloaked figure of Thaedis, still in a body identical to Rexion's.

"Where are we? What did you do to me?"

Thaedis said nothing and simply stared ahead toward the center of the cave. A few moments later, a man entered. He wore a brown robe and had black hair and a bearded face that bore an uncanny resemblance to Rexion's, although this man appeared gaunter. The man placed a bundle of cloth onto the dusty floor and began a deep chanting ritual.

Rexion's attention shifted to the moving bundle and realized it was a baby. His heart slowed in his chest, and his blood froze.

A dark-gray cloud appeared before the man. It deepened further until two glowing amber eyes appeared in its midst. A rumble emanated from within the cloud, and long, inky-black tendrils extended to grasp the baby. The apparition lifted the baby free of the wrappings, examining every inch of it with the viscous appendages. A few moments later, it placed the child back into the father's arms and gathered a heap of sand from the cave floor.

The cloud grumbled deeply, and the man resumed chanting. This time he uttered a different verse.

Rexion felt a dark magical power seep into the cave, and the sandstorm outside intensified. He watched in awe as the apparition sculpted the sand into a replica of the baby and then remodeled it into the adult version of Rexion.

Another deep rumble issued from the heart of the cloud, and the black tendrils reached out once more. This time, they pried open the back of the sand sculpture.

A black viscous but skeletal arm burst out of the cloud and dug its ghoulish fingers into the cave's floor, clawing their way forward an inch at a time. Another arm followed, and then a decrepit skull of the same substance that seemed contorted in a silent scream. When its whole form had emerged, the viscous skeleton ambled forward into the sand sculpture and immediately animated the golem, which began its transformation into an organic Zenorian.

The newly formed, naked, adult version of Rexion opened his eyes and took a moment to marvel at his physical form. He flexed his fingers and then ran them over his face and through his hair. A smile crossed his face for a fleeting moment and then faded just as quickly. He clicked his fingers and was instantly adorned with the outfit Thaedis now wore.

The exiled Guardian in the memory turned to bow to the cloud while the old man headed to the exit with the baby.

Another rumble issued from the cloud, and Thaedis reached under his cloak. However, a warbled exchange of words occurred between the man and the Exiled. Thaedis took a moment to gather his thoughts and then simply nodded. The man departed with the baby.

The memories continued to flash past Rexion's mind, recounting his life as a wandering orphan who'd never aged past his current appearance—until one day when he found himself hiking a mountain range on an alien planet and lost his footing.

They passed through a period of darkness, and when the memories resumed, he saw himself lying in a hospital in Kel-Ardimus.

Rexion's mind fell back into the present. His hands clutched his temples, and he keeled forward.

"What in the name of the spirits was that?" he demanded of Thaedis, who had returned his hood over his face.

"Those are the memories you lost," the Exiled answered simply. "Your father wandered into my cave seeking the means to avenge the wrongs done to his people by the richer lords of the kingdom. His desire for vengeance was what drew him to my soul, which had found refuge in that cave after my death. Nethriziin and I offered to show him the means to gain the revenge he desired. In exchange, we asked for one condition."

"That he bring you his child," Rexion whispered in horror. He had always felt that a curse lingered over him, and now he knew why. No! This could not be true. This sorcerer was trying to manipulate him. But what if there was some truth to it?

"Once my vessel was created," Thaedis explained, "Nethriziin saw no further need for the infant and demanded that it die. However, your father said he would see to it himself."

Rexion's face grew more ashen.

"Needless to say, that never happened. I believe that, using what we had taught him, he cast a spell to prolong your lifespan. Only the most ancient magical civilizations learned such power."

"Does this mean that I am…" The soldier's mouth grew dry. He could not bring himself to utter the words.

"You are the heir to Lord Aeron."

"No! This is a trick!"

"Your father bestowed the gift of immortality upon you so that you may serve in bringing order to this galaxy."

"Aeron was a monster who started Zenor's first interplanetary war. He butchered countless innocents!"

"He furthered the legacy of all great Zenorian rulers. He gained the power of the Vaux and exerted his rule to create justice and order. You can join me in continuing his legacy. Together we can free ourselves of Nethriziin's enslavement and bring righteous order to the galaxy. We can continue our fathers' work and ensure Zenor is the center of a new age of peace across the realms."

"That is not my destiny," Rexion said firmly. "Even if what have you shown me is true and I am Aeron's heir, he was not my father. He is not the man I wish to become."

"He bestowed upon you the blessing of immortality!" Thaedis insisted. "You are chosen for a greater purpose!"

"This immortality was no blessing," Rexion snarled. "I have been cursed to watch countless friends die at the hands of your marauding armies, and I am plagued to keep losing people!"

"You have the power of a god within you," Thaedis snapped, "yet you whine like a petulant child?"

"No. I am not the son of Aeron or the benefactor of your demonic rites," Rexion replied defiantly. "I stand with Rezaaran Valhara!"

"Then you are an imbecile," Thaedis snarled.

"Now that I know the truth," Rexion replied with a half smile, "I can stand before you truly fearless, for I cannot die."

"There is much you cannot even begin to fathom," Thaedis sneered. His eyes flared orange, and a purple flame erupted across his sword. "There are fates far worse than death."

Orin stopped in his tracks and reached for his heart. The echo of every council member had disappeared into darkness. Now it had consumed Rexion's essence. The last of his friends had fallen. But he did not stand alone. He felt the echoes of Rezaaran and the Sentinels approaching. Rezaaran Valhara, the boy on whose shoulders Orin had placed the hopes for galactic peace. The son of his dearest friend. He owed it to Zaran to protect the last Valhara.

General Libranth drew himself tall and boldly strode through the dark corridors into a large open space. Although bathed in darkness, Orin stood unafraid, for the Vaux guided his vision.

"You are brave to stand before me once more," Thaedis said softly, appearing in a burst of smoke and cinder. "Is it valor or foolishness that brings a blind man to face an adversary who has bested him?"

Orin extended the dual blades of his sword and raised his guard. "It is the conviction that justice be upheld," he replied firmly.

Thaedis's straight, dark blade ignited with a purple flame. "It is perhaps ironic that we should both stand against a coming darkness," the Exiled said slowly. "Much like you, I am on a quest to free this realm from evil. I merely seek to instill order."

"Your sense of order exists beneath the edge of the sword," Orin replied. "The Dominion over which you preside crushes freedom and offers singular choice as the only option."

"Freedom is a delusion," Thaedis said, bristling. "You cannot understand this truth, for you lack perspective. I have seen civilizations with freedom waste this gift and squander their opportunity to grow, thanks to the trivial whims of leaders who did not have the vision to progress. People can see only the next few steps before them. I can unite every world in this realm and move us forward together. Peace and unity is what we both seek."

"The freedom to act as individuals is what every person deserves."

"That is the road to anarchy," Thaedis replied coldly. "If you will not kneel before my rule, then prepare to meet your end."

The Exiled hurled a shrieking shadow toward Orin and leaped forward. However, the general stood resolute and parried the strike. Their blades flashed through the darkness and sparked as the metal edges rang aloud as they met again and again.

Despite his blindness, Orin was a match for Thaedis, as he relied on the Vaux to guide his defenses. Thaedis suddenly appeared in a cinder cloud behind him and slashed at Orin—but he met the lower edge of Orin's dual blade. The general pivoted sharply, seized the initiative of the duel, and drove Thaedis across the dusty floor. He spun swiftly, blades striking multiple times where his adversary stood. However, the Exiled dispersed into smoke and reappeared several paces behind Orin.

"I am impressed, General Libranth," Thaedis said, smirking. "This is more of a challenge than last year, when I left my mark upon you. However, you cannot stop my quest. I will free myself of bondage and then bring order to this realm."

Sensing a stirring in the dust beneath his feet, the Exiled held himself back from attacking. His black gloves grasped some of the gray ash, and he gained flashes of Rezaaran and the others within a golden room and subsequently their destruction of the chamber.

"No!" he whispered, and a growing fury pulsed through his body. That meddlesome child had destroyed the Ark, and this ash no longer held the memories of the Ark's contents. "My only chance to free myself lay within these ashes, and now they are no more!"

"Then your reign has reached its end," Orin boomed. "You will face justice for the crimes you have perpetrated."

"Do you think mortal men can pass judgment upon me?" he snarled. "I am Thaedis Silvermire, the exiled Guardian. Thanks to your damnable Rezaaran Valhara, I am now the eternal slave of Nethriziin. If such is my fate, then I shall carry forth his will and scorch this world into oblivion! IRIS never had a means to stop our cause, and their end shall begin with yours."

With that, Thaedis hurled a blast of dark fire at Orin. The general telekinetically seized the attack and reversed it onto the Exiled. A wave of heat reached Orin, who rolled aside and marginally avoided a series of dark-fire explosions.

The general fixed his attention on Thaedis and attempted to drain the Exiled's essence from a distance. However, he could not siphon the villain's energy. His grasp tightened on his sword, and he charged forward to strike at the abomination.

Rezaaran felt his skin bristle. His mouth grew dry, and his heartbeat slowed.

"No, don't do it, you fool!" he whispered, his eyes distant.

"What is it?" Ashana asked with concern.

"Orin is fighting Thaedis," he replied hoarsely.

Flames licked across the War Mage's body, and he encased himself in their amber wrath. The heat lifted him into the air, and he blasted along the corridor as a ball of molten plasma, searing through the walls before him.

Rezaaran swung his fist toward Thaedis, but the villain evaded the strike and reappeared across the dusty room. The War Mage rose to his feet and dispersed his scorching armor. Each plasma fragment scattered to the periphery and held fast beneath the War Mage's telekinesis. Their light pierced the darkness brought in the Exiled's wake.

"My nemesis," Thaedis sneered. "It seems you too cannot accept defeat and are compelled to crawl back for more. You will find that I am all too willing to oblige."

"You cannot fight both of us together," Rezaaran said. He drew Harkenathor and summoned five plasma orbs to his free hand.

Thaedis's eyes lingered on the weapon he had once held. "Is that a challenge?" he asked, chuckling. "You have taken the only hope I had to break free of Nethriziin's rule."

"What?"

"You think the Maelinthian has seen horror?" he asked. "The Edarian army I unleashed on Tarlok is but a taste of what shall come to pass. When Nethriziin controls all of Anmor, it will become a wasteland, and all mortals shall serve beneath the Edarians and his rule."

"If that fate befalls Anmor, then it is because of your complicity. You cannot twist this tale to be the savior."

"History is written by the victors," Thaedis whispered.

In a burst of smoke and cinder, the Exiled set upon the soldiers. His black cloak twirled in a tempest, and his purple-flaming sword sparked against the blades of his adversaries.

Rezaaran swung a fiery fist, but Thaedis evaded the punch and thrust a kick into the War Mage's chest. He then turned his attention to Orin, and they resumed their frenzied duel in a flurry of metal and sparks. The War Mage recovered his feet and rejoined the fray. Harkenathor's edge whistled through the air and resoundingly struck Thaedis's weapon. Thaedis locked his blade against Rezaaran and with his free hand attempted to wrest control of Orin's mind. However, the strong-willed general fended off the spell and charged toward him.

"That is enough!" Thaedis cried. The Exiled slammed his sword into the ground and telekinetically blasted Rezaaran and Orin away from him. Raising his fist, he summoned a wall of smoke around their arena.

Rezaaran's apprehensive eyes took in the extent of the Torementhian construct. Within the churning smoke, he heard the screams and cries of tortured souls. Shapes of swift-moving, screeching specters emerged from the ground and swarmed through the smoke wall.

"Your friends will be busy for some time," Thaedis said, smirking. "There's nobody to save you now!" The Exiled fired a congregated blast of dark fire at the War Mage.

Rezaaran instinctively released the flame guard over his hand and then hastened to raise his sword to block Thaedis's strike through the explosion. Orin charged forward once more, but his attack halted when Thaedis seized him in a spectral grasp and flung him aside. The War Mage's rage ignited at the sight of this fiend once again injuring his mentor. His eyes rose from the deadlock of their swords and looked beneath the hood of the Exiled. The glowing orange embers that glared back at him reminded him immediately of his fatal mistake on Zynoo.

Rezaaran relinquished his fury and drew on Kashari to return to a peaceful center. Summoning the wind magic he'd gained from Nish Ira, he heightened the tempo of their battle. However, Thaedis responded in kind and drew deeper from the Obsidious to further augment his speed. Meanwhile, the Exiled had not forgotten his other adversary and intermittently bombarded the general with blasts of dark fire to keep him out of reach. The War Mage was more difficult to contest than he had been a few months prior, but Thaedis glimpsed an opportunity to cripple his adversary.

The pair blasted a powerful telekinetic force toward one another, and their physical frames quaked beneath the intensity of power growing between them. Eventually the sheer force repelled them away from one another.

In preparation to charge his adversary once more, Rezaaran leaped to his feet and infused himself with electricity. However, his heart grew cold when he saw that Thaedis had seized Orin in an Obsidian snare.

"I did not understand the connection between you two," he sneered. His eyes flared orange, and a red spot burned into Orin's forehead. "You have taken Orin Libranth to be a stand-in for the father you lost."

"The father that *you* murdered," Rezaaran snarled. He felt his resolve for serenity falter.

Thaedis tightened his snare around Orin's neck and telekinetically drew his sword from the ground to his hand.

General Libranth relaxed his body, and his blindfolded eyes found Rezaaran. *In times of darkness, the only light remains within the hearts of men who dare to believe in virtue. Your greatest strength has always been your unshakeable resolve.*

Orin then offered a simple nod and disintegrated into luminous yellow particles moments before a barrage of congealed dark tendrils ravaged the metal armor he'd left behind.

The twisted and scorched debris of the general's armor fell to the ground, and Thaedis turned to face the War Mage once more. He expected to feel his seething rage, his anguish, his hatred. Instead, the young Zenorian closed his eyes and, with both hands on the hilt, brought Harkenathor before him once more.

Rezaaran set upon Thaedis in a flash of white and crackling electricity. Harkenathor's whistling edge rang aloud and sliced at Thaedis, striking his guard repeatedly as the contenders passed through the dusty arena in flashes of black and white. Deflecting Thaedis's strike, the War Mage connected a powerful cross to the villain's jaw. He followed through with a flame blast, which Thaedis deflected with his sword. Upon absorbing the magical attack, the black blade released the screaming soul of one of his victims. However, black tendrils from the smoke wall around them swiftly snared the freed spirit and dragged it into the darkness.

Thaedis again flew toward Rezaaran, and they resumed their high-speed duel. Magic and blade sparked across the arena—until the Exiled found a breech in the War Mage's defense and thrust his weighted fist into Rezaaran's chest. The War Mage gasped for breath and looked toward his approaching adversary.

"You have trapped me in servitude to Nethriziin," Thaedis said, scowling. "I shall see your soul ensnared in the Obsidious to endure eons of torture. Tyrel cannot save you this time!"

Thaedis drew back his weapon to deliver the death stroke when an arrow pierced his heart and detonated in his chest. The Exiled reached for the gaping hole now filling with smoke that congealed until the wound closed. Turning abruptly, he spied the intrepid archer atop a column overlooking the arena, another arrow nocked. She loosed the arrow, but it disintegrated in a blaze of dark fire.

"You fool," he said, chuckling. "You cannot kill what no longer lives."

Thaedis telekinetically yanked Ashana from her vantage point down toward him and drew back his sword.

"*No!*" Rezaaran watched her fly through the air toward the Exiled in distorted time. The Vaux heeded his desperate call. White ribbons of energy infused his body and lifted him to his feet, while his legs filled with the swiftness of Halsyn's winds and powered him toward Thaedis.

Ashana fell upon the glowing purple blade. A white shimmer of herself separated from her body and was instantly consumed by the weapon.

The War Mage sprinted through where Thaedis had stood and caught Ashana before she hit the ground. Holding her close to his chest, he wept bitterly. The heat was already escaping her body, and her vacant eyes stared straight through him.

"No, Ash!" he wept. "Come back to me!" Without Ashana, what world was there to save? What life was there to live?

His fingers reached for her neck as tears streamed down his face. Despite her waning pulse, she was already devoid of life, bereft of her soul. Rezaaran gently lowered her body to the ground and sobbed over her still form. His world fragmented around him. His breath arrested in his chest, and his vision darkened. His hands grew limp, and his heart stilled. He did not feel the coldness of Thaedis's mystical weapon when it seared through his chest. He did not feel the impact when his body hit the ashen ground. All he remembered were the vacant eyes of the only woman he had ever loved.

CHAPTER SEVENTEEN

THE SCION OF DARKNESS

Rezaaran opened his eyes slowly to a tranquil, gray-clouded sky. He immediately sat upright and looked for Ashana. However, rather than within the dusty, dark fortress on Tarlok, he sat in a lush green field of waist-high grass that swayed in a gentle breeze.

The War Mage's eyes passed to his hands. He was free of his armor and instead wore a relaxed white doublet over a white thermal suit. Cautiously he rose to his feet and took in the serene plains around him. A morose but hopeful melodic hum coursed through the verdant valley, buoyed along the trickling stream that ran from the white stone mountains and nourished the fields.

An echo pulsed beside Rezaaran with an intensity he had never before felt, and he turned to face a colossal blue crystal with runes etched into its largest facet. A celestial column of white light bathed this crystal and warmed his face as he drew nearer. His eyes closed in the stone's presence, yet in its aura, he felt its gentle, maternal touch upon his soul. A serene voice whispered in his mind, directing his attention toward an expansive sanctuary carved out of the white-stoned mountainside.

His feet crossed the flagstones of the sanctuary entrance, and his hands, shaky with trepidation, pushed open the golden doors. Although decrepit from the ravages of time, the sanctuary retained vestiges of grandeur beneath the vine creepers and dust. The cracked tiles in the central courtyard bore the weathered sigil of the Anmorian Guardians. Despite the fissures that disrupted its edges and the scorch marks that sought to obscure it, the familiar symbol riled hope within Rezaaran's heart.

At the center of the courtyard stood a solitary, charred, barren tree. Its branches reached high into the roof of the sanctuary and channeled whispers of the echo from the crystal on the plains. Intrigued by the rumbling power within this dead tree, Rezaaran touched the gnarled, cold bark. A torrent of memories flooded his mind, and the War Mage sharply withdrew his hand.

From the deluge of recollections that swathed his mind, he clearly discerned the most recent. A horde of Edarians had stormed the sanctuary. Most of the damage to the building had occurred in their standoff with Luminara before the Edarians succeeded in subjugating the Guardian. Those who remained proceeded beyond this tree in search of Lord Salvidawn.

Rezaaran persevered onward and followed the trail branded into his mind. He passed into a cavernous room with eleven thrones arrayed around a wide, low platform. A shifting silver-and-cerulean liquid filled the platform and occasionally assumed the Guardian's symbol. Overhead, numerous stained-glass murals filled the roof and bathed the chamber in multitudinous hues. Each frame depicted moments in the history of Anmor as well as the Guardians themselves. Despite the gray skies beyond the walls of this sanctuary, Rezaaran felt the pleasant warmth of the summer day waft through the numerous archways around the chamber, which provided a view to the verdant fields of the Aetherealm. The War Mage's attention wandered to the throne in the center of the room, for it emanated great power that fluctuated between light and dark.

As he approached the throne beneath the golden shine of Lord Salvidawn's mural, he felt the conflict between these primordial forces grow stronger. It was a battle that crackled in the air around him yet also brewed within his heart. His fingers gently touched the regal golden arms of the throne, and his mind flared with the memories of Lord Salvidawn's valiant last stand before the Edarians overpowered him and thrust him through the portal that had led to his end.

"It feels a lifetime ago that I was upon that throne."

At the familiar voice of Tyrel Salvidawn, Rezaaran turned and saw the Guardian King standing beside the platform—although this form of Salvidawn seemed far older and more serene, dressed in a white doublet and cloak instead of his usual battle armor. His silver hair and crisp white beard glistened in the soft light.

"Are you still alive?" asked Rezaaran, walking beside the liquid pool toward the Guardian King.

"I have not been alive since the day I became a Guardian," he responded wryly. "In the fleeting moments after my death, my soul entered the Aetherealm. Here I met Alaris, who bequeathed me the gift of immortality in exchange for my upholding the sacred duty and presiding as a Guardian over Anmor. When you found me on Aardii-Atia, I was a shade of that Guardian, only barely tethered to Anmor because of Isiel's sacrifice. Luminara released me from those confines and allowed me to become one with the Vaux. At long last, my soul has found rest within this sanctuary that I once ruled."

"Does that mean that I am dead too?"

"Your soul is in the twilight of its existence," Salvidawn explained, turning to face the wide pool of liquid. "It appears that Thaedis has defeated you once again."

"I can't beat him," Rezaaran said. His eyes lingered in the depths of the liquid, and for a fleeting moment, he glimpsed Ashana. "He's too strong for me, and this time you weren't there to give me a second chance. It was never my destiny to defeat him."

"Or perhaps this is simply another part of your destiny," Tyrel replied as he gestured toward the pool. "This is the Augura Nexus. Its waters draw their power from the Vaux, and at the apex of the Anmorian axis, it grants the ability to witness events that have unfolded within the Vaux."

Salvidawn waved his hand across the shimmering waters. Streams of light filtered through the stained-glass panels overhead and struck the water, displaying the extent of Anmor with the axis that bound the four realms in the constant ebb and flow of the Vaux as it shifted between the Valinthian and Torementhian stones. The Guardian King magnified their view to the Maelinthian, and the galaxy came into view as a sprawling network of trillions of luminous spheres.

"Is this a star map?" Rezaaran asked. "I don't recognize any of the systems."

"No, my young friend," Salvidawn replied with a warm smile. "These are the souls of every individual in the Maelinthian. Every soul ensnared by the Obsidious grants power to Nethriziin. This power lust, this insatiable hunger, drives his conquest and invigorates his followers. Thaedis made a shortsighted deal with Nethriziin in his quest for vengeance. Now he is enslaved to the will of a force he barely understood. None of us truly knew what we were contending with."

A shadow crept upward from the Obsidious to ensnare the Maelinthian. Its tendrils engulfed and extinguished the lights of souls caught in its wake while a shadow strengthened over a bright cluster of souls. The battle at Tarlok.

"The war against the Dominion rages on," Salvidawn noted. "However, only the Sentinels can end Nethriziin. We fought him once and gained the advantage of a surprise assault. But we lacked the strength and unity your group has developed. Together the Sentinels have displayed the resilience only mortality may confer."

"Our group is down to two people now," Rezaaran murmured with a downcast gaze. "Diothur is beyond redemption, and Ashana…"

His voice trailed off, his eyes lingering on the image of Ashana falling deeper through the Augura Nexus.

"Yet despite all that has happened to you, I see in your heart that you still hold the hope that this evil can be defeated."

At that moment, a powerful blast of light burst through the roof and struck the Augura Nexus. Around the blazing column of light, Rezaaran saw his memories in the waters as clearly as the day he had lived each of them. He saw the day he learned to walk and the delight of his parents, the first time he tried rock climbing and injured his leg in the fall.

"And I will say it to you now, as I did then: when we fall, it shows us that we are strong enough to rise and try again."

Rezaaran turned in amazement to see his father and mother standing in the sanctuary behind Lord Salvidawn. He ran and embraced them, unable to believe that he could see and hold them again.

"I've missed you both so much," he said, sobbing and laughing at the same time.

"We've missed you too, my dear, sweet child," his mother whispered, kissing his head as the War Mage squeezed them tighter still. "There are no words to tell you how much we missed you."

"Nor to tell you how proud we are of everything you have accomplished thus far," Zaran said, beaming. "I knew you were destined for great things in your lifetime!"

"I...there is so much to tell you," Rezaaran said, releasing his parents but scarcely containing his excitement.

"Oh, I believe I know quite a bit already," Zaran replied with a wink. "I've had quite a retelling from an old friend."

His father extended an outstretched arm and drew Rezaaran's attention to Orin. The venerable general walked toward his friend, bereft of his armor and wounds, restored to his former self.

"It has been my honor, Zaran," Orin said, also beaming. "You raised a fine young man, my friend."

The general clasped Rezaaran's shoulder and walked him back to the Augura Nexus, where the War Mage's memories continued to replay. The waters displayed his capture, his training with IRIS, and his every conquest against the Archlords. Interspersed among his victories were the various memories of the friends he had made along his journey, as well as the worlds they had freed—and his straying from the path of the Light and his entanglement with Tolbetrius.

"Your road has been arduous," Orin remarked. "But because of the passion I saw in you that first day we met, I trusted that at heart you were a good person. And I have seen my faith in you rewarded at every turn."

The memories shifted to Rezaaran's role in uniting the Dorassi and the Zenorians, ending millennia of unwarranted hatred between their peoples. His role in uniting the Sentinels unfolded as he drew Jet and Quirt from their painful pasts and directed them toward the hope of a better future. Finally, the rippling waters of the Augura Nexus showed the Sentinels' last stand against the Dominion's armies and Rezaaran's valiant battle against Thaedis, which ended in a haze of darkness.

"Every moment to this point in your life," Tyrel explained, "has unfolded as the Vaux intended. Each act of kindness, every valiant and defiant stand, was the Vaux acting through you and guiding you to this point."

"I don't understand how I am destined to defeat Thaedis," Rezaaran murmured. "In every instance I have fought him, I have lost."

"In the first instance," Salvidawn explained, "you were brash and not ready. Yet the defeat you were dealt humbled you, and the Vaux guided you through a path that helped you learn what mattered most to you."

The Augura Nexus shimmered once again and revealed the numerous memories he had shared with Ashana, ending with the final moments he had looked into her vacant eyes on Tarlok.

"She is beautiful," his mother remarked with a gentle smile. "And she has a pure, fiery spirit. I see why you love her so dearly."

"But now she is gone," he replied softly.

The nexus's waters shimmered and revealed a pearlescent form of Ashana in a dark-walled maze.

"Her soul still endures in the Obsidious," Tyrel said. "With the destruction of Thaedis and Nethriziin, she can be freed."

"Then I will do whatever I can to save her," Rezaaran said fiercely through gritted teeth.

A glimmer began over his chest, drawing his attention.

"What is happening?"

"You stand in the Aetherealm," Tyrel explained. "Here you are not the dull matter of a corporeal form as you were in the Maelinthian. Here you are a soul of pure, boundless energy. Intention and character define you within this realm. Here you are no longer Rezaaran Valhara. You are Loradún, the Sentinel of Valor."

As Rezaaran watched in awe, the shine on his chest brightened in harmony with the pillar of light at the center of the nexus.

"You have always held an indomitable spirit. It is what gives you the strength to keep fighting. This is why your second defeat to Thaedis served to mark the end of a journey and bring you before the Valinthian stone to be judged if you were ready."

"Ready for what?" Rezaaran asked.

"To become the hero we have always known you to be," Orin replied proudly.

The general indicated the blazing pillar at the center of the waters of the Augura Nexus. Rezaaran gathered his thoughts and stepped forward intently. The Vaux reached through the waters and cradled his feet as he walked across the surface toward the pillar of light.

As he passed his hand into the blazing white light, he felt a solid object beneath his grasp. The power that coursed through it paralleled the Valinthian stone itself. Streams of white light laden with gold-and-white particles reached from the pillar and connected with the shine over Rezaaran's heart. The ribbons of energy coated him in a shimmering gold-and-white suit of armor.

The War Mage drew his hand from the pillar with a magnificently elegant blade in his grasp. The sleek golden hilt housed a blazing light and connected to a large, glowing, crystalline blade. It was a broadsword, yet it felt weightless in his hand.

"Behold the mighty Dawn Shard," Tyrel exclaimed. "A gift from Alaris herself to bequeath the power of the Guardian of Light."

"I thought this weapon had been destroyed," Rezaaran said. "Twice."

"Such an item is born of the Vaux itself. When Thaedis's construct destroyed Aardii-Atia, that Dawn Shard merged with the Vaux and found its way to the other relics in the Ark of Torementhias. When you destroyed the Ark, you destroyed a manifestation of this weapon and returned its essence to be forged anew. Now Dawn Shard has a new master. Only a pure-burning soul can summon it from the Vaux, and its edge can quell any darkness. Before this blade, Thaedis and Nethriziin shall know fear as they did once before."

"How will I return to the Maelinthian?"

"Well, you didn't think I would leave you without any help, did you?" Orin replied with a wink.

Thaedis reached down to retrieve Harkenathor from beside the corpse of the War Mage and his lover.

"Such a waste of talent," he muttered. His fingers ran lightly along the blade. Although the Ark had been destroyed, he remembered that Salvidawn had a penchant for enchanting items to contain memories. Perhaps within this weapon lingered some answers to how he might free himself of Nethriziin. After that, he could reclaim the splinters of his soul laced within this ancient weapon. Within the blade, he felt a bristling power resist his touch. "I shall see that your meager spirit is scoured from this blade, Elder Mage. I am sure the Edarians will delight in seeking vengeance upon the slayer of their brother."

The tyrant was walking away from the two fallen Zenorians when he noticed a glow lighting the darkness. He turned—and felt his fingers lose their grip on Harkenathor.

Streams of yellow energy flowed into the corpse of the War Mage, lifting his still form into the air. A blazing white light erupted from within the Zenorian's chest and enshrouded his being. Moments later, the glowing figure slammed his fist into the ground. Streams of lucent energy flowed from his back and connected him to the Vaux.

A robust figure covered in gleaming gold-and-white armor rose to face Thaedis. The helmet obscured his face, but there was no mistaking the emblem on his breastplate or the weapon he carried. It was Tyrel Salvidawn!

Thaedis calmed his seething and looked closer at his adversary. He lacked the anvil jawline and the height of his friend. No, this was definitely Rezaaran, resurrected once again by Tyrel's interference. How had the Vaux found this wretched slave worthy of Dawn Shard?

Rezaaran aimed Dawn Shard at Thaedis.

"Submit, and let us avoid a needless battle," he said. His ethereal voice resounded across the chamber.

"Submit?" Thaedis asked, his rage rising once more. "Do you think an armor and weapon change will scare me? I may have found defeat at the edge of that blade once before, but a better man than you commanded that sword then. I have defeated you twice now, child, and Subjugator hungers for the burning light of your soul."

The Exiled lunged forward and dispersed into smoke. When he reappeared, though, his strikes met the unyielding edge of Dawn Shard. While his alacrity had previously proven overwhelming to

Rezaaran, now Thaedis's movements seemed lazy to the War Mage's perception.

Rezaaran deflected a slash from the glowing purple blade and struck Thaedis solidly in the jaw with Dawn Shard's hilt. Thaedis staggered and snarled at the War Mage. He disappeared in a burst of smoke, but Rezaaran pursued him in a crackling flash of white-and-gold lightning. Dawn Shard's edge sliced through the smoke and bit into Thaedis's leg. Staggering, the Exiled sought to disperse once more.

Rezaaran caught Thaedis by the shoulder, yanked him from his smoky form, and flung him to the ground. The War Mage came to a hover and cast his gaze upon the Exiled. Flashing aside, he evaded a blast of dark fire. In an instant, he set upon Thaedis and grappled Subjugator from the tyrant's hand. The Exiled leaped up and grasped Rezaaran's helmet to scour the Toremententhicite in his being—but nothing happened.

"This is impossible," he whispered, aghast. "Every mortal has a trace of Torementhicite in them. Unless...this cannot be!"

Rezaaran threw a swift cross that lifted Thaedis off his feet and then telekinetically blasted him across the chamber. His hand ignited with a brilliant glow, and the War Mage hurled a cluster of incandescent orbs at Thaedis. The particles pierced his robes and exploded in blasts of light amid his agonized roars.

Dawn Shard slammed into the ground and triggered a barrage of light-bound swords to imprison Thaedis as Kashari had once captured Tolbetrius. Moving as a streak of white and gold, Rezaaran struck Thaedis with the edge of Dawn Shard from twenty different directions in the blink of an eye. This time, the glowing blade did not bite into his flesh, but its sacred light scoured the darkness at his core and attenuated his potency. Once certain the Exiled was crippled, Rezaaran swiftly summoned an enormous cataclysm overhead, triple the size of the one his mentor had conjured against Tolbetrius.

"Now the nightmare of your tyranny ends."

A blazing column of light, brighter than a supernova, blasted from the cataclysm and incinerated the crouched form of Thaedis.

When the assault ended, when the smoke had cleared, the tyrant was no more than a battered and broken man. Crushed beneath the mortification of losing to a child, broken by the memories of the last time he had lost his very existence to that damnable sword, Thaedis dragged his heaving form to a standing position. His charred robes slumped off his body as he shuffled forward. He raised a shaking hand to summon Subjugator once more, but the blade scarcely shifted.

Thaedis's knees buckled, and he collapsed in front of the War Mage. His cowl slipped aside, revealing the pallid replica of Rexion. Unlike the fallen commander, though, this being had the callous eyes of a soul tormented through the ages, its last vestiges of humanity shattered at the core. No hatred or wish for vengeance marred his gaze; he looked to Rezaaran with neither menace nor rage. Rather, his eyes held the gaze of a man who stood broken and resigned to the inevitability of something too vast for him to contest.

"So it passes that despite my misgivings," he murmured, "you were always the one chosen by Tyrel. Very well, then. If you are to be his champion, then I have but one choice to ensure that the legacy of that Zenorian traitor is erased."

The Exiled closed his eyes and chanted in a strange guttural language. Streams of viscous Obsidian energy crept from the walls around the chamber and swirled about Thaedis as he chanted into the darkness. Rezaaran watched apprehensively, unsure whether to attack or prepare for defense. When the last syllable left Thaedis's lips, the streams viciously pierced his own flesh, causing him to scream in anguish. Black skeletal hands reached from the streams flowing through him and clawed into his skin, binding the energy tighter against his body until it embroiled him entirely.

Smoke bellowed from the Obsidian walls and enshrouded Thaedis as the streams of magic shredded into his flesh. From the heart of the gathering smoke clouds rumbled the gut-twisting sounds of cracking bones and shredding skin mixed with the odor of burning flesh. A pair of glowing orange eyes pierced through the smoke and fixed on Rezaaran.

When the product of this dark ritual strode out through the smoke, the ground trembled. Whatever Obsidian force now resided in Thaedis's body had grown its corporeal vessel to a height of twelve feet. Where the skin had fissured and the bones fragmented to accommodate this change, lava pulsed with a steady orange that matched the arcane runes burned through the flesh on his chest. His visage, although identical to Rexion's in appearance, held a grave solemnness. The glowing orange eyes added to its blank expression. Whatever the apparition was, it emanated an echo of darkness stronger than anything Rezaaran had ever felt.

The creature raised its hands to its face and swept a gaze across the chamber. Its view pierced the Obsidian veil and admired the battle in the valley.

"At long last I have arrived," it said in a measured, rasping voice. "This realm is rich with conflict and ready for the taking. Finally, Anmor is mine."

It fixed its sights on Rezaaran once more. The only obstacle before it was this lone soldier.

"Kneel before Nethriziin, Scion of Darkness."

Rezaaran defiantly raised Dawn Shard, ready to attack. This being was the monster the Guardians had collectively stood against. This mythic figure was real, but his power felt greater than the combined might of every Archlord Rezaaran had faced. Lord Salvidawn had said that Nethriziin would be wary of Dawn Shard, for he had fallen to it once before. If this were so, then therein lay Rezaaran's path to victory.

"You may wield that blade," Nethriziin said slowly, seemingly reading Rezaaran's mind, "but you are not Salvidawn. He defeated me once, but not with that blade alone. I had relied on my legion of Edarians in that battle. It was a miscalculation on my part, yet his hubris would see him carve history with himself as the superior commander. You are merely a boy who is wearing the armor and brandishing the weapon of my nemesis. I crushed the spirit of Alaris until she lost the taste for battle. I defeated her champions, and you think you alone can stand against *me*?"

Rezaaran called upon the Vaux, and Valinthicite immediately infused his body. He set upon Nethriziin in a light-speed sprint. However, the Scion sneered and siphoned the War Mage's magic into his hands, and Rezaaran stumbled. Meanwhile, Nethriziin's hands flared alive with a molten glow. Every step scorched the ground as Nethriziin charged toward Rezaaran.

The War Mage slipped beneath the Scion's swinging molten fists, but his attempt to counter halted when Nethriziin grabbed his wings and ripped them off his back, severing his Vaux connection.

Rezaaran staggered away from the reach of the monster and took aim. Concentric rings of light appeared in front of him, and he unleashed a ferocious blast of energy. The attack landed squarely on Nethriziin's chest. Yet once again he absorbed the power into his being and augmented his strength, this time growing a pair of igneous horns from his forehead. The Scion charged forward with a pace unexpected given his lumbering size. His molten fist slammed into Rezaaran and smashed him across the arena.

The War Mage rose to his feet, and his hands traced the cracks in his breastplate. His fingers closed tightly around Dawn Shard's hilt. As Nethriziin lifted two fingers skyward, columns of lava erupted through the ground around Rezaaran, while tendrils of Obsidian magic slithered from the walls to ensnare his limbs.

Dawn Shard sliced through the restraints, and the War Mage rushed toward Nethriziin, who closed the distance between them in a burst of smoke and cinder. One molten-lava hand wrapped around Rezaaran's neck, while his other pressed against the cracked breastplate and drained the magic from the mythical armor. Each moment he maintained the connection, he grew larger and transformed closer to the form of his Edarians.

Suddenly a stone pillar slammed into Nethriziin and pushed him away from Rezaaran. The War Mage fell to the ground and gasped for breath. What had that monster done to him? Lying a few feet from him, Dawn Shard's blade dimmed, and the light in the hilt flickered. Rezaaran turned his attention to the pillar's origin and saw Quirt in his VERITAS standing beside Jet, who was flanked by Reikon and ADAM.

The Erebonian walked over to his friend and offered him a hand. "I see that you found yourself some new toys in our absence," he remarked with a wry smile.

"You dare to strike me?" Nethriziin roared. He hovered over the battlefield, shrouded in a cloud of orange and red Torementhicite. The Scion released a powerful blast of dark fire toward Rezaaran.

Jet immediately placed himself in its path and with an agonized grunt absorbed the full power of the assault onto his back. "That packed more than I expected," he growled. The intensity of the attack had incinerated his coat and fragmented his armor plating. The crystals along his head pulsed orange with increasing frequency, and soon his whole body was alight. Cracks appeared in the crystals along his head, and fragments disintegrated into the stream of dark fire.

"Jet, you have to stop!" Rezaaran wheezed, using Dawn Shard to prop himself to his feet. "Stop now, or you're going to die!"

"If that's what it takes to keep my friends safe," Jet grunted, "then that is a price I will gladly pay!"

Nethriziin stopped his assault and took a moment to regard the creature shielding Rezaaran. "I feel Torementhicite coursing through you," he mused. "I can taste that rage and pain fills your soul. You are an Erebonian, yet you have shown resilience beyond any mortal I have previously encountered. Perhaps there may be a use for you in my Dominion."

Jet drew himself to his full height and stretched his arms out to shield Rezaaran completely. "Kiss my ass!"

Enraged by this lesser creature's audacity, Nethriziin unleashed a more powerful blast of Obsidian power into his body. ADAM flew forward to strike Nethriziin's face but was caught midflight. The Scion ripped an arm and a leg from the android and then kicked his falling shell past Rezaaran and Quirt. Meanwhile, Reikon called upon the spirits of his ancestors and charged at Nethriziin. However, the Torementhian ruler swept his arm aside and swatted away the powerful souls that had decimated his Edarian army moments earlier. Reikon recovered quickly from his surprise and flung his thunderbolt spear at their foe. Although it found its mark, the weapon did little more than further incite his rage.

"I am Nethriziin, Scion of Darkness! I will not be disrespected by the likes of mere mortals!"

Suddenly, to his surprise, the Erebonian grabbed Nethriziin's ankle and threw him through three stone walls. Undamaged, the Scion rose to his feet with incandescent fury and received a hefty strike with a stone pillar to his face. He stumbled backward, and when he turned his gaze to the culprit, he saw Jet's body glowing orange and a burning white flare in his eyes. The Erebonian punched his open fist and fixed a glare upon Nethriziin.

"Someone's cruising for a bruising!" he snarled. He leaped at his foe and pummeled him beneath an avalanche of fistfalls.

How can we hope to stop such a monstrosity? Reikon asked his ancestors as he watched Jet assaulting the behemoth with unholy strength and yet still struggling to contain the monster.

Ultimately, none of you can defeat him, an ancestral spirit bluntly replied. *That task lies with only one person.*

Reikon turned his attention to Rezaaran, who healed rapidly with Dawn Shard in his grasp. A blazing light reignited in the hilt, and its essence infused the War Mage with renewed strength and vigor.

"Rezaaran," Reikon said, "you are the only one who can end this war."

"Nethriziin completely counters my abilities."

"Only because he can see the incoming spells. Jet and I will keep him distracted. You think of a way to destroy him."

Reikon dashed to aid Jet in his assault on Nethriziin. Streaks of golden lightning buzzed around the Scion, marking the path the Dorassi Tetros followed. His electrified spear sliced into the Torementhian's flesh. Although his ancestors could not lay a hand on Nethriziin, the spear rent his flesh as Jet continued to wear him down with his relentless assault.

With weighted sorrow, Quirt knelt down to examine the remains of ADAM. His armored hand gently touched the silver Arkanian helmet and triggered a flicker of the eyes.

"I believe I am all right," ADAM informed him amid sparks from his severed limbs. "Well…mostly all right. I was by no means straight out of the box."

"Out of the box," Quirt whispered. "That's it! Rezaaran, do you remember when we entered the Ark?"

He completed his healing with Dawn Shard's magic. "Yes. What about it?"

"When we accessed the repository we found 'Sahar's Requiem.'"

"Nethriziin draws his strength from conflict," Rezaaran murmured, recollecting the memories from the Ark. "I remember the spells to cast him back into the Obsidious and seal him within a confine but it will take some time."

The Scion threw a punch at Jet, which the Erebonian caught with an open palm, forcing his opponent to kneel. Enveloping himself in a tachyonic field, Quirt flew at light speed into Nethriziin's face and broke off an igneous horn. Together the three of them kept the Scion's attention fixed on them while Rezaaran summoned a series of luminous yellow runes in an ever-growing network of complex patterns amid a steady Sirantanian chant to forge the sequence of magical seals.

"We need to bind him!" Quirt shouted.

I believe we may be able to assist, an ancestral spirit said to Reikon. A thick chain of golden light appeared in the Tetros's hands.

Quirt surrounded himself in his tachyonic field once more and used his heightened speed to knock Nethriziin off balance. Seizing the opportunity, Jet shoulder-barged the Scion into a thick stone pillar. Reikon tossed an end of the chain to Jet and drew his end taut around Nethriziin's waist. Fifty of the ancestral spirits rushed to Reikon's aid and anchored their end while Jet coiled the chain around his forearm to bind the Scion in place.

We can help the Erebonian, a spirit said to Reikon. *Your purpose is no longer here.*

Reikon offered a simple nod and in a bolt of lightning appeared beside Rezaaran. While they had battled to subdue Nethriziin, the War Mage had successfully constructed thirty-nine seals around a series of rotating concentric circles.

"I believe it is time, my friend," ADAM said quietly to Quirt. "Until you are able to repair me, this body is useless for any further fighting. However, I may have one last opportunity to assist."

ADAM's eyes powered down, and the crumpled armor of his torso opened to reveal a shining, self-perpetuating power core.

Quirt nodded acknowledgment of his friend's final request. He extended his graviton field, captured the power core, and hurled it toward Nethriziin. Reikon took aim and flung his lightning spear toward the flying power core. The core detonated the instant the bolt struck its shell. The fifty Dorassi ancestral spirits released the chain and swarmed to shield Jet from the blast.

"Now, Rezaaran!" Reikon roared over the explosion.

Rezaaran fired the blast of energy toward Nethriziin, and a powerful pillar of light erupted between him and the primordial deity. The War Mage relinquished control of his senses, offering himself as a conduit to the Vaux's raw power as it sought to expunge the wound in its harmony.

The concentric circles of light spun faster, moving along the pillar to frame Nethriziin's form between the mystical seals. The Scion's glowing-ember hands seized the boundaries of the frame. Although his vessel was bludgeoned from the punishment, his malevolence drove an unholy fighting spirit.

Rezaaran swiveled Dawn Shard in his hand and hurled the ancient weapon at Nethriziin's torso. The crystal blade pierced his runic chest, and the star within the hilt flared alive. Its magic flashed along the blade and permeated throughout Nethriziin. Light shone from the fissures in his vessel.

"You think this is a victory?" he snarled at Rezaaran. "Although this vessel may disperse into oblivion, I will endure! Wherever there is darkness in the hearts of mortals, I shall live on! My presence is eternal! I cannot be forgotten! I will not remain a memory!"

"I know," Rezaaran said. "But wherever you may appear, the Sentinels will be there to defeat you!"

Nethriziin released a final roar, and the power of Dawn Shard finally overcame his might. His fingers flailed and the Scion of Darkness disappeared into a vortex that cast him beyond the edge of Anmor.

Ash fell from the roof where the portal had closed. Jet coughed loudly and emerged from a dust-laden cocoon born of the remains of the pillar to which he had bound Nethriziin.

Dawn Shard flew across the arena into Rezaaran's hand. The star in the hilt resumed its gentle glow, belying the intense power it had displayed.

"Is it over?" Quirt whispered in disbelief.

"I believe so," Reikon replied. Although his Tetros armor distorted his voice, his elation was more than noticeable.

"There is still something else I need to do," Rezaaran said quietly. He knelt beside Ashana, his armored hand gently caressing her ashen face. Jet placed a comforting hand on his friend's shoulder.

"I am sorry, Rez. I know the pain of losing the one you love."

"She is not yet dead," Rezaaran replied defiantly. "I can save her!"

Jet looked at him blankly.

"Thaedis tore away her soul and cast it into the Obsidious," Rezaaram said. "I can retrieve her soul!"

If you choose to pursue this course, Lord Salvidawn informed him, *it will be without the protection of Dawn Shard or the Guardian armor.*

In response, Rezaaran embedded Dawn Shard in the ground, and the armor plates tumbled off his body.

"Very well, then," he replied, fixing his eyes on the shifting walls of darkness around them. "Kashari, how do you feel about one more journey?"

You need not ask, his mentor replied.

Harkenathor flew into his hand, and the War Mage charged into the darkness, unsure what awaited him past the veil of reality—yet assured in the knowledge that he could save Ashana.

CHAPTER EIGHTEEN

A LIGHT IN THE DARK

The moment Rezaaran passed through the Obsidian veil, he plummeted off an edifice into an abyss. Streaks of red energy and lightning flashed past his face while the corrupted souls of the Obsidian prisoners ravaged him throughout his descent until he crashed onto a gray, dusty plain. He rose to his feet beside an enormous red crystal that pulsed with a dark presence akin to Nethriziin's power. However, with the Scion of Darkness banished, the Torementhian stone's power felt attenuated, and Rezaaran could feel the repressed fear this thought raised among the Edarians. They hid it well, fearing their prisoners would revolt if they relinquished their pretense, but it clung to their fiendish bodies.

The bloodied skies cracked alight with a storm of red lightning. Ash and cinder filled the air, and an incessant heat wave flooded the dark-walled maze.

Well, we are here, Kashari remarked mirthlessly. *Rezaaran, your hands...*

The War Mage turned his attention to his wrinkled, wasted hands.

"Let's get going," he said firmly, fixing his grasp on Harkenathor's hilt. "If this is happening this fast to me, then Ashana needs our help that much faster."

Rezaaran set off at a sprint through the maze. The overpowering shadows suppressed his animusense. It should have been difficult to track Ashana amid the agonized screams of souls ensnared in eternal torment or the hideous cackle of Edarians who delighted in their torture. However, one path through the maze lay littered with the corpses of Edarians. They were peppered with arrows.

"This seems to be the right way," Rezaaran said grimly.

He felt the Obsidian magic wearing him down. At every turn through the maze, a wall of Torementhicite washed over him and whittled away at his strength. His bones grew heavier with each passing moment. Each step aged him a little faster, but he could not stop. He had to endure. He had to reach Ashana. With renewed vigor, he pushed through the next magical barrier and felt a barrage of power slice through his flesh. Yet he persisted and trudged onward.

Ahead of him, an Edarian fell with two arrows through his skull. Then he saw her. Ashana stood defiantly, firing an arrow at a time into any Edarians attempting to strike her. The ravages of Obsidian magic had weathered her skin and silvered her hair, but her tired eyes still held the glint of her fighting spirit. Arrows no longer flew with the same alacrity she usually displayed, yet her aim never wavered. Beyond her, Rezaaran saw several pearlescent souls beneath her protection. When the last Edarian of the raiding party lay dead, Ashana cast her tired gray eyes across the maze in search of enemies. When her gaze met Rezaaran's, she offered a small smile and sank to her knees.

Rezaaran ran forward, accepting the small boost his ailing knees reluctantly afforded him. He wrapped his arms around her and cradled her silver hair to his chest.

"I thought I would never see you again," she whispered. Tears crept from her eyes, and she set her bow down beside her.

"I'm here now," he replied gently.

"It feels like I've been here forever, Rez," she said. "I arrived next to the red crystal and looked for a way out. That's when I found these souls. They were scared. Alone. I couldn't let them be tortured. Every Edarian I killed brought us closer. But we have been trapped. I have lost track of how long we have wandered this maze."

"I'm going to get us out of here," Rezaaran said, and a smile stretched across his haggard features. His gnarled hand caressed her wrinkled cheek. "We're getting out of this place together. I promise."

Ashana's eyes drifted closed, and her breathing slowed.

"No...not again," Rezaaran croaked. "Open your eyes, Ash."

"You shouldn't have come here," she whispered.

Around them, a larger raiding party of Edarians scaled the walls of the maze and bared their fangs. The fiends leaped toward the Zenorian souls.

"Ashana Binarjiin, you listen to me," he said. "You are the most important person in the four realms to me. But you are also the strongest woman I know. And I refuse to believe that this place has taken your fire! Now get up! We are going to fight this together! Because there is no other option. I love you too damn much!"

Rezaaran kissed her passionately.

Immediately a brilliant light erupted from their chests and repelled the inbound Edarians with a forceful blast. The Obsidian magic reversed, and the souls of both Rezaaran and Ashana returned to their younger forms. Ashana's hand reached into Rezaaran's hair, and the light from their hearts merged with one another as their kiss lingered. Powerful tremors rocked the Obsidious and shattered the walls of the maze. Cracks of light appeared all around them in the dark walls, and the souls of the unjustly imprisoned sought their escape. From the light between their hearts, a familiar screech sounded, and Simarata spread his enormous wings to shield the pair as a scouring column of light engulfed them.

Rezaaran's eyes drifted open, and he found himself back on Tarlok. He looked down at Ashana in his arms. The archer shifted and gazed at Rezaaran with a small smile.

"Are we back?"

"We are," he said, beaming. The War Mage kissed her deeply once more.

"Well, it is fantastic that you two are back," Jet interjected gruffly but with a relieved smile. "But there is a war we still have to win!"

The Sentinels laughed this off as Rezaaran helped Ashana to her feet. All around them, souls freed of the Obsidious floated through the fortress and sought a reprieve from their ages of darkness. Quirt watched them in amazement and gasped at the sight of his family appearing before him. Frintly and Kitrina flashed their toothy grins at their father. Beyond them, Jeena appeared, a kind smile lighting her features. She gently touched her husband's face and placed a soft kiss on his forehead. Although her soul did not utter a word, it warmed his heart to see them free and happy once more. With a final loving look into his eyes, Jeena placed her hands on the children's shoulders, and the three dispersed into a stream of lucent particles that drifted away with the other free souls.

Tears welled in the Thyrillian's eyes, and a smile lifted the corners of his mouth. His heart swelling with emotion, he pulled Rezaaran into a tight embrace.

"Thank you, my friend," he whispered in a choked voice. "By allowing my family to rest, you have given me all I have wished for."

Jet, also watching, saw the soul of Hera toss him a wink before she merged with the Vaux.

"Aye, our loved ones may have found rest," he said with a wide grin, clapping the shoulders of Rezaaran and Quirt, "but you've also given us a new family."

"Then let's go get our home back," the War Mage replied with a broad smile.

Blaylock's hammer slammed into the jaw of a Kalaran and knocked the possessed cyborg away from his brother. Meanwhile, a pack of spirit creatures heeded Luminara's call and rallied behind the Dorassi brothers. The three drew closer, continuing their defense of Ikso's fallen body as the battle raged around them.

Suddenly, Simarata's screech sounded through the valley. Luminara turned her attention toward the fortress in expectation. Moments later, the familiar havaka conjuration burst through the Obsidian bubble that encased the fortress. The four Sentinels and Reikon rode atop its back and pelted a barrage of attacks onto the battlefield.

Quirt leaped off the back of the magical creature, carrying Jet with his one hand. They skidded into the fray and widened the perimeter around Ikso. Their surprise assault allowed the other IRIS soldiers a moment of respite to retrieve their wounded. However, the assault of arrows and fire blasts from the back of the mythical beast repelled the

Edarians the most, for in that moment, they sensed that their master lay vanquished beyond Anmor.

Simarata set Rezaaran and Ashana down at the command post from where Orin had led the battle and then took to the skies once more. The havaka set upon a flight path calculated to decimate low-orbital fighters and artillery vessels while the Zenorians retrieved information on the overhead space battle.

"Well, it seems that despite gaining the advantage on the ground," Ashana informed Rezaaran after she read the reports, "we are in a deadlock with the Citadels. They can't reach the *Sedah Destroyer*, and there are endless waves of capital ships appearing."

Rezaaran looked upward as an enormous shadow filled the sky. The terminal of the control panel flickered alive, and Diothur glowered at them with a maniacal glint in her bruised eyes.

"How does it feel to have come so close to victory?" she cackled. "After today there will be no Thaedis! There will be no Sentinels! I will finally be the master of my own fate! Justice will prevail!"

A large red glow flared alive at the heart of the low-orbital flagship's main cannon, bathing the battlefield in a bloody hue.

Rezaaran watched the scene unfold in slowed time. The red shine dominated the thousand explosions of the space battle overhead. He turned his gaze to Ashana beside him, her fingers readied to connect to the Citadels. Jet and Quirt stood defiantly with the three Dorassi and Luminara to shield Moya as she mourned her sister. These past few months, his dreams had foretold this moment, and now he faced it in the company of his friends.

The time has come, Rezaaran, Luminara said sorrowfully.

The War Mage saw her offer a slight nod toward him. His perception returned to real time.

"According to the scanners," Ashana said, reading the figures off the terminal, "that weapon is charging far beyond the previous attack. If she unleashes that blast—"

"This planet will be obliterated," Quirt said across the communication channel.

"I am going to order all Citadels to focus their fire on the main gun!"

"That won't help, Ash," Rezaaran replied serenely. "Tell all Citadels to enter a Torus tunnel immediately."

The archer looked at him and fought back the stinging tears. "You're the only one who can stop it," she said quietly. "I have seen it in your dreams."

"You knew?"

"I've known since the first time you dreamed it," she admitted. "Although I wish it could be otherwise. I wished we could have had our end together. But I know this is what has to happen."

Rezaaran wrapped his arms around her waist and drew her into a kiss as the tears streamed from their eyes.

"Zenor is going to need a strong leader to rebuild," Rezaaran said, wiping Ashana's tears away. "I can't think of anyone better. Wherever you go, I will be with you, Ash. One day we'll find our way back to one another."

The archer simply nodded and kissed him once again. Finally Rezaaran released her and turned his attention to Jet.

"If it's all the same to you," the Erebonian said with a sad half smile, "I think I'll pass on kissing you."

"But I know you're going to miss me," Rezaaran said, laughing slightly.

"Indeed I will, my brother," Jet said and pulled Rezaaran into an embrace.

The War Mage took Quirt's hand firmly in his grasp. "Make sure you keep an eye on him. Good-bye, Quirt."

"I shall endeavor to give my best effort," the Thyrillian replied. "Thank you for my second chance."

Rezaaran turned to face Reikon and his Enchiridion knights.

"I understand the burden of duty that you face," Reikon said with a bow. "It has been my honor to stand with you."

The Dorassi offered the War Mage a salute.

"It has been my honor to have your friendship," Rezaaran replied with a warm smile.

Finally, he turned to Luminara.

"Thank you for all that you have done," she said, holding his shoulders. "You have ensured that the sacrifices of the Guardians were not in vain, and I know no better man to have returned the light to Anmor."

"I was blessed by the spirits to have had the company I did."

Luminara offered him a final warm smile and looked skyward at the growing glow within the *Sedah Destroyer*'s cannon.

Rezaaran whistled loudly, and Simarata landed beside him. "Ready once more, my friend?"

For Anmor, Kashari said as they took flight and careered toward the *Sedah Destroyer*'s cannon.

"For our friends," Rezaaran replied.

Simarata swept back its wings and powered higher into the bore.

Rezaaran felt the approaching heat of the gathering blast. It crisped his hair and singed his cloak. The War Mage released his grip on Simarata and siphoned all the Valinthicite from the construct into himself. His eyes flared white, and his hair glowed with the power surge. A blast of light escaped his screaming mouth, and the power ripped through him as momentum carried him toward the Obsidian blast within the chamber.

A few moments of silence ensued. Then a chain reaction began within the chamber.

On the surface of Tarlok, the Sentinels watched with mounting anticipation. Simarata's screeching flight had caught the attention of every soldier on the battlefield. They awaited the outcome with hearts stilled and breaths arrested.

A tremendous wave of light filled the sky from the annihilation detonation within the *Sedah Destroyer.* Seconds later, a sonic boom escaped the eye of the explosion, and the ensuing wave of force obliterated every Dominion capital ship in the sky.

Waves of fiery debris rained down, a spectacle received differently by every observer. While the soldiers whooped in exhilaration and the Edarians made a hasty escape into the regressing darkness, the Sentinels watched the falling debris with somber appreciation.

"It's finally over," Quirt whispered.

Reikon walked over to Moya, who still held Ikso close to her chest as she whispered her final prayer.

And so our duty here is done, an ancestral spirit said to the Dorassi. *We are proud to serve you and call you our Tetros.*

The army of Dorassi spirits faded from the battlefield. Reikon's armor disintegrated into billions of golden fragments and returned him to his modest brown robes. He offered a respectful bow to the departed spirits and crouched beside Moya to comfort her.

"Alas, it is my time to bid you all farewell," Luminara said, casting a kind and loving look over her friends. "Today a new era of peace dawns, and this epoch will be the legacy of the Sentinels."

"It feels hard to embrace peace," Quirt said, his head downcast.

"In time, the Vaux shall reunite you all once again," Luminara replied.

"I am going to miss your cryptic riddles, lady," Jet said, chuckling.

"He's gone," Ashana whispered. A tear rolled down her cheek, and her gray eyes scanned the sky, hoping against reason that Rezaaran had survived. Yet in her heart, she knew there had been no other option.

"Perhaps for now," Luminara said softly to the archer. Her form began to merge with the Vaux as lucent yellow particles. "However, through the Vaux, he shall always be linked to you, and you continue his legacy as long as he is in your heart."

Sunlight crept through the clouds and warmed Ashana's face. For a fleeting moment, she thought she felt Rezaaran's touch upon her cheek.

CHAPTER NINETEEN

A BRAVE NEW WORLD

Rezaaran awoke to the kiss of a warm summer sun upon his face, and a gentle breeze blew through his brown hair. He stood once again in the lush field of the Aetherealm, dressed in a full white suit.

"Well, this is a bit too familiar," he muttered. His hands searched through the tall grass for Harkenathor, but the weapon was nowhere to be found.

Simarata's screeching drew his attention to the clear azure sky. He followed the spirit's call toward the sanctuary, knowing he would find answers from Lord Salvidawn within its hallowed walls. Within the confines of the Sanctum, he sensed that the darkness had lifted. Despite the damage caused by the battles of old, this wondrous structure stood redeemed. The War Mage entered the throne room, where an aged Tyrel stood beside Luminara, who beamed proudly at the Sentinel.

"You were born Loradún," Tyrel proclaimed, "yet as Rezaaran Valhara you achieved so much more than I could have expected!"

"Well, I had a lot of help along the way," the War Mage replied.

"Indeed you did," Luminara said. "Rest assured that their sacrifices will not be lost in the stream of time."

She spread her arms, and the souls of the IRIS council members materialized from the Vaux, each manifested beneath the glass murals embedded into the roof.

Several of the soldiers marveled at the splendor of the sanctuary. However, only two recognized their setting and the presence of their hosts. Xephyrus and Muraka knelt in reverence to the Guardians.

"It is an honor to stand before you, my lord," Xephyrus said steadily, scarcely containing his elation that he should behold the wonders of the Aetherealm.

Tyrel rested his hands on Xephyrus's shoulders and lifted the soldier to his feet. "Rise, my friend," he said kindly. "We are all equal."

"Forgive me, my lord," Xephyrus said, his cheeks flushed, "but to be in the presence of a Guardian is something I had not imagined I would experience in my life."

"No?" asked Tyrel with a sparkle in his eye. "Well, would you imagine that you should become one?"

Xephyrus looked at the silver-haired Guardian with astonishment. Tyrel strode toward the Augura Nexus and took Luminara's hand before he faced the IRIS soldiers.

"We are all that remains of the old Anmorian Guardians," he said. "With our brethren, we protected Anmor for eons against a varying array of threats. However, within us lay the greatest threat to the peace we dearly cherished, the peace we were duty bound to preserve. As I stand before you all now, I declare that I have seen the errors of our ways. We became detached and eventually indifferent to the plight of the people of Anmor. The Guardians could no longer protect Anmor in the vision of Alaris."

"However, Anmor will always need those to watch over it," Luminara continued. "There will always be darkness lingering beyond the horizon. But you have all proven that a spark of hope always exists within the hearts of those committed to stand for the Light."

"So, by the power vested in us by the mighty Alaris," Tyrel exclaimed, "I confer our power to a new generation of Guardians."

The Augura Nexus flared alive. A stream of Valinthicite flowed from its heart and forged eleven relics.

Tyrel grasped the hilt of Dawn Shard once more, savoring the feel of its comforting warmth within his hand. His electric-blue eyes sought Rezaaran, who stepped forward.

"This blade called to you before," he said proudly, "for the Vaux has awoken to the strength of your spirit, Rezaaran. May Dawn Shard serve you in your watch as she has served me throughout mine."

Rezaaran offered a respectful bow and upon grasping the hilt was covered in the Guardian armor he had worn on Tarlok.

"It will be your duty to lead the Guardians through this new era," Luminara said. "Their hearts are loyal to your cause."

"That may be so," Rezaaran replied, "but there is another who ought to lead us as he has in life."

"Do not worry about me," Orin remarked with a laugh, striding toward the nexus to clasp Rezaaran's hand. The general stood restored to his former uninjured self and dressed in a crisp black suit. "I have led enough in my lifetime. That role has fallen to a better man than I. Now is my chance to retire and spend quality time with a few good friends."

Rezaaran looked back toward the Sanctum's entrance, where he saw the souls of his parents and a fully Zenorian Cosmonox holding the hand of his wife.

"In that case," Rezaaran said with a growing smile, "General Orin Libranth, I relieve you of duty. Effective immediately."

"I am relieved," Orin replied with a proud smile.

The former IRIS council members knelt in reverence to their erstwhile leader, who reciprocated their respect and departed the sanctuary.

Rezaaran turned his attention once more to the Augura Nexus and saw Harkenathor floating within the Vaux that streamed through the roof. He telekinetically summoned the weapon to his reach and summoned Kashari from the confines of the blade.

The Elder Mage looked around her in disbelief. "This is the Aetherealm," she whispered. "That means that I am—"

"You are free, my friend," Rezaaran replied with a smile. "You were bound by a Guardian of Light to Harkenathor so that your spirit could serve Anmor. As the new Guardian, I release you from your duty."

Kashari's eyes welled with tears.

"However, if you would do me the honor, I have one request, my dear friend. Having been your student for so long, I know no better or wiser mentor to remain custodian of the Sentinels, both present and future. Would you grant me the honor of remaining their advisor and mentor as needed?"

"It would be my honor," she replied with a small bow. Her eyes wandered past Rezaaran toward the sanctuary entrance. "Mehara," she whispered in astonishment.

"I think we have spoken enough in our time together," Rezaaran said with a kind smile. "Now there is someone else who would like to have some time with you...and I believe there are a fair number of unspoken things that need to be said."

Kashari embraced Rezaaran tightly. "Thank you, my friend."

The War Mage released his mentor and watched her leave the sanctuary, feeling her elation deep within his own heart. No matter the distance, their bond remained, regardless of Harkenathor.

Luminara offered a Rezaaran a slight nod of appreciation for ensuring that Kashari received her due right for her service to Anmor.

Inspired by Kashari's uniting with her beloved, Leta felt emboldened and approached Xephyrus. Her cheeks flushed, and she struggled to find the words. However, the Elder Mage simply took her hands in his own and gently kissed her.

"Well, it's about time," Moraya said, rolling her eyes. But she allowed herself a small smile, knowing that her friend had found her happiness at last.

Tyrel looked over the Zenorians with a fond smile, glad that the sanctuary once again held the cheer of camaraderie. He approached Gerrin and handed him a scepter with a swirling orb atop its spiraled end.

"Gerrin Mordakai," Tyrel said. "Throughout the conflict, your greatest strength remained your ability to remain steady under pressure. You have humbled yourself and learned humility, a trait I entrust you shall continue to display as the Guardian of Frost."

The commander grasped the weapon, and his eyes turned light blue as a crystalline armor encased his being.

Tyrel moved on to Krayzar and Atomauran. "In life, your destinies were resolutely interwoven, and so it shall be in your watch as Guardians of the Storm."

He gifted each of the brothers a single buzzing metal gauntlet. Although perplexed, they each took the item onto opposing hands and felt a strong magnetic pull toward one another. They clasped hands, and in a burst of lightning, they formed into a single storm spirit who sparked electricity off its steely, spiked armor, which mirrored Krayzar's appearance as a council member.

Luminara approached Muraka and placed a hand on his bowed forehead.

"Within you I feel a kindred spirit," she said softly as she assessed his soul. "You have always sought to use your strength to protect others, and you possess a heart that yearns for the forests. I can think of no better Guardian to preserve the forests of Anmor."

Luminara gifted Muraka a sealed green bud that opened in his hands to reveal a glowing pink flower. Tendrils reached down and formed into the handle while the petals reformed into a lithe hammer. The glowing flower settled to a bright white, reminiscent of the Valinthicite shard at the heart of his old weapon.

The Woodland Maiden turned her attention to Stryker, who stood proudly at attention back in his uninjured state, his organic arm reattached to his body.

"While Muraka held a heart for the forest," she said with a kind smile, "your heart has always bonded to the souls of the creatures of this realm. While IRIS fought for the freedom of all civilizations, you ensured that you freed and kept as many creatures as possible from harm. I am proud to pass my title to such a worthy successor."

Luminara touched her hand to Stryker's forehead, and a glow passed from her heart through her fingers and into the soldier. An amulet of glowing Valinthicite formed around his neck and materialized to a silver disc. In the center of the amulet, the Anmorian Guardian emblem was engraved deeply into the metal. An etching of a mighty sabersteed lay superimposed over the emblem. Surrounding the engravings was a series of runes.

"It's truly magnificent," Stryker whispered in amazement. "What do the runes say, my lady?"

"They're Sirantanian," Luminara explained. "They translate to 'I see your soul, I know your journey.' You will be able to confer sentience, draw upon the strengths of all creatures of the galaxy, and summon them to your side. You will also be able to see their souls and know their history. I have seen your soul, and I know that you shared a remarkable bond with a sabersteed in your time."

"Arion," Stryker murmured. A tear formed in the corner of his eye as his finger traced the carving of the sabersteed. "It's perfect. Thank you, my lady."

Luminara bowed her head slightly and stepped over to Aloric.

"Aloric Melias," she said slowly after assessing his soul. "A pure and powerful soul burns brightly within you. I feel that your heart is heavy with regret. You sought to purge this with aggression, yet you have found the virtue of humility. A proud soldier of Novanithor. I believe I have the perfect item for the future Guardian of the Flame."

A bright-saffron egg passed from the Augura Nexus into Aloric's hands.

"An egg?" he asked with a raised eyebrow.

Within his hands, the egg trembled, and from within it hatched a sparkling red-scaled dragonet. The little creature shook away the remnants of its shell and turned its yellow eyes to Aloric, uttering a shrill, excited chirp.

Stryker stepped forward and gently touched the dragonet's head. The runes on his amulet flared blue. His eyes clouded with the same color, as did the eyes of the dragonet. In amazement, he turned his gaze down to the creature. He had known this soul once before.

"Kabuura," Stryker whispered, removing his hand from the dragonet.

"What?" Aloric asked, aghast.

"This dragonet is the soul of Kabuura," Stryker explained.

"The soldier who died under my command?" Aloric asked in disbelief, peering into the yellow eyes of the dragonet.

"I saw the pain in your heart from this loss," Luminara explained. "The Vaux has felt this pain, and now you have regained your dear friend. Your souls are henceforth bonded to serve the Vaux and uphold justice."

Aloric touched his fingers to the side of Kabuura's head, and the dragonet climbed along his hand to perch on his shoulder. Both their eyes briefly flared blue, and the dragon's spirit bonded with Aloric's, his body set alight in flame and the sigil of the Novanithorian dragon blazing across his chest.

"Thank you, my lady," the Gundancer said with a deep bow.

Tyrel turned his attention to Albeinius and passed him a metal ring forged from Valinthicite.

"I have watched you for some time. In many ways, you remind me of Itara Zelzo. You have an insatiable curiosity and an innate understanding of how any manner of machinery operates. This ring confers the power of Guardian of Metals and Industry, and the metal within it adapts to any function, as you require."

The former Guardian King then turned to Xephyrus and Leta, who stood beside one another, their fingers interlocked. He offered them a slight smile, seeing a familiarity in their genuine love. He presented Xephyrus with a white-hooded cloak that allowed him to control the winds and take flight with ease. To Leta, he presented a bag of enchanted dust that allowed her to alter time, along with the power of terrakinesis.

Luminara approached Moraya and looked into her blue eyes.

"There could only ever be one calling for your soul," she said with a wry smile. She passed Moraya a long staff topped with a spiraling conical shell. The newly anointed Guardian of the Seas tapped the hilt against the floor, and three prongs erupted from an extension atop the shell.

Walking toward Rexion, Tyrel placed his hands comfortingly on the young soldier's shoulders.

"I know you have had the hardest road reaching here," he said kindly. "I know what Thaedis showed you, and this could not have been easy to handle. I have seen the many losses you experienced and then forgot over the span of your eternal life. For whatever it may be worth, you deserve to know one truth that Thaedis failed to share with you."

"What truth is that?" asked Rexion, his gaze full of sorrow.

"Your eternal life was not a curse from the Obsidious. It was a gift from your father. Whatever his shortcomings and ambitions may have been, in the end, when he looked into the eyes of the trusting baby he had handed to a lost soul, Aeron realized the error of his ways. Your extended life came from Aeron cutting his own life short in the ritual to ensure that you survived to contest the evil he had set in motion. He sacrificed himself to save the one thing he believed to be solely good in his life."

Rexion averted his gaze and rubbed his eye.

"Although born into the darkness, you lived a life of honor in the Light and turned away from temptations. Your steadfast virtue is why Orin Libranth chose you to be his second-in-command on Zenor, for you are a man of integrity. This team of Guardians cannot work without you by their side."

"I second that," Rezaaran said and started to clap.

"And so do I!" Muraka boomed, joining the applause.

Rexion offered them all a bow of appreciation and graciously accepted a thin silver disc that split into two crescents. The first remained within a ring and formed a cloak pin, while the second formed a circlet that wrapped onto Rexion's head.

With the circlet settled into his hair, the Sanctum came to life once more. Light filtered through the glass murals in the roof, which now depicted the new Anmorian Guardians. Out in the atrium, the grand tree blossomed once again, and a chorus of souls sang in jubilation across the verdant plains of the Aetherealm.

Rezaaran stepped over to the Augura Nexus and placed his hand upon the Anmorian axis. In an instant, he felt his mind connected to every soul in the Maelinthian. Those on Tarlok were still celebrating, save the somber souls of the Sentinels as they thought about their losses. He felt a tug in his heart and knew that they mourned his death. However, his attention was drawn away by the thick fear that still enshrouded the rest of the Maelinthian. Word had yet to spread that the Dominion was defeated, and he could not allow these people to live in terror another second.

"While in contact with the Anmorian axis," Tyrel explained, "your soul is directly connected with every other soul. Although your words will not be heard in the sensory manner, your voice will resound within the souls of all who draw breath."

Rezaaran stilled his mind and took a moment to gather his thoughts.

"To all the people who are still wondering when they will know peace again, when their fortunes shall change, I want you to know that today is that day. The Dominion is defeated. The war is over."

Instantly, he felt an intense yet pleasant warmth reach through the axis and back into his arm. The people had felt his presence and his message within their core.

"Although our oppressor is vanquished and his forces are scattered, there is something that we need to remember. This war was a warning to us all that the truest evil resides within our own hearts. To those who remain oppressed and outcast, you are not alone. IRIS fights on, as do the Anmorian Guardians. Together we outnumber the darkness. Together we can bring about a golden era of peace for Anmor. We set aside our differences and fought against a common enemy. Now let us embrace and celebrate those differences as we look together to the Light. Together let us shape this brave new world."

Rezaaran felt the darkness across Anmor falter, its grasp loosened marginally yet enough for a resurgence of warmth. The Guardian King stepped aside from the Augura Nexus and walked with his predecessor to an open archway overlooking the Aetherealm field.

"That was quite a sentiment you shared," Tyrel remarked proudly.

"I sense the whisper of a darkness," Rezaaran admitted, looking beyond the horizon of the Aetherealm. "It is faint and elusive, but I sense its presence still."

"Yet you do not seem too worried."

"Throughout this war, we were constantly surrounded by danger and darkness, yet there was a singular constant that kept us fighting. When I touched the axis, I felt it stronger than ever before, for it is now within the hearts and souls of every person."

His gaze wandered beyond the edge of the Aetherealm and focused on the blazing echo of Ashana burning far brighter than any single person around her.

"Hope. That is the legacy of the Sentinels."

THE JOURNEY WILL CONTINUE IN

THE ANMORIAN LEGENDS:

LORDS OF TORETHIAS

ABOUT THE AUTHOR:

Dhesan Neil Pillay is a South African medical doctor who started his writing from a young age. Always a lover of stories, he began working on what would become The Anmorian Legends series from the ninth grade. Over the next few years, he slotted writing the manuscript between homework and classes, taking a momentary hiatus in his matriculation year. While studying medicine at the University of Cape Town, he continued finding time between studies to expand on the journey of his characters. Driven by a passion to share the surreal experience of his story he released his debut novel The Anmorian Legends: Wrath of the Exiled in 2014. This was followed by the release of The Anmorian Legends: Legacy of the Sentinels in 2018. Currently Dhesan is looking to diversify his writing portfolio with several new projects that are in the planning stages. To keep updated with the latest news, visit his website at http://dhesanpillay.wix.com/dhesan-pillay

www.ingramcontent.com/pod-product-compliance
Lightning Source LLC
Chambersburg PA
CBHW031756260626
47154CB00027B/1971
9780620795623